In Her Hands

Matilda Latham

Contents

Chapter 1

"Reynolds, Murphy."

Our supervisor pushed through the door of the break room, eyeing the two of us before he looked down at his clipboard. "Can you two stay for a bit and make sure that everyone in hallway D is taken care of?" he asked. "Check their vitals, make sure they don't need anything, and deliver the left over meal orders to the front desk."

Glancing at my watch, I tapped my leg anxiously, hoping that this extra work wouldn't cause me to miss visiting hours. It was already closing in on seven 'o'clock, and having missed the visiting hours the previous night due to my orientation, I didn't want to have to go another night without talking to my mom.

"Sure," Claudia said, dropping her bag back into her locker as I nodded in agreement, "We'll head over there now."

He dipped his head in acknowledgement. "Thank you," he said, waving as he turned his back on us, "Have a good weekend."

"You too," Claudia returned before the door shut completely. When it did, she sighed, looking over to me while rolling her eyes. "Come on. The faster we get this done, the faster we'll be able to leave."

Having told me that she had two young sons at home, I'm sure she wanted our shift to be over just as much as I did.

Grabbing my stethoscope, I stood and plucked a new pair of gloves from the bin at the door before following behind her.

Luckily, none of the patients had any major issues, and we weren't held back too long. Claudia checked everyone's IVs and administered pills to the patients that needed them, while I recorded the data that was flashing on the monitors in each room.

When all of the patients were checked, we'd made sure to notify them that a new nurse would be around shortly to check in with them. Claudia handed me the small pile of meal cards for the patients who had yet to be fed, asking me to submit them before calling it a day. The nurse at reception wasn't extremely busy, so after handing them off to her, I headed back to the break room, ready for my first shift to end.

I'd been hired by the local hospital as a nursing assistant, and I was extremely grateful for the opportunity. Having another year left of school, I'd been worried that I wouldn't be qualified to fit the role. However, since a lot of the staff had become familiar with me because of my mother, they'd given me a shot, and I didn't intend on wasting it.

"You did good today," Claudia smiled, turning my way as I pushed through the door. She'd already changed out of her work clothes, and was shutting her locker as I entered. "I was worried this morning. I could see that you were nervous, but you seemed to fall into a routine as the day went on."

The corners of my lips tilted upwards as I smiled nervously. "Yeah – first day jitters you know."

She nodded. "I get it. This job can be stressful, but I think you'll fit in here just fine," she said, giving me the impression that, while it was only my first day, I hadn't done all that bad of a job. "Just remember that there's always more to learn, and don't ever hesitate to ask me something if you're unsure of what the proper procedure is."

"Thanks," I said genuinely, "I'll remember that."

She smiled, her lips crinkling at the sides. "Have a good night," she said.

"You too."

When I was alone, I quickly stripped off my scrubs, ignoring the way the sheen of sweat on my skin caused them to stick to some areas, and pulled on my clothes in a rush. Glancing at the time on my phone, I breathed out a sigh of relief.

I still had almost forty-five minutes.

On my way to the elevators, a few of the other nurses and staff that I'd been introduced to throughout the day threw me a friendly smile or said hello, but as the lift doors slid shut and I ascended up three floors, the questions started circling my mind.

What if her condition had worsened? When she was asleep, could she hear what I was saying? Would I finally be able to tell her about my job? Would she be awake?

The worries and nerves came back full-throttle as the doors slid open and I walked the familiar path to her room. It'd been over a year that I'd been visiting, after she'd been deemed unwell enough to have permanent residency in the hospital – needing daily care that I couldn't provide to her while working through my degree.

And while I would've given it all up just to stay home and look after her, I knew she wouldn't have wanted that. She wanted me to succeed in life, and in her fragile state, I couldn't stand to see her unhappy.

Coming to her room, I stopped outside, taking a deep breath before hitching my bag further up on my shoulder and pushing the door open.

My mom was lying on the sole bed that occupied the majority of the space in the room, like she always was when I visited. However, her doctor was also in the room.

I hovered in the entryway as the door closed behind me, watching as she noticed me and threw me a tentative smile. "Hey Katie," she said, moving her attention back to my mom as she scribbled away on her clipboard while checking my mother's IVs, "I'll just be a few more minutes, and then I'll leave you two alone."

"Okay," I said hesitantly, stepping forward as I dropped my bag onto the chair next to the bed. "Is there, um, have there been any changes?"

Pity and sadness clouded her eyes as she glanced my way. "No, I'm sorry." She shook her head. "We're trying to be as careful as we can when helping her. In her weak state, we don't want to push her body in case she can't handle the side effects, but we'll keep you updated when things change."

I took the information solemnly, familiar with the standard response that I received each time I asked, and nodded. Watching as the doctor finished with the check-up, I stood silently and felt a pull at my heartstrings as my gaze landed on my mom. Her skin was sickly pale due to her treatment, and her weight was withering away to nothing.

I was helpless in the situation, and it was painful to know there was nothing I could do to help her.

Minutes later, when it was just my mom and me in the small, antiseptic smelling room, I was seated by her side. I had my right hand resting atop of her pale one, and though she was asleep, it didn't stop me from talking.

"Hey mom," I said softly, my eyes on our joined hands instead of her face. "I'm not sure if you realized it or not, but I'm sorry I couldn't visit yesterday. Orientation ran late. I'm working here at the hospital now, isn't that surreal? I didn't think they'd hire me, but today was my first day, and even though Claudia – the nurse I'm working under – had to go over a lot of the procedures a few times, I thought it went well. I wish you were able to celebrate this with me. Remember when I got my acceptance letter to Duke, and you opened an expensive bottle of wine to celebrate?" I sighed, knowing that I was reminiscing. "I miss those days. I'll probably just head home soon and get a start on some of the readings for my classes the start next week. Fun way to spend my Sunday night, eh?"

"Anyways," I continued, "Theo called a few days ago, wanting to know how you were doing. I told him that there haven't been any changes lately, and I don't think that's what he wanted to hear. He's scared that, when the time comes, since he's all the way in London, he won't have a chance to say goodbye. But he loves his job, and he has friends over there, so I think the distance is the only thing he doesn't like about being overseas. The apartment is lonely though, without the both of you, but I'm dealing."

I always found myself going off on a tangent when I was speaking to my mom, because she was usually asleep, and there was nobody to stop the conversation from going off in a million different directions.

Babbling on until the clock struck eight, I sighed, knowing that I'd used up the limited amount of time I had with her today.

I could hear the bustling in the hallway as other visitors left their loved ones, as I stood up from my chair. "Goodnight mom," I whispered into the air, squeezing her hand with the hope that she'd have the strength to squeeze back.

But like always, my hopes were dashed when I was met with nothing but the stillness of her haggard hand beneath mine.

On the way home, I was one of the only people on the bus. It was a quiet journey through the streets of Durham, North Carolina, though with my headphones in, the time passed quicker. It was merely eight thirty when I arrived back at my apartment complex, riding the elevator up to the fifth floor.

Unlocking the door, I was hit with the usual wave of thoughts at how lonely it was to still be living here. This had been the home that I'd shared with my brother and my mom since I could remember, as my father had died when I was young, and now I was left alone, not able to give up the space that held so many great memories.

Heading up to my room, it was a sad reality that, with nothing else to do, I pulled out my textbooks and began to look over the material that would be covered in my classes once the new term started. Even though I knew my hours at the hospital would be worked around my schedule, it wouldn't leave a whole lot of time for studying. I figured reviewing now would only help, considering there was a possibility that things could arise at work that I hadn't covered in class yet.

My headphones were still in as I settled down at my desk, distracting me from the silence of the apartment as I flipped through a few chapters. Paying attention to nothing other than the words on the page in front of me, my studying trance was only broken when my phone rang.

Swiping to accept the call, I held it between my shoulder and my cheek as I jotted a few notes down. "Hey Stella, what's up?"

"Are you not home from the hospital yet?"

Rolling my eyes with amusement, I wasn't bothered by her bluntness. It's just who she was, and after a long road of friendship that started back in middle school, I'd grown accustomed to it.

"I am," I replied, furring my eyebrows as I tried to figure out why she was asking. To my knowledge, we hadn't made plans tonight. "Why?"

"Because I've rung the bell for your apartment more than five times, and I'm standing outside looking like I'm trying to break in or something."

I chuckled, standing up from my desk as I made way to the entryway. "Sorry, I was listening to music," I said, pressing the buzzer to let her in. "There, the door should be open now."

"Finally," she said teasingly.

Opening the door to my apartment, I stayed on the phone until I saw her emerge from the elevator at the end of the hall.

"Hey," she greeted with a smile, entering the apartment as I closed the door behind us, "How was your first day?"

I shrugged, waiting as she slipped off her shoes before heading back towards my room. She followed me, knowing exactly where I was headed. She'd been coming around for years, and for the past few months, she'd spent more time here with me than back at her own house. "It was good," I said simply, sitting down on the bed as she leant back against my dresser. "I was kind of worried that I wouldn't know what to do, but the nurse I'm working under is really nice, and explained a lot of the paperwork to me. I mostly just recording the information from the monitors in the recovery rooms, but I really didn't expect to be doing much else."

"That's good then," Stella said, "At least you're getting experience." I agreed. "Did you get to see your mom today?"

Nodding, I picked up a pillow and placed it on my lap, picking at the threads hanging from the end. "Yeah," I said quietly. "She was asleep, and the doctor said there hadn't been any changes, but I still got to talk to her for a while."

"No change is a good thing though, right?" Stella asked. "I mean, even though there's no good news, there also isn't any bad news."

"I guess."

"And next time you go, tell me. It's been a while since I've seen her."

My lips pulled upwards into a soft smile. "I go everyday Stella, you just have to come."

"Right," she laughed, though as her eyes began to wander around the room, they narrowed when they saw the textbooks I'd left open on my desk. She turned back to me with an eyebrow raised. "Were you studying before I got here?"

I bit my lip, shrugging sheepishly as a reply.

"Katie!" she exclaimed bewilderedly. "Classes don't start for another week, why are you putting yourself through that torture before you have to?"

I laughed at her reaction. While she was going into her final year of her history major, she wasn't the most enthusiastic about studying. Stella was naturally smart, and just preferred to put the extra effort into having a full social life.

We were complete opposites, but we balanced each other out.

"It's not like I had anything better to do," I said, "But if you wanna watch a movie or something, we could do that instead."

"Actually," she trailed, her eyes sparkling with excitement as a grin formed on her lips.

Suddenly, I was wary of the reason that she'd come over. "What?"

"There's this party – "

I was already shaking my head before she could explain any further. "No."

"Oh come on," she begged, coming over to sit next to me on the bed, "You don't even know what I was going to say."

"I'm guessing it had something to do with the two of us going out tonight," I replied, quirking an eyebrow in suspicion. "Am I wrong?"

Stella bit her lip, only to sigh and shake her head a moment later. "No," she said, before the willing gleam in her eyes returned, "But it's been ages since the two of us have had a night out. And I know you don't like clubs, so I thought this would be a good compromise."

"And how is a party a compromise?"

"Because it's a small party," she insisted. "It's away from the city, and I promise that I'll leave with you whenever you want."

"You know I work tomorrow morning, right?"

She waved me off. "You don't work until ten, and that's plenty of time to sleep once we get home tonight," she said, a gleeful grin playing on her lips. "And I didn't hear a no."

"I'm not drinking," I said firmly, knowing that she was getting to me.

The glimmer of hope that flooded her irises grew quickly as she realized that I was wordlessly agreeing to go. "You don't have to," she said, "But can you drive there? We can take my car."

I sighed, a defeated smile on my lips. "Sure."

"Great," she chirped, engulfing me in a hug as her plans fell into place. Pulling back, she nudged me gently. "I promise you'll have fun – just you wait."

The party ended up being out near the edge of town, in an open field that was completely surrounded by trees. According to Stella, it was the extended property of someone's family that she knew off the basketball team. It was a wide clearing, and was private enough that no one in the surrounding area would be able to hear the music as it blasted from the speakers propped up on the tailgates of two trucks.

"How does this constitute as a small party to you?" I asked Stella.

The two of us were standing further back from the crowd, lingering closer to the forest than most guests. The evening air was less humid than I wished, leaving a chill to gloss down my spine as a result of the clothes that Stella had forced me into before leaving. She had a stockpile of outfits stored in my closet, and after I'd agreed to come tonight, she'd thrown a pair of black denim shorts and a cropped t-shirt my way.

Letting my eyes travel out across the grass, I spotted a few familiar faces, having been Stella's plus one to these parties since our senior year of high school, but I didn't actually know many of them. Stella was the one who made a point of making friends with the jocks and frat boys, but I preferred to stay in my own company.

I had enough to deal with, and most people didn't under-stand why I would rather spend my hours at a hospital than out enjoying my life.

"Because it wasn't really advertised," Stella replied simply, answering my earlier question as she took a swig of beer from her cup. The first thing she did when we arrived was drag me towards the coolers, but while she'd quickly poured a beer into an empty cup, I'd stuck to soda. "A lot of people are still back at home, soaking up the last of summer, but I guess people decided to invite a lot of friends – which is fine by me."

A satisfied smirk glossed her features as she cast her gaze towards a group of guys that were standing a few meters away from us, laughing obnoxiously.

I rolled my eyes. "Please tell me you're not going to leave me alone to find a guy tonight."

Stella smiled innocently as she finished off her drink, shrugging. "I won't leave you alone," she said, and when I raised an eyebrow in disbelief, her innocent façade dropped. A sly smile appeared on her lips as she nodded subtly to the left. I noticed that she hadn't been eyeing the group of guys after all, but two guys that had been lingering behind them. And to my surprise, they were slowly heading towards us. "But I might leave you alone with the blonde one."

That meant she had her eyes on his friend, and while both of them were attractive, I just didn't have the confidence that she did when it came to approaching guys.

And for the first time that night, as I looked down shyly at my cup, I wished it were filled with something stronger than soda.

Chapter 2

My hair was matted to my forehead as I made my way up the stairs to my apartment. The elevator had been broken for nearly a month now, and even though basketball kept me in shape, trudging up ten flights of stairs after a grueling practice was certainly not ideal.

The rookies had ventured up to campus a week early for try-outs, and coach had pushed us all to our limits to show them how our team was run. It wasn't by luck that we were one of the highest rated teams in the country. The whole team worked together, day in and day out, putting in the hours and the effort to improve and show our fans why we fell in love with the game.

Basketball had been something I'd fallen in love with as a kid. While my brother had been keen on science and drama, I'd been the one who spent hours out in the yard with my dad, practicing and learning more about the game. After all the time I'd invested into the sport, it'd still been a shock when I'd received an offer from Duke to play for their team on scholarship, but it had been something I couldn't refuse.

The past three years I'd put all I had into the sport – my blood, sweat, and tears – and I was only a few weeks away from finding out if I'd made captain. It wasn't a for-sure thing, since some of my teammates deserved it just as much as me, but I had a gut feeling that things would end up in my favour.

Pulling my team lanyard out from the side of my gym bag as I reached my floor, I jiggled the key in the lock before pushing into my apartment. The air conditioning was on, which was a breath of relief as I could feel the beads of sweat dripping down my skin, but not much had changed since I'd left for the gym.

The dirty dishes were still piling up in the sink, the curtains were still shut to prevent the sun from heating up the place, and Holden hadn't moved from the couch. He was still stretched out, lying comfortably with a hand behind his head, as he watched a copious amount of re-runs on the television.

"Hey," Holden said as I let the apartment door shut behind me, "How was practice?"

I shrugged, tossing my shoes next to the door before dropping my bag. "Okay. It looks like the new players can handle it so far, so that's a bonus."

"You grabbing a shower?" he asked, smirking at me with a glint of humour in his eyes. "Cause I hate to tell you this, but you seriously reek."

I chuckled, well aware of the fact that I currently smelled as though I'd gone a week without a shower. Shedding my tank top, which had been dripping in sweat just minutes before, I scrunched it up and threw it towards him. "Thanks man, I appreciate it."

He flung my dirty shirt right back at me as I passed by the couch, which he'd managed to catch just before it'd landed on his face. "No problem," he grinned, shouting after me as I headed down the hall, "Someone's got to be the one to tell it like it is."

Grabbing the first clean clothes I saw after I pushed open the door to my room, I backtracked across the hall and into the bathroom. Standing under the spray of the shower, I let the cold temperature shock the tightness out of my muscles before turning the heat up until I was surrounded by steam. It was relaxing and just what I needed to clear my head. I only emerged half an hour later, once the constant downpour of water had begun to cool down on its own.

"So," I started, walking back into the living room fully dressed as I ran a towel through my hair, "What are we doing for dinner?"

Holden's eyes flicked to mine as a set of commercials began. "I don't know," he shrugged nonchalantly, "Pizza?"

I rolled my eyes, taking a seat at the end of the couch and forcing him to sit up. "We've had pizza twice in the last week," I pointed out.

"Then what about Chinese?"

"Or how about we actually cook?" I asked sarcastically, "I mean, that is why we bought all that food in the fridge, right?"

He glared my way as he readjusted the beanie that covered his dark mop of hair. "You know Juliet was the one who cooked most nights," he said bitterly, speaking of his recent ex-girlfriend that had left quite the scar on his heart.

When I'd met Holden during freshman orientation, the two of us had become fast friends, despite the fact that we ran in different social circles. And being friends with Holden meant that Juliet had been part of the package. They'd been dating for over a year at that point, and even though she seemed like a great girl, over the years, something just hadn't sat well with me. I could never pinpoint it though. That was until I came home a few months back to see Holden drinking himself into a depression.

After four years together, and without a clue as to what he'd done wrong, Juliet had broken up with him.

She'd told him that their relationship was becoming too predictable for her, and instead of working for it; she'd simply fallen out of love. But I knew right away that there was more to it. I'd noticed the way she'd been pulling back from Holden, but he hadn't believed me when I told him the next morning, as he nursed a killer hangover, that she'd more than likely found someone else.

The two of us had lived in silence for almost a week before he finally caved. Holden had gone over to Juliet's place to talk – only to find another guy there. Not only had she already moved on, but she also admitted to seeing him before she'd officially ended things.

He was pissed, and as the weeks passed, he'd sunk into a sullen hole of cynicism and sadness.

I nodded, acknowledging his hostility, but knew that it was time for him to get over her. "And I also know that you helped her a lot of the time," I said. "You know how to cook, you just don't want to because it reminds you of Juliet."

Narrowing his eyes, he slouched back into the couch. "What's your point?"

"My point is that you need to get over her, because honestly, I'd much rather have my best friend back than have to share this apartment with a bummed out couch potato."

"Just because you never really liked her – "

"Not true," I cut him off, "She was fine. She just wasn't for you, and I knew that."

"So what?" he asked sarcastically, "Do you want a medal?"

I shook my head, though my lips did tilt upwards at his comeback. "No, but I do want to help you get out of this funk that you're in," I replied. "You need to get out and move on, instead of holing yourself up in the apartment all day."

"I'm not here all the time."

I sent him a flat look. "You leave for work, and you haven't come out to a party since the break-up."

"Maybe I'm just not in the mood for a party," he groaned, pausing as he quirked an eyebrow, "Besides, I can't even remember the last time you had to get over a girl."

I shrugged. "I don't have time for relationships," I said simply.

Between classes, basketball practices, and away games, I just never found the time to really date. I'd see girls here and there, but nothing serious, and I'd always be the one to break it off.

He smirked. "Yet you somehow find the time to learn a girl's name long enough to sleep with her."

"Hey," I nudged him as he laughed, "Don't try and pretend that I'm even half as bad as some of the guys on the team. And I'm your best friend, so I know what's good for you. And tonight, you need to get out of this apartment."

He closed his eyes and sighed. "And what have you managed to cook up to get me to forget about Juliet."

"Matt's throwing a party out at his parent's place," I said. "I wasn't gonna go, but if it'll help you get used to being single, then I'm going, and you're coming with me."

"If we're going, then we're ordering pizza," he scowled, "And you're driving."

If held my hands up in mock surrender. "I'm fine with staying sober, but you my friend, can drink as much as you want."

He grumbled as he pulled his beanie further down over his eyes, casting me a frown. "I'm so going to regret this."

I clapped a hand on his shoulder reassuringly as a smirk pulled at my lips. "Trust me, I'll make sure you have a good night."

Matt's parents lived on the outskirts of town, and with no nosy neighbours, they'd been letting him use the field on their property for parties since I could remember. Their house was far enough away that they wouldn't be bothered, and all Matt had to do was make sure that nobody attracted the attention of the cops.

By the time we arrived, there was a backlog of cars down the trail that led through to the field, parked every which way in an effort to stay unnoticed by passersby. Pulling my car in between two trees near the entrance, I rounded the car as

Holden climbed out of the other side, the two of us following the soft lull of music that grew louder the farther we trekked.

The trail ended as the party came into full view, and it seemed as though it was already in full swing.

I passed by a few of my teammates, guys I'd met from class, and groups of girls who thought they were being covert when their eyes lingered one too many seconds on the guys they had their eyes on. Unfortunately, some of those gazes were pointed towards me when, tonight, I needed all the attention to be on Holden.

Holden followed behind me, not thoroughly thrilled to be here in the first place, as I made my way to the drinks. Matt's family was better off than most, and his parties always seemed to have a decent supply of alcohol that usually disappeared by the end of the night.

"Here," I said, grabbing two beers from one of the coolers and tossing one towards Holden.

He caught it with little effort, expecting as much as he popped it open and took a long swig. Nodding down to the second beer in my hand, he raised an eyebrow and cast me a curious look. "I thought you weren't drinking."

"I'm not," I replied, cementing the point as I picked up a cup before filling it with soda. "This is for you once you finish that one, because I don't feel like walking all the way back over here in just a few minutes."

He tipped the beer in his hand so that the liquid ran smoothly down his throat. When he pulled the can back from his mouth, he tossed it into the garbage bin that had been set up, grabbing the second beer from my hand. "You might want to grab another one then, because I'm going to need a bit more of a buzz to have any kind of fun tonight."

I chuckled, doing as he said before the two of us made our way around the field.

It didn't take me long to realize that, with a quite a few tents set up near the edge of the field, I was one of the only ones actually staying sober for the night. Most of the guys on the team were on their way to being drunk, and the girls that they had their eyes on didn't seem to be holding back on the alcohol either. The guys and I got along great, but there was a reason that I'd decided to share an apartment with Holden and not any of them, and that was because, outside of basketball, we didn't have much to talk about.

The night wore on, and it was as if the music got louder as the darkness evaded the field. The fresh air was nice, covering up the underlying smell of pot and cigarettes as Holden and I moved away from the crowd.

"So, having fun yet?" Holden asked with a smirk, taking another swig of his fourth beer. Once the buzz that he'd been looking for hit him, he'd slowed down, not wanting to get completely trashed for the night.

"I will be once I find you a girl to talk to," I replied slyly, scanning the field to find any likely candidates.

He clenched his hand tighter around his beer, his knuckles turning a paler shade of white. I knew he wasn't completely psyched about the reason I'd dragged him here, but I was going to make him forget about Juliet for the night by what-ever means deemed necessary.

And right now, the easy solution was to get someone else to do that for me.

The options were limited however, considering most of the girls here had either come with their boyfriends or were already cozying up to another guy.

A movement to my left caught my attention. For a moment I believed it to just be my teammates, whom I'd left to enjoy their drunken states of mind, but before my gaze shifted once more, I noticed two girls that were standing across the field. While the blonde was unfamiliar, I'd seen the other one before at parties. Her black hair has pulled back into a ponytail, and her golden brown skin complemented her piercing brown eyes, and though I'd never talked to her, I knew she'd been a friend of the local guys for years.

When I noticed her eyes lock with mine for a moment, I smiled, completely satisfied as they shifted to my right. She was more interested in Holden than me – which made her the perfect girl for him tonight.

"And I think I found just the one," I said confidently, clapping Holden on the shoulder, making him choke slightly on the beer in his mouth. Looking back to the pair, it seemed that they'd both noticed Holden's little mishap, smiling to themselves as I nodded subtly towards them. "The one with dark hair, what do you think?"

Holden eyed her curiously, and I had a feeling she knew that he was watching as she spoke happily to her friend. I saw the spark of interest in his eye, but he was nervous. I knew he'd never been with anyone other than Juliet, and maybe he just needed a push in the right direction.

"Come on," I urged him, nudging him ahead of me as we headed towards them.

I noticed that the blonde girl seemed on edge as we approached, quite opposite to the girl that seemed confidently happy to be eyeing Holden.

"Hey ladies," I said smoothly, sticking my free hand in my pocket as I nodded in greeting. The blonde's eyes were cast downwards at her drink, and for some reason, it intrigued me as to why she was here when she seemed so uncomfortable.

"Hey yourself," the other girl grinned, her eyes flicking between Holden and I. "What brings you guys over here?"

Holden stayed silent, and while it seemed as though him and the blonde would make a great pair, I needed him to get back to his usual up-beat self.

I smirked slyly, nodding my head in Holden's direction. "Well, I'm really just the wing man on this one, but this guy could really use your company tonight," I said slyly, and when I saw a thrilling gleam in her gaze, I knew that I'd done my job.

"I guess in that case," she said, biting her lip as she glanced back at her friend with an undecipherable look, "I'm Stella, and this is Katie."

Nodding, I softened my smile as Katie's head tilted up and our eyes met. "It's nice to meet you," I said, though I was thrown off slightly as Holden all but grunted a return greeting. "I'm Dean, and this grumpy idiot is Holden."

He glared at me as he finished off the last of his beer, something that Stella took an interest in as she laughed at my words.

"Well Holden, if you're up for it, I need another drink, and I'm sure these two will be just fine if we get you one too."

I raised my eyebrow in surprise, and silently gave Stella props, because even I wasn't that forward. Though as she glanced my way to make sure I was fine with her suggestion, I shrugged, glancing quickly at Katie. "I'm cool with it."

Katie sighed, so quiet that I barely heard it before she spoke, "Me too."

Stella's grin widened as she quickly grabbed Holden's hand and pulled him towards the coolers. And though he glared at me, I knew he wasn't bothered all that much.

"So," I trailed, turning back to Katie, "Your friend's pretty forward."

It surprised me as I heard her laugh, and while it wasn't all that loud, I found it strangely cute. "That's one way to put it," she said, trailing her pointer finger along the rim of her glass as her gaze stayed lowered. "Stella sort of goes after what she wants, and it seems your friend is the lucky guy on her radar tonight."

"And do you?" I asked impulsively, though when her eyes widened, I instantly regretted the question.

"I don't, um – "

"I'm sorry."

Her eyebrows furred as the red tint that had graced her cheeks slowly began to fade. "Why are you sorry?"

"I don't know," I shrugged, "It just seemed as though the question made you uncomfortable."

Her lips tilted up at the corners. "It's fine," she said softly, "I just didn't expect to be at a party tonight."

"To tell you the truth, I didn't either," I admitted, "But I think Holden really needed the night out, even if he doesn't want to admit it."

"Is there something wrong with him, or...?"

"It depends on how you look at it," I replied, causing a curious expression to gloss across her features. "His girlfriend broke up with him a few weeks back, and he's kind of been down since he found out she'd already gotten with someone else."

"Well how long were they together."

"Since their junior year of high school."

"Shit," she whistled, and even though the word slipped from her lips so easily, I couldn't help but think that it sounded foreign coming from her. As far as my first impression of her went, Katie seemed like the type of girl that was shy and innocent, keeping out of everyone's way and lingering in the shadows. Yet somehow, I'd managed to see her through the dark. "Then maybe Stella wasn't the best choice for a rebound since, how do I put this?" she paused, genuinely thinking of her next words. "She can be a bit overwhelming when it comes to guys."

I grinned, lifting my cup up to my lips. "As long as she makes him forget about his ex tonight, then my job is done."

"And what made you choose her in the first place?" she asked inquisitively, drinking from her own cup as she waited for my response.

"Not taking into account that most of the other girls here have already met Holden at one point or another," I started, "I saw that she'd been looking over at him, so I thought I'd give it a shot. Plus, the fact that she had an attractive friend kind of sweetened the deal for me."

She raised an eyebrow skeptically, though I didn't fail to notice the trail of heat that had risen on her neck. It somehow made her more appealing, especially since she didn't shy away from my words like I somehow expected her to. "And none of the other girls here appealed to you more?"

"Maybe you're just different than the other girls here."

She laughed - loudly and fully. And while I could see some of the guys looking over at the two of us curiously, most of them smirking as they assumed she was the latest girl I'd set my sights on, I ignored them. Katie intrigued me, and it was something that didn't happen with the girls I'd previously been with.

"What?" I asked, a smile forming on my lips at the sound of her laugh. It was like I was sinking deeper into a vortex that I hadn't even noticed, and I needed to know what I'd said that had caused this reaction from her.

"Is that the best line you could think of?" she asked cheekily, a grin tugging at the corners of her lips as her laughter died down. "Telling me that I'm not like most girls so that I'd think I'm special? Because if it was, then I think you'd better cut down on the drinks, because they're starting to affect your brain."

I chuckled, swirling what was left of my drink in the bottom of my cup. "I hadn't meant for it to be a line," I said with amusement trailing my words, "And I'm driving tonight, so I think my brain is safe."

"Same," she replied, her voice softer than before as she nodded down at her own cup, "But now I'm curious."

I quirked an eyebrow. "About what?"

"What the best line that you use to get girls is," she replied teasingly.

It was my turn to laugh, but suddenly, for reasons other than getting Holden hooked on someone other than Juliet, I was glad that I'd come out for the night.

It was a few hours later when the crowd slowly began to dwindle.

After I'd told Katie the best pick-up lines I could think of off the top of my head – making sure to point out that a majority of them were just used to get the girl to laugh – we'd found a couple of free seats near the bon fire that had been set up. It was closer to the crowd, but that didn't matter so much to me, because I couldn't seem to tear my attention away from Katie.

I'd offered her my sweater once the night air had gained a distinct chill, and while she'd been resistant at first, I'd insisted. And thank god I did, because her zipping up my sweater over her chest somehow made her look better than she did in the shirt that she had on underneath.

"I can't believe school starts in a week," she said once midnight hit, crossing one leg over the other. We were already sitting close to one another, and this action caused her knee to knock against mine, and while I acknowledged it, she didn't seem to. "I mean it's crazy that we only have one year left."

We'd been talking for hours, and I had learned that she did go to Duke; she just didn't frequent parties as much as Stella seemed to. I figured she was more of a fly on the wall than a social butterfly, but that didn't bother me in the slightest. I'd also told her that I was on the basketball team, which she had already assumed, and that I'd had NBA scouts looking at me for the past few years, but I wanted to finish my degree before deciding to play professionally.

"I know," I said, "And soon enough we'll be out in the world, all by ourselves."

There was a flash of something in her eyes – and I'd noticed it a few times over the course of the night – but it was fleeting, and I couldn't understand what it meant.

"I don't know about that Mr. Hot-Shot-Basketball-Player," she teased, "It seems like you have your future pretty well planned out for you."

"Still..." I trailed, not really knowing what to say, because while we'd spent the night talking, we really didn't know each other that well.

Katie seemed to feel the same ounce of awkwardness that I suddenly did, as her eyes moved around the open field, looking anywhere but directly at me. Her gaze stopped however, as she spotted Holden and Stella standing out near the trees, almost completely hidden from the view of onlookers.

"It seems like your plan worked," she said, pulling the long sleeves of my sweater over her hands.

As I saw Holden smiling down at Stella, I knew that it had. It didn't matter if the distraction was just for tonight, because Stella had managed to get Holden talking and acting like himself again, so it was clear that Juliet hadn't completely wrecked his heart.

"That's because I'm secretly a creative mastermind," I replied jokingly, easing the tension that had sprung up between us over the past minute.

It worked, as she laughed. "Sure you are," she mused, though she couldn't hold in the yawn that made its way past her lips. "But I think it's time to break them up for the night."

Agreeing with her, the two of us made our way over to the pair, interrupting their conversation as we appeared next to them.

"You ready to head home?" I asked Holden, the smallest of smirks playing on my lips as my eyes travelled between him and Stella, and what little space separated the two before he took a step back.

He coughed, disguising his discomfort as he shot me a glare. "Um," he started, turning to look at Stella for a moment, "I was actually thinking of heading back with Stella."

I raised my eyebrows in surprise, though I masked it quickly.

"I thought you were staying at mine?" Katie quickly interjected, looking to her friend quizzically.

Stella smiled sheepishly. "Do you mind an extra person taking the couch?" she asked pleadingly.

Katie sighed, shaking her head. "I guess not."

Her reply seemed to satisfy both Holden and Stella as I turned to her and smiled. "So, I guess I'll see you around campus?" Katie's smile was shy as she nodded, and as she went to unzip my hoodie, I shook my head, causing her eyes to glaze with confusion. "Keep it. That way I've got a reason to see you again."

I was satisfied as I saw Katie's cheeks blush a dark hue of red before a goodbye escaped her lips, and I backed away, winking at my best friend as I left him in the company of the two girls.

The drive home seemed longer as I traveled alone. I had turned the radio off, having had enough of background music over the past couple of hours, and I'd rolled the window down. It was an end of summer night that I hadn't anticipated, and while I'd gone out solely with the purpose of helping Holden, I was shocked that I'd managed to meet someone like Katie.

It wasn't something I was expecting, and she was still on my mind as I made my way home.

And maybe that was why I didn't see the car coming at me from the right as I passed through a set of stoplights. I had the green light, but that didn't stop the other driver from speeding up, and before I had time to break or accelerate to avoid it, I turned my head and my eyes widened.

The lights were bright, and they felt were all I could see as the car jolted sideways at the force of impact.

I could tell that I was screaming – but whether it was out of fright or pain, I didn't know.

Glass was shattering around me, and a searing pressure felt like it had exploded over my entire body. I didn't know which way was up and which way was down as my car was pushed off the road. There was a familiar taste of blood in my mouth as my mind raced a mile a minute.

I wasn't sure when the car had stopped moving, but the seconds that ticked by were agonizing. My thoughts were jumbled and my whole body was aching as I tried to move, but realized I was trapped when my head lulled forwards onto the steering wheel.

And the last thing I heard was the sound of sirens approaching from the distance as the outside world faded to black.

Chapter 3

It was just past eight in the morning when my alarm sprung to life, effectively waking me up.

Daylight broke into my room through a crack in the thin curtains as I rolled over and silenced the constant beeping. Letting my head fall back against the pillows, I simply relaxed into the peaceful lull of my surroundings. I could hear the vague sound of birds chirping outside my window, and for a moment, I let my thoughts drift to the previous night.

Soon after Dean had left, the three of us – Holden, Stella and I – had made our way to the car. The two of them had slipped into the back seat while I was behind the wheel, and even as I nudged the volume of the radio up, I could still pick up on their hushed conversation.

Thankfully though, they'd not resorted to PDA in the back seat.

I had to hand it to Dean, because while his matchmaking skills had more than likely been a complete fluke, Stella and Holden had genuinely seemed to hit it off.

Dean.

He'd been an enigma that I couldn't quite work out. He was undeniably attractive, with his dirty blond locks and winning smile, but that had only made my nerves accelerate when Stella had left me alone with him. It was more his easy-going personality, and the way that he just went with the flow of things that got me to loosen up. He shared tiny bits of himself with me, prompting me to do the same, and as the night progressed, everything just felt simple.

It was strange. I wasn't normally that open with people, especially someone I'd just met, but there were moments when I was listening to him talk that the thought of kissing him had crossed my mind. They were fleeting feelings – the kind that floated happily around your head as a means to make you smile. They were only a blossom of what could be, and only time would tell if the feelings would bloom or fall from the stem.

Stretching my arms above my head, I bit my lip as I'd realized I'd fallen asleep in Dean's sweatshirt. He'd insisted that I keep it, and while it was a smooth attempt at getting to see me again, I'd been too tired when I'd climbed up to my bedroom the night before to shrug out of the comfort that it offered.

Getting up for the day, I knew I had almost an hour of spare time before I had to catch the bus to work. I took my time in the shower, letting the refreshing downpour wake me up before pulling on a pair of yoga pants and a loose t-shirt from my wardrobe.

Making my way downstairs, the lights were still off, and the only hints at life were the soft snores that both Stella and Holden were making, as they laid asleep on the pull out couch. Thankfully, even with the blankets covering them, I could see that their clothes were still on, which made the situation considerably less awkward on my end.

And while Holden was someone that I truly didn't know, I'd let Stella bring friends over plenty of times before, so this occurrence wasn't far out of the ordinary.

Pouring myself a bowl of cereal for breakfast, my stomach grumbled in anticipation. I spent the next half an hour feeling as though time was passing dreadfully slow, and while I scrolled through all the apps on my phone and finished my food, I had yet to hear anything from the pair currently occupying the living room.

As I finished rinsing off the dishes that I'd had piled in the sink the night before, I glanced at the clock, and knew that I had to wake them soon if I wanted them up before I left for work.

Flicking the lights on in the living room, I'd hoped that the action alone would be enough to wake them, but when they barely moved a muscle, I sighed, walking over to the couch. Leaning over, I nudged Stella's shoulder a few times with my hand, pulling back as I noticed her squirming awake.

Stella groaned as she stirred, and I chuckled as I saw Holden's eyes slowly open with confusion.

When I was sure that both of them had noticed me, I quirked an eyebrow as I smirked. "Hey."

Stella turned her head away from me, avoiding the morning light as she snuggled deeper into her pillow. "What time is it?" she asked in a mumble.

I laughed, pulling her pillow out from under her head. "Almost nine."

Holden sat up, running his hand through his messy hair. It was almost impossible not to see the guilt swimming in his eyes as they moved between Stella and I. "I should probably get home," he said, his voice catching Stella's attention as she raised herself up on her elbows. He grabbed the beanie that had fallen off his head during the night, tugging it on.

Stella yawned, covering it with her hand before she smiled at him. "I had fun last night," she said to Holden, causing him to crack a smile.

"Me too."

I motioned towards the entryway when nothing else was said. "I'll walk you out."

Holden nodded, smoothing out his clothes slightly as he followed me to the door. "I'm sorry if I ruined your plans with Stella last night or anything," he said hesitantly, his hands venturing into his jean pockets as his shoulders hunched. "I'm not usually – "

I cut him off with a soft smile as I opened the door. "It's fine," I shook my head. "Dean kind of explained to me what was going on with you last night, and if Stella happened to get your mind off your ex, then it's all good."

"Great," he muttered, ducking his head with embarrassment. "But thanks for letting me stay here."

"No problem."

"Maybe I'll see you around," he said awkwardly as he stepped out into the hall.

My lips pulled up at the corners. "Maybe."

Letting the door shut as he made his way down the hall and towards the elevator, I turned on my heel and headed back into the living room. Shaking my head with amusement, I saw Stella curling herself back up under the blankets.

"You know I'm leaving for work in a few minutes, right?"

She mumbled an incoherent reply, and as she pulled her pillow over her head, I made the assumption that she was suffering from a mild hangover.

I let her be as I collected my things from my room - throwing my scrubs, keys, and wallet into my bag – but once I returned a few minutes later, I saw that she hadn't moved a bit. I sighed. "Make sure you lock the door before you leave."

I saw her sneak a glance at me, the edge of her lips turning up tiredly as I flicked the lights back off. "You know I always do," she said, yawning as her words slurred together. "Have a good shift."

Seeing her lay there comfortably had me wishing, on some level, that I could do the same. In fact, as I stepped out of my apartment and shifted my bag higher up on my shoulder, I tried and failed to remember the last time I'd been able to truly relax without worry clouding my thoughts.

"Katie?" Claudia asked, gaining my attention as my eyes snapped up to meet hers. I was standing at the foot of the patient's bed, having just finished writing down the updated information appearing on the monitor as she changed the patient's IV. "Would you be able to get the latest dose of pain medication for him?" she asked, nodding to the boy in the hospital bed.

I nodded, and after telling her that I'd be right back, I took the clipboard with me as I stepped out of the room. Heading towards the medical reception, my footsteps echoed off the walls, and there was still the small voice in my head that found it surreal I'd been given a job in the place I'd visited so frequently the past year. As the reception desk came into view, I joined the short line, noticing how quickly it dwindled down to nothing.

"I need the next pain dosage for the patient in room 54D," I said politely, sliding the clipboard across the desk so that she could look it over.

"Sure thing," the middle aged nurse behind the counter said, checking over the details I'd handed her. She turned and grabbed the required medication from the locked cabinets, handing me one small box of pills before signing off on them.

"Thanks."

"No problem," she said, handing me back the paperwork. "So, I heard Claudia let you give your first sponge bath before lunch."

Her words were heavy with humour as I visibly shuttered at the memory. The elderly man I'd been tasked with bathing had seemingly enjoyed my company a little too much as I'd scrubbed him down, all while Claudia had watched with a small smirk on her face.

Only after it was over did I learn that it was a tradition that the nurses did with the new hires.

The nurse saw my grimace as I nodded in confirmation and let out a laugh. "Don't worry, you'll get a lot more familiar with patients the longer you work here," she said with amusement.

I smiled wryly at the thought of working here for a while longer. It might not be the most glamorous job in the world, but it was what I wanted to do with my life. " I look forward to it."

Making my way back to the young boy's room, I delivered Claudia the medication and grabbed a glass of water. Handing it over to the boy, I watched carefully as he tossed the two pills into his mouth, and swallowed them.

"Are we done with the checkups then?" I asked as I followed Claudia out of the room. The boy's family had been allowed in as we finished up, and she began leading me away from the patient sector of the floor.

"We have a few minutes free," she replied, looking back over her shoulder as she went to push through a door, "So I wanted to show you – "

I never got to find out what she'd been about to say, as our supervisor called out for her. "Claudia," he said from a few feet behind us. Her attention immediately shifted as she saw him jogging towards us. "Are you and Katie able to tend to a patient right now?" he asked, his eyes flicking between the two of us.

Without a second thought, she nodded. "Sure," she said, taking a new clipboard from him.

He let out a breath of relief. "Thank you," he said. "He's being moved into room 29D right now from the ICU, so you're going to need to do a full examination before you let his family into the room."

"Will do."

When he turned and headed out of sight, I saw Claudia grimace as her eyes scanned the pages that he'd passed her.

"Is it bad?"

Her gaze shifted towards me and she nodded. "Drunk driving accident," she said, reading from the medical notes on the top page. "A young male was hit and veered off the road with critical injuries, and the impaired driver didn't make it to the hospital."

The words caused a small amount of pain to prick at the edge of my heart. "Is the male stable?" I asked hesitantly, falling into stride with her as we ventured back towards the patient's wing.

"It depends on how you look at it," she explained. "He's alive, and he'll recover with time, but right now he's not in good condition."

We stopped in front of room 29D, waiting back a moment as a group of workers piled out of the doors before stepping inside.

A tiny sound escaped my lips as soon as the door closed behind me - so quiet that Claudia didn't bat an eyelash towards me as she walked around the bedside – and I froze mid-stride. Dean was lying, beat and battered, in the hospital bed in front of me, and I could've sworn the sight caused my heart to stop beating.

Memories of the night before quickly began flashing through my mind, because the guy I'd met then, looked completely different to the one laying unconscious in front of me now.

He was almost unrecognizable, as he laid motionless in the bed, having been stripped of his clothes and thrown into a white-checkered gown. His eyes were closed and his hair fell raggedly flat against his forehead. The doctors had elevated his right leg, as it was wrapped extensively with gauze to cover an operation site, and they'd stitched up a few cuts on his forehead where a few drops of dried up blood were clotting.

I couldn't even begin to imagine the pain he'd gone through, as I had yet to see a strip of his skin that wasn't covered in a scratch, bruise, or cut.

When Claudia handed me the clipboard with his information on it, my shock seemed to wear off slightly as I noticed that she hadn't noticed my falter. With instructions to fill out the basic information as she hooked Dean up to his monitor, I nodded numbly. Watching as the numbers leveled out on the screen after just a few moments, I scribbled down the readings haphazardly. My mind was still unclear - wondering how this could have happened – which was dangerous. I was only half coherent, nodding and doing my best as Claudia told me which boxes to check off as she checked him over.

She pulled back from Dean's side minutes later, seemingly done with her inspection and checks, but as she readjusted two of his IVs, my muscles tensed as I noticed his fingers twitching.

That was the first sign, and when I saw his eyes peel open seconds later, I held my breath and tightened my grip on the pen I was holding. There were bruises surrounding both of his eyes, and his skin was ghostly pale, but as he slipped into consciousness, I zeroed in on the way his irises glassed over, flicking aimlessly around the room.

"What's happening?" he croaked, his voice dry and scratchy.

Something heavy settled within my chest as his gaze bore straight through me with no recollection of who I was.

"You were in an accident," Claudia replied, keeping her composure as she turned to me. "Would you be able to grab his family from the waiting room? They're allowed in now, and I'm sure they'd like to know he's alright."

I nodded wordlessly, clutching the clipboard to my chest as I walked briskly from the room. The hallway was empty, making it easier to collect my thoughts and even out my breathing, but it didn't change the situation.

Dean had been in a car wreck, and right now, I was one of the people helping him recover.

My steps were automatic as I walked towards the waiting room, and as I pushed open the double doors, I was met with a room full of hopeful, piercing eyes. The room was on edge, as everyone waiting there wanted me to tell them that their loved ones were okay – that they'd get better. I couldn't do that however, and knowing that put the weight of the world on my shoulders.

"Um, Mr. and Mrs. Adams?" I called out, feeling an ounce of guilt as so many sighed with defeat.

A small group of people to my left stood up though, seemingly frazzled and deterred by the news of Dean's accident.

The man and women who stood up first were clearly Dean's parents, and a pair beside them seemed as though they were family as well. They were younger, maybe a few years older than myself, and the man looked uncannily similar to Dean, though the woman holding a child to her chest with comfort showed no resemblance.

Dean's dad intertwined his hand with his wife's, gripping tightly for support as tears welled in both of their eyes. "Yes?" he croaked, watching me with carefully.

He was terrified for his son.

I gulped. "Dean's allowed visitors." I said slowly, nodding back through the doors that I'd just emerged from. "If you'll all just follow me," I trailed, watching as they took the steps forward before I turned around.

The footsteps resonated loudly off the bare hospital walls, and the air was clouded with a tenseness that couldn't be described. It was hopeful, scared, and frightening all at once. Glancing back to make sure the group was keeping up, I stopped in front of Dean's door, pushing it open as Dean's family hurriedly rushed inside.

The steady beeping of his pulse transmitted loudly through the monitor, though it's sound was drowned out by his mother's sobs as she let her hand fall from her husband's and rushed to Dean's bedside. His father walked up behind his wife, wrapping his arm around her shoulders to steady her as she wept, while the other two people moved to the other side of the bed, taking a seat in the small, plastic chairs that lined the wall.

I kept my tears at bay, knowing that I was meant to stay strong in these situations. It was a part of my job. It just hurt when the person you were treating was someone you knew.

After awhile, as Claudia and I stood back to let everyone get settled, Dean's father finally turned to us with confusion and worry filling his eyes. "What happened?"

"It was a drunk driving accident," Claudia said, and before she could utter another word, I saw his brother's facial features harden as his eyes snapped to Dean.

"You better not have been the one driving drunk," he ground out lowly, his voice menacing and angry.

"I wasn't."

"He wasn't."

Two voices spoke at the same time, and while the first one was undeniably Dean in a dry tone, it took me a few seconds to realize that the second person who had spoken was, in fact, me.

Curious eyes flitted to me, as I drew my gaze downwards, ignoring the soft bundle of heat that bubbled on my cheeks.

Claudia once again broke the silence as she nodded in confirmation. "They're both right. Dean wasn't the one driving drunk, and the culprit did die on impact. He was speeding through a red light before he rammed into the side of Dean's car. Luck was on Dean's side however, as a cop was patrolling near by and saw the accident, so help was there immediately to save him from the wreckage."

"So what's wrong with me?" Dean asked bluntly.

"Well, your car seemed to crush a good amount of your lower body, which is where a majority of your injuries were,"

Claudia said, glancing down at the clipboard I'd returned to her for a clear reference. "Your right knee was shattered and you had an immense amount of damaged tendons surrounding the site. The doctors did what they could to repair it, but you also have a broken fibula, which luckily, didn't pierce through your skin. Two of your ribs were cracked, and six were bruised, which is why you may be finding it difficult to breathe. There were signs of a concussion once the doctors sealed up the wound on your forehead with stitches, so you may experience a load of nausea, dizziness, and memory loss for a short amount of time. The rest of your body is simply covered with cuts and scratches that will heal, but you'll be staying here for at least a week or two until you're able to function semi-permanently again."

"And what about my eyes?"

His voice lacked any sort of emotion, as though he had hardened himself up to the tragedy, while his parents, his brother, and the woman and child had tears welling and streaming down their faces at the news.

Claudia nodded. "That's the tricky part, you see, as the doctors were able to remove the glass from your eyes, but in doing so, the procedure caused several bruises and scratches. While your vision may be incredibly blurry and weak now, there is a great chance that your full ability to see will return within the next 48 hours or so. But if it doesn't, we'll run more tests to see if there's anything we can do to speed up the healing."

The explanation caused my eyes to widen the smallest amount. Dean was currently blind to his surroundings, which meant that he had no idea that I was there, and even though there was a tiny contraction of pain in my chest at the thought, I figured it was better this way.

Dean currently had way too much on his plate, and even though last night was vivid in my mind, his memories may have been tainted from the crash. He was better off healing with his loved ones by his side, and certainly didn't need someone he'd met less than twenty-four hours earlier worrying about him as well.

As the news and reality of the situation sunk in for everyone in the room, Claudia and I made our exit. The door clicked shut behind us, and I dragged in a deep breath. The sounds of sobbing and worried words coming from inside the room was saddening, but lifting my head up high, I knew there was nothing more I could do as I followed Claudia to see to our next patient.

Chapter 4

Hopeless. A burden. Useless.

Three words that described exactly how I felt as I laid – still and cramped – in the hospital bed.

My parents had flown out from Los Angeles as soon as they'd been called about my accident, while Ryan, Zoe, and Abbie had driven out from their home in New York for support, and yet, I didn't have the ability to look them in the eyes and thank them.

The room was heavy with despair as the nurses left to tend to other patients - the constant beeping of the ECG monitor and the underlying smell of disinfectant filling the air. I could feel a maze of wires and tubes connected to different parts of my body, and while I was sure that my green eyes roamed around - unfocused and delirious – I was thankful, just for a moment, that I couldn't see the state I was in.

I was a wreck – physically, emotionally, and mentally.

It seemed as though, with my eyes out of commission, my ears were on high alert. I picked up on the quiet sniffles to my left, no doubt coming from my mom as she tried to keep her tears at bay, and I could hear the awkward shuffling of chairs and feet as my family moved around.

The silence was thickening as nobody knew what to say, and while my mind was completely blank, having not yet made sense of the situation, I was able to break the quiet with a fit of hoarse and painful coughs. Every muscle felt like it was shaking as I brought my hand up to cover my mouth, only to have a plastic cup placed in my grasp as I did so.

"There," my dad said quietly, and I assumed that it was him that had given me the cup.

Tipping the plastic up against my lips, I felt a small amount of relief as the water slid down my throat. "Thanks," I forced out, my voice still raspy.

No one replied as the cup was taken from my hand and I heard the thump of footsteps moving away from my bed-side. I was still trying to understand what had happened, even though the nurse's explanation had been clear. I assumed it was due to the concussion and head trauma, but nothing was making sense to me, and it felt easier just to keep a clear mind.

"So... did you know the nurse or something?"

Ryan's voice was hesitant, but also curious, as though he thought that saying the wrong thing would cause me further pain.

I furred my eyebrows, turning to my right where I'd heard his voice come from. "What did she – " I started, though I was cut off as another coughing fit invaded my body. "What did she look like?"

"Blonde hair. Blue eyes. Around your age."

The description immediately brought my thoughts to Katie. The image of her blonde hair tied up loosely on her head, wisps escaping as the wind caught them, and her captivating eyes that lit up in the moonlight. She'd been a curve ball at the party – someone I hadn't expected to meet – and now, lying in a hospital bed, there was an internal sting that ignited at the possibility of never seeing her again.

I didn't dwell on her though, not wanting to stress any further.

And besides, she'd said she was going into her last year at Duke, so there was no chance that she'd been my nurse.

I shook my head, clenching my eyes shut immediately as I felt a throbbing pain in my temples. "I don't think so."

A dismissive noise escaped his lips. "Okay," he paused, "I just thought it seemed weird that she was so worried about you."

"Why?" I asked dryly, "Because it's strange for someone to be worried about me?"

"You know that's not what he meant," Zoe stressed with insistence, stepping in for my brother.

"I know," I spoke, though I didn't have the energy to lift my lips into a smile. My body was drained. Sighing, I dropped my head back on the pillows. "Just forget it."

A quiet lull followed, because what could anyone say in this situation? There was nothing that could be done to turn back the clock, but as the silence dragged on, the thoughts that I'd been keeping at bay began to fill my mind. There were so many things to think about – the accident, what I could've done to avoid it, my friends, my family, my future – and I didn't know when the turbulence of my mind would subside.

"Honey?" My mom's voice pulled me from the nightmare inside my head. I wasn't able to see the tears in her eyes or the crease of worry in her forehead as I shifted my head to the left, but the underlying fear of her words rang clear in my ears. "Are you okay?"

The truth was – I wasn't sure.

"I don't know."

I heard a sharp intake of breath and the legs of plastic chairs scraping against the tiled floors. I could hear Zoe talking quietly, and I assumed her words were directed to Abbie as I felt a pull on the covers beneath my body. Her tiny hands grabbed one of mine, grasping carefully to avoid the cuts and scrapes that covered my skin.

"I think you'll be okay Dean," Abbie said, with more confidence than a seven year old should have in a situation such as this. "You survived, and that means that you weren't supposed to die, so everything will be okay soon."

And for the first time since I opened my eyes and saw my blurred surroundings, I felt my lips quirk upwards.

They were just words from a young girl who had wormed her way into my heart years ago. While her assurance was nice to hear, as Zoe and Ryan pulled her back towards them as she struggled to climb up next to me on the bed, I wondered how long it would take for everything to truly be okay.

Because at the moment, I was failing to see the light at the end of this dark and dreary tunnel.

In all honesty, there wasn't much that my family could do but stick around for moral support. I wasn't allowed to eat much – not that I would be able to stomach it if I could – and I couldn't heal my injuries.

It seemed as though every few minutes, nurses were in and out of the room to readjust my bedding, keep me hydrated, and to make sure I took my painkillers. They were helpful, and I appreciated their expertise while they made sure I was comfortable, but the constant hassle was exhausting.

The longer I lay in the bed, the more irritable and annoyed I became at my situation. My mom's doting nature was starting to annoy me, and Zoe, my brother's girlfriend, seemed all too positive with her daughter at a time like this.

I knew that they meant well, but with everything going on, I just wanted some time to myself – some time to digest my situation.

Eventually, as the sounds of heavy voices and wide yawns hit my ears, I managed to convince the majority of my family to head to a hotel for the night after insisting that I'd be okay, but Ryan wouldn't hear of it. He wouldn't budge, and while he sent Zoe and Abbie off with my parents, he stayed by my side until I let my exhaustion take over.

All I could do, as I fiddled around uncomfortably trying to fall asleep, was pray that the next time I opened my eyes, this reality would cease to exist, and this whole ordeal would simply be a dream.

My body was rigid and stiff as the constant beeping of the monitor pulled me into consciousness hours later. I'd always been a morning person, ever since I'd begun morning training, so it wasn't a surprise when I opened my eyes to see darkness consuming the room.

For a moment I forgot what had happened over the last 48 hours. The accident seemed like a far off memory and the beeping replicated the persistence of an alarm, but as the room slowly came into focus, the unnerving feeling of hopelessness crept its way into my head.

Turning my head to the side, my sense of logic was somewhat halted, though I quickly recognized that the figure hunched over in the plastic chair was Ryan, still sound asleep in the corner of the room.

When my thoughts veered through the mess in my mind and eventually found the correct track, the realization came that I wasn't visualizing the room around me – I could actually see. It was blurry of course, and not at all the quality of vision I'd had just days before, but my eyes widened in surprise that at least something seemed to be going right.

My gaze instantly snapped downwards, taking in the mass of wires and injuries that covered my body, though seeing everything made it all the more real.

There wasn't enough time for me to truly take everything in as the door to my room pushed open, and a nurse walked in. Her tired eyes grew slightly and her posture straightened when she realized I was no longer asleep. "Oh, you're awake."

"Yeah," I said, slowly and with uncertainty as I attempted to push myself up into a sitting position. Though I was too weak, and she was able to take notice of that quickly, coming over to ease me upwards as I begrudgingly leaned back into my pillow.

"And it looks to me like you've regained your sight?" she asked inquisitively, picking up on how my eyes no longer darted around aimlessly. I grimaced, giving an affirmative as a sharp pain ignited underneath the gauze that covered my injured knee. Noticing my discomfort, she recorded the readings on the screen quickly before looking over my injuries. "I'm just gonna change the bandage on your head, and then I'll be back with some medication to ease your pain."

As she fiddled with the wrapping around my head, it was unlike any pain I'd ever felt during a game. I was used to getting banged around, and the usual headache after a particularly rough game, but as the nurse loosened and tightened the bandage, it felt as though a jackhammer was repeatedly pulsing inside my head. There would be seconds where the pain was intolerable and my face screwed up as I fought against it, but there were also the moments, brief as they may be, where the bandage tightened and the pain significantly decreased.

I had no sense of time as the pain continued, but thankfully, after what felt like an eternity – but was surely only a minute or two – it reduced to a semi-bearable level when the nurse finished up.

"There, all done," she said, giving me an encouraging smile as she stepped away from my bed.

With one final note on her clipboard, she promised she'd be back momentarily with my pills, and as she stepped out into the hall, the door swinging shut behind her, I felt like I could breathe a bit better.

Now there was no one I had to pretend for.

It must've simply been my state of mind following the crash, but it seemed now, with my sight returning and the ability to see what the accident had done to me, I was simply overwhelmed. Every small scrape seemed so much larger, the broken bones seemed like they had cracked into a million small pieces, and though the pain was bad at the moment, with my thoughts beginning to pile up quickly, it seemed like my brain was intent on making everything much worse.

The nurse returned, causing me to quickly pull myself together as she administered my medication. Ryan hadn't cracked an eye open the entire time, continuing to rest in the most uncomfortable position I'd ever seen, and as the nurse left once again, with a message to simply press the call button if she was needed, I felt a familiar heat prickle at the corner of my eyes.

The last time I had truly cried was at my grandfather's funeral when I was nineteen, and now, laying beat and battered in a hospital bed, I felt as though there was nothing else I could do.

Tears were slow to build beneath my eyelids as I laid my head back, closing my eyes in turmoil, but soon enough they were streaming down my cheeks, with only silence to accompany them.

When the tears began to subside and the pain medication slowly began to work it's way into my system, the sun was beginning to peak through the cheap curtains that covered the large panel window to my left.

It seemed as though the light was enough to wake my brother up after a rather eventful night, as he began to shuffle in his seat before peeling his eyes open. When everything became clear to him – where he was and why he was here – he stood up abruptly. Worry flooded his eyes as they trailed up and down my beaten body before zeroing in on my face, or more specifically, the partially dried tears that stained my cheeks.

When his gaze met mine, there was a mixture of relief, fear, and uncertainty merging together, and while we'd always been there for each other, through thick and thin, we both had no words. There was nothing I could say to assure him that I would be okay, and there was nothing he could do to help me out of my current situation.

Seconds passed and the tension in the room grew before Ryan cleared his throat. "How are you?"

I knew from the intensity of his gaze that there was more he wanted to say; he just couldn't form the words.

"Well considering the nurse brought me a high dose of pain meds while you were asleep, I'd say I'm doing alright."

It was an attempt to lighten the heavy atmosphere as I tried to act as though there was nothing wrong, but as Ryan cracked the smallest of smiles, there was still a definite sense of hesitancy between us.

"That's good," he said stiffly, digging his hands into the jeans that he'd fallen asleep wearing, "Any word from the doctors?"

I shook my head, ignoring the slight pain that ignited as I managed to pull the side of my lip up slightly. "No, but I got my sight back."

His eyes widened, as though he hadn't noticed the way my eyes were no longer moving blindly around the room. "You did?"

"Yeah," I replied. "I mean, it's not the same as it was, and you're a bit blurry, but I can definitely see you."

This news seemed to make Ryan release the largest of breaths. "Well it's good you're getting better," he said sincerely, before a joking edge latched onto his tone, "I wasn't ready to have a blind best man."

Even though I hated it growing up, in this moment, the teasing was just what I needed – though I didn't fully process what he'd said until a few seconds ticked by.

Best man.

My eyes widened. "You proposed?" I asked with shock, watching as a happy grin spread across my brother's face. However, as he shook his head in response, the confusion began to spread.

Pulling one of his hands out of his pocket, he brought a small velvet box out as well. Popping open the clasp, I jolted with astonishment at the ring that was nestled inside. It was small, but stunning - a silver band with an intricate diamond decoration.

"I've been carrying it around for a few weeks," he admitted, not taking his gaze off the ring as he ran his finger over the top of it. "I was planning to take her out to dinner yesterday, but after dad called me saying you'd been in an accident, my plans went out the window." He shrugged. "Besides, making sure you're okay is more important."

It was evident that he hadn't said it to make me feel bad, but I couldn't help but feel slightly responsible for ruining my brother's intentions.

The whole family knew that a wedding was in the cards for Ryan and Zoe. Ever since they worked over their rough patch at the beginning of their relationship, dealing with Ryan's lack of privacy as an A-list actor, they'd practically been joined at the hip. We all realized that it wasn't a matter of if they'd tie the knot, but simply a guessing game as to when.

"Take her out tonight."

My sudden and forceful words caused his eyes to widen, and it was clear he thought something besides a concussion was screwing with my head.

"Wh...what?" he stammered.

The pain in my chest was minimal as I took a deep breath, settling myself as I replied. "You shouldn't wait to do this because you feel like you have to," I explained. "Mom and dad will more than likely be here all night, and I know you said that Abbie starts school on Monday. If you really want to propose to Zoe, take her out for a walk tonight and just do it – I'll be happy to keep Abbie company in here for a while."

The idea was slightly insane – I knew that. I was lying in a hospital bed, and after having my brother drive all this way to be by my side, I was telling him that this was the perfect time to propose to his girlfriend. I could tell that, as he stood silently, taking in the suggestion, the wheels were turning in his head. The paparazzi didn't know he was here, he would have the privacy he wanted, and there was no doubt that if he asked, Zoe would agree in a flash.

"I don't think – "

"Don't think," I cut him off, "Just do it. I'm sure Zoe knows that you'll ask sooner or later, but this way, you'll catch her off guard."

The room was silent for a moment, bar the constant beeping from the monitor, and just when I thought he'd made up his mind and would shake his head in refusal, Ryan sighed. "You better be right about this," he said, and although there was a worried undertone to his words, the smile that pulled at his lips showed his true feelings.

"When am I ever wrong?"

Later that night, a little while after I had sat smirking as Ryan convinced Zoe to head downtown for dinner, the nurses had cleared out my room as the doctor that had operated on me came in to further explain what was wrong.

And the explanation managed to crush the small amount of happiness that had begun to sprout in my mind.

"After looking over your results from various scans performed while you were treated in the ICU yesterday, I can confidently say that you've sustained a grade 3 concussion due to the force of impact," he said seriously, waiting to continue until he knew that both myself and my parents had understood. "I would like to run a few more tests now that your eye sight has returned and you seem to be functioning better, solely to detect any permanent damage that may have been done."

"On a brighter note, your bruised ribs and broken bones have all been set, and should heal with the right amount of down time and therapy, but the brunt of the trauma was sustained in your right knee," he continued, pointing down to where my leg was elevated at the end of the bed. "While working around the shatter site, it was clear that your ACL was torn halfway through the tendon and your meniscus had torn as well. I was able to perform the surgery quickly to fix both problems, however, that does mean that you won't have use of your leg for a prolonged period of time, as we'll be wrapping it as soon as some of the cuts on your legs close up."

The tips that followed – which mostly ranged from different physiotherapy options and ways to continue with my everyday life – more or less flowed in one ear and out the other. The thought that I wouldn't be able to get around by myself was disheartening, and with one sorrowful look from my dad, I knew, without asking, that the chances of me continuing with my dreams of basketball were quite far-fetched.

I supposed that, with nothing but countless horrid scenarios floating around inside my head, I must've fallen asleep. I didn't know how long I'd passed out for, but with my medication acting as a sedative, I could only assume that it'd been a while.

When I wretched my eyes open, my mom had taken immediate notice, while my dad reached over to press the on-call button.

Ryan and Zoe were still yet to return, and as I waited for my next dose of pain medication, Abbie was seated beside me on the bed, attempting to cheer me up with a tale of fairies she believed to be true.

"Knock, knock," I heard minutes later as the nurse walked into the room.

What I wasn't expecting, was for a familiar blonde haired girl to be following shyly behind her. She was dressed in scrubs, and while I knew that my brain wasn't completely okay in that moment, I was sure that, through the blurred edges, my eyes weren't playing tricks on me.

"Katie?"

Chapter 5

I froze as soon as I heard my name slip from Dean's lips.

The last time I'd seen him he'd been experiencing difficulty with his vision, though after returning home, I'd not thought to check in on the progress of his healing. It was evident that, while I highly suspected his sight was not fully back to normal, he'd definitely gained a fraction of it back.

It seemed as though, in that moment, everyone's eyes were on me as I let the door swing shut behind me.

"So you do know her?" the little girl sitting beside Dean on the bed asked, flitting her gaze questioningly between the two of us.

I finally gained the courage to meet Dean's squinted gaze, and even in their damaged state, I could feel his eyes piercing right through me.

"Yeah..." Dean trailed slowly, though his facial expression was blank as he continued, "We met the night of the accident."

The air in the room became heavier as I sucked in a breath, receiving curious looks from Dean's parents as no one sought to reply.

Though, as the seconds ticked by, it was Claudia, with full professionalism, who broke the silence with an encouraging smile. "How about we complete this check-up?" she asked, directing her words towards Dean, "Are you hungry?"

"Starving," Dean said.

Claudia nodded, turning back to me as she hovered at his bedside, nodding towards the door. "Do you mind grabbing his dinner while I check his vitals?" she asked, though the look she was sending me was clear. It said 'I'm giving you a chance to duck out for a few minutes, so take it.'

"Sure," I stuttered, and while I tried to play it cool, I'm sure everyone in the room realized that, as I turned on my heel, my pace was rushed.

Stepping out into the hall, I took a left at the end of the hallway before halting my steps and leaning back against the wall of the empty corridor. The silence seemed somehow suffocating in a way, as the hustle and bustle of the rest of the hospital ceased to exist and my thoughts became louder.

Just yesterday I'd experienced the unthinkable as I stepped into Dean's room to see him lying on the bed. I didn't know what to do, I didn't know what to think, but after hearing what he'd gone through, I'd told myself that I wouldn't get involved. That I'd keep it professional – act as his nurse and nothing more.

I certainly hadn't expected to show up to work today and for him to be able to see me. Hearing my name had worried me, but at the same time, it had also sent a brief spark of happiness through me, knowing that the accident hadn't completely messed with his memory.

But that wasn't something I could dwell on at the moment, and as I continued my way towards the cafeteria, there was a new purpose to my step. My first priority was to do my job, but maybe, when I found the time, and the courage, I'd stop by Dean's room as a friend. He may not need the extra support, but I'd be there to offer it if the need arose.

Despite my new found determination, I still took my time returning to Dean's room once I collected his meal. Pushing open the door to his room, I immediately felt the underlying awkwardness in the atmosphere. The curious eyes of his family members followed me as I stepped up to Dean's bedside, my head ducked in shyness as Claudia finished up his check-up.

I wanted to say something – anything – as I situated the tray of food on Dean's lap, but his facial features were immensely impassive, betraying no clues as to what he was thinking. Staying silent, I could feel the weight of his gaze as I turned and followed Claudia out of the room.

"You know that you don't have to tend to patients that you know, right?" Claudia asked, though she didn't turn to face me as the question left her lips. She was focused solely on finishing up the paperwork in her hands as we headed further down the corridor.

I let out a deep breath. "It's fine," I admitted, and while my voice sounded stern, my insides were jumbling with nerves.

"Are you sure?" she continued, glancing back at me with a raised eyebrow as she exchanged clipboards with another nurse.

"Positive," I said with affirmation, tilting my lips upwards, "I don't know him that well anyways." The words left an unfamiliar taste on my tongue, because although it was the truth – I'd only spoken to him once – it felt as though a connection had been built in that short amount of time.

It was clear that Claudia didn't completely believe me, though she didn't push any farther, which I was grateful for. She simply nodded in acceptance before leading me further down the corridor, giving me hope that, with other patients to tend to, the rest of this shift would fly by.

I spent a majority of that night tossing and turning underneath my covers. My mind just wouldn't shut off, and for some reason, every time I closed my eyes, all I saw were glimpses of a car crash. I figured this was my subconscious urging me to just talk with Dean, but when I got out of bed for work the following morning, sluggishly and yawning frequently, I wished there was a simpler way.

I just wasn't ready.

Or maybe I was, but I was much too shy, and couldn't fathom what to say.

It was times like these that I wished my house wasn't so empty – when I wished that Theo hadn't moved halfway across the world, and I wished my mom hadn't gotten sick. Because as much as I appreciated the friendship that Stella and I had, I couldn't find it in me to let her know about Dean yet, or more so, I didn't even know how to bring it up.

That's how, even with a minimal amount of rest, I found myself heading to work an hour earlier than need be, but as I walked through the sliding doors of the hospital, instead of heading for the break room, I took the elevator up to my mom's room.

Every time I visited, there was always the voice in the back of my head that urged me to think positively. That somehow, overnight, maybe she'd made a miraculous recovery, but similar to every other time, my hopes were dashed as I pushed open the door to her room to see her lying still in her bed, the same as she always was.

I let the door fall shut, taking a seat in my normal chair next to her bed.

"Good morning mom," I said softly, as I readjusted a bit of her bedding. "I guess I just wanted to let some stuff off my chest, and even if you're not awake, I knew that you'd be willing to listen."

After all, even the strongest people needed someone to lean on during tough times.

"So, I guess I should start off with the fact that I met a guy a few nights back," I admitted. It was a sentence that I hadn't spoken since high school, before everything in my life began to fall off of its axis. It seemed foreign coming from my lips, but I still felt a light heat dust across my cheeks as I ducked my head and continued. "Stella dragged me out to another one of her parties, and while she was off flirting as usual, Dean just seemed to be there. He was nice, funny, and everything just seemed effortless that night. I left with a smile on my face, but when I turned up for work the next day, he ended up lying in bed as one of my patients."

I continued on, telling her all I knew about the accident and his current condition.

"It's complicated," I sighed, once I realized I only had about ten minutes left before my shift was due to start. "I want to see him get better, but I don't know how much support I can give when I barely know him."

"Anyways," I trailed, "I'd better get going, but I'll be back tomorrow, alright?"

Squeezing her hand gently as my eyes scanned her face, I noticed, not for the first time, how peaceful she seemed when she was asleep. The odd times I dropped by to see her awake, she'd be talking to doctors, stress lines creasing her already pale skin, and the ghost of a frown would almost always grace her lips. While resting however, she was just as beautiful as the days when she used to sing in the kitchen while baking with Theo and I.

Bringing my free hand up to wipe the stray tears that had escaped over the past hour, I went to pull my hand from hers when I felt the faint pressure of hers latching onto mine. My eyes flashed up to her face quickly, wondering if she was awake, but when she showed no further signs of consciousness, a smile twitched on my lips.

Maybe she'd heard me, and maybe she hadn't, but either way, as I made my way down to meet Claudia and start my shift, I couldn't help but think that maybe that small gesture was a sign that things with Dean would work themselves out – one way or another.

For training purposes, in the days that led up to the start of my school term, I was scheduled with daily shifts to adjust to my role as a nursing assistant. It was easy to get familiar with the main gist of the job, but things like proper drug dosages, where to store certain files, and memorizing the different medical routines of each patient were much more complex.

It seemed as though I was learning something new every day, and while I was nervous to begin juggling school and my job, Claudia assured me that I'd be just fine making the adjustment. After all, my shifts would start to become shorter, and I'd been taken off the on-call list until my classes ended.

And although thoughts of Dean were very much still floating around my mind, it was seldom that Claudia and I would visit his room. Whether it was due to scheduling, or because Claudia had mentioned to someone that I knew him, it didn't matter. I still hadn't managed to speak more than two words to him at a time, and anything that minimized the awkwardness and tension was a plus in my mind.

When Monday finally rolled around, and my alarm clock went off just after seven, I felt reenergized. It had sunk in that this would be the last year that I'd be stuck sitting in a classroom, because once the next eight months passed, there would no more weekly lectures or tedious lab reports.

It was bizarre to think about, and somewhat scary, but as I pulled myself out of bed and headed for the shower, I didn't dwell on it.

After I had pulled on a pair of shorts and a striped t-shirt, my phone dinged with a text from Stella, telling me that she was just leaving her place and would be here to pick me up in a few minutes.

Typing out a quick reply, I threw a few of my notebooks, my wallet, and a cardigan into my bag, while making sure I hadn't forgotten anything. Minutes later, I was waiting on the sidewalk outside my apartment building when I saw Stella's car round the corner and roll to a stop right in front of me.

I'd barely managed to close the passengers' door when Stella pulled back onto the road.

"In a hurry?" I asked teasingly, having become used to her style of driving over the years.

She rolled her eyes as I fastened my seatbelt, only turning to look my way when she came to a red light. "You seem to forget that getting up this early for class is not something I enjoy."

"Which constitutes the question as to why you chose early classes on a Monday?"

"I didn't have a choice," she grumbled, causing me to laugh as the traffic began to move. "What kind of professor only teaches on Monday mornings? I don't know how he thinks everyone will be able to stay awake for three hours."

"Doesn't your class only start at nine?" I asked, raising an eyebrow, as I vaguely remembered helping her with her schedule a few months previous.

"Yeah," she said, raising an eyebrow, "What's your point?"

I shook my head with amusement. "Because for someone who claims to hate the mornings, you picked me up more than an hour earlier than you needed to."

As she flipped on her signal and slowly took a right, heading for the university, she gave me a look that I couldn't quite decipher – with her eyebrow raised and her gaze pointed.

"That's because we're stopping by William's for breakfast, and you're going to tell me what's been going on with you the past couple of days." Her words caused my throat to go dry for a moment as my eyes widened. Her gaze flitted back towards me for a moment, though her irises were now much softer. "Did you really think you could hide something from me? Give me a bit of credit. I've known you since you were thirteen – I know when something's bothering you."

Stuck for a reply, I felt an ounce of guilt begin to worm its way around the pit of my stomach. If I was being honest, Stella and I usually didn't keep things from each other. She was always forthcoming with information, even when it was something I didn't needed to know, mainly regarding details about whatever guy she was with at the moment, but I was always quieter. The last time I'd kept a secret from her had been the summer before we started university, when my mom had fallen ill. Even then, she'd picked up on my mood swings and sudden unwillingness to go out, so it shouldn't have surprised me that she managed to figure out I was hiding something.

I sighed, resting my head in my hand as my gaze stayed glued to the window. "I'll explain everything once we get there."

Seemingly satisfied, the sound of the radio filled the remaining minutes of the ride, covering the otherwise heavy silence that surrounded us.

When she pulled into the William's parking lot, the both of us headed inside without saying a word, in fact, neither of said anything until the waitress headed back towards the kitchen with our orders.

"So... are you going to tell me what's been on your mind, or am I going to have to start guessing?" Stella quipped.

And that was how everything came out.

It was easier to explain things to Stella than it had been to my mom – mostly due to the fact that she'd been there the night of the party. As I spoke about the crash, and how Dean was still in recovery at the hospital, her expression turned pale with disbelief.

"And you've kept this all to yourself since you found out?" Stella exclaimed after a short lapse of silence between us. Her voice was loud enough to echo across the café, causing me to turn and send an apologetic look to the surrounding customers.

"I spoke about it with my mom," I offered, though my voice was quiet as I slumped lower in my seat. She knew everything about my mom's condition, including the fact that I often talked to her when she was sleep. "I didn't know what to say I guess," I continued, "I mean, I didn't expect to go into work and see him there. It just sort of threw me off."

Her gaze held sympathy as her lips pulled upwards with a supportive smile. "Of course it did," Stella replied. "You didn't even have to tell me what happened that night at the party between you two, I could just tell by the smile you had on your face when we were driving home that you were happy."

I felt colour flood my cheeks as the waitress returned with two coffees, resting a mug in front of both of us as I ducked my head, letting a few strands of hair fall in front of my face.

"So, have you talked to him?"

My head snapped up and a frown creased my forehead. "Hmm?"

"Dean," she said softly, taking a sip of her coffee before continuing, "Have you talked to him at all?"

My grasp tightened around my mug as I shook my head slowly.

Stella's gaze turned curious at my response. "Why not? I'm sure he wants to know that you care enough about him to check in on him."

"The only times I've seen him over the past week are when I'm bringing him his pain medication or his food, and it doesn't really seem as though he particularly wants to start a conversation with me."

Stella shrugged. "Sometimes it's the girl that's got to make the first move," she said an encouraging smile flashing across her face before she sighed and looked down at her drink. "At least now I know why Holden didn't answer my texts a few days back."

I straightened up in my chair as I realized that, even though Dean was the one who'd been injured, Holden probably hadn't known what to do once he found out that his best friend had been in a car crash.

"I honestly haven't seen him around the hospital Stells."

She shook her head to clear her mind. "Don't worry about it," she said, "Besides, I'm sure it wouldn't have gone anywhere anyways. But you, missy, have to talk to Dean, and soon."

Realizing that she simply didn't want to talk about it, I took the hint. "And how do you suppose I do that?" I asked jokingly, though I really was open to any suggestion she had, because currently, courage was something I significantly lacked.

"Well," she started, pausing as she sought to rack her brain around an idea, "Do you still have that hoodie he leant you? You could always go and return it after a shift."

Her idea began to turn the cogs in my mind, and as I realized that it wasn't such a horrible plan, I noticed the satisfied smirk that Stella wore as she saw me contemplating it.

I stayed silent, choosing not to reply, and though the conversation dropped as our breakfast finally arrived, I found her idea circling the back of my mind. It was definitely something I could consider, because really, what could go wrong?

As the first week of classes passed in blink of an eye, I managed to stay on top of the pile of assignments I'd been given, but when it came to Dean, there had still been no progress made.

I knew he was healing, that much was obvious from his extended stay in the hospital, but from what I'd gathered from Claudia, he was being released over the weekend, which meant there was only a small window of opportunity left for me to talk to him.

Over the course of the week, I'd managed to slowly build up enough courage, and as my shift ended on Saturday afternoon, I lingered around the break room, waiting until the last bit of willpower found its way into my heart.

"You're still here?" Whirling around, I saw Claudia coming out from the bathrooms, changed out of her scrubs with her bag slung over her shoulder. "I would've thought that you'd be out of here as soon as possible to catch the bus."

"Umm, no," I stuttered, "I'm actually going to visit someone, so I'm sticking around for a while."

Her eyebrows raised, and while I knew that she was aware my mom was residing a few floors up, there was a certain gleam that sparked in her eyes, telling me she clearly knew it wasn't my mom I was waiting around for.

"So, you're waiting until the day he checks out to go talk to him?" she guessed, a sly smile on her face as she nodded to the sweater that was hanging in my locker that was clearly too big for me. "Cutting it a bit close, aren't you?"

I smiled sheepishly, ignoring the blush that graced my face. "Better late than never, right?"

Claudia laughed as she shook her head in amusement. "Have a good night Katie," she said, waving goodbye as she headed for the door, "And good luck."

"Thanks," I replied, dropping my voice to a whisper as the door swung shut behind her to leave me alone, "I'm going to need it."

Taking a few extra moments to collect my things, I threw my bag over my shoulder, grabbing Dean's sweater just before I shut my locker. Moving with determination, I headed towards corridor 29, knowing that his room was the last one on the right.

Standing outside the door for a few seconds, I finally brought my hand up to knock, clutching Dean's sweater in my arms as I waited for an indication that I wasn't interrupting anything. That came seconds later, when a small weight shifted just above my stomach to launch a flight of butterflies as I heard Dean's voice, hoarse and barely audible, inviting me in.

Holding my breath, I placed a palm against the door and pushed it open, letting the air out of my lungs slowly as I saw Dean pushing himself up in his bed. His expression morphed from bored and tired to surprised and intrigued as he noticed me enter the room. I resisted the urge to turn and head back into the hall as his eyes bore intently into mine, but as the door fell shut, I realized it was just the two of us.

"Umm, hey."

My voice was timid as I used my free hand to play nervously with the zipper on my bag, waiting for him to say something.

"Hey," he said simply, his voice devoid of all emotion.

Stepping further into the room, I couldn't help but let my gaze drop to his injuries. For the most part, the smaller cuts and scrapes he'd obtained from the crash had healed drastically over the time he'd spent in the hospital. There were still a few noticeable injuries however, including his right leg, which was now secured in a full leg brace, and the cut on his forehead which, with the stitches gone, was beginning to scar. I had no idea how much his sight had improved, though with the way he was watching me, almost calculatingly, I'd have to guess that it was almost as good as new.

"Why are you here?"

I faltered as his voice cut through the air, much stronger and more pronounced than it had been previously. "I, umm, I have your sweater, and – "

"I meant why are you here now?" he asked again, though this time the bitterness and anger rang through in his voice. "You've known I've been here the entire time, hell, you're one of my nurses, and yet, you never came to talk to me."

Tears pricked at the corner of my eyes. He was right, because while I'd been contemplating how to strike up a conversation, he'd always been here. I'd just been too nervous and afraid to face him.

"I was scared," I admitted quietly, letting the sweater of his that I held drop on the edge of his bed. "I walked into work the day after the party, and I definitely didn't expect to see you here. I wanted to make sure you were alright, but when your vision was impaired, I thought it'd be better if you didn't know I was around. That all went out the window when your eyes improved, but I couldn't really think of anything to say."

He was listening, and as I stopped to meet his eyes, they were less hostile than before. "I wouldn't have found it weird if you would've just stopped by."

"I didn't think you wanted me to."

He laughed dryly, though when he began coughing a few seconds later, worry flooded my eyes.

"I'm fine," he insisted as I made a move to get closer to him, though he did take the glass of water I offered him, gulping it down greedily. "And I did want to see you, mostly just because it would've been nice to know that I wasn't the only one who felt something that night at the party."

My heart squeezed at his confession as flashes of us smiling and laughing around the campfire appeared in my mind.

"You weren't," I said softly, the edges of my lips turning upwards, "But the way I was looking at it, there was more important things that you had going on, like healing, and getting out of here."

"Well you got your wish, because the doctors say I can leave later today, as long as the tests they did this morning have nothing wrong with them," he said, "though I'm guessing you already knew that."

Biting my lip, I nodded, subconsciously letting my gaze fall back down to his damaged leg. "I don't, umm, do you want to talk about it?" I asked anxiously, "Because I'll be here to listen if you do."

I had let my hand fall to his bedside, and as his eyes met mine, I felt the warmth of his skin gently touch mine. "Not really."

My lips turned up at the corners as I nodded in understanding. "Then we don't have to," I said, "We can talk about whatever you want," I continued, before my nerves got the better of me. "Or if you want me to leave, I can – "

"Don't go," he cut me off, clearing his throat as my eyes widened. "I just want someone to talk to me as though I'm not stuck in a hospital bed if I'm being honest," he admitted, his voice tired and raw as his head sank back against the pillows.

"Okay, well umm, what do you want to talk about?" I asked nervously, sitting down in the plastic chair that was seated next to his bed, not wanting to pull my hand away from his just yet.

He raised an eyebrow jokingly. "How about you start by explaining to me why you said you were still a student at Duke, when you've clearly got a full-time job here?"

"About that," I started hesitantly, "I didn't lie." Dean still seemed unconvinced. "I started classes last week, just like everyone else, but I started here at the hospital a few weeks back. The money helps pay for school, and I couldn't turn down the opportunity for the experience."

His facial features shifted from ones of disbelief to seemingly curious and impressed. "You're telling me that you have a full course load and a full-time job?"

"It's not exactly full-time – "

"Katie," he said sternly, though a smile was threatening to appear on his lips, "You know it's okay to boast about things every once and while, right?"

Biting my lip, I looked anywhere but directly at him. I'd never been one to talk about myself all that much, especially things that seemed impressive or would make me stand out. I was a fly on the wall, and I'd gotten quite good at perfecting that persona over the years.

Noticing that I'd gone silent, Dean cleared his throat, and when I finally tilted my head up to meet his eyes, wariness flooded his gaze. "So, school..." he trailed unsurely.

It took me a few moments to catch on, tilting my head sideways until everything just clicked when I saw him shift uncomfortably in his bed.

My eyes widened. "I'm so sorry," I babbled, my voice apologetic, "I didn't even think. We can talk about something else, I don't mind. How about how – "

"Katie, it's okay." I froze. "I actually, umm, wanted to know how everything was the first week?"

"You did?" I asked tentatively, watching as he nodded. "Well, I mean, I don't really run in the same social circle as you, so I can't really say much, but I didn't find anything all that different."

It was evident, as his expression deflated, that those weren't the words that he'd wanted to hear.

"Oh."

"But I'm sure things will change when you go back to school on Monday," I offered.

"That's just it though," he said, pausing as a frown twisted its way onto his face and his eyes averted towards the door, "I don't know if I want to go back."

His confession was quiet, and in that moment, I realized that he probably hadn't had anyone else to talk to about this. At least no one who would understand. His family wanted to know that he was getting better, not that his thoughts were on the verge of depression, and somehow, I'd become the one who could listen as he spoke his mind.

I masked the surprise that coursed through me. "Can I ask why?" I questioned carefully.

Dean closed his eyes and sighed. "I just don't think I'll be able to deal with the way everyone will look at me," he admitted in defeat. "Last year I was spending half my time in the gym and focusing on getting my team on the same page, and now I'll be in a wheelchair for a few weeks before I can even start to walk with crutches. I don't want to see the pity in everybody's eyes, because it just makes it more evident that maybe I won't have the future I always dreamed of."

I wasn't going to lie – I could see where he was coming from. He was used to being looked up to and praised by his teammates and friends, but sometimes, even the greats had to fall to find out where they truly belonged.

I squeezed his hand, as it hadn't moved from mine over the course of our conversation. "I don't think you should give up just yet," I said softly and with encouragement. "You still have your degree to focus on, which is, umm – "

"Biology."

I smiled, not figuring him for someone who had an interest in science. "Right, and you never know what could happen. Trust me, everything will get better. Maybe not today, and maybe not tomorrow, but eventually, it will," I promised. A beat of silence passed. "You'll see."

He managed a weak smile in response, though I could see the hope and light slowly glimmer in his eyes. And in that moment, something came over me that I couldn't explain. It was an impulse – something I couldn't control – which had me leaning down to kiss his cheek with affection and support.

And maybe it would've been okay, that is, if he didn't turn his head towards me just before my lips met his skin.

Our lips pressed together in a way that was completely unrehearsed, and I heard the quick hitch of his breath as my eyes widened in surprise. His lips were warm, if not a little chapped due to his condition, but that didn't stop my heart from accelerating as I pulled away quickly.

Biting my lip, I blushed as I saw the way his eyes regarded me with surprise. "I'm sorry," I whispered, "I didn't mean to do that."

An unreadable expression crossed his face, but was gone before I could decipher it. "Don't worry about it," he said calmly.

Realizing I was still all too close for comfort, I went to pull back when the door pushed open to reveal Dean's older brother, causing the both of us to wrench our hands apart, embarrassment filling the air around us.

"Well, well," he relished in amusement, "Either of you want to explain what's going on here?"

Chapter 6

Ryan's grin was wide, his eyes sparkling with amusement as they flitted between Katie and I.

Looking back at the last half an hour, I couldn't begin to comprehend what had transpired between the two of us. I'd been angry and confused when I saw her, but that had quickly been diminished when I realized that she was just as shy as she had been the night of the party. She was the same girl that I'd been interested in, and even though it took longer than I would've liked, I was glad that she'd worked up the confidence to come and talk.

In fact, it was difficult to keep my eyes from drifting in her direction. She sat on the chair next to my bed, fingers folded nervously on her lap as her hair fell in front of her face to mask the flush of her cheeks. I assumed that she hadn't meant to kiss me, and even though the thought of her regretting it put a thorn in my side, she was clearly embarrassed to have my brother, who she didn't know, walk in immediately after.

"So..." Ryan trailed teasingly, "Anything interesting happen while I dropped everyone off at the airport?"

"Nothing too exciting," I said dryly, glaring at my brother as he chuckled silently to himself, "We were just talking."

"Sure you were," he quipped in reply, turning towards Katie with a smile on his face, "But I don't think we've ever been properly introduced."

I swivelled my head towards her as she looked up at my brother shyly, her lips twitching upwards as the pink hue that graced her cheeks dulled. "I'm Katie," she said softly, picking up her bag that hung from the back of her chair before standing up and smoothing down her clothes. "But I think I've just about overstayed my welcome, so I'll just leave you two alone."

"You don't have to you know," I protested, "Leave that is."

Katie smiled, though the way she readjusted her bag atop her shoulder told me that she wasn't going to change her mind. "It's fine. The next bus comes in a few minutes any-ways, and if I don't catch that one, I'll be waiting around for a while." She turned back towards my brother. "It was nice to meet you," she said, looking back over her shoulder at me as she made her way towards the door. "I'll see you around Dean."

"See you."

When the door shut behind her, and I was sure she was out of hearing range, I directed a flat look towards Ryan.

"Couldn't you have hopped on that plane back to New York with your fiancée and her daughter?" I asked with irritation.

He smirked, shaking his head as he stepped closer to my bedside. "They'll be fine on their own for a week or two," he replied, "Plus, mom more or less expects daily updates from me until you're back on both feet."

"I didn't know you'd been hired as a full-time babysitter," I said sarcastically.

"I'm not," he replied, "But because I know that you're not going to have the easiest time over the next couple of days, I'm sticking around to do what I can."

His words were sincere, and if I was being honest with myself, I was glad that he'd decided to stick around, even though it was going to be weird having him bunk on my couch for a prolonged amount of time. But before I could say thank you, he had to ruin the moment by eyeing the sweater that Katie had left at the end of my bed with a grin plastered across his face.

"I don't remember bringing you that from your place," he commented slyly.

"That's because you didn't, nimrod," I returned, rolling my eyes. "I leant it to Katie a few hours before my accident, and she was just giving it back."

Ryan's eyes glazed with amusement, but before he could reply, the door swung open once again. Holden appeared, a quizzical look on his face as he held up a backpack of things I'd asked him to bring from the apartment.

"Did I just see Katie leaving?"

"That you did young one," Ryan replied, his tone still teasing as he looked between the two of us.

Holden's eyebrows rose in surprise, as if he truly hadn't believed what he'd seen as his gaze met mine hesitantly. "I didn't realize you two were still talking," he trailed unsurely.

I shrugged. "She works here, so I've seen her around," I said offhandedly, "And she knows I'm heading home today, so she dropped by to talk."

He nodded, accepting my words as he hovered near the door. Ever since the first time he'd visited a week ago, I realized something was off with Holden. I didn't know if it because of the accident, because he was now living with a cripple, or another reason entirely. Whenever he visited, which was seldom, and only for short periods of time, his words were clipped and he'd often avoid looking directly at me.

It was disheartening, but like Katie had said, I had more important things to focus on as my body recovered.

Though the air began to grow heavier as the time ticked on, it was levelled as Ryan pulled Holden into a conversation about university. Holden answered, only somewhat enthusiastically, and it didn't take a master of observation to sense the uneasiness and turmoil that being here caused him.

Thankfully, not much time passed when a doctor strode into the room, halting conversation and turning everyone's heads.

"Well Mr. Adams," the doctor smiled, jotting down a few notes, "Correct me if I'm wrong, but I'm sure you've been waiting anxiously to be cleared for release."

My lips turned upwards and a chuckle breezed through my lips. "You could say that."

The doctor let loose a laugh in reply, though sobered up as he looked down at his clipboard. "Then I'm happy to say that everything looks good with the results from your blood tests yesterday," he explained professionally. "You're going to be stuck in the full cast on your right leg for some amount of time, but we've scheduled you an appointment back here in two weeks to see if things have been healing alright to switch you to a normal cast. If all goes well, that's when you'll be able to be upgraded to a pair of crutches."

Nodding along as he continued, I realized how he generally avoided the injuries to my eyes. I know they were getting better, as my vision was clearing up, but it was also apparent that everything was not as it used to be. I waited until he finished speaking though, before asking, "And what about my eyes?"

His smile dimmed slightly as he sighed. "That's one thing I can't really say much on," he said reluctantly. "Your cornea seems to have healed completely, but with your vision still appearing blurry, you're being given a recommendation to visit your local optometrist to see if a pair of glasses will solve the problem."

"And if it doesn't?"

"Then we'll go over your other options if, and when, the time comes," he returned. Pulling off a sheet from his clipboard and handing it to Ryan, he continued. "But if that's all the concerns you have, you'll just have to get that prescription filled in the pharmacy on the first floor before you leave. The dosage has been lowered significantly to what you've been taking, but if you find yourself in an immense amount of pain, come back and we'll do a few tests to adjust it. Other than that, if you're ready to head home, I'll get a nurse to come around with your release papers and the wheelchair that's been set up for you."

"Sounds good doc," Ryan said, shaking the doctors hand before glancing my way. "What do you say, are you ready to get the hell out of here?"

A huge weight lifted off my chest as I let out, what felt like, my first breath of relief in ages. Nodding, my lips curved into a smile of satisfaction as I replied, "Most definitely."

It turned out that the thought of heading home, and actually going home, were two different matters entirely. In my mind, getting out of the hospital and back into my own apartment would be a breath of fresh air – as though things would begin to go back to normal when my surroundings were once again familiar.

However, I quickly realized how naïve I'd been to think that way.

The first dilemma occurred before we left the hospital parking lot. After signing the release papers and filling my prescription, I was wheeled out into the fresh air, but was faced with the problem of fitting my wheelchair into the car Ryan had rented. It was a struggle, but after numerous attempts, Holden had managed to squeeze the wheelchair in with him in the backseat, while Ryan helped me into the passenger's seat.

The car ride that followed was silent for the most part, as I kept my eyes transfixed on the window while Ryan navigated his way through the city. My gaze scanned over the normalcy of everything – how the buildings and streets looked the same as the sun shone down through the clouds, and how couples and friends were laughing on the sidewalks without a care in the world.

"Dean?" Ryan's voice shook me out of my thoughts as I turned towards him, "Did you hear what I said?"

"Sorry," I shook my head, running a hand through my messy mop of blonde hair.

"It's fine," he said, his lips twitching upwards as he pulled the car into a parking spot a few buildings down from our apartment. "I was just asking if you wanted take-out for dinner?"

"I'm good right now," I replied, sighing as I realized that I no longer had to rely on the food that the nurses brought for me, because while it was edible, it definitely didn't do much for my taste buds. "I'll eat something from the fridge when I get hungry."

Ryan nodded, taking the keys out of the car before climbing out and walking around the front.

My forehead creased in confusion as he pulled open my door. "Why aren't you parking at mine?" I asked, knowing that with my car in the dump, there was no longer anything occupying the space.

Ryan's gaze flicked to Holden for a second, though when my curiosity shot to him, he averted his gaze, focusing on prying my wheelchair out from the backseat. As my attention slid back to Ryan, I noticed him sigh. "I guess it wasn't going to be a secret much longer."

"What secret?"

"Well, I know you worked hard to save up the money to buy your car a few years back," he began to explain, "And since it wasn't your fault that it got totalled, I thought that you could do with another one without having to deal with your insurance."

"What do you mean?" I asked, though as a sheepish grin appeared on his face, everything clicked. My eyes widened in shock. "You bought me a car?"

"Now don't be mad," he rushed out in defense, holding me up as my balance began to sway. "It's a few years old, and was leased by someone else before you, but Holden and I thought that you'd like it once you're cleared to drive."

"I'm not mad. I just," I paused, letting out a deep breath, "You know I won't be driving again for a while, right?"

"I know," he shrugged, helping me down into my wheelchair, "But once you're healed, and feel ready to drive again, it's there."

I didn't know what else to say, except, "Thank you."

"Don't worry about it," he said offhandedly, pushing me forward as Holden lingered a few steps behind us. "Besides, what's the use of having an actor as a brother if you can't reap the rewards every once and a while."

Letting out a laugh as the lobby doors of my apartment slid open, I quickly sobered up as I realized how drastically different things were since the last time I'd been home.

It'd been just over a week, but it felt like a lifetime.

Two neighbours were lingering in the lobby, their conversation falling quiet as they caught sight of me as Ryan pushed me in the direction of the elevators. I caught their eyes, and all I could see was the pity and confusion that swirled in their irises before I averted my gaze and ducked my head down towards my chest.

The three of us – Ryan, myself, and Holden – rode the elevator up silently to our apartment, emerging to the marble hallway seconds later. Taking out his key, Holden wiggled it around in the lock for a moment before the latch clicked, and with a simple push, waved me in.

"Welcome home," he said, his voice scratchy and wavering as he stepped aside to let me through.

I expected the familiarity to calm me down, for it to help the doubt in my mind and the fear in my chest, but simply looking at the living room, it was crystal clear that things wouldn't just bounce back to normal because I was no longer in the hospital.

The furniture had been moved around, presumably by Holden, sometime over the last week. There were clear cut paths constructed so that maneuvering around in a wheelchair wouldn't be unbearable, and to accommodate our new roommate, the couch had been set up as a pull-out at the far corner of the room.

I looked back to Ryan, and in turn to Holden, but they were both just standing behind me, watching me carefully as though I'd explode at any moment.

Sighing, I gripped the wheels of my chair the best that I could and slowly inched myself across the room. "I'll just be in my room," I said, not speaking directly to either them, and more so just notifying the two of them that I'd be alright on my own.

The voices were hushed as I made my way into my room, and while I tried to pick up on some of what they were saying, it was just too hard. Shaking my head and choosing not to eavesdrop, I struggled for a few moments as I moved myself from my chair and onto my bed, lying back against the pillows in comfort.

I settled for getting my thoughts straight, but it seemed as though no time had passed before a knock on my door caused my head to turn, seeing Holden standing there with his hands shoved deep into the pockets of his jeans.

"I know you said you weren't hungry," he said, clearing his throat, "But Ryan's cooking up some bacon and eggs, considering that's pretty much all that's left in the fridge."

"Okay."

It seemed as though he wanted to say more, as his forehead creased with a frown and a jolt of confliction danced across his features.

"Are you okay?" I asked, the words an instinct response, as the last time I'd seen him look this upset – this recluse – was when Juliet had broken up with him.

Holden's eyes widened in shock, his turmoil fading slightly as confusion overtook it – as though he couldn't quite believe that I was asking him if he was okay.

"I'm fine," he muttered, though with the way he averted his eyes and moved to step back into the hallway, it was clear he was lying.

"I just want to know what's been going on with you lately," I said dryly, anger beginning to pulsate through my veins. His presence had been sparse in the hospital, a time when I'd needed him for support, and now, he seemed as elusive as ever. "It's not like you're the one in a wheelchair here – "

"But it's my fault!"

His words hit me hard, causing me to stop short as a range of emotions flitted across my face. Any thoughts that were growing in my mind shattered to bits at his outburst. "What – " I started, my voice strangled and my eyes wide. My head was spinning, and it wasn't because of my injury. "What are you talking about?"

Holden's posture fell hunched as his fingers shot up, running through his hair in a mess. He began pacing around the room, hurriedly and in no real pattern, my eyes following his movements as I waited for him to pull himself together. He looked as though he'd been defeated, and was grasping at the little hope within him that was holding him together.

"If I had just gone home with you that night, if I'd just stuck to the plan, I would've been in the car with you," he said, his voice strangled as though the weight of his guilt was crushing him. "I would've been sitting in the passenger's seat, and I might've seen the car. You could've avoided all of this and – "

"Stop," I said, cutting him off as I found my voice, "Just stop."

"But – "

"There's nothing that you could've done to stop this," I spoke levely, gesturing to my damaged leg and the wheelchair next to my bed. "The drunk driver slammed into the passenger's side of my car, so if you would've been in the car that night, you might not have survived. That guilt would've fell on my shoulders, considering I'm the one that forced you out that night, and I don't know if I'd be able to cope."

He sighed, his facial features stressed as he sat down in my wheelchair. "I just wish there was something I could do to help," he admitted quietly. "I know everything's going to shit for you, and right now, if I could switch places with you, I would.

I don't know why his words sparked hilarity, but I found my lips tilting upwards as a laugh escaped. "Sorry," I said, meeting his eyes to see that he was looking at me as though I'd gone insane. "It's just, even though things are going to shit, I'm still going to need your help with things."

And for the first time in a while, I saw the wry tilt of his lips as he shook his head. "If you're expecting me to give you sponge baths, you're going to be very disappointed."

I chuckled. "What about helping me get dressed in the mornings?"

He shook his head in amusement as he stood up, motioning for me to take the seat he'd just vacated. "How about I bring you out to the kitchen so that you can finally eat some real food," he offered, watching as I scooted myself to the edge of my bed and sat up to the best of my ability. The smell of Ryan's cooking was wafting across the apartment, and though there was a burnt undertone in the air, it was still more appealing than the food I'd been eating all week. "After all, bacon makes everything better."

The claim was true, to some degree, as the return to normal food felt like a feast to me. It was a small step back towards normality, on top of returning home, but the climb ahead was a steep one. All I could do was hope that, as time went by and the dust settled, things would return to the way they used to be.

Chapter 7

The pressure of his lips on mine was driving me wild. My eyes were closed, and as strong hands came up to cup my cheeks, I felt his tongue delve deeper into my mouth, adding fuel to the blazing fire that ran through my veins.

He was evading all of my senses. I could feel his hair as I gripped the strands gently between my fingers, smell his woodsy cologne that lingered on his skin, and hear the quiet moan that escaped him as he pulled me impossibly close. A gentle nip to my bottom lip caused a quiet whimper to escape me, causing his lips to move feverishly on top of mine.

It was thrilling, it was beautiful, and it was –

A dream.

I was startled awake, and pulled from my fantasy, as my alarm sprang to life. With wide eyes I quickly racked my brain around my surroundings, realizing that I'd fallen asleep in the early hours of the morning at my desk. Papers were crumpled slightly from where my head had been resting, a half empty mug of coffee sat near the edge of my desk, and one of my notes had a particularly large spot of drool that caused me to cringe as I stood up. Stretching my back muscles as I strode across the room to stop the incessant beeping, a yawn escaped my lips, and for the first time in weeks, the thought of insomnia popped into the back of my mind.

In my teenage years I'd been very focused on studying, and while I kept up a decent social life, there were times – during exams and while working on projects – when my sleep patterns began to suffer. I hadn't thought much about it at the time, as it was periodic, and I'd usually be able to get through the days with a few cups of coffee.

However, everything went downhill when I collapsed on campus right after my last exam during my first semester at Duke.

My study habits had worsened, and with my mom being diagnosed just months earlier, I'd more or less stopped sleeping. After being taken to the hospital, several blood tests and physical check-ups had given the doctors all the evidence they needed to diagnose me with chronic insomnia. The cause – a mild case of depression, as well as the constant stress I placed on myself.

The year that followed was a hard one. I'd been put on a small dosage of medication to help with my depression, Theo had accepted a job across the world, and my mom's health had slowly begun to deteriorate. My social life suffered, though Stella was fully supportive, and I managed to push through and succeed in school, my job, and helping out my family anyway that I could.

Slowly, the insomnia began to fade, though it was still a reoccurrence during extremely stressful points of my life. At times, I would find myself sleeping through the night, or waking up once during the week, but at other times, I could go weeks with only one to two hours of sleep per night.

I tried my best to keep a sleeping schedule, though with my new position at the hospital, and my final year at Duke starting up, I'd just not been able to stick to it over the past couple of weeks – and the effects of doing so were beginning to catch up to me.

Taking a deep breath, and a minute to collect my thoughts, I realized that following my afternoon shift the day before, I'd been so concentrated on getting my assignments done, that I'd stayed up until three in the morning.

Shaking my limbs out, I headed into the bathroom, hoping that a stream of warm water would sufficiently wake me up and give me enough energy to get through the day.

Though with the thoughts of insomnia ebbing out of my brain, flashbacks from my dream began to race through my mind once more.

Closing my eyes, the brief moment between Dean and I on Saturday replayed. I didn't know what had come over me, but as I leant in to kiss his cheeks, I certainly hadn't meant to meet his lips. But while it was an embarrassing accident, I didn't regret it. The soft touch of Dean's lips against mine had sent a small spark of electricity through my veins, and our conversation had given me hope that, while he needed to heal, he wouldn't hold my avoidance of him during his stay in the hospital against me.

That maybe, just maybe, we could build a friendship, or something more, in the future.

Once I slowly began to feel the tightness in my muscles unwind, I shut the water off and stepped out, feeling much less tired and ready for the day ahead. It took me only fifteen minutes to get ready, after tossing on a simple outfit and braiding my damp hair down the back of my head, but as I sipped on my steaming cup of coffee and picked a fresh apple out of the fruit bowl, I heard my phone ringing from where I'd left it in my bedroom.

Scampering quickly towards my room, I picked up my phone, and thinking it was Stella telling me that she'd be leaving soon to pick me up, I answered the call without looking at the screen. "Hey, Stella," I said, bringing the phone up to my ear.

A throat cleared on the other end of the line, followed by a deep voice that certainly didn't belong to Stella.

"Umm, it's not Stella," the voice said unsurely, "It's Holden."

"Oh, sorry," I said, furring my eyebrows, as I made my way back towards the kitchen, "I just assumed it'd be her."

"It's cool," he said awkwardly.

"So, umm, you called because...?" I asked, as he paused, as though he forgot the reason for his call.

"Oh, right," he started, "I was wondering if it was possible for you to come over here for a bit?"

Surprise fell over me as his words registered and my eyes widened. "Now?" I asked, knowing that it couldn't have been much after half past seven.

"If you can," he trailed, and I could imagine him scratching the back of his neck awkwardly. "It's just, Dean's kind of having a rough time this morning, and he mentioned your name, so I thought maybe, if you were free, you could come help Ryan and I."

Opening and closing my mouth as I attempted to formulate a response, the brief emotion of happiness that registered in my mind at the thought of Dean mentioning me vanished, quickly being replaced with turmoil. He'd mentioned Saturday that he was hesitant to return to school, so this morning must not be the easiest on him, especially with the added pressure from his brother and best friend.

"Katie?"

"Sorry," I shook my head, weighing my options. I didn't start class for at least two hours, but if I ditched my usual morning ride from Stella, I'd be stuck taking the bus to campus. I sighed, knowing that without much thought, my mind was already made up. "Text me the address, I'll leave in a few minutes."

Double checking the message Holden had sent me to confirm the address, I gazed up to see the sun coming through the clouds above the five story apartment. It was a similar building to my own, not anywhere close to grand and luxurious, but perfect for students, and surprisingly, less than a ten-minute walk from my place.

Adjusting my bag on my shoulder as I pressed the buzzer for their apartment, it didn't take long for Holden's voice to come through the intercom, inviting me in as the door unlatched. I was fidgeting as I rode the lift up, ignoring the slight creek that it had as it came to a stop on the third floor. My anxiety heightened as the metal doors slid open and I saw Holden standing there, waiting for me in the open doorway of his apartment.

What was I doing here? What could I really do to help Dean more than his brother or best friend could?

"Hi."

With a wry tilt of his lips, Holden nodded me in, staying quiet as I stepped in front of him and into the living room. I could hear, who I assumed was Ryan, banging on Dean's bedroom door, pleading with him to unlock his door and go to school.

Cringing as I heard a crash, I turned to Holden to see that he'd closed the door and was now shaking his head, seemingly frustrated with his roommate's actions. "Now you can see why I called you over."

"About that," I started quietly, "How did you get my number?"

A sheepish expression crossed his face as he rubbed the back of his neck. "I asked Stella for it," he admitted, "I hope that was okay."

My eyebrows rose slightly, not knowing that the two of them kept in contact much after the night of the party, though apparently, Stella was holding out on me. "It's fine," I nodded, biting my lip, "But what do you really think I can do to help?"

"Well, I guess I just thought – "

His thought was cut short as Ryan stomped out into the living room, grumbling angrily under his breath as he raked his fingers through his hair. My movements halted as his eyes landed on me, and his shoulders visibly relaxed as a deep sigh left his lips.

"Thank god you're here," he voiced, coming over to stand next to Holden, "Maybe you can talk some sense into him."

I looked to Holden for an explanation, my facial expression bewildered. All I knew so far was what I'd been told– which was that Dean was having a rough time – but it seemed apparent that their issues with him were much more complex.

Holden, picking up on my evident confusion, sighed and replied, "He's beginning to realize that things aren't going to just snap back to normal now that he's back at home. Yesterday he seemed determined to maneuver around here on his own, and even though we offered to help him, so he wouldn't have to use his chair, he refused."

"He's used to doing things on his own – it's been that way for a long time – and I think the mental and physical frustration of his injury is starting to get to him," Ryan chimed in while Holden nodded along in agreeance.

"A crash was what woke me up this morning," Holden stated. "I don't know what happened – "

"And neither do I."

" – But by the time we were out of bed and at Dean's door, he'd locked himself inside, adamant that there was no chance he was going to campus today."

Their statements simply confirmed the thoughts that had gone through my head when I'd been on the phone. Dean, although strong, was feeling defeated, and as a star athlete, it was seemingly something that he wasn't accustomed to.

He needed reassurance and a game plan – something that would get his spirits rising again – and for some reason, that appeared to be me.

"And you two think I can help?"

Ryan shrugged. "Honestly, it's worth a shot," he muttered, though as he continued, his lips turned upwards with amusement. "The last time I saw you and my brother together, you seemed quite close, so I think right now, you're the best chance we've got."

I ducked my head, blushing as I brought my hand up, pointing towards the hallway. "So," I cleared my throat, "Dean's room is that way right?"

Holden nodded, while Ryan just stood there, entertained at the sight of colour filling my cheeks. "First door on the left."

Turning on my heel, I made my way across the room, disappearing from the two men's views until I stood still in front of Dean's bedroom door. Closing my eyes as I took a deep breath, I exhaled quickly before bringing my clenched hand up to knock gently against the wood. Waiting a few seconds, I heard nothing, and just as my fist made contact with the door for the second time, Dean's voice, loud and abrasive, split through the air.

"Didn't I tell you guys to leave me alone?" he exclaimed, his words accompanied by a small crash that caused me to flinch.

"Dean?" I spoke softly, though my voice did have a notable squeak to it, "Will you please open the door?"

Silence followed my plea as I stood alone, gripping the shoulder strap of my bag. When I heard jostling from within his room, I turned my head to see that Holden and Ryan were watching me curiously from the end of the hall, and when the latch to the door opened, I expected a quizzical look or a raised voice.

Or anything other than Dean wrenching open the door with a neutral expression on his face, nodding me inside, and preceding to lock the two of us inside once I'd stepped over the threshold.

My eyes roamed unsurely around the room, noticing the pulled drapes, a dent in the wall across from his bed, and a broken alarm clock left lying on the carpet.

"Who called you?" he deadpanned, his voice breaking through the silence, causing my gaze to snap towards him as he wheeled himself slowly towards his bed.

My eyebrows knitted together. "What?"

"Ryan or Holden," Dean questioned further, repeating himself as he asked once again, "Which one of them called you?"

"Oh," I said, "It was Holden." Dropping my bag to the floor, I slowly moved towards the edge of his bed as he helped himself up, taking a seat as I continued. "He said that you were talking about me this morning, or something, and – "

"It's not what you think," he said in a rush, as though my thoughts could only have gone in one direction. "The two of them were just pushing and pushing this morning, and I may have said something about you coming to talk to me in the hospital. How you were just there for support and to listen," he explained in a stressed out tone. "I didn't think they'd actually call you over here and – "

"Dean," I cut him off, my hand reaching out to touch his own, "It's okay, really. My classes only start at ten, so I have a bit of time to spare."

It was only when the last syllable rolled off my tongue that I realized my words were falling on deaf ears. Confusion forced a frown onto my forehead as I noted that Dean's posture had stiffened, and while at first I thought he was in discomfort over his injury, when his eyes flickered briefly to our joined hands, my eyes widened in realization.

Snapping my hand back from his, I inched further down the bed as I clasped my hands together in my lap. "Sorry," I said quietly, ducking my head.

"It's fine," he said, his voice sincere, while I, on the other hand, wasn't the least bit apologetic.

He clearly needed the support this morning, and as silence took a hold of the atmosphere, I racked my brain around another way to show him that I was here for only one reason – for him.

"So," I started slowly, turning to meet his gaze as I chose my next words carefully, "Do you want to talk, or...?" I trailed, leaving the choice up to him.

The stiffness in his shoulders dissipated as he sank back against his pillows, closing his eyes. "Do you remember how I said I didn't know if I wanted to go back," he said, referring to a brief part of the conversation that had come up on Saturday.

"Yeah," I replied softly.

There were a few beats of silence as Dean's eyes opened to meet mine. "Well," he paused, "I think I meant it."

I bit my lip, remembering what Holden had said to me when I arrived. "Did something happen this morning?"

Irritation flashed across his face. "Nothing's happening, that's the fucking problem," he all but growled in frustration. And while I felt the need to flinch back in response, I stayed calm, watching as his hands clenched into fists and he drew in a deep breath. "I know recovering takes time, but it just feels like nothing is changing." His green eyes flashed with a mixture of anger and defeat. "If I step foot on campus today, I'll be the outsider. I won't be able to see the lecture notes or what my professors write on the chalkboards, I'll more than likely be late to all of my classes because I'm forced to wheel myself around, and I don't want to see the pitying looks on everyone's faces as I pass by."

I faltered for a moment as he flared his nostrils and took a deep breath. "You know; everyone has things that they have to overcome," I said. "Granted, right now you're not in the best of shape – "

Dean snorted. "That's an understatement."

" – But try thinking about your future," I continued as though I'd not been interrupted. "A month from now, or even a year from now, you'll look back and wonder why you let a bump in the road stop you completely. If you're worried about pitying looks, just try to faze them out, and if today doesn't go as planned, there are other options. You can ease up on your course load this semester and take an extra year to graduate, or try doing online courses if they're offered, but don't give up before you've even given it a shot." I took a deep breath. "There are two people out in the hall that really care about you, and want you to get through this, but you also have to want things to get better, and put in the work, or else you're just going to struggle."

As I spoke, Dean's anger began to dissipate, and a range of emotions flitted across his features. Surprise, confusion, and sadness all made an appearance before his eyebrows finally knitted together in curiosity.

"You said everyone has things that they have to over-come," he spoke after a few moments of silence, his voice skeptical and slow. His gaze was calculated and hard, causing my eyes to drop down to his navy comforter, knowing what question was coming next. My finger was running a mindless pattern along the fabric as he asked, "Even you?"

The question itself was enough to send my thoughts whirling to the parts of my life that very few people knew about – my insomnia, the constant loneliness, my mom – but I quickly reigned them in and masked my emotions before replying. "Of course," I said softly, "Even me."

It surprised me, however, when he leaned forward slight-ly, reaching for my hand and intertwining our fingers. The friction between our hands was warm and comforting, as I saw the remaining tension leave his shoulders and his irises lighten. Neither of us said a word, completely content with savouring the moment, but as the corners of his lips began to lift into a hesitant smile, and his grip tightened momentarily to show support, feelings I'd been trying to hold at bay began to fly free.

And right now was surely not the best time to deal with those feelings.

Clearing my throat, I stood up, letting our hold on each other slip. "I can't force you to make a decision, but if you're feeling ready to go to campus today, I'll stick around in the living room for about twenty minutes and go in with you. If not," I shrugged, my lips tilting upwards, "Just get my number off of Holden and text me when you are, because I'll be there for you then too."

Grabbing my bag off the floor, I stepped towards the door, glancing back over my shoulder to see him watching me, though I didn't say another word as I pulled the door open and let it close behind me.

Ryan and Holden's conversation ceased as they heard my footsteps rounding the corner, and their sharp gazes followed me as I settled down on the open lounger in the living room.

"So?" Holden asked, breaking the silence moments later, "How'd it go?"

"Did he say anything?

I shrugged in response, turning towards the two of them. "He said some things," I said vaguely, "But I don't know if I did any good."

"You're saying you got nowhere with him?" Ryan muttered, looking hopeless and a bit angry as his fists clenched. Holden, on the other hand, seemed defeated – shoulders hunched with a sea of guilt drowning his features.

I smiled sadly at the pair. "He's just dealing with everything, and I think he believes that you guys just want him to be the guy he was a few weeks back," I explained. "From what I can tell, Dean's a strong guy, but he's also doubtful of himself, and the best thing you guys can do is just be there for him, and don't push him to do things before he's ready."

A frown creased Ryan's forehead. "So what are we supposed to do on mornings like this?"

"I can't give you all the answers, but whatever Dean decides to do – "

I faltered as the clear sound of a bedroom door opening caught my attention, as well as the two other's. Dean, having pulled on a clean t-shirt and a pair of cargo shorts, wheeled himself to the entryway, his face impassive as he said, "Just give me a few minutes, and I'll be ready to go."

Trying, and failing, to hide the smile that pulled at my lips, I nodded, while Ryan and Holden simply stared at Dean blankly, surprise taking over their expression.

Dean turned and wheeled himself into the bathroom when no one replied, and the sound of a running tap seemed to snap Holden out of his trance, appearing unmistakably impressed as he said, "Well clearly whatever you said worked."

Ryan however, surveyed me with intrigue, his eyes flashing with amusement and a knowing grin pulling at his lips. "That," he mused, "Or it all had to do with the person he was talking to."

Rolling my eyes to divert the attention off of myself, I ignored the smirk that grew on Holden's lips, as well as the knowing laugh of Ryan's that filled the room, choosing instead to busy myself on my phone until Dean was ready.

"So how are we doing this?" Dean asked.

As the four of us lingered near the front door I'd turned into more of a background character, noticing Dean looking to his brother and best friend for an answer. I'd done what Holden had asked me here to do – to boost up Dean's confidence enough that he'd give school a shot – and now I was fine fading back out of the picture while he recovered.

It was evident, with his injured leg and wheelchair, that Dean could no longer drive, which left the question as to how we were getting to campus. My assumption was that Ryan would be driving us, as walking and bussing were out of the question, and to my knowledge, Holden didn't have a car.

"Aren't I dropping you guys off?" Ryan replied.

Holden shrugged, though Dean's head moved back and forth in a negative response. "Your car was tight on Saturday, and that was with one less person."

"Then what's the plan?" Holden asked, arching his eyebrow as he looked down at Dean.

There was a lengthy pause as Dean racked his mind for a solution, his fingers grasping tightly at the arms of his chair. "We can take my car," he offered quietly, much to the surprise of the rest of us.

"Umm..." Holden began hesitantly, "I don't really think you'll be able to – "

"I know I can't drive," Dean cut him off, dragging in a breath and shaking his head, "And neither can you," he continued, and for the first time since he'd emerged from the bathroom, his gaze met mine, "But I was thinking maybe Katie could."

Hearing my name sent a jolt of surprise through my veins. "Me?"

A brief moment of hesitation and regret crossed his face. "If you have a license that is," he backtracked, suddenly unsure of himself.

"I, uh, I do," I said, repositioning my bag atop my shoulder, "It's just, didn't your car get, uh, damaged?" Dean's lips thinned as he nodded. "Then how...?"

Ryan sighed, running his hand through his already frazzled hair. "I got him another one," he replied, causing my mouth to fall open in shock. "I thought he could use it once he was cleared for driving," Ryan explained. As he spoke, he made his way into the open kitchen, pulling open a drawer and grabbing a new set of keys from within it. "But I guess if it's easier," he held the keys out towards me, dangling them until they were within my grasp, "You guys had better get going, if you don't want to be late."

It seemed that he wanted to say more – as though he wanted to be there for his brother – but also wanted to respect Dean's decision.

With a short goodbye, and a wish good luck, the three of us headed down to the parking garage, where Ryan had said he'd left the car.

Riding down in the lift, I hesitated a moment before asking, "Can I ask you something?"

With my question being directed towards Dean, his head tilted upwards, looking right at me as confusion creased his forehead. "Sure."

"How did, uh, how could your brother pay for a whole new car out of the blue?"

Dean arched his eyebrow, though a small amount of amusement glossed his features, and I quickly noticed that Holden's expression nearly mirrored Dean's.

"Are you serious?" Holden asked.

The way the pair were staring at me, made it crystal clear that I was missing something. "Yes," I trailed, waiting, curious and confused, for one of them to reply.

"Well that explains a few things," Dean mused, an airy laugh escaping his lips. "Ryan's an actor," he explained, "Has been for a while actually. He used to live out in Los Angeles with my parents and I, but when the press got too much, and started harassing both him and his girlfriend, Zoe, a few years into their relationship, they moved out to New York, and into a gated community for a bit more privacy."

"Oh," I said, fiddling with the set of keys in my hand, "I didn't know."

"It's cool," Dean shrugged, "Besides, sometimes people who know we're related try to get close to me for the wrong reasons. It's good to know that you're not one of those people."

A rush of happiness welled up inside me at his words, and I offered him a shy smile. I was able to catch an upwards twitch of his lips as the lift came to a stop, but the smile was fleeting, disappearing as quickly as it had appeared. The doors slid open to reveal the dimly lit parking garage, smelling vaguely of propane and mold, located in the basement level of the building.

With Dean adamant to wheel himself around, Holden and I stepped back, waiting for him to exit the lift first before following closely behind. Looking around, most of the cars were a few years used or cheaply leased – ones that most students and young adults could easily afford. Though when we neared the end of the aisle, and Dean started to slow down, my steps faltered and I mentally gaped as my eyes landed on a car that stood out from the rest. It was a rich shade of midnight blue with an evident shine to the coating, and though it wasn't overly flashy, the Porsche symbol that graced both the front and back of the car was a giant nudge to the worth of the car.

As I took a step towards the driver's side, I was stopped by Holden. "Can I get your help for a second?" he asked sheepishly. "While I'm helping him into the front of the car, would you be able to squeeze the wheelchair into the backseat?"

Giving it no thought as I nodded, I waited as Holden's arm came around Dean for support, holding up the bulk of his weight, and once the chair was vacant, folded it up like I'd done to many before in the hospital. It took a bit of extra maneuvering, but once the hassle was over and the keys were in the ignition, I noticed Dean skittishly moving in the seat next to me.

As he noticed me staring, he arched an eyebrow and I cleared my throat. "Are you comfortable being in a car yet, or...?"

His eyes scanned my face briefly, catching the worry and hesitation that crossed my features, though a bit of my nerves faded as the smallest of smiles pulled at the corner of his lips. "Katie," Dean started.

"Yeah?"

"I'm fine, really," he pressed, leaning back to get comfortable. His eyes met mine, and the mixture of thinly-veiled dread and genuine happiness sparked such an intensity that my heart thumped a sporadic beat. "Just drive."

Chapter 8

Sitting in the passenger's seat of my own car was something that didn't happen often. Holden couldn't drive, and it was only once in a while that one of my teammates would offer to be designated driver after a party, but other than those odd times, I always preferred to drive. I liked being in control of the situation, and ever since I'd gotten my license, being behind the wheel was something that had the power to relax me.

Since the accident however, the thought of eventually having to get back in the saddle hadn't crossed my mind, that is, not until Ryan had mentioned my new car. It was apparent that driving while injured, overall, was a bad idea, but what worried me was what would happen once I recovered. Something as simple as driving had turned my whole world on end, and I didn't know if I would have the courage to jump right back behind the wheel.

As grim thoughts began to clog my mind, I tried to shake myself out of it. I eyed the rear-view mirror with hopes of catching Holden's eye, though his head was ducked with his focus on his phone, and when I turned to Katie, her attention was fixed on the road ahead. She seemed at ease, though it was hard not to notice that she pulled the corner of her bottom lip between her teeth every time she checked her mirrors or flicked her turning signal on before rounding a corner.

I should have realized I was staring, though the fact failed to register with me until we pulled to a stop behind a stand-still line of traffic near a university crosswalk and Katie's gaze turned to me. Quickly turning my attention to the window, the lone student sat at the bus stop adjacent to us didn't exactly entail anything interesting, and I found my eyes shifting back towards her only a few moments later.

There was a quizzical edge to her gaze, curiosity spreading through her features, and all that filled the silence was the low lull of the music that drifted out of the speakers. "Are you okay?" she mouthed, her eyebrows pinched closer together.

Feeling as though I'd already unloaded enough of my problems onto her this morning, I simply nodded, trying to hide my emotions the best that I could. I wasn't able to put my feelings into words just yet, and as I noticed the traffic beginning to move, I nudged her attention away from me.

Pulling into the parking lot, the normal mass of students that filled the campus grounds on the first day of the semester were non-existent. There were a few people loitering in the parking lot, or walking between buildings, but the whole scene just felt different.

And then I remembered that it wasn't the first day of the semester, but in fact the second week. The sudden realization did nothing to calm my uneasiness, and make me slightly regret leaving my bedroom this morning.

The car came to an indefinite stop as Katie pulled the keys from the ignition and Holden jumped at the chance to escape from the cramped backseat. Quickly gathering his things, his focused shifted to wiggling my wheelchair out from its wedged position.

Katie had yet to move from her seat, and while I could feel her gaze on me, I pushed the car door open, accepting Holden's help as I maneuvered my way into my wheelchair.

"So," Holden said, sounding rather uncertain as he adjusted his bag, "I've actually got class in less than ten minutes on the other side of campus, but if you need help getting around, I'll gladly miss the beginning of my international finance lecture."

I shook my head in amusement, knowing that while he wasn't particularly keen on his professor, Holden wasn't one to show up late for things, especially when his grades were involved. "You know I can get around on my own," I said, a teasing undertone to my words, "It's not like I'm gonna get lost on my way to class."

"If you're sure."

"Go," I smiled. "I'll see you this afternoon."

He nodded. "Just text me if anything goes wrong." As he turned to walk away, he shouted back over his shoulder, "Oh, and good luck."

With Holden heading through the courtyard, I braced my hands against the wheels of my chair, and with a series of unskillful movements, managed to turn myself in the direction of my first class. After a few more adjustments, I began to push the wheels again, only to be stopped as a cough from behind me caught my attention.

I turn my head to see a mirror picture of this morning when I opened my bedroom door to see Katie standing there. Her blonde hair was pulled back from her face in a braid, she was clutching at her bag's shoulder strap tightly, and the expression on her face told me that she didn't exactly know what to do in this situation.

"Sorry. I just didn't know if – " She looked between the car and I, holding the keys in her palm. " – you wanted the keys back. Or do you guys need a ride home?"

Realizing that my plans for her to drive had come with some complications, which I'd overlooked in the first place, I sat still for a moment. "Oh," I replied lamely. "Well, when are you done classes?"

"Around three," she replied, shifting her position so that she stood beside me, her gaze holding mine.

"I think that's about when I finish too, Holden maybe a little earlier," I said hesitantly. "And if you wouldn't mind – if it's not an inconvenience – do you have time to drive us home? Because if you don't then I'll just leave my car here overnight and Ryan can come pick us up."

"It's fine," Katie said, her voice soft as the edges of her lips lifted into a smile, "I don't mind."

And because I couldn't seem to end the conversation there, I opened my mouth and said, "Good, though if you're really not doing anything this afternoon, would you maybe want to tag along to my eye appointment? They're more than likely going to say I need a pair of glasses, and no offense to Holden or Ryan, but I don't exactly trust them to help me pick out the best pair."

With a small laugh, she replied. "And you trust me?"

Her eyes lightened as I shrugged. "Enough not to make me look like an idiot."

"Well then, I guess I could," she said, and as a grin slowly made its way onto my face, she hurried to continue, "Though I work at five, so I might have to duck out early."

I nodded in understanding. "That's fine. So, I'll meet you in the quad around three?"

"Okay," she said, shuffling her feet as beats of silence passed between us. Her eyes shifted to my chair, biting her lip as she glanced at the path towards the closest buildings. "Are you sure you don't need any help?"

"I think I'm good. You don't have to worry about me."

She smiled wryly. "It's kind of hard not to, considering I know you don't exactly want to be here."

I paused, taken aback by the caring tone that accompanied her words. "Really Katie, I'm good," I repeated, "Besides, I have to get used to this eventually."

"Well, like I said," she began, pulling a scrap piece of paper and a pen from her bag before scribbling something down quickly, "I'll be there if you need me." Passing me the note, ten digits were scrawled out, presumably denoting her phone number, and when I looked back up to meet her eyes, she smiled. "See you later."

Nodding in response, she turned to head in the opposite direction, and as I wheeled myself over towards the accessibility ramp, a fragment of optimism coasted into my mind, making me believe that, maybe, today wouldn't be as bad as I'd initially thought.

As soon as I wheeled myself through the doors of the building, my hopes of a good day shattered around me.

Students were mulling around the hall, on their way to class or simply meeting up with friends, and as I made a move towards the elevator, it was as if I was a magnet for everyone's attention. The gentle murmur of voices slowly grew in volume as several hushed conversations molded together and pointed looks were shared between friends.

It was an uncomfortable sense of paranoia on my end – thinking that everyone was watching me – but as I heard my name and the words car crash numerous times over, I knew it wasn't completely unjustified.

When I reached the elevator and the doors closed on the whirlwind of chatter, I was able to take a second to breathe – to prepare myself for a multitude of stares and whispers. A ding denoted the passing of each floor, and as I climbed closer to the fourth floor of the building, my grip on the wheels of my chair tightened. The doors slid open to reveal an empty hallway, and as I caught the time on the clock outside my classroom, I realized why.

I was late.

A hush fell over the room as I entered, facing a room of classmates that I'd interacted with for the better part of the last three years. The professor, who'd been addressing the class, turned to me with a flat look, thinking I was just another student trying to sneak in unnoticed, though his eyes widened when he saw my chair. He seemed completely thrown, not knowing what to do, but after a few moments, he cleared his throat. "Do you have the wrong class, sir?"

Having had a different professor in my earlier year physiology courses, it wasn't a shock to see he didn't know who I was.

"No," I replied, my voice rather emotionless, "I just, uh, couldn't make it to class last week."

He nodded in understanding, not wanting to refute my words as he gestured to the front row. "Very well. Take a spot in the front and make sure to stay behind after the lecture."

The front row was full, and with that realization, I rolled awkwardly towards the side of the table, watching as a pair of students, who were seemingly unimpressed, scooted their chairs down and closer together to give me a sliver of room to maneuver in behind the table.

As the professor continued with his lecture, I reached into the bag I'd situated onto the back of my chair to grab a notebook and pen, trying to ignore the stares that were pointedly placed in my direction. Every time one person averted their eyes, I could feel another pair turn towards me.

It shouldn't have thrown me off guard – being the center of attention – having grown accustomed to it over the years of playing the game I loved in front of cheering onlookers. But now things were different. People were no longer watching me on the court in awe or in anticipation, but rather with pity and curiosity.

Now, the stares made it nearly impossible to concentrate.

With not much written down as the professor wrapped up his lecture more than an hour later, students began to pack up and slowly leave the room, most of them sparing me one last pity-filled glance before heading out the door.

When the last of them were gone, and just my professor and I were left, I said. "You wanted to see me, sir?"

He nodded firmly, moving his reading glasses up further along the bridge of his nose. "I did," he said with affirmation, "And your name?"

"Dean Adams."

"Well then Dean, seeing as it's evidently clear why you weren't able to make it to the first lecture last week, I just wanted to speak to you briefly about the course require-ments." He reached into his briefcase and pulled out a sta-pled handout, passing it to me as he continued. "That's an overview of the course. The topics we'll be covering are listed in order, as well as the dates of the tests, when the three major assignments are due, and the recommended textbook you should purchase to keep up to date with the material. In regards to the lab portion of the course, you've already been paired up with a partner, whose name should be listed on the last page of the handout. Now," he paused, and I fought the urge to squirm as he eyed my wheelchair, "If you would like a more convenient classroom for us to meet, I can talk to a few department heads and inquire about switching to a room on the first floor."

His words shocked me for a moment, not anticipating the generosity, though I found myself shaking my head. "It's okay sir," I replied, "I'm on track to be on crutches once my leg starts to heal, so you don't need to worry."

He eyed me for a moment before he responded, trying to see if I was telling the truth. "Alright," he nodded, "Then I'll see you here for Thursday's lecture then."

With a semi-awkward goodbye, I wheeled myself out of the classroom. It was no surprise to me that, as the day wore on, I didn't make it to a single lecture on time, though most of my classmates and professors wore a jolted look of shock each time I arrived late. When I wasn't being observed like a lab rat as I sat in on my lectures, I was tasked with dodging the ignorant hordes of students in the halls that only seemed to notice my chair at the last possible second. By the time my last lecture ended, the exhaustion was beginning to settle in, though I felt a wave of relief wash over me knowing that, while it hadn't been the best day, I'd made it through.

Knowing that Katie and Holden would more than likely be waiting for me, I tried my best to move quickly, though was hit with a snag when I came to the bottom of the ramp and turned towards the quad.

Coming towards me, dressed in their practice jerseys, were a few of the guys from the basketball team with their gym bags slung over their shoulders.

I stopped, wishing that I'd brought some kind of disguise with me and hoping they wouldn't notice me. Laughter erupted from the group when they were no more than a few feet away from me, and thinking they were going to pass me by, I held my breath. However, one by one their laughs faded while I let out a breath of distress, realizing that they were slowing to a stop in front of me.

"Uh hey Dean," Matt said, scratching the back of his neck with uncertainty, "How's it going?"

I raised my eyebrows in response, pausing for a moment before replying dryly, "Fine."

"It sucks that you're out man," another guy chimed in, "You were a shoo in for captain."

"Yeah, and now coach gave it to Dallas," Scott muttered, a hint of anger lacing his voice as he scuffed his shoes in the gravel. It wasn't a surprise though, knowing that Scott had been eyeing the title of captain as much as I had been.

"Well hopefully you guys start the season off right," I said, smiling as I let an ounce of optimism sink into my system, "That way I won't be joining a losing team when I'm back on my feet."

"But coach said that you were out for the season."

Not letting their ignorance get to me, I shrugged. "There's always hope."

They eyed each other doubtfully, and it was clear that none of them thought I'd be able to recover.

"Okay..."

"See you around."

"Yeah," I nodded, feeling dejected as they headed towards the gym, "See you."

By the time I made it to the quad, Katie and Holden were already there. They were sitting on one of the benches closer to the parking lot and chatting happily to pass the time, though as I neared, their conversation came to cease as Katie's eyes swept the area and collided with mine. Rolling to a stop next to them, the two of them stood up.

"Are you ready to go?" Katie asked, smiling a little as she raised an eyebrow.

My heart skipped unsteadily in response to what was nothing more than an innocent question. Truthfully, it was much more. She was coming along this afternoon for support – though having invited her, I had a hard time understanding why I was so nervous.

Hiding the way my hands clammed up as I gripped the wheels of my chair, I smiled in return. "Ready."

"What about these?"

Putting the glasses I was holding back on the stand, I turned towards Holden, my eyes narrowing as I did so. He was holding a pair of bright red frames that had pointed edges and were taken from the women's section.

Rolling my eyes, I asked. "Is this funny to you?"

"A little," he said in response, chuckling as he placed the frames back where they belonged. "I don't know, I just never pictured you with glasses."

"Yeah, well neither did I," I muttered, averting my gaze back towards the counter where the optician sat.

With the optometrist's office only a block away, the four of us had forwent the car in favour of walking as I wheeled along behind them. Though, in actuality, I'd suggested it just so that I could prolong the inevitable.

I knew that it wasn't her fault, that she was just doing her job – confirming what the doctor had already told me the day I'd left the hospital. What had once been 20/20 vision was now significantly less, and according to the optometrist, with the damage that had been done to my corneas, I was lucky to have regained my eyesight at all.

"It's not the end of the world," Ryan stated, looking down at me as he stepped up next to me.

"That doesn't mean I have to be happy about it."

"Yeah," he shrugged, "Though you might not hate it as much as you think you will. It'll just take some getting used to." The sides of his mouth twisted upwards into a smirk as he continued, "Besides, some girls like a guy who wears glasses."

Noting that he was staring pointedly in Katie's direction, I shook my head, throwing him an irritated look, but I couldn't help the pull my eyes had towards her. She hovered on the other side of the store, completely oblivious to Ryan's comment as she scanned a wall of frames. She'd been fairly quiet this afternoon, and while she'd given her opinion on most of the glasses, it was usually just a word or two. It was as if she wasn't completely comfortable, and having invited her, it made doubt creep into my mind, wondering if I'd made a mistake.

Countless of options later, I'd more or less resigned to the fact that glasses just didn't suit me. Every pair I tried on was either too big, too small, or, with some of the frames Ryan and Holden had chosen, a complete joke.

Just when I was about to ask the optometrist to pick a pair at random, Katie spoke up. "What about these?" Her voice was meek as she picked up the frames from a stand that I hadn't looked at yet, and as she walked towards me, her lip sat in between her teeth nervously.

Taking the glasses from her hand, I slid them up the bridge of my nose and turned towards the mirror. Surprisingly, they didn't look all that bad. The frame wasn't too thin, too square, or too feminine, and they sat nicely on my face. It still seemed strange to be looking at myself with glasses, but with a bit of time, I could see myself getting used to the black pair I was wearing now.

"What do you think?" I asked, pivoting my chair around to face everyone.

"Looks better than the other pairs."

"You don't look like a complete dork."

Rolling my eyes at Ryan and Holden's generic responses, I met Katie's gaze and raised an eyebrow inquisitively. "And what about you?"

A moment passed as she took me in, and just as I began to worry that maybe they weren't as suited for me as I believed, the edges of her lips drew upwards. "They look good," she said, her eyes bright as they met mine, "But if you don't like them – "

"Katie," I said, cutting her off before she could finish her thought, "I like them."

"That's good then," she nodded awkwardly, not knowing what else to say as she readjusted her bag atop her shoulder. "Well, I've actually got to head to the hospital for my shift, but I'll see you tomorrow."

She turned to walk away, to head towards the exit, but I stopped her before she could. Gripping her hand a little too hard, I pulled her back towards me, stretching so that my lips grazed her cheek, pulling away to catch her shocked expression. It was a peck, nothing extraordinary, though the feeling of her skin under my lips was still unnerving.

"Thanks for coming."

It seemed as though my voice caused the surprise to clear from her features, a tint of red dusting across her cheeks before she smiled.

"Goodnight."

Ignoring the grins on Holden and Ryan's faces as Katie stepped out of the building, I slid the glasses off my face and wheeled towards the front counter. "I'll take these."

Clenching my teeth in agony, I tried to ignore the sharp pains shooting up my leg as I sat on the plastic bench in the physiotherapist's office. It was my third time in this room this week, and while Tuesday and Thursday's session were painful, this one was definitely the worst so far.

Tuesday morning through Friday afternoon, Katie had continued to show up when I needed her. When she'd knocked on our apartment door before nine on Tuesday, we were all surprised, but when she claimed that she didn't want to see me discouraged after a not-so-great first day, she volunteered to drive. Day after day she was there, and while I had taken it upon myself to tell her that it truly wasn't necessary to keep on chauffeuring me to campus if she didn't want to, she insisted.

On Wednesday, when Holden had morning classes, Katie had come over to eat breakfast with me, and on Thursday, when Katie had classes until five, I spent the extra time catching up on my assignments in the library. She didn't seem to mind the arrangement, and honestly, getting to spend time with her wasn't something I was going to object to.

"Are you almost done?" I all but growled, my narrowed vision clear as I glared down the physiotherapist.

As he looked up from where his gaze had been focused, his smile was sympathetic, though I was able to catch the flash of amusement cross his face as he continued on. With my right leg out of commission and wrapped in a cast, he had decided to focus all of today's session on getting the muscles in my left leg used to movement again. With the lower half of my body having been more or less immobile since my accident, my muscles had begun to experience atrophy. The rehab visits were helping with this of course, but the stretches and exercises certainly brought a burn to weakened muscles they were directed at.

When the physiotherapist stepped back a few minutes later, I breathed a sigh of relief. "I think that's enough for today," he spoke, grabbing his clipboard and jotting down a few notes, "Though if you want to be able to support yourself on crutches within the next few weeks, you're going to have to start working up the muscles in your arms again."

"Isn't pushing myself around in my chair enough?" I asked dryly, shifting myself to the edge of the bench I was seated on. Reaching for my chair as I readied myself to drop down, the physiotherapist moved to help me, but I shook my head. "I've got it."

Landing safely in my chair, he looked down at me and smiled. "You're pretty mobile, which is good, but you should try using some light weights during down points in your day, just to make sure all your muscles stay in good shape. Other than that, if you keep up with the scheduled rehab, you should be back on two feet in no time."

Nodding in acceptance, I left the physiotherapist's office, located on the second floor of the hospital, but as I dodged the other patients and workers on my way to the elevator, I noticed a clock on the wall and realized I still had another half an hour until Ryan would be here to pick me up.

Deciding to head down to the cafeteria, I moved quickly enough to catch the elevator, stopping inside just as the metal doors slid shut. As the doors opened again, I just about rolled out, believing that we were on the ground floor, however, while I'd been focused on catching the elevator, I hadn't thought to check if it was actually going down. Slumping my head back in frustration, I waited as a stream of nurses, patients, and visitors all moved in and out during the ride to the top.

Finally, as the elevator seemed to slowly make its descent, the bell chimed as the doors slid opened on one of center floors. Waiting as a nurse stepped inside, my gaze moved out passed the doors, latching onto a familiar blonde-haired girl as she moved farther down the hall. It was as if my instincts suddenly kicked in, my hand reaching out towards the closing doors to stop them as I wheeled myself into the hallway before my brain could fully comprehend my actions.

Watching as Katie smiled at her fellow nurses, I noticed that, while she seemed to be a few floors up from where I'd always seen her work, she also wasn't dressed in scrubs.

That meant she wasn't working.

My curiosity peaked as she rounded the corner and fell out of sight. Not knowing exactly where I was heading, or what floor I was even on, I tried to act casual and appear as though I belonged as I followed her. Catching sight of her again when I reached the hall she'd turned down, I noticed from afar that she seemed tired. Her hair was thrown up messily on top of her head and her shoulders were slouched as she hovered next to a closed door.

My eyebrows creased together as a doctor stepped out of the room, nodding to Katie and holding the door open for her as she entered.

That was the moment I could've turned around. The moment where I could've simply headed back down to the lobby to wait for my brother like any sane person would have.

Instead, I moved towards the door, stopping just outside and brought my hand up to knock.

When no response came back, I took one last look up and down the hall, making sure I hadn't gotten the room wrong before taking a risk. Twisting the handle and peeking inside, I let out a breath of relief when I saw Katie sitting in a chair next to the bed. "Don't you know it's rude to walk away from a guy in a wheelchair?" I teased, wheeling myself fully into the room as the door swung shut behind me.

I didn't know what I was expecting her reaction to be, but as her head whipped towards me with shock and her eyes widened in disbelief, she seemed to be at a loss for words. Through the prolonged silence my thoughts found time to catch up with my actions, and watching as her expression paled, I realized that, maybe, this hadn't been the best idea.

Chapter 9

The sound of Dean's voice had succeeded in stunning me into silence. Disbelief and shock rained over me, suffocating the room with a thick tension that he had yet to sense.

"Dean?" I asked breathlessly, my voice strangled, "What are you doing here?"

He wasn't supposed to be here. He didn't need to see this.

I'd taken the early shift this morning after Claudia had switched hours for the weekend, which meant that I'd been awake and on my way into work just as the sun was beginning to peek out from behind the clouds. It hadn't been an overly stressful shift, but with my exhaustion growing heavier as the day drew on, all I had wanted to do was to come up and visit my mom. For it to just be the two of us. Alone.

I certainly hadn't expected Dean to appear, and though I'd known he had his appointment downstairs in the physiotherapy wing, it hadn't crossed my mind that he could possibly follow me up here.

My heart had sped up in worry and I didn't know what to do.

"I'm not sure, if I'm being honest." His voice seemed normal and an element of surprise was missing from his face, which meant that he had yet to realize that the two of us were not alone. "My appointment finished early so I thought I'd explore a bit, but I got on the wrong elevator. I was heading down to the cafeteria actually, but when I spotted you I thought I'd take a look around."

I barely heard a word of his explanation as I sat frozen, letting the uneasiness of the situation consume me. It was when I saw his eyebrows draw close in confusion that I realized he had figured something was off.

There was no stopping this – he was going to find out.

"If you want me to leave," he started again, this time slow and unsure of himself, "I'll just – "

"No," I protested all too quickly, causing him to flinch back in surprise. I was positive I looked a state, my emotions flustered as I tried again. "I mean, it's fine. I just, I don't..."

I'd been caught speechless, not knowing what to say, but as my eyes flicked to the bed where my mom laid asleep, I noticed Dean's gaze follow mine. It was the first time he'd looked around the room since he'd entered, and I ducked my head as I heard a sharp intake of breath.

"Katie..." he trailed softly, his tone warm and sympathetic.

Clenching my eyes shut for a moment, I rang my hands together tightly in my lap before lifting my gaze to meet his.

"Dean – " I spoke quietly, a definite strain to my voice as I forced out my next words, " – meet my mom."

I had only ever told one person about my mom, and that had been Stella. My brother, Theo, had been there the day my mom broke the news to us, and my mom had taken care of telling our relatives, one by one, as her condition worsened. I hadn't been nervous about Stella's reaction when I'd told her, as I knew she'd be around as a shoulder to lean on, but Dean was another story. I hadn't known him all that long, and honestly, I didn't know how he'd react.

When it seemed as though my words had sunk in, Dean's face paled. He looked as though he'd had the air taken straight from his lungs and was trying to regain stabilization. He didn't know what to do or what to think, but amongst the tense lull, I kept my focus on him, too scared to look away.

It was because of this that I didn't hear the stirring. The rustling of sheets was lost on me, and when the silence was broken, it was neither Dean nor I who broke it.

"Katie."

My breath caught in my throat and my heart leapt. I turned my head just in time to see my mom's eyes blink open hazily before they landed on me. I sat frozen for a moment, gripping the arm of the chair to brace myself, not believing that this was happening.

But it was.

She was awake, and she was my mom.

"Mom," I said as I rose to my feet, my voice cracking with an overwhelming wave of emotion, "You're awake."

It'd been over three weeks since I'd last seen her awake, and happiness was bubbling through my veins as I looked down at her. Her chapped lips stretched wide as she smiled and I noticed a sparkling glow that fought hard to hide the tiredness in her eyes.

"How are you darling?"

Feeling tears begin to fill the corners of my eyes, my lips tilted upwards at the edges as I leaned over and planted a kiss on her cheek. "I'm good," I nodded. Pulling back, I brought a hand up to wipe a stray tear away before gripping her hand in support.

It was when her heavy eyes travelled past me and landed on Dean that a mixture of worry and nerves overclouded the joy of seeing my mom awake. "And who's this?" she asked, an unmistakeable croak to her voice as her gaze flitted curiously between Dean and I.

"Oh," I started. Glancing back towards him, I offered an encouraging smile when I noticed the sense of discomfort in his features. "This is Dean."

Raising his right hand with hesitation, he said, "Hi mam."

"Call me Marcy dear," my mom responded, though the violent coughing that followed sent a spark of worry through me. I rubbed her arm as she went through the worst of it, having done this one too many times to know that the doctor didn't need to be called just yet. As her painful fit subsided, she looked back to Dean as though nothing had happened. "Are you a friend of Katie's?"

It was clear that he was out of his element on this, but he was powerless when it came to this situation. He tried his best to shield the concern on his face as his eyes shifted to me. "You could say that," he replied, the smallest of smiles pulling at his lips.

"Well it's nice meeting you. It's rare that I get to see any of Katie's friends."

Dean's gaze was soft as he turned to me, noticing the pink tint to my cheeks that flared up in response to my mom's words, and while it was true, I had a feeling it was just the confirmation he needed to know that he really shouldn't have followed me.

"I've actually got to get going," Dean said, moving his atten-tion back to my mom as he gripped the wheels of his chair, "My brother will be here soon to pick me up and I don't want to keep him waiting."

"That's fine Dean," my mom replied, nodding in under-standing, "But hopefully I'll get to see you again soon."

Dean smiled, though he kept quiet with his words as he maneuvered his chair in a semi-circle so that he was facing the door. "I'll see you," he said as he reached for the door.

There were no more words exchanged as he wheeled into the hallway and disappeared from view, and while I felt a small weight of relief rise from my shoulders, it was imme-diately replaced with a load of embarrassment as I saw the gleaming look in my mother's eye.

"So," she began slowly, "He was certainly cute."

My cheeks tinged faintly of crimson as my eyes jolted wide with embarrassment. "Mom!"

"What?" she asked innocently, sounding quite under the weather as she struggled to pronounce her words. "I'm just saying, he must be someone special if you invited him along today."

It was easy to pick up the teasing undertone to her voice, flashing me back to the times when she'd talk to me about boys in high school.

"I didn't invite him though," I replied with a fluster, "He followed me up here."

Her eyebrows rose. "He's a stalker?"

Laughing in response, I shook my head in silent mirth. "Definitely not." I shrugged my shoulders, a serene smile spreading across my lips. "He's just Dean."

Though I hadn't, in any way, made the situation any clearer to her, a sense of understanding settled into her fragile features, making me wonder what exactly I'd said as she settled back into her pillows.

It was then that I pressed the call button next to her bed. With her awake, while I'd love nothing more than to keep this time to myself, I knew that her doctor had a few tests to run to make sure nothing had suddenly changed. I was gifted an extra two minutes of privacy with my mom before the doctor, followed by two nurses, strode into the room. I sat by her side in support, watching her struggle to swallow a few pills and get her blood drawn, but as one of the nurses stuck around, I saw my mom's eyes slowly flicker shut in exhaustion.

Knowing that my time had run out, I planted a gentle kiss on her forehead, promising her that I'd be back tomorrow. Collecting my bag off the floor and bidding the nurse goodbye, I stepped out into the hallway, turning to leave as the sight of Dean made me jump back in surprise.

He was still here, half an hour later, and as confusion spread through the crevasses of my mind, I stood frozen for a moment as he noticed me.

"Dean, what are you doing here?"

He was idling next to the door, seemingly stressed and crestfallen. "I didn't want to ruin the time you had with your mom," he admitted apologetically, raking a hand through his hair in self-deprecation. "God, if I would've known, I would've never – "

I shook my head as I interrupted him, stopping him from completing his thoughts. "Don't worry about it. It's okay."

He looked at me with disbelief clouding his irises. "It's not though," he said adamantly. "It's not fair to you. If you didn't want me to know – "

"Really Dean, it's okay." I paused, biting my lip nervously as I saw his knuckles turn white. He was clenching his fists, trying to stop himself from fighting my words. "Just, can you not mention this to Ryan or Holden? At least not right away."

My plea appeared to surprise him, but his gaze softened immediately in response to my quiet voice. "Of course."

I couldn't understand why he didn't look away – I could see my reflection in his glasses, and certainly didn't look my best as exhaustion laced my every bone. The air was charged and my heart began to race as his gaze dragged over my features, stopping one too many seconds on my lips before he met my eyes once more. I was more than aware that we were currently in a hospital hallway, but while our gazes stayed locked, it felt as though we were alone.

The moment was broken eventually however, and it was me who damaged the silence between us. "Speaking of Ryan," I started, clearing my throat, "Didn't you say he was picking you up?"

"I told him to wait." He shrugged, as though it was no big deal. "I wanted to apologize – "

"I've already told you it's okay."

" – And I wanted to know if you'd come over for dinner tonight."

Surprise graced my face at the unexpected invitation. " Wh... what?" I managed to force out, stumbling over the syllables.

"I mean, if you're not busy and you're not sticking around here," he was quick to backtrack.

I smiled, though there was a sadness to the way my lips stretched. "I was actually heading home," I replied timidly, though it was the truth, "And just because you found out about my mom, that doesn't mean that you have to – "

"That's not why I asked," he clarified, shaking his head, "Holden's already got plans for the night and Ryan was thinking about ordering pizza." He paused, a shyness beginning to cloak him as he shrugged and looked down at his lap. "It's not that exciting, but if you wanted to come over, the offer's there."

A warmth grew in the pit of my stomach, gratitude accompanying it as it began to spread.

"Plus," he added softly, "If you did want to talk, about anything, I'd be there to listen."

My lips pulled upwards, recalling the recent times that I'd spoken the exact words to him. Except now the roles were reversed, I needed someone to talk to, and maybe, that person was Dean.

"I'll keep that in mind."

Two hours later, I had the end of a pen caught between my teeth as I struggled to keep my focus. Sitting in my apartment with nothing but emptiness surrounding me made it impossible to concentrate on my work, but I knew that wasn't the only reason.

Dean was on my mind, and I couldn't seem to shake the thoughts away.

I'd gotten home from the hospital and immediately dialed Stella's number, needing her advice on what to do now that Dean knew, but when she picked up I couldn't get a word out before she told me she was on her way out the door. I hadn't wanted to ruin her plans, so I kept the events that had transpired at the hospital to myself.

As I sat staring at my barely started essay, Dean's offer of pizza was looking pretty tempting.

I didn't know what to think. Dean had seemed almost spooked when he saw my mom today, his usual colour paled and his emotions unsure, though it was understandable, considering I'd given him absolutely no information about my home life. He'd offered to talk, and I was stuck as to whether it had been genuine, or if it was just a debt he assumed he owed because I'd been there for him over the past week.

Biting my lip as I glanced at the time, I mulled my thoughts over for a moment before grabbing my phone from my nightstand. Pulling up the last message I'd sent Dean, I began to type.

That offer for pizza still stand?

The seconds ticked by slowly once I pressed send, and I waited in anticipation until his reply popped up.

We're just about to order. What toppings do you want? :)

A burst of relief flooded over me, and my smile grew to the match the one he'd ended his message with.

I'm good with anything but onions & mushrooms!

So meat and hawaiian are okay?

Perfect

See you soon.

Leaving my essay forgotten on the couch, I gathered up my keys and wallet, throwing them into my purse in a hurry before heading out the door. The air was humid but the gentle breeze was refreshing, and when I reached the familiar apartment building, I was immediately buzzed in.

Knocking on the door, I waited a few moments until it was pulled open to reveal Ryan, as lazy smile playing on his lips as I stepped inside.

"I thought you were the pizza," he said jokingly, shutting the door before turning towards me.

I shook my head in half-hearted mirth. The events from earlier were slowly seeping back to the forefront of my mind, and though his eyes held no sympathy towards me, I wondered what – if anything – Dean had told him. "Unfortunately not." Letting my eyes sweep over the room, it became immediately apparent that Dean wasn't here.

My actions however, didn't go unnoticed by Ryan. With a teasing glint in his eye and a smirk growing on his lips, he nodded towards the back hallway. "He's in his room."

Realizing with embarrassment how much of an open book I could be at times, I ducked my head to conceal the rising colour to my cheeks. "Thanks," I muttered.

Not giving him the time to continue to tease me, I turned on my heel and headed towards Dean's bedroom, opening the door without a knock. In hindsight, that might not have been the best idea, but nothing seemed out of the ordinary as I stepped into the room. Dean was resting in the middle of his bed, his headphones covering his ears in an attempt to drown out the world around him.

My steps faltered quickly, though my movements didn't go unnoticed. Sliding the headphones down around his neck, he shot me an apologetic look as he forced himself into a sitting position. "Sorry," he said, running a hand through his tousled locks, "I didn't hear the intercom buzz."

I waved him off. "Don't worry about it," I replied, "Your brother let me in."

Sitting down on the edge of the bed, I could feel Dean's gaze on me as I fiddled with my fingers, unsure of what to do or say.

As though he could sense my discomfort, the edges of his lips quirked upwards. "I don't exactly know what you want to do until the food gets here," he started lightly. "I've got some books you could sift through or we could sit here and talk, but you probably don't want that."

He continued with his suggestions, and while some were rather extravagant, I slowly began to tune him out as my eyes flickered down to the headphones on his neck.

"Or we could just listen to music," I offered with a shrug, abruptly cutting him off.

Blinking in surprise, it took a moment before his gaze softened and he nodded. "Sure," he replied in agreement. Unplugging the headphones from his phone, he raised his eyebrow. "Your music or mine?"

"Yours is fine."

It took no time at all for the room to be filled with the beginning chords of a classic rock song, but with the volume turned low, the music was melodic and soothing. Feeling myself relaxing by the second, I noticed as Dean shifted over slightly, making room for me beside him as he got comfortable once more.

Hesitant at first, I hiked my legs up onto the bed, involuntarily shifting myself closer to Dean as I did so. As I laid beside him, only a sliver of space was left between us, leaving me to feel the warmth radiating off his body as one song ended and another began. My eyes were drawn to his profile, noting the bruises and cuts that had faded significantly over the weeks. Some scars however, still remained. The dim light that soaked into the room enhanced his flaws, while at the same time, illuminated his strong cheekbones and slightly crooked nose.

Turning towards me, Dean lifted an eyebrow and watched me with a glimmer of curiosity. "What?"

He spoke quietly, and was close enough that his breath tickled the skin of my cheek.

"Nothing," I said softly, "Nothing at all."

The pizza arrived twenty minutes after I did, forcing Dean and I to migrate into the living room to eat with Ryan. Though once the conversation died out and the food disappeared, Dean and I were left sitting on the couch as Ryan shuffled around in the kitchen.

"So..." Dean trailed, unsure of himself and apprehensive as he cast his gaze my way, "Do you want to talk?"

It was a simple question, and all it required was a simple answer. Though knowing that he was no longer talking about making light conversation – that there was a specific topic he was wordlessly suggesting – my hands clammed up and my heart beat unsteadily.

My eyes flickered towards the kitchen, knowing that, whether he wanted to or not, Ryan was eavesdropping on our conversation. "Um, I don't know."

Before either of us could say another word, Ryan's footsteps grew louder as he emerged from the kitchen. "I'm heading out to pick up some groceries," he said, and though his voice was nonchalant, the fact that he was giving the two of us some privacy warmed my heart. "I should be back within the hour."

"Don't get mobbed," Dean quipped, a grin pulling at his lips.

Ryan chuckled in response. "I'll try not to," he replied, grabbing his keys from the counter as he headed out the door.

And now we were alone, with me being the first to break the silence.

"My mom," I started quietly, sadness welling in my eyes, "She has cancer."

Although I'm sure he'd already guessed as much, there was still a sharp intake of breath as his movements froze still. I couldn't let the sympathy that clouded his irises deter me though, because if I was telling this story, I needed to do it before the strength I was mustering got shattered to pieces.

"My dad died when I was young, so growing up, it was just me, my mom and my brother, Theo. We were a close family, and even though it seemed lame at the time, I thought of my mom as my best friend." I gulped, pausing to work out my thoughts. "It was the summer after I graduated high school that she got diagnosed with breast cancer."

"It didn't start out horribly," I continued, though my voice dropped an octave as I focused my gaze on my lap. "The doctors had said they'd caught it in time, and after a few months of chemotherapy and a small surgery, she was cleared and sent into remission. That was around the same time my brother moved to London after accepting a job offer straight out of university, and even though he had tried to reason with himself to stay, our mom pushed him to go."

"Six months later however, the results of a mandatory scan had shown that the cancer had come back at full force. Theo flew back as soon as he could, but my mom didn't want him putting his life on hold just to take care of her – so it fell on me. The cancer spread to her lungs, and eventually her blood, and by the time I finished my sophomore year, I was overworked and was leaning towards dropping out. Her doctors knew that I was her only real support, and seeing what the stress was doing to me, they advised that she be transferred and stay as a permanent resident at the hospital."

"So your mom's been staying at the hospital for over a year?" Dean asked, frowning thoughtfully as I nodded. "And you've been on your own this entire time?"

His stared at me in incredulity as I stuttered. "I mean... Stella stays around some times, and it's not that much different from you living on your own, but – "

"Geez Katie," he said, cutting me off as he inhaled a haggard breath.

The next second he was shifting towards me, wrapping his strong arms around my torso as he pulled me closer. I froze as my cheek met his chest, but the tension in my posture didn't deter Dean as he held on tighter, one hand weaving up into my hair as the other ventured to wrap securely around my waist.

"You should never have to be on your own."

As he mumbled his words against my forehead, I felt the tension seep from my body as I fell safely into his embrace. I closed my eyes and took comfort in the support he was offering, allowing my senses to become overpowered his clean scent and steady breathing.

We stayed like that for a few moments, though when I felt him drawing back, the quick pressure of his lips against my temple was enough to let me know he wasn't going far.

"Is your mom okay?" he asked, unsure of himself as I felt his arms tighten around me once more.

It was like he was afraid that I'd push back from him, as though he didn't know how unlikely that would be.

"Overall she's stable," I sighed, taking a deep, shuddering breath while my hand unconsciously gripped the fabric of his shirt. "There hasn't been much change with her treatment or recovery in the past couple of months. The doctors are still treating her with chemotherapy, as well as some additional medication, but what she has to go through everyday takes a toll on her. She's tired, but she's fighting to stay alive."

"She's fighting for you, because you're the strongest person she knows." Dean's words hit home and made my heart beat quicken as his hand moved in slow, soothing patterns on the base of my back. "Is that why you're studying to be a nurse?"

Tilting my head back, I rested against his shoulder and met his gaze. "I want to be able to help people. I knew I wanted to go into nursing before my mother's diagnosis, but now – " I gulped. " – If I can't help her, then at least I can help others."

A response didn't come. I didn't know if he was holding back with a fear of pushing me too far, or if he was simply speechless, but the lull in conversation wasn't entirely unwelcome. I was tired of appearing strong, and as I inched closer into Dean's arms, that was when I finally allowed the tears that I'd been holding at bay to fall.

The longer I stayed there, the heavier my eyelids became – a result of exhaustion settling in as the effects of insomnia caught up with me. With dried tears staining my face and my head resting against Dean's chest, my surroundings began to slowly fade away as my eyes fell shut.

"Sweet dreams Katie."

Chapter 10

Watching Katie break down that night was heartbreaking. From the first night that I'd met her she always appeared to be strong and independent – striving for success as though nothing could get in her way.

But that was why you could never judge a book by their cover.

Katie was strong and she was independent, but she hadn't been given the choice to be that way – it'd been forced onto her when her mom fell ill to cancer. Not on purpose, but that was just the way the cards fell, and she'd learned to live with it. There was a wall she'd built up over the years to protect others from seeing her inner agony and bouts of loneliness, and somehow, I'd stumbled across the boundaries and discovered who she truly was.

A myriad of emotions had struck as I kept her close to me the night her past had come out. With her eyes shut and the remnants of tears staining her rose coloured cheeks, I blocked out the soft lull of the television as her words looped in my mind. She was losing her mom. She was fighting and she was scared, and seeing her like that had shifted my perspective on my own injury.

I had the ability to get better, and while things may begin to shift in my life, I still had my family. I had a life that I could build up from the wreckage, but from the way that Katie spoke, it seemed like her mom didn't have much hope left.

The worry that I'd pushed her too far – that I'd made her uncomfortable – had been at the forefront of my mind, especially when I awoke the next morning to see that she'd disappeared. Panic set in immediately, and as I struggled into my chair, banging around the room, Ryan was quick to stop me. He told me that she'd slipped out in a hurry, that she had another early shift at the hospital, and though it made my fear subside slightly, the text message that came through later that afternoon was what curbed my concern fully.

Thank you.

She wasn't keeping me at a distance, and for that I was thankful.

As the days passed Katie didn't bring up her mom again, though I could tell from her eyes when she'd been to see her. Whether they were guarded with thinly-veiled sadness after talking to her mother's doctors or shining with happiness after seeing her mom awake, I was there to offer her my silent support.

With my thoughts preoccupied by a certain blonde, time seemed to speed up. With a will to focus, I managed to catch up with my classes before my midterms started at the beginning of October, and because I was getting used to having to maneuver around in my chair, I was less bothered than I should have been when my doctor kept pushing back my appointments to give me a better opportunity to heal.

By the time the autumn-coloured leaves had begun falling from the trees, six weeks had passed since my accident, and I was sitting in an observation room, hopeful but non-expectant as my doctor entered.

"Dean," he nodded his head in acknowledgement, jotting down a note before slipping his pen into the pocket of his white coat, "How are you today?"

"Pretty good," I replied indifferently, shrugging my shoulders, "All things considering."

The ghost of a smile pulled at his lips. "Well then, I guess I'll just cut to the chase." He paused, paging one of the nurses as he flipped through the pages on his clipboard. "After looking over your physiotherapy progress and mirroring it to the results from your most recent tests, I can safely say that your ACL and meniscus seem to be healing greatly. Your bones have more or less healed, but because of the severity of your injury, I can't advise that you put much weight on your leg just yet."

My eyebrows drew closer in confusion as a bubble of hope popped inside of me. "And that means...?" I trailed, encouraging him to continue.

"We'll be switching out your cast for a smaller one, which means you should have the ability to move around on a pair of crutches," he affirmed, pausing as a nurse pushed through the door and into the room, "But if you end up finding it too difficult, you'll be able to go back to the wheelchair."

"I'm sure I can manage," I was quick to rush out, because while I'd gotten used to moving around in a wheelchair, I was growing tired of the looks I received and the inferiority I felt as I moved at half the height of everyone else.

It was clear to the doctor that I was more than willing to do the work as he let a small chuckle escape. "Alright then," he replied, nodding to the nurse as she readied the small device to remove my cast, "I'll be back to check in once you're situated."

It was simple and painless as the plaster encasing my leg was cut, and as a breeze hit the bare skin for the first time in weeks, I felt as though a gigantic weight had been lifted from my shoulders. Before my new cast was given however, my physiotherapist came in to work some life back into the muscles that had been still since my accident.

And the pain was excruciating.

It began slow but built quickly as cramps flared up the entirety of my leg. The therapy was in no way intense, but as soon as the muscles were budged awake, I felt a sweat break. My blond hair stuck to my forehead and my jaw was clenched as I held my lip between my teeth to stop myself from shouting profanities at the physiotherapist for simply doing his job.

With a small dosage of pain medication, the aches finally subsided and I sat back watching as the nurse rewrapped my leg. When blue fibreglass was secure and the nurse stepped back, I was content to see the cast only spread a few inches above and below my knee. My doctor returned soon after it was completed, a pair of crutches in tow that he passed off to the nurse before looking me over.

"Is that comfortable?" the nurse asked minutes later once the doctor had left. She'd readjusted the height of my crutches for the second time before passing them over to me to use.

Placing my weight on them, I was supported for the most part, but it felt strange to be stable while standing up. "I think so," I replied, wobbling slightly to the left as I began to move around the room.

Listening as she showed me the best techniques for using the crutches, it didn't take long before she was walking along beside me as I limped my way through the hospital wing. Rounding a corner, I stopped short as I spotted Katie huddled some ways down the hall with a few other nurses. Through the corner of my eye I could see my nurse turn to look at me in confusion, but before she could ask what was wrong, her gaze followed mine and a small grin pulled at her lips as she kept quiet.

Over the past couple of weeks, I'm sure most of the nurses at the hospital had picked up on my affection for Katie, and while I was okay with them knowing how much I wore my heart on my sleeve, I wasn't so sure I ready for Katie to know.

I hadn't even realized I was staring until one of the nurses talking to Katie looked my way, a teasing smile on her lips as she nudged Katie. Turning my way, her smile widened and her eyes crinkled up at the corners.

"Looking good on two feet there Adams."

It was embarrassing, on some level, the way the rest of the nurses smirked and chuckled silently as a shy flush graced my cheeks. Noticing quickly the proud gleam in Katie's eyes, an idea popped into my mind and my lips twisted upwards. Without thinking much about it, I replied, "Good enough to grab some food with after your shift?"

I could see the tips of her ears turn pink as the nurses cooed in amusement. "I get off in an hour," she mumbled, though it was loud enough for me to hear as I grinned in response.

"And I'll be waiting."

Her gaze softened as she shook her head happily, moving along with her colleagues as her pager beeped and she set back to work.

Once my nurse had deemed that I was able to maintain some form of stability with my crutches, I headed down to the ground floor cafeteria to wait for Katie. When I'd made myself comfortable at a table towards the back of the room, I pulled my phone out from my back pocket. There were a few missed notifications, though I had just noticed the two missed calls from Ryan as another incoming call from him lit up my screen.

I swiped a finger across my screen to accept the call, bringing the phone up to my ear. "Hey sorry," I said, "My phone's been on silent. What's up?"

"I figured, and I'm just leaving an audition," he replied. I could hear a lot of background noise for a few moments before it quieted down. "I just wanted to know how everything went today."

After bunking on our living room couch for close to a month, it was evident that while he felt the need to be there for me, Ryan missed his family. He'd caught a red-eye flight back to New York almost two weeks ago now, and while he still called to check in at least twice a day, it was strange not having him around.

"I'm back on two feet. Well, technically. I've got a smaller cast and I'm on crutches for the next couple of weeks, but I'm not stuck in a wheelchair anymore."

"That's great," he said, the relief in his tone flowing through the line, "And you're doing okay with school and everything?"

I began to nod, only to realize that he couldn't see me. "Yeah. I'm caught up with all my assignments and stuff, and Katie's still dropping by in the mornings to pitch in and give me a ride."

"So... Katie eh?"

I rolled my eyes at his suggestive tone. "Yeah, you've met her, remember? Blonde, average height, really nice, cute smile."

"I remember," he chuckled, "But I'm wondering if you've asked her out yet."

"No – I haven't."

"Well get on with it then." Ryan's amusement was crystal clear as he continued. "You like her don't you? So why not ask her out?"

"I seem to remember me having to force you and Zoe together four years ago, so I don't really think you're the best one to be offering up any advice."

"Whatever, keep living in denial," he replied, "Just make sure you don't wait forever, because you're gonna need a date for the wedding in a few months."

My eyes widened in surprise at this unexpected piece of information. "You guys set a date already?"

"May 20th – out here in New York."

"That's great," I said, running a hand through my already tousled hair, "Uh, congratulations."

"Thanks, just don't go spreading that around to anyone else. I don't need Zoe upset when photographers that we haven't booked start crowding the place." His tone was joking, but I knew he was serious on some note. He'd do anything for Zoe and her daughter, including moving across the country for privacy reasons, and they deserved a private ceremony if the possibility was there.

"I won't."

"I should probably let you go," he continued, a little reluctantly, "The car's pulling up at the house. Are you sure you're alright?"

"I'm fine," I said, stressing my words with hope that he'd believe me. There was no need to worry. "Say hi to Zoe and Abbie for me."

"Will do," he promised. "Talk to you soon kid."

"Yeah, you too," I said, saying goodbye before ending the call and sitting back as I waited for Katie's shift to finish.

Being that it was only three when the two of us hopped onto the bus from the hospital, I offered up grabbing some ice cream, which Katie was more than happy to agree to. Knowing just the place, we got off the bus a stop early, and while our pace was slow, we stepped into the small shop a few minutes later, a mixture of sweet scents clouding the air as a bell dinged above our heads.

"This place is cute," Katie said as we moved towards the front counter. Glancing her way, I saw her admiring the brightly coloured walls that were decorated with encouraging quotes that I'd read a thousand times over.

"Yeah," I shrugged, "I like it here. Found it when Holden and I first moved into our apartment sophomore year."

"Well then," she spoke with an amused undertone, an eyebrow raised as she nodded to the display case of flavours, "Any suggestions?"

"It depends," I mused, "What do you like?"

"Umm, something sweet I guess," she offered, her eyes glazing over the forty flavours unsurely.

My lips pulled upwards reassuringly. "Then I think I've got just the flavour for you." Turning towards the teenage boy that stood behind the counter, I rattled off my own order – consisting of one scoop of banana and one scoop of cookie dough – before ordering a medium waffle cone of strawberries and cream for her.

It took a few moments, and as Katie took both our cones, I led the way to one of the empty tables.

"Thanks," I said once I was situated, my crutches lying flat underneath my chair as Katie passed me my cone. Taking a lick of my own, I watched as Katie tried hers for the first time, a smile on her face as it melted on her tongue. "So, what do you think?"

"It's really good," her smile wide as she took another lick. Her eyes flitted to the glass windows, where streaks of rain were starting to blur the view outside. "And it looks like we got here just in time."

"I guess we'll just have to stay here until the rain lets up," I replied cheekily, and while I knew it wasn't realistic, I hoped the rain didn't last long. It wasn't a long walk back to my apartment, but I knew using my crutches on a wet sidewalk, with nothing but a hood to block out the rain, was not an ideal situation.

She rolled her eyes. "A bit of rain won't hurt us," she said. "Plus, I'm sure you've got just as much work to do as I do."

I shrugged. "Not really," I replied, which caused a look of skepticism to be thrown my way. "I mean, I've finished all my assignments and I've done my half of the lab report I have due. All I really have to do is start studying for a midterm on Thursday, so I've got plenty of time."

A wry smile pulled at her lips, an impressed expression gracing her features. "Who would've thought that the star athlete was actually a good student?" she asked teasingly. Her words opened up the wound that I'd tried to seal tight, and as my face reflected the sadness coursing through me, I saw the exact moment she realized what she'd said. "Oh god," she said quietly under her breath, apology flooding the blue of her irises, "I'm so sorry, I didn't think."

"It's okay," I breathed adamantly, although the words themselves left an unsettling feeling in my mouth.

With everything that'd been filling up my time – managing my injury, physiotherapy, and my course assignments –

there'd only been a few instances when my thoughts drifted towards basketball. It used to be a constant in my mind. The daily fitness and training schedule had been grueling, but I would always be excited for the games. Now, since my accident, I'd barely spoken to me teammates, my coach had been dodging my attempts to chat, and all I'd heard were whispers through the campus that the team had been faring well thus far in the season.

Her shoulders were squared in a defensive manner, like she assumed I was mad, and her gaze was fixed on her ice cream. "Sorry."

"Really," I spoke softly, "I'm okay. It's just, I haven't really had a chance to think about it much, but the thought's always been there, you know? I've been pushing so hard with my therapy – trying to heal so that I can get back to training like I used to – but I never fully realized how much work it'll actually take to get back to normal."

"I didn't mean to be a downer," she admitted shyly, biting down hard on her lip as her gaze met mine.

"Trust me," I said, "You're not."

We sat quietly for a few minutes as the rain outside hit gently against the window pane, consuming our ice cream content with the muted atmosphere. Though it came to an end when a buzzing from Katie's bag caused an repentant look to cross her face.

Pulling her phone out, she apologized as she looked at the caller ID, glancing back towards me. "Do you mind?" she trailed unsurely.

I shook my head. "Go ahead."

Smiling as she brought the phone up to her ear, she stood up, gesturing to the store front as she stepped away from the table. "Hey Stella," I heard her speak into her cell, walking in the direction that she'd pointed before hovering around the entrance.

My eyes trailed after her as she walked, and as she leaned up against the full glass window, the rain-stained reflection caught the curve of her smile and the lightness in her limbs. A bout of laughter escaped as she talked with her best friend, and though I tried my hardest not stare, it was hard when she appeared so magnetic.

Katie was a light amongst the darkness. She found the good in every situation, appeared strong on her weakest days, and she'd played a huge part in shifting my life back onto a stable axis after everything around me had been torn to pieces.

Even when she tried her hardest to fade into the shadows, the goodness in her heart illuminated her in ways nobody could describe – and she didn't even know it.

"Everything okay?" I asked when she returned to the table a few minutes later.

She nodded with a vague trace of amusement on her lips as she sat back down. "Yeah," she replied, "Stella's just got a date tonight and wanted some advice on what to wear."

Though it didn't concern me, that tidbit of information sparked a memory from earlier that morning. "You know, Holden's going out tonight too," I remarked breezily, not exactly sure of his plans, but suddenly thinking they had something to do with Katie's dark-haired friend.

Her eyebrows rose in surprise. "Seriously?" she asked. I nodded, finishing off the rest of my cone. "So you think they're seeing each other?"

Truthfully, I wasn't sure, but the possibility wasn't that farfetched to assume.

"Who knows."

"Remember to pick up your midterms on your way out," my professor announced as he called the lecture to an end.

Letting out a sigh of relief, I packed up my things with the knowledge that I'd officially made it through my first day of classes on crutches. I'd learned that, just because I was no longer in a wheelchair, it didn't stop some of my more ignorant classmates from staring, but it did make it a lot easier to move around campus.

Joining the growing line near the door, I inched forward slowly until my professor held out the exam I'd taken the week previous.

"Great job Mr. Adams," she said as I took the exam from her, "Keep up the good work."

Moving outside the classroom, I stopped for a second, leaning my crutches up against the wall as I looked down, surprised to see a 96 marked in red and circled at the top of my exam. Apparently the lack of training and extra studying was paying off this term, but as the thought drifted into my head, I found my good mood dampened.

Stuffing my exam into my bag, I knew I was meant to be meeting up with Katie fairly soon, but my mind overruled my feet and sense of direction as I headed across campus and towards the gymnasium.

Not wanting to be seen, I pushed open the back entrance, struggling up the stairs until I reached the rooftop bleachers. Looking out over the barrier and onto the court below, the sounds of squeaking shoes and dribbling balls echoed off the walls. The practice was in full swing, everyone either running laps or shooting perfect shots towards the baskets.

It was fast-paced and adrenaline pumping, but it wasn't the same as I watched from above. It wasn't healthy, I knew, to watch the group of guys I used to call my teammates in jealousy, but I couldn't help but think about how it'd be different if I hadn't crashed that night.

I tortured myself as my eyes stayed glued to the court, watching the practice go on for what felt like an hour, though it was really only ten minutes. "Okay boys, that's enough for today!" my coach yelled, unbeknownst that I was watching as he called the team in. "Practice tomorrow afternoon will be drill based so we're all set for the game against Kansas on Wednesday, so rest up tonight and I better see you all in weight room in the morning."

I could hear some noncommittal groans from a few of the freshmen as everyone headed for the locker room, but I knew that most of the guys had long since grown accustomed to the training regimen coach swore by.

It was how we got to be one of the top teams in the country – through hard work and never giving up.

Waiting until the gym was empty, I felt myself drowning in a flood of self-pity as the lights dimmed. I sighed, knowing that it didn't matter how down I was feeling, I was making Katie wait, and she'd done absolutely nothing to deserve it.

Successfully making it out of the gym without anyone noticing me, I headed towards the quad, which had come to be mine and Katie's meeting place after classes. Once in view, it made me feel slightly better to see that Katie wasn't waiting alone, but was talking to Stella as I made my way towards them. It was Stella that noticed me first, as Katie's back was facing me, and I noticed the outline of a smirk trace her lips as she nudged her friend, her mouth moving with words I couldn't make out before Katie glanced back at me.

"Hey," she greeted, a smile on her face and a faint blush to her cheeks.

"Sorry I'm a bit late. I was in the library and lost track of time."

The lie slipped through my lips easily, and while it added a level of guilt to the range of emotions flitting through my mind, I didn't have it in me to tell her the truth. Not right this moment.

"Don't worry about," she said reassuringly, taking my words as they were as her hand fluttered to the strap of her bag, "I was just catching up with Stella."

"Yeah," Stella agreed, a teasing tone lacing her words. "Since you've been stealing my best friend away from me lately, I've had to resort to staying on campus to get some time with her."

"Sorry about that," I mused.

Katie rolled her eyes, and though she was trying to hide it, I saw the crimson flush that slowly climbed up the skin of her neck. "Ignore her," she said to me, causing both Stella and I to chuckle, "Are you ready to go?"

"Yeah," I said, readjusting my crutches and pushing away the weakness I felt for keeping my thoughts and emotions hidden, "I'm ready."

Chapter 11

Tossing the used needle into the disposal bin as Claudia applied a small band-aid to the young girl's arm, my gloves were quick to follow before I hunched in front of the patient with a friendly smile.

"See, wasn't that quick?" I asked, watching her lips pull up slightly as she nodded, forgetting about the pinch of pain that the needle had caused. Reaching into the jar of small lollipops, I pulled one out and held it towards her. "And because you were so brave, you get a treat to enjoy on the ride home."

Her eyes shone happily as she quickly grabbed the candy. "Thank you!"

I chuckled at her reaction, offering her my hand as I nodded at the door. "Let's get you back out to your mom then, shall we?"

The waiting room was only two hallways away, and as soon as her mom was in sight, the little girl released her grip from my hand and ran towards her. Making sure to remind the mom to sign out at the front desk, I didn't linger long, returning diligently to where I'd left Claudia.

"So, how many more kids have appointments today?" I asked, leaning up against the side table as I watched her. I tried my hardest to make it appear as a casual action, but truthfully, I was exhausted. My alarm clock had woken me up this morning just after nine, and even though that was considered a lie-in for me, it didn't do much good after only managing to catch two hours of sleep.

"There's six written down in the books for appointments," Claudia replied, her eyes trailing the papers in front of her as she finished jotting down the notes for the last patient, "But we have to accommodate the people who just walk in to, so probably around ten."

I nodded, and after a quick calculation, figured that we'd be administrating the flu shots for the remainder of our shift. "Sounds good," I replied, turning my gaze to the list of appointments. "Did you want me to go and grab Samuel then?" I asked, reading off the next name, and while I attempted to conceal it, a yawn managed to escape me.

Claudia had seen it, there was no doubt about it, and while it wouldn't normally be a strange occurrence near the end of a full shift, she'd already caught me zoning out while filing paperwork and rubbing my temples in an attempt to curb an on-going headache.

"Katie," she spoke carefully, her eyes softening with worry as her gaze met mine, "Are you sure you're okay? Because if you're feeling overworked, or stressed, I can see if your hours can be cut back or – "

My lips pulled up tiredly as I jumped in. "I just didn't get much sleep last night that's all." The words were true but a guilty taste lingered on my tongue afterwards. "I'm fine, really. You don't need to worry."

I wasn't fine. I was disoriented, overworked, tired and experiencing regular headaches as a result of my lack of sleep, but I couldn't admit it. I'd worked hard for this job, and having made so much progress, I wasn't ready to stumble backwards. I could get a hold of my insomnia. I'd done it before and I could do it again.

Swallowing hard, hoping that she didn't catch the slight waver to my voice, I let out a silent breath of relief when she accepted my reply a few moments later. "Okay." There was still an ounce of skepticism to her voice, but for now, she was letting the issue drop. "But before you fetch Samuel, can you drop these files off at the front desk?"

Detouring to the staff room for a cup of coffee, I returned five minutes later with Samuel in tow, hoping that the caffeine would give me enough of a boost to get through the rest of my shift.

Two hours later I was considerably more awake and less drowsy. My headache had subsided and my thoughts were more fluid, which seemed to please Claudia. We were just finishing up with the last walk-in client before shift change, and though he looked to be a young teenager, I was still tasked with distracting him as Claudia administered his flu shot.

"Katie?"

Knowing that it wasn't Claudia's voice, I turned curiously to the doorway to see another nurse, who I vaguely remembered meeting, looking at me in an expectant manner.

Arching an eyebrow, I glanced back to see that Claudia had used this distraction to inject the vaccine into the child's arm. "Yes?" I replied slowly, moving towards the candy jar that had been serving its purpose all afternoon.

"You're wanted upstairs," she said hesitantly.

Halting my steps, a frown creased my forehead. I didn't understand what was going on, and with one glance back at Claudia, she didn't seem to know either. Noticing that the nurse was fidgeting with the material of her scrubs, I asked, "For what?"

The sympathy that she'd evidently been holding back flooded across her features quickly, her blue eyes muted and her tone somber as she said, "It's your mom."

A cold chill made its way down my spine as I froze, my shoulders stiffening as my lungs contracted painfully. I felt like I couldn't breathe. My heart was thundering above my rib cage and my mind was running a mile a minute, racing through different, gut-wrenching scenarios.

"Wh...what?" I managed to force out, my voice croaky and dry as my hands began to shake with worry.

"I don't know much," she continued softly, "They just wanted to talk to you."

Any prior feelings of exhaustion had rushed out of my body as my emotions were set to high alert. I was holding it together for the moment, keeping my tears at bay, but I didn't know how much longer it'd take before things went downhill.

"Go," I heard Claudia say persistently, "I've got everything handled here."

Nodding mindlessly, my legs moved on their own accord, breezing passed the nurse whose name I couldn't remember and towards the elevator. When the metal doors slid open, I stepped inside quickly, pressing the button for my mom's floor before repeatedly tapping the button to close the doors, hoping that it'd speed up the process, even though I knew it wouldn't. The elevator ride was constricting, even though there was only me to take up space, and as the seconds ticked by as though they were minutes, I could feel myself begin to hyperventilate.

I had almost lost my mom once, two years back when she'd contracted a bad strain of the flu just as she was finishing up her first round with chemotherapy. I'd been a wreck, and the thought of having to replay that nightmare made panic bubble in the pit of my stomach as the elevator doors finally drew open.

Moving as quickly as I could through the halls, I weaved my way around patients and co-workers before I reached my mother's room. The door was closed, and through the small glass window, I could see two nurses tending to my mom as she laid awake while one of her doctors stood at the foot of the bed.

I paused only for a second. Taking a deep breath, I placed my palm against the door and pushed it open. "What's wrong?" I asked, and while I'd tried to sound concerned and level-headed, I was sure that, as all eyes turned to me, I sounded hysteric. "I was told to come up here." My words were quick and full of worry. "Is she okay? What happened?"

"Katie," the doctor spoke calmly, cutting off my nervous ramblings. "We've got everything under control, we just wanted you to be here to hear what's going on."

"And what's going on?"

The only thoughts that were running through my mind in that moment were grim and terrifying.

"Your mom woke up about half an hour ago, and when we began to take her vitals, we saw that she was dehydrated. We increased the amount of medicine in one of her IVs and succeeded in levelling out the water supply in her body after a meal, but she is running a slight fever." His voice was professional as a way to appease my fears. "All of the tests we've run since have shown nothing out of the ordinary, so we don't believe it's affected her condition by any means. We'll be checking in at least once an hour for the rest of the day, and once the fever disappears we'll go from there."

My heart was beginning to slow down as the situation was explained. There was no sympathy hidden in his eyes, which meant that I could trust that his words weren't altered to put me at ease, and for that I was thankful.

"Am I okay to stay here for a while?" I asked softly, feeling small as I looked to my mother. The pale skin of her forehead had a sheen layer of sweat and her features were laced with exhaustion.

I could see the doctor nod in my peripheral vision. "That's completely fine, though I should let you know that your mom is running low on energy and she's likely to fall asleep within the next few minutes."

Nodding in understanding, I waited stilly until everyone vacated the room, leaving my mom and I alone. Moving towards the bed, I leaned over her. Until then, I'd managed to hold my tears back, but as water lined my eyes, I couldn't find the strength to blink it away. "Please tell me you're okay," I pleaded, clutching her hand with my own in a desperate attempt for a connection.

"No need to worry sweetie," she spoke slowly, though the unusual scratchiness to her words felt like a spike to my heart. Her lips cracked slightly as she smiled. "I'm okay."

"Good," I choked out, "Because I can't lose you."

Just as her doctor had predicted, my mom didn't stay awake more than a few minutes after we'd been left alone. She asked how I was doing, ignoring the tears that leaked from my eyes as I replied, but when I was left alone to stew in silence, I pulled the plastic chair in the corner of the room next to her bed.

Claudia had dropped by at the end of her shift, not at all worried about the fact that I'd left her to deal with the end-of-shift duties alone, but sincere as she voiced how glad she was that everything was okay. She'd departed just as another nurse entered to check on my mom, wishing me a good night as she disappeared down the hall.

I didn't know exactly how long I'd stayed in the same position, but when the harsh glare of the setting sun beat through the glass windows, I knew I couldn't stay all night.

I packed up my things slowly, but when all was said and done, I left the nurses to be with my mom for the night, a hopefulness in my blood that this truly wouldn't have long-term effects.

As I was waiting patiently for the elevator, I pulled out my phone, shocked to see that Stella had blown up my inbox with more than a dozen messages. Choosing not to bother with reading them, I dialed her number quickly, knowing exactly what the reason was for the sudden burst of texts.

She answered on the second ring. "Hey."

"Stella! I'm sorry I didn't get your texts, I just got held up at the hospital, but I'm leaving now."

There was a pause on her end, and just when I was about to repeat myself, thinking she hadn't heard me, she replied. "You know, if you need to be at the hospital tonight – " Her voice was soft and knowing. " – We can just do this another time, I don't mind."

"No, everything's good," I insisted, feeling like an awful friend. First I'd offered to help Dean out by driving him to campus, effectively ending our morning drives to campus, and with my extra workload, I'd already cancelled and postponed plans one too many times. "If you pick up the snacks I should be home in half an hour and we can order take-out."

There was a low sigh from her end as the elevator doors finally slid opened and I stepped inside. "If you're sure."

"I am."

"Okay then, I'll meet you at yours."

"Great. See you soon."

On the way down the elevator stopped on several floors, many people crowding into the small space as I was pushed towards the corner in a claustrophobic attempt to give myself some breathing room. When we finally reached the ground floor, I was the last one to step out of the elevator, my legs on autopilot as I headed towards the exit.

Though maybe if I was paying more attention to my surroundings I would've seen Dean approaching before he managed to sneak up on me.

"Katie," he started with amusement, though when I jumped in surprise, whirling around to face him with wide eyes, I saw the light in his eyes slowly dim as a calculating curiosity overtook it. I was almost positive that I looked a mess. My eyes were red-rimmed from the tears I'd shed upstairs, the exhaustion that I'd pushed aside was slowly starting to seep back into my body, and I was hyperaware of the fact that the bus I had to be on would be leaving in less than five minutes. "Are you okay? I called your name three times and you didn't respond."

Shaking my head to try and even out my thoughts, I replied, "It's just been a stressful day." I'd known Dean was scheduled for his usual physiotherapy appointment, though since I hadn't expected to stay this late after my shift, I hadn't expected to run into him.

He quirked an eyebrow. "Anything I can help with?"

I relaxed slightly, tension seeping from my muscles as my lips quirked upwards. "It's okay," I replied softly, "I'm actually meeting up with Stella tonight, so I've got to get going before I miss the bus."

"If you're sure," he trailed with a wary look in his eye.

"I am."

Knowing that I wasn't going to say much more on the subject, he sighed, a satisfied smile stretching across his lips just a few seconds later. "Then have fun tonight."

"I'll try," I replied breezily, readjusting my bag as I moved to head towards the exit. "And I'll see you Monday."

"That's only if I don't die during physio," he called after me with a teasing tone.

"It's not that bad," I said, ignoring the looks sent my way as I gazed back over my shoulder, "You just have to suck it up."

"Easy for you to say."

Our exchange seemed to be causing the patients loitering the lobby some form of amusement, but as the glass doors slid open and I saw the bus rounding the corner, I let him have the last word.

Crossing my eyes and sticking my tongue out childishly, I pulled a ridiculous face with no further explanation before turning away and catching the bus home.

"I still can't believe that that flawless face is related to Dean."

Stella's voice had a teasing undertone as she watched Ryan Adams grace the screen of my television. It hadn't been my choice of movie because, in my opinion, watching Dean's brother act as though he was the tortured prince of a long lost kingdom just didn't sit well with me after having actually met him. However, when I'd given Stella free reign over my movie collection, she'd grinned especially wide as she slid the disc she'd chosen into the DVD player.

It was strange – knowing somebody famous and then having to watch them take on new identities and personalities as they furthered their career – and if I was finding it strange watching him act, I couldn't even imagine how Dean felt when he watched one of his brother's films.

"And I don't know why I even told you that Ryan is Dean's brother," I replied, pulling a blanket tighter to my chest as a chill hit my shoulders.

The two of us were spread out across the couch in my living room – one of us at either end with our legs taking up the middle and a mound of blankets covering us. There were empty takeout containers littering the coffee table, as well as a mix of opened bags of chips and candy packages – the essentials for a girls' night in.

"Because you love me," she replied cheekily, and though the lights in the room were off, and the only source of light was the harsh glare of the television, I could see a gleam of amusement in her eyes. "Or maybe it's because I was bugging you about Dean and you can't control what slips out of your mouth when you're thinking about him."

Holding down the blush that threatened to appear, I narrowed my eyes. "I can to," I said adamantly.

"Maybe when he's around," she continued teasingly, "But when he's not, it's completely obvious how you feel about him."

This time I couldn't prevent the heat that spread to my cheeks, painting them a bright crimson that was more or less hidden in the dark. "I don't – " I started, struggling to get the words out, "I mean – "

"You what?" she asked, urging me to continue with a smirk. As I stayed quiet and the blush spread down my neck, her eyes flashed knowingly. "Come on Katie, you can't even deny it – you like him."

I bit my lip timidly, my voice meek as I replied, "Is that so bad?"

"Of course it's not," she said reassuringly. "I'm actually happy for you, and looking back at the guys I've dated over the years, you could've done a lot worse."

"Gee thanks," I drawled, rolling my eyes.

She laughed. "I'm just saying, Dean seems like a great guy. Just be sure to keep me up to date about what's going on; I like hearing about your love life."

"What love life?" I muttered embarrassedly, very aware that she knew I didn't date much since my mom had gotten sick.

"You know what I mean."

When I lifted my head, my eyes catching hers, it threw me off slightly to see such a genuine look of happiness dance across her features. Her eyes were bright and her smile wide, and as a thought popped into my head, I wondered, for a moment, if it was because of Holden.

"What about you?" I asked nonchalantly, attempting to conceal my curiosity as I continued. "You've been calling me at least once a week since the end of September about dates you're going on. Anyone special?"

"Nobody you need to worry about," she said with a dismissive wave of her hand. She shrugged. "Anyways, you know how I am with guys."

It was true that she'd never really been one for a serious relationship, but if Holden – or whoever she was seeing – was breaking down her walls, then I was happy for her.

"But we aren't talking about me right now," she continued before I could get a word in. "We were talking about you and Dean." She paused, the movie now forgotten as she quirked an eyebrow in amusement. "So... has he kissed you yet?"

I flushed as the memory of me accidentally kissing him back in the hospital flooded my thoughts, causing Stella to laugh and squeal. As she begged for details that I'd previously withheld, I found myself smiling, this afternoon's events being safely pushed to the side knowing that, even though it wasn't all that exciting, tonight was just the kind of night I needed.

Chapter 12

"Are you sure you're okay?" Holden asked one morning, his voice slow as he eyed me skeptically and with worry.

My breathing was heavy as I dropped a pair of weights to the ground, hearing the groan of the floor boards underneath. My hair was matted to my forehead with sweat, and while I was in desperate need for a shower before Katie arrived, I knew that to build my strength back up I had at least two more reps before I could quit.

"I'm fine," I replied, my throat dry. Reaching for my half empty water bottle that I'd left beside the couch, I gulped down a healthy amount before returning my grip to the dumbbells.

It had been more than a couple of weeks since my physiotherapist had recommended I get back into a routine – something to help rebuild the strength I'd lost as a result of the accident. I hadn't seen much of a point whilst I'd been confined to a wheelchair, but once I'd regained a chunk of mobility, and had gotten used to my crutches and cast, I'd taken his advice.

However, thinking I could get right back into my old routine had been a mistake, as well as an eye opener.

The gym was fairly empty the first night I'd tagged along with Holden. There were a few people I recognized, but I hadn't paid much attention to them as I stretched out my muscles and started with a few simple exercises I was able to do without putting much pressure on my leg. When I'd begun loading the weight plates onto the the iron bar, Holden watched me warily, especially as I continued until I was at a weight I had once been comfortable with. He hadn't stopped me – afraid to knock down my determination - but had stood silently behind me as a spotter, and I was thankful he did.

The weighted down bar had nearly dropped down on my chest, Holden catching and supporting it at the last minute. It was as he slid the weights off, one by one until I could properly lift the bar, that I felt my heart sinking. It hadn't truly registered until that moment how much I'd lost.

Leaving the gym that night I'd been embarrassed. With my crutches supporting me and my glasses hanging on the bridge of my nose as I ducked my head, it felt as though everyone was watching me. Heavy gazes bore into my back, full of pity and amusement, and I found myself unable to turn around as Holden walked along beside me.

It wasn't fair. I'd worked hard and this is the hand I'd been dealt.

But I'd grown up being told that if I wanted something bad enough, the work I put in along the way would be worth it in the end.

And right now I wanted to heal – more than anything.

So a routine formed. I found myself waking up earlier than normal, stretching out my muscles and working with the dumbbells I'd kept in the apartment. The mornings were the hardest however, because as I finished with a workout and showered, I was cutting it close most days when Katie arrived to find me forcing down my breakfast in a hurry.

It wasn't that I didn't want her to know that I was getting back into shape, but a small fear kept me from talking about it, believing that, instead of encouragement, I'd receive sympathy as I overworked myself.

At school I'd take the stairs, and while challenging, I found it rewarding in a way – knowing that I was on my way to a full recovery.

The evenings were when I really tried to push the boundaries. Keeping up with my assignments was still a priority, but instead of relaxing once they were finished, I made my way towards the gym nightly. Sometimes Holden would come with me, and other times, when he was focusing on his coursework or had other plans, I went by myself. This was when I tried to rebuild the strength in my entire upper body, switching my focus daily between my arms, my shoulders, and my back. I made sure to talk with one of the professional trainers, and listened to his recommendations on exercises I could execute safely without putting strenuous pressure on my injury.

It made me motivated – like I was working towards something – and I craved that feeling.

What I hadn't planned however, was continuing to sneak into the campus gymnasium and overlook the basketball practices. It seemed to be something I couldn't let go of, and almost every day I found myself up in the rooftop bleachers, hidden from view as I watched my teammates on the court below.

With each drill I watched, frustration and jealousy coursed through me. It used to be me driving towards the net for a lay-up or practicing offensive plays to get around the toughest defense, but now I was a spectator. I simply watched, all too aware of the fact that the longer I didn't play, the smaller my chances were at continuing at all.

Maybe that was why, one afternoon in early November, I'd stayed. Waiting until the lights dimmed and I saw the last of my teammates trickle out from the locker room, I made my way downstairs and into the gym. The sound of my crutches repeatedly hitting the floor echoed through the air, stopping only as I halted my steps at the edge of the court. It'd been over two months since I'd been on a court, and as I took a few hesitant steps forward, it felt like nothing had changed. Two nets still hung ten feet high at either end, the lines etched into the wood were the same, and the balls were loaded onto the same trolley they'd always been.

Indecision clouded my mind, but after casting my gaze around the empty gym, I made my way towards the rack of balls, grabbing one from the top row. Limping closer to the free throw line, I let my crutches drop and shifted my weight onto my good leg as I found my balance. Getting a feel for it, I dribbled the ball a few times, the sound radiating loudly in the air before I lined up the shot – one I'd made a thousand times before – and let the ball fly.

It missed.

Believing it to be a fluke, that I just had to warm up a bit more, I retrieved the ball again, shooting again, this time with a little more power behind it.

Except the ball barely grazed the netting before hitting the floor with a dull thud.

I tried again and again, though each time I missed the basket a mixture of discouragement and irritation ran through my veins.

Half an hour later, I was still there, defeat washing over my features as collected the ball once more. Attempting to calm myself, I closed my eyes for a quick moment, releasing the pent up anger in my muscles before zeroing in on my target. With my elbows bent and my feet spread shoulder length apart, I let the ball roll up my palm and off the tips of my fingers as it headed towards the basket.

And to my surprise and satisfaction, the sound of the ball swishing through the hoop met my ears.

It was then that the lights flickered to life and I froze, knowing the only way to turn them on was a switch located near the main entrance. I gulped as I turned towards the doors, expecting my coach to be standing there with a mass of questions.

But it wasn't.

Instead, Katie stood there with her bag tossed over her shoulder and an undecipherable glow to her eyes. As my gaze caught hers, her lips twitched upwards and she took a few steps towards me. "Hey."

"Hi," I forced out, my voice gruffer than I intended it to be, "How long have you been there?"

"A few minutes," she replied, bringing the corner of her lip between her teeth nervously.

"How did you know where to find me?"

"I saw you one day after class," she admitted sheepishly, causing a sinking feeling to grow in the pit of my stomach. She knew – but she'd never said anything. "I thought you were just talking to your coach that day, but when I kept seeing you head over here after classes, I figured it was something else, so I just left you to it." She was standing next to me now, and her eyes moved to the ball that had rolled to a stop against the wall before meeting mine again. "Is this what you've been doing?"

Her voice was curious, and surprisingly, there was no hint of judgement as she tilted her head slightly, waiting for me to reply. "Not really," I sighed, bending down to pick up my crutches. Positioning them to better my balance, I noticed Katie shifting closer to me. "I've kind of just been watching my teammates practice," I replied, a hint of embarrassment seeping into my voice as I nodded up to the rooftop bleachers.

Her eyebrows rose, surprise flitting across her face. "And none of them know?"

As my lips thinned out, my silence was enough of an answer.

"I'm guessing that's why the lights were off then?" she asked bemusedly, lightening the mood enough for me to crack a smile in return. "Do you have to hide though?" she continued, "I mean, I'm sure your coach wouldn't mind you watching from the sidelines."

I shrugged, not really knowing how to explain the thought process that was going through my head. "I don't know," I paused, trying to formulate some kind of response, "It's just not the same. If I'm down here I feel like I'm a part of the team, and since my accident, I haven't felt that way. My coach barely spoke to me when he visited in the hospital and my teammates have their own lives – none of them have time to worry about if and when I can play again."

"It looks to me like you're pretty determined to play," she pointed out, the edges of her lips tilting upwards in encouragement.

"I am." I nodded in confirmation. "But this is the first time I've been on a court in a few months."

"Well," Katie began, a gleam in her eye as she went to retrieve the ball I'd been using and passed it back to me, "Show me what you've got."

The words got stuck in my throat as I tried to protest. "I don't... I can't – "

"Dean," she said gently, cutting me off. Unexpectedly, she reached out until her hand was on my arm, squeezing encouragingly. "I'm not here to judge you. I just want to see you happy, and I know this sport does that."

Several beats of silence ensued as her optimism caused gratitude to well in my heart, and knowing that it was just her and I in the gym, I found myself nodding, wordlessly agreeing to her request. My nerves came alive as a smile grew on her lips and she headed for the bleachers, her eyes trained solely on me as they lit up with expectation and reassurance.

It took a few moments to compose myself, taking a few calming breaths as I took to dribbling the ball again. When I finally began to shoot, I found myself missing almost every time, but when one hit the backboard and fell through the hoop, the confidence that had begun to fade started to return. I took a few extra shots, sinking two and missing three, and glancing nervously to the sidelines to see Katie still sitting there, I moved backwards a few steps. Angling my shot differently as I aimed for a three-pointer, I was stunned as the ball flew through the air and swished almost effortlessly through the basket.

"See," Katie chirped happily, leaving her bag on the bleachers as she moved towards me, "I told you could do it."

Unable to stop a smile of my own, I nodded in affirmation. "You did."

What happened next was unexpected. I didn't know if Katie had meant to bump my hip, or maybe she'd try to hug me, but whatever the case, as her body collided with mine, I felt my balance falter. My arms reached out for her waist at the same time her hands landed on my chest in an attempt to stable me.

A flicker of panic crossed her features as she looked up at me with wide eyes. "Sorry."

It was hard to be mad in that moment, our close proximity registering with me right away. If I'd been braver, I might have taken the opportunity to lean in and close the distance between us, kissing her like I'd wanted to since our lips brushed accidentally all those months ago.

But I couldn't find it in me to take that chance just yet, and so I said, "It's fine Katie."

My words had a breathy tone to them, which only seemed to make Katie realize our current position. She drew her hands back quickly and casted her gaze downwards, but while I loosened my grip on her waist, I couldn't bring myself to let my arms fall just yet.

As an idea popped into my head, I pulled her closer, forcing her gaze upwards as I smiled down at her.

"Do you have to work tonight?" When she shook her head, biting her lip nervously, it took all the strength I had not to stare. "Did you want to go for a drive?"

Her eyebrows drew closer together as curiosity and intrigue encased her features. "Where to?"

"You'll see."

"Are you going to tell me where we're going?"

Katie looked over at me skeptically, returning her gaze to the road ahead a moment later. After leaving the campus parking lot, I'd directed her onto the highway, but had kept our destination a secret. We'd now been driving for almost forty-five minutes, and with the traffic moving smoothly, I knew we were getting close.

I could see her glancing at every road sign we passed, but since the place in mind wasn't all that advertised, and more of a hidden gem for the locals, I knew there was a slim chance of her figuring it out.

I shook my head in response, a grin curling on my lips. "We'll be there in a few minutes."

"You know, if you're just making me drive all this way just to grab a burger, you're gonna be the one driving home."

I hadn't meant to inhale sharply at the mention of me driving, but the reaction was automatic. Getting back behind the wheel was something I hadn't really thought about, but I knew that eventually my cast would come off, which meant I'd be cleared to drive. She'd said it as a joke, laughing lightly until she sobered when she noticed how uncomfortable I'd suddenly become.

"I, uh," she said, struggling to come up with the right words, "I'm sorry, I didn't mean it."

I breathed out heavily, running a hand through my hair messily. "It's okay," I replied sincerely, though my voice wavered slightly. "Honestly, I'm fine being in a car, it doesn't bother me. I just haven't been in the driver's seat since the accident, and I don't know if I'll feel as composed when I'm the one in control."

"Okay," she nodded, "Well when you're feeling up for it – "

"You'll be there," I finished for her, a gentle smile pulling at my lips to mirror her own. "I know."

Averting my gaze to the window, I found myself enjoying the silence. Katie and I had long since given up on trying to choose a radio station we both agreed on, but the atmosphere in the confined space of my car wasn't the least bit awkward – it was comfortable.

Realizing we were nearing our destination, Katie's nose scrunched up in confusion as I told her to take the next exit, though she turned her blinker on and moved into the right line. Veering off the highway, we headed down the side roads, and with a sparse amount stores and houses, I figured Katie's confusion was only increasing. It wasn't long before the open grounds came up on our left, and as I pointed out our destination to Katie, the car slowed and her eyes widened in surprise.

Raleigh Road Outdoor Theatre.

The words were scripted onto a large marquee-type sign that stood at the front of the field. Underneath them, there were letters stuck on, one by one, to display the movies that would play tonight as a part of the double feature, along with what times they were projected to start.

"What is this place?"

"It's a drive-in," I said, though it was self-explanatory as she eased the car slowly along the mostly-dead grass.

"I can see that," she rolled her eyes, "But in November?"

The temperature had definitely dropped over the months, the chilling breeze currently blocked as the windows of the car were sealed tight. It was strange that this place was still open, but after I'd subtly checked their website on the way here to make sure they hadn't closed down for the season, I didn't see a reason not to come.

There was a big screen set up at one end of the field, and even though it was late in the year, there were already a few crooked rows of cars already parked up front. Finding it difficult to maneuver much closer, Katie pulled the car to a stop behind a slightly rusted pickup, taking the keys out of the ignition and dropping them onto the center console.

"I guess if people are still willing to sit out in the cold," I started, nodding to a few brave souls who had brought a mound of blankets and were setting up to watch from the grass up front, "Then why close down." She looked over at me for a moment, and while she didn't say anything, I could see in her eyes that something was running through her mind. "This is okay right?" I asked, breaking the silence as a sudden worry flooded over me, thinking that maybe this wasn't the best idea.

"It's great," she replied, sounding more than a bit excited. "Do you know what movies are playing?"

My lips tipped upwards. "It's a comedy double feature night, so they're playing Neighbours and Trainwreck."

She quirked an eyebrow. "And we're staying for both?"

Gesturing around us, where other cars were beginning to box us in, I let loose a chuckle. "I don't really think we have a choice."

"Well in that case," she began, "We're gonna need some snacks." She unbuckled her seatbelt, pushing open the car door, but when I went to do the same, she waved me off. "You want anything specific?"

I shook my head, settling back against my seat. "Surprise me."

The concession building was tiny and located back near the entrance and ticket booth, and while there was a crowd of people piling inside, I didn't lose sight of Katie as she made her way across the field to stand in line. Her blonde hair was pulled up in a bun on top of her head, and as she reached the front of the line and ordered, moving over to the side as she waited for the food, my stomach began to grumble quietly in anticipation.

It wasn't long before one of the workers behind the counter stepped up with the food, and when I saw Katie turn, her arms were wide as she struggled with the amount of snacks she was carrying. Guilt creeping over me, I stepped out of the car and limped forward until the two of us were face to face.

"You didn't need to get out of the car," she said, though I could tell she was grateful for the help as I took a soda and a bag of popcorn from her hands, "I had it handled."

I quirked an eyebrow as we returned to the car, though I followed her around the front, gripping the door handle to pull it open. "But how would you have opened the car door?"

Leaning down to drop the snacks onto her seat first, she turned back to me, shaking her head in amusement. "I'm sure I would've managed," she mused, causing a laugh to escape my lips as she got into the car.

When I'd settled back into my seat, I realized how much food Katie had bought. There were two bags of popcorn, both salted and buttered, but it wasn't long before one had a bag of M&M's mixed into it, as Katie claimed it was the only way to truly enjoy both snacks. She'd bought two giant Cokes, which were now in the cupholders, along with two personalized pizzas and a variety of candy and chocolate bars she'd picked out.

By the time the loudspeakers burst to life, announcing that the first movie would be starting momentarily, the field was packed, and there was no escaping without making a multitude of people mad. Pushing our seats backs as far back as they would, settling comfortably in the small amount of space, it wasn't long before the large screen flickered to life.

When the credits rolled for the first movie and the large stadium lights flickered on, we'd made it through a good amount of our food. Wrappers were strewn messily across my dashboard, and since the sun had slipped from the sky, when you looked out the windshield and up over the mass of cars, there was nothing but an expansive sea of darkness.

"Do you believe that wishes made on stars come true?"

We were some of the only people who had stayed in their car, as everyone was looking to refill on snacks or stretch out their legs, but content with where I was, I looked over at Katie to see her eyes on the sky. "Don't you mean shooting stars?"

She shook her head, glancing my way. "Have you never heard twinkle twinkle little star?" she joked, though her voice became quiet as her gaze returned to the darkened sky. "I never understood why people tell their children that they can only wish on the first star they see. It's not as if it simply just appears, and if you're lucky enough to see it, a wish is granted. The stars are always there, immersed in their own gravity, and just because not all of them are bright enough to see, that's no reason why they all shouldn't be wished on."

It was like her mind was up in the stars, everything else fading out of view. Her cheeks were flushed and her irises seemed to be sparkling with wonder, but what I quickly realized, was that she was also shivering.

"Are you cold?"

I hadn't meant to snap her out of her supposed trance, but as she blinked and turned to me, I realized my mistake. Repeating the question slowly, I watched as she crossed her arms, trying to warm herself up. "Uh, a bit, but I'm okay," she stuttered shyly.

Not believing her, I reached into the backseat and pulled a sweater out of my bag. Handing it to her with a pointed look, a sheepish smile pulled at her lips.

"Thanks."

"No problem."

As she pulled it over her head, it took a moment for me to realize that it was the same sweater I'd loaned her months ago. The one she'd returned when I was in the hospital – the day we had kissed. It was clear to see, as she fiddled with the long sleeves nervously, that she had noticed the same thing, and when she sent a smile my way, holding my gaze for a moment before looking back up at the sky, I ignored the chill seeping into my skin as a burst of warmth spread through me.

"Make a wish," I said encouragingly, my voice just above a whisper.

"What?"

"Make a wish," I repeated. We were looking at each other, our faces somehow closer than they'd been before. "You were talking about wishing on the stars, so why don't you?"

I was nervous – a good nervous – as her eyes scanned my face. There was nothing but silence between us as her eyes closed, taking the moment to herself, and when a soft smile emerged on her lips, I knew she'd done it.

"Aren't you going to make one too?" she asked curiously, opening her eyes and tucking a stray piece of hair behind her ear.

Taking a chance, I reached across, resting my hand on top of hers. "I don't think I need to."

Because other than being able to play basketball again, the only thing I could think to wish for, was her.

Stunned by my response, her cheeks flushed crimson, but as the large screen in front of us lit up once again for the second movie, nothing else was said. We settled back comfortably, encased by darkness and a charged atmosphere, and I found myself smiling as she turned her palm up, threading her fingers through mine.

Chapter 13

"So... what happened with Dean?"

Rain splattered against the windows of William's coffee shop, blurring the view of early morning traffic towards the university. Stella and I had stopped in for a quick breakfast before our classes started, but our conversation had been stagnant, up until her sudden question caused a sharp inhale on my behalf. Choking on scolding coffee, my eyes wide, I regained my composure a few moments later to see her expression blank and her brow quirked.

"What do you mean?"

"Considering you asked for a ride this morning," she began slowly, a rush of worry flooding her eyes, "I didn't know if something had happened, or – "

"Oh," I said, realizing where her train of thought had led her, "No. Everything's fine. Dean just had a check-up this morning." I shrugged, cracking a smile. "I thought it'd be weird if I dropped him off at the hospital and then left with his car."

"Isn't it a little weird already though? You driving his car most of the time?"

"I thought it was at first," I admitted, taking a sip of coffee before continuing, "But I get why he's weary about driving." I cast my gaze downwards shyly. "Plus, it's not like I mind spending time with him."

A small grin pulled at Stella's lips. "Speaking of which," her voice now laced with delight and intrigue, "Is there anything interesting I should know about?"

I rolled my eyes with amusement. "This again?" She laughed, though pulled a face of mock innocence as I sighed. "We've hung out a lot, as friends, and sometimes I think that there's something there, you know?" I couldn't stop the smile that spread across my lips. "He's sweet, funny, insanely attractive," I paused, "But he's also putting so much effort into recovering and getting back into basketball, and I don't know if I want to talk to him about it just yet."

"But..."

"But," I continued, "It's hard to bite my tongue or hold myself back."

"Sometimes you just have to take the risk."

I couldn't think of a response as we finished our breakfast, and when I sat in the passenger's seat of Stella's car minutes later, the radio filled the otherwise comfortable silence up until she killed the ignition in the campus parking lot. Just as I went to reach for the handle, I noticed that Stella was sitting nervously in her seat, and when she glanced over at me to see me eyeing her, she bit her lip.

"Can I ask you something?"

Her question was calculated as she rang her hands togeth-er in her lap, making it seem like she'd spent the entire ride from the coffee shop trying to pull together the right words.

"Yeah," I replied, letting my bag drop down to the floor, "Of course."

She inhaled deeply. "Are you okay?"

Maybe it was because her pointed stare seemed to carry a lot more weight than simple curiosity that a swarm of dread sprouted in the pit of my stomach. At the sudden realization of what she was talking about, I could feel the colour drain from my face.

"I don't – " I stuttered, "I'm not – "

"Katie, I'm your best friend," she stated, no louder than a whisper, "Did you really think I hadn't noticed?" My chin hit my chest as I dropped my gaze, feeling small as embarrass-ment coursed through me. "Don't get me wrong, I think it's great that you're somehow staying on top of everything you have going on, but with the bags under your eyes and the waver in your steps, I don't think it's worth it if you're putting your health at stake."

Her words cut through me, but even the guilt of not con-fiding in her sooner couldn't push the truth through my lips. "I'm handling it."

It came as no surprise to me when her eyes surveyed me, narrowing in suspicion while also casting a swell of pity and sympathy over me. Breaking the somber silence, she said gently, "I'm just worried about you. I know you have a lot on your plate with work and classes and your mom, but I just don't want to see you fall apart again."

Flashbacks of my life three years ago flooded my mind, causing me to cringe as I remembered the state I'd been in. Stella had been there through it all, watching me unravel and fall because of the stress, but she hadn't been as perceptive as she was now. Now, she knew, and there was no way she believed the words I said next. "I've got it under control," I said quietly, though I couldn't meet her eyes as I stifled a sigh, "I promise."

I spent the rest of the day too self-conscious to fully focus during my lectures. Up until now I'd forced myself into believing that I was fine – that I had a control on my insomnia. Or more specifically, that I'd done a good job at hiding it.

Now, knowing that Stella had picked up on the clues that I'd been trying so hard to keep hidden, I was worried about others doing the same.

By the time my last class of the day finished, I'd downed more coffee than I should've to wake me up and simultaneously calm my nerves. Heading to the hospital for a short shift, I declined a ride from Stella, instead choosing to take the bus to save me from the inevitable look of worry.

At work, I found myself constantly on my feet, following Claudia around the hospital wings to check in with patients. I tried not to let my exhaustion show, plastering a smile on my face for the duration of the shift, but when I finally clocked out, all I wanted to do was see my mom.

"You have any plans for your weekend off?" Claudia asked, turning to me as she closed her locker.

"Not really," I shrugged.

I hadn't planned on having the weekend off, but when I'd gotten my schedule at the beginning of the month, I'd been surprised to see that a few of my usual shifts had disappeared and two weekends had been cleared. I had a suspicion that it'd been Claudia who advised our supervisor to give me a bit of a break to rest, but when I'd asked about it, the only answer I received was that I should take advantage of the time off.

"I'm sure you'll find something to do," she said, her smile shifting into something more mischievous as she continued, "Especially if you happen to talk to that boy of yours."

Fighting down a blush as I shook my head in amusement, I said, "Have a good weekend."

She chuckled as she headed for the exit. "You too."

Making the familiar trek up to my mother's room, I clutched the strap of my bag a little too tightly, my knuckles turning white, realizing that this was the first time I was hoping for her to be asleep. I wanted to open my mouth – to speak to someone about the return of my insomnia – and my mom was the perfect person, but I was scared of her reaction. If she was awake that meant that she was doing okay, and all I would succeed in doing would be giving her more to worry about.

Pushing open the door to her room, I felt the strange surge of relief wash over me as I saw my mom lying in bed, peacefully asleep. Moving closer to the bed, I leant down and placed a gentle kiss on her forehead, ignoring the paleness to her skin as I moved a few stray pieces of hair away from her face.

I backed away slowly, inhaling deeply as I dug deep to find the courage to say the words I needed to.

Just as I was about to sit down and let everything spill out, the door was pushed open. My eyes widened and my head swivelled around as I met the surprised gaze of a nurse I'd seen plenty of times, but had never bothered to ask her name. She frowned thoughtfully, her forehead creasing.

"Oh, Katie... I didn't know you were here."

I faltered for a moment, a chill running down the length of my spine as I detected the underlying sorrow to her words.

"Yeah," I began carefully, "I just thought I'd drop by for a few minutes."

"In that case," she bit her lip, glancing down at her clipboard for a moment before meeting my gaze frankly, "You're going to want to see Doctor Edmonds before you head out. He wanted to discuss something with you."

Her words struck a chord with me, sucking the air out of my lungs. I'd been around the hospital long enough to know that talking in private was never good.

"Do you – " I started, my voice raw as the words got caught in my throat, "Do you know what he wants?"

She shook her head, though the sympathy that glimmered in her eyes was enough to wedge a crack in my heart. "I'm sorry, but you'll have to wait and speak with him," she replied. "As soon as I check your mom's vitals I'll bring you to his office."

Nodding numbly, I couldn't blame her for the professionalism she displayed as she stepped further into the room, going about with performing a quick checkup. I knew it was standard practice for the doctors to deliver important news to family members regarding a change in a patient's health, whether it was good or bad, but I wish that now, for me, they'd make an exception.

As the seconds ticked by, the sudden stillness in the air registered with me, causing my muscles to tense in anticipation of what was to come. I wasn't ready to hear what Dr. Edmonds had to say, but as I followed the nurse down the tight corridors, I knew there was no delaying the inevitable.

When we reached his office, the nurse opened the door for me, greeting Dr. Edmonds with a nod before leaving the two of us alone. Stepping further into the room, I suddenly felt claustrophobic, the walls seemingly closing in as my heart began to beat rapidly. Hooking my thumb over my shoulder, I gulped as I gestured towards the door. "She said you want to see me."

Shuffling a few papers around on his desk until he found the one he'd been searching for, he replied, "Yes." Nodding, his expression gave nothing away. "Have a seat."

Falling into the cushioned chair, I was hyperaware of the fact that my leg was beginning to shake and my hands were clenching on their own accord. My gaze was drawn momentarily to the ominous grey skies visible through the window, and while it had stopped raining a while ago, I was left wondering if they were foreshadowing the direction this conversation would take.

"You're aware of your mother's diagnosis, correct?" Dr. Edmonds asked evenly, waiting to continue as I shakily nodded in accordance. "The cancer cells have taken over a large amount of her body, and, up until recently, have been primarily targeting her breast tissue, lungs, and blood."

My heart lurched. "Up until recently?" I asked shakily, my breathing shallow as I sought further clarification.

"I'm afraid, a few days ago, the results of a few tests we'd taken came back to show that the cancer cells were beginning to affect your mother's immune system." I inhaled sharply, knowing that wasn't good. "We altered the dosage of her current medication as soon as we could, increasing it to help fight back, but as of this morning, it doesn't look to be doing anything significant."

"Is this because of her dehydration a few weeks back?" I asked, my tone close to hysteric as my eyes welled up with tears. "Because you said that everything had gone back to normal – that everything was going to be okay."

"Things did go back to normal," he replied, "But that doesn't mean that normal for her was much better." He paused as he looked down at the piece of paper in his hand. "We're going to try switching out her medication with a more effective one later today, as well as intensifying the next round of chemotherapy she has scheduled. The hope is that this will help to correct, or at the very least, slow down what's happening, but right now, I'm sorry to say that your mother's health is quickly deteriorating."

Flashes of my mother lying in bed, her ECG flat lining, suddenly flooded my mind. The tears that I'd been holding back began to fall, staining my cheeks in a matter of seconds as I snapped. "And you didn't think to tell me this any sooner?"

"We didn't think – "

I didn't let him finish as I stood up, anger pulsing through my veins. "You didn't think to tell me that the cancer was getting worse?" I asked, my voice rising significantly. "You didn't think to tell me that my mother's body was getting tired of fighting? You didn't think to tell me that my mother was dying?"

Shear panic had washed over me, and while I took a deep, shuddering breath, trying to regain an ounce of control, it didn't do much good. My heart was still hammering inside my chest, my mind was still racing, and I knew my mother was still dying.

"I'm sorry," he said slowly, and though he tried to remain professional, clasping his hands together in front of him, the sympathy that crossed his features was clear. "We're doing all we can."

My next words were just above a whisper. "Except that's not much at all."

There was nothing else he could say, and as the silence in the room quickly became suffocating, I turned swiftly, picking my bag up off the floor as I ran from the room.

Moving through the corridors, it felt like I'd been swallowed by quicksand, falling deeper and deeper into a dark abyss with every step I took. Everyone was looking at me as I passed, my hair falling in my face to hide the tears that were falling as I rushed towards the elevator.

Stepping inside as the doors slid open, I felt a small amount of relief when I realized I was all alone. As the metal doors sealed shut, giving me the privacy I desperately desired – even if it was just for a moment – I let myself drop to the floor, the truth finally sinking in. I shut my eyes tightly, pressing the back of my hand against my mouth to catch the sobs that escaped as my emotions unraveled and I fell apart.

My head rested against the streaked windowpane of the bus, a dull throbbing developing the further away from the hospital I travelled.

It hadn't been pretty when I'd stepped off the elevator and into the lobby of the hospital. Gazes were drawn towards me, curiosity and sympathy filling each and every one of them. Wanting nothing more than to escape the building that had caused the heart-wrenching pain in my chest, I'd rushed towards the sliding doors, though not even the fresh air could help me.

I'd caught myself staring blankly up at the darkening sky, wondering what I'd done to be cursed with this life, and why nothing ever turned out the way I wanted it to.

The tears were still flowing as I dialed Theo's number on my cell, leaving him a message that was half-hysterical as I tried to explain that he needed to come home – that I needed him to be here. It wouldn't exactly be a voicemail he was expecting when he woke up, but he needed to know.

And now, as I watched the familiar streets and scenery whiz by, the anger and frustration had faded, leaving behind only the sadness and disbelief that chewed away at my thoughts.

Why did this have to happen? Could I have done anything to stop it? What will happen when she's no longer around?

It was hard to fight against the voices in my head telling me that I wasn't strong enough to handle this, that I needed someone to rely on, and as that thought crossed my mind, I knew that there was no way I could spend the night alone.

Though it did little to help my appearance, I swiped roughly at the moisture on my cheeks as I stood up, gathering my stuff as the bus pulled to a stop a few blocks away from my house. I didn't think as I headed into the familiar building, riding the elevator anxiously up to the third floor. My hands were shaking and my breathing had become anxious as I reached up and knocked, biting my lip hard enough to draw blood.

Hearing the lock unlatch, it was as though a burst of relief spread through me, only to be replaced with worry moments later as Holden pulled open the door. His hair was dishevelled, his cheeks were flushed, and all he was wearing was a pair of sweatpants hung low on his wait, but none of that registered with me as he took in my appearance with wide eyes. Suddenly aware that I'd come here for a reason, he opened the door wider, letting me inside as he glanced nervously towards his room.

"Katie?" he started, scratching the back of his head as I looked around frantically. Dean wasn't in the living room, and that only made my breathing speed up as I began to hyperventilate. "Are you okay?"

"Is Dean here?" I drew out, resting my hands against the back of their couch for balance. I knew I was seconds away from falling apart again, and there was no I would be able to get back to my apartment by myself.

"He's in his room, but – "

My attention was snagged as a door to my left cracked open with a squeak, and as I turned my head, I saw Stella peeking out guilty. I stared at her, my jaw unhinged as I found myself unable to form words. She stepped out of what I assumed to be Holden's room, a large t-shirt draped over her small frame and her bottom lip securely between her teeth. She was nervous, and even though I'd expected it to come out at some point, I would've thought she'd tell me before I walked in on whatever was going on.

"Katie..." she trailed softly, her gaze pleading, though she was stopped from continuing as another voice cut her off from the opposite side of the apartment.

"What's going on?"

Maybe it was everything happening at once – the chaos of it all that was messing with my mind – but my resolve quickly crumbled and I sank to the floor as Dean limped into the living room. My vision blurred and my throat constricted while the dam that had been holding back my cries finally burst, causing tears to flow quickly down my cheeks.

My sobs filled the apartment as I pulled my knees to my chest, but through my hazy vision, I saw Dean's eyes widen as he rushed to my side. He dropped to the ground beside me, wrapping his arm around my shoulder and pulling my head close to his chest. I could hear the worried questions coming from Holden and Stella, but I couldn't bring myself to force my gaze upwards.

Zoning everything out, all I could hear was the loud pounding of my heart and the strangled sounds that escaped my lips. My surroundings had blackened as I forced my eyes shut, and the only thing that kept me tethered to sanity was the feeling of security that Dean's embrace offered me.

At one point, after an immeasurable amount of time, Dean's voice managed to break through my haze. "Please... tell me what's wrong," he murmured softly, "I need to know what happened."

Lifting my gaze up, I saw the devastation and alarm in his eyes, which only made me cry harder as I choked out, "It's my mom."

His hold on me tightened as he inhaled sharply, tucking my head underneath his chin, but not pushing me to say anything further. He knew what was going on without having to ask, and from the way I could vaguely hear him speaking to Holden and Stella, they did as well.

"Come on," Dean whispered into my hair a while later, holding me close as he helped me to my feet. When he spoke again, his words were directed towards Stella and Holden. "I'm gonna take her home."

"Are you sure you don't need any help?"

Although I knew Dean was on crutches, I selfishly hoped that he'd deny Holden's help. I could pull myself together long enough to make it home if it meant that I didn't have to be alone tonight.

"We'll manage," Dean responded, taking a small weight off my chest as I lifted my head.

While Dean turned and headed back to his room to gather his crutches and a few other things, my gaze drifted towards Stella and Holden. Holden had his arm around Stella as she leaned into him, water brimming her eyes as she fought to keep it together. I knew I'd unintentionally ruined their night together but, pulling a wobbly smile onto my lips, I tried to convey that I was happy for her. Our conversation was completely silent, something we'd done a thousand times, but this time I was thankful I didn't have to say anything.

Because, if I was being honest, I didn't know if I could form my thoughts into words if I tried.

When Dean returned, his goodbye was quick, ushering me out the door as though he thought if I stayed in one place for too long I'd fall apart again. And to be fair, it was a likely assumption.

There was no possibility of me being in the right mindsight to get behind the wheel of Dean's car, which left us to walk. It wasn't a long way to my apartment, and since the sun had long since set, we strolled leisurely along the sidewalks, the light from the streetlamps brightening our path. Somehow, Dean had managed to make it the entire way with his right hand tightened around my left one, and though I was grateful, I knew it made it harder for him to maneuver around.

This was the first time that he was coming to my place, and that thought registered just as I turned the key in the lock and pushed open the front door. There was a bit of a mess in the living room from where I'd been studying the night before, as well as where I'd fallen asleep on the couch around four in the morning.

"My room's upstairs," I mumbled, almost incoherently as I shed my jacket and shoes at the door, nodding to the staircase.

Taking it slow, I waited at the top until he limped up onto the platform before moving further down the hall and stepping into my room. My bed was made, as it hadn't been slept in for two nights now, but as I sank down into the mattress, I found myself curling into a ball, seeking comfort after the longest day.

Dean followed my lead, except he inched onto the bed as though he was waiting for me to tell him to leave. When it was evidently clear that those words would not be escaping my mouth anytime soon, he relaxed slightly, resting his head against the same pillow I was using, moving closer so that our faces were only a hairsbreadth apart.

"I'm sorry."

"You're sorry?" he questioned, his brow furring as he brought a hand up to move a lock of hair behind my ear. "For what?"

"For ruining your night, for breaking down, for making you walk back with me on crutches."

"Don't worry about it. Seriously," he pressed as I gave him a doubtful stare, "None of that matters right now."

With his eyes trained on my face, I was struck with the sudden realization of how I must look. I could sense that my face had swelled up as a result of all of the crying I'd done over the last couple of hours, and I figured my eyes were red-rimmed and my cheeks were tear stained. He'd seen me like this before, when I'd first told him about my mom, but this was different. He was so close, his breath fanning my face, that my heart began to race due to something besides immense worry.

Trying to wipe the evidence of it all away, I brought my hand up to my face, but my actions didn't escape Dean's notice. He pulled my hand away, replacing it with his own as he rubbed the residue of tears gently away from beneath my eye.

"Tell me what I can do," he begged. "There has to be something I can do that will make everything okay again."

I'd thought about it more times than I could count, but in that moment, with a mixture of emotions flooding my head, my mind settled on one thing that would get my mind off of everything.

Bringing my hands up to his face, I didn't think as I pulled myself towards him and slanted my lips on top of his.

The action caught him off guard and I felt him still against me, and while it was disheartening that it was one-sided, if he wasn't pulling back, then I wasn't stopping. I started off slow, trying to convey how much he'd come to mean to me in just a short amount of time, and much to my surprise, it took a few seconds, but he finally began to respond.

The kiss quickly turned into something different – more passionate and rough then I'd imagined. My breath caught in my throat as one of his arms fell on my hip, pulling me closer and eliminating the sliver of space that had been hovering between us. His tongue slid slowly along my bottom lip, stopping the quick exchange of nips and sucks and instead drawing out a breathless sigh from the back of my throat as I matched his fervour with my own.

It was when my hands travelled down his chest, lifting the fabric of his shirt just the smallest amount that the frenzy came to a screeching halt as he wrenched himself backwards, his eyes widening as he took a hold of my wrists.

"We need to stop," he said, though his words were laced with pain, telling me that stopping was the last thing he wanted to do.

I leaned in again, pecking his lips gently at first. "It's okay," I said, looking into his eyes, "I want to."

His grip on my wrists was weakening with each second that passed, but that didn't stop him from shaking his head adamantly. "You have no idea how much I want this – how much I want you," he said, visibly torn as he shakily continued, "But not like this. I can't take advantage of you."

I gulped, tears brimming my eyes once more as I pulled my hands free, crossing my arms across my chest protectively. "Then will you stay with me tonight?" I asked, suddenly feeling ten times smaller. "I just... don't want you to go."

"Of course." He pulled me closer, his lips searing an imprint into my forehead. "You don't even have to ask."

Chapter 14

The next morning, the first thing to hit my vision was the bright rays of sunshine streaming in through the window. The curtains had been left open, and while I found myself blinking to adjust to the light, I felt disoriented for a moment as I realized I wasn't in my own bed.

But it all came rushing back quickly; the memories of last night yanking at my heartstrings as my gaze rested on Katie. Even as she slept, her brows were creased with worry and a frowned adorned her lips, making me wish that I could do something to run the nightmares from her mind.

Shifting in her sleep, she moved closer to me, pressing against my chest and causing me to hold my breath and keep completely still, hoping that I wouldn't wake her. She'd had the worst night imaginable, and while I didn't know the exact details yet, it wasn't hard to guess.

Katie's mother's fight against cancer was coming to an end, and not in the way that she had hoped.

Moments later, when her breathing evened out again, I inched my arm slowly away from her waist. Rolling slowly on the mattress, I was careful not to make much noise, pulling a blanket up over Katie's sleeping frame and grabbing my glasses from her side table before creeping down the stairs.

The silence in the house was maddening, my footsteps echoing heavily, and I wondered, for the first time, how Katie managed not to let the loneliness of living here get to her. It was clear that this was where she'd grown up – well-loved furniture and knick-knacks scattered around the apartment accompanying the framed pictures that lined the walls.

Moving into the kitchen, I located the coffee maker with ease, flipping it on and brewing a fresh pot as I rested my weight against the counter. Now that I was alone, it wasn't just the flashbacks of Katie's sobs filling my mind, but a vivid replay of the way she'd kissed me, as though it was the only thing that could help heal her heart. It had all but killed me to pull away from her, having wanted nothing more than to brave the line that separated a friendship from something more, but it'd been the right thing to do.

She didn't need to rush into something she wasn't ready for. Her heart was breaking with the news of her mother fresh in her mind, and she was the only one who could slowly piece it back together.

When my gaze drifted around the room, I was hit with the realization that we'd slept through the majority of the morning, and for a good reason. Katie's strangled cries returned as she'd curled up to my side, her hot tears soaking through my shirt until a quarter past three, and even after her cries had quieted down, I'd struggled to shut my brain off. It was no wonder we were exhausted.

The smell of fresh coffee filled my senses moments later, and after locating two mugs from the sparse collection, I headed back upstairs. Careful not to trip or spill the scolding liquid, I placed one cup on the side table in Katie's room for when she woke up, circling the other in my hands as I eased back onto the bed.

Warmth from the coffee was soon accompanied by a spark of happiness as Katie, still sleeping, edged closer to me, burying her face into the side of my chest. Guilt was quick to creep in however, banishing the pleasant thoughts as I sighed dejectedly, moving one hand to run softly atop her head in comfort.

Sitting there in silence, I found my thoughts trail off in unimaginable directions, and without realizing it I'd finished the last of my coffee just as Katie began to stir awake.

Her eyes blinked tiredly, still rimmed with redness. "What time is it?" she croaked, and noticing how close we were, scooted towards the other edge of the bed.

Ignoring the thorn of pain that pegged my chest, I glanced at my phone that rested on her side table before turning back to face her. "It's just after noon," I replied softly.

Pushing herself up, resting back against the pillows, she ran her hands over her face and through her hair stressfully. "I'm so sorry about last night," she began, a flush of embarrassment creeping up her neck. "I have no idea what I was thinking, and – "

I cut her off before she could continue. "Seriously Katie, there's no need apologize." Her head was bowed, hair covering her face as she wrung her hands together in her lap, and despite my better judgement, I set my mug aside and wrapped my arm around her shoulder, pulling her to my side. The surprise was clear in her eyes as they widened. "I know your emotions were all over the place last night, and even though what I said was true – that I do want you – I'm not about to jump in when you're clearly not ready."

Holding my breath as I waited for her reaction, I could feel my heart beating into overdrive.

Tears welled up in the corner of her eyes. "So you're not going to leave?"

Her words were wobbly, vulnerability showing clearly in her irises, and my heart squeezed in sympathy. "I'm not leaving," I reassured her, and while doubt still radiated off of her, I knew there was nothing else I could say; only keep my word and stick by her side.

Reaching out to grab the coffee I'd made for her, I tugged one side of my mouth upwards in a lopsided smile as I handed it to her.

"Thank you."

No words were exchanged as she sipped at the coffee, though I did notice her posture relax slightly as she pulled her knees to her chest. It was when the coffee was done that she sighed, running her fingertips around the rim of the empty mug.

"The cancer started to attack my mom's immune system a few days ago," she said at last, biting back her emotions as my hold on her tightened. "I found out just before I showed up at your apartment. The doctor said they tried increasing the amount of medicine they're giving her, but it doesn't seem to be working, and even though they're going to intensify her chemo, he doesn't see much hope."

The gutted look on her face had my chest contracting with pain, but I put on a brave face as I saw the tears start streaming down her face.

"It'll get better," I said as she rested her head on my shoulder and I kissed the top of her head. "Maybe not anytime soon, but she's still here, and eventually, it'll get better."

When Katie had stopped crying, I'd managed to get her to eat something despite her protests. It wasn't much, but I'd found a few things in the kitchen and had whipped up an omelette for each of us, and it'd stopped me worrying about her reverting to a shell of a human being as grief consumed her. Other than that however, we'd pretty much stayed in her room, my arm around her for comfort as everything truly sunk in for her.

It was just after two however, when a frantic knocking echoed through the apartment, alarming the both of us. "I'll get it," I offered, realizing that whoever it was wasn't leaving anytime soon.

Once I'd made it down the stairs, I limped towards the front door, the banging getting louder the closer I got. Unlocking the door, I pulled it open slightly to come face to face with a man a few years older than myself. He wore a jacket that was open just enough to see his wrinkled dress shirt, matching the condition of his dress pants, and though he looked exhausted, his features were strained with tension.

It took me a second, but when his eyes widened in surprise, noticeably similar to the blue eyes that'd been stuck on my mind for months, I realized that this was Katie's brother.

"Shit... sorry man. I must've gotten the wrong apartment," he trailed, seemingly deflated as he dragged a hand stressfully through his hair, moving to head back down the corridor.

"No," I stopped him, "You've got the right one." Opening the door a little wider, I hooked a thumb over my shoulder. "Katie's just upstairs."

Incredulity crossed his features, clearly caught off guard by a stranger greeting him, though he didn't dwell on it long as he moved past me in a hurry, dropping his briefcase and moving in place anxiously.

"Sorry," he apologized, the trace of an English accent accompanying his words, "She just never mentioned she had a boyfriend, so I just assumed – "

I coughed uncomfortably as I shut the door, cutting him off again. "I'm not her boyfriend," I replied uneasily, watching as he arched an eyebrow in disbelief. "We're just friends."

His reply was delayed as he eyed me carefully for a moment longer before his head fell heavily to his chest. "So I'm guessing you know."

There was no reason to ask what he was referring to; the pain in his voice a definite indication.

"Yeah," I replied quietly, shoving my hands into my pockets.

He sighed. "Well, I guess it's good she has someone to – "

"Theo?"

Both our heads turned towards the staircase, where Katie stood at the top, a blanket drawn around her shoulders. Her jaw was hanging open and disbelief had clouded her features as her gaze fixated on her brother.

His lips pulled upwards sadly. "Hey kiddo."

It took another moment for her to realize that she wasn't dreaming this, that this was real, and when she did, she bolted down the stairs with lightning speed and launched herself into her brother's arms. He hugged her back just as tight, and when she pulled back, it was clear seeing him again was overwhelming.

"What are you doing here?"

Theo tossed her a look of bewilderment before pulling her back into his arms. "I was on my way to work this morning when I checked my voicemail," he explained, pain crossing his features as the memories were tossed back to the forefront of his mind, "And shit Katie, I headed straight to Heathrow and hopped on the next flight. Did you really think I was going let you go through this on your own?"

Katie sniffled, bringing a hand up to wipe the tears from her eyes. "But what about work?"

"I called in on my way to the airport. I've got a few weeks off, and they know if things take a turn for the worse I'll be taking a leave of absence, but if something major comes up, I can work from here."

Casting her gaze around the entryway, Katie's eyebrows creased. "Where's your suitcase?"

"I didn't really have time to go home and pack first," Theo admitted sheepishly. "My friend is getting my luggage flown over soon, and until then, I have a few things left from the last time I visited. Now will you stop with the questions – none of that matters right now."

Katie's eyes glassed over in sincerity. "Thank you," she said softly. "Really. I'm happy you're here."

Watching all of this unfold, an awful feeling spread through the pit of my stomach, knowing I shouldn't be intruding on their family moment.

I waited a bit longer, thinking they'd completely forgotten that I was here until I coughed, grabbing their attention. "I'm uh... just gonna go grab my stuff and head out," I stuttered, reaching for the staircase, but wasn't able to move much further as Katie was quick to block my path.

"I thought you said you weren't leaving?"

Her gaze was pleading as her fingers latched tightly onto my arm.

I gulped, shifting my gaze to her brother, who was watching us with a vague hint of curiosity in his eyes, before looking back to her. "I just thought, now that your brother's here, you two should use the time to catch up," I spoke carefully, not wanting to upset Katie any further.

"Don't worry about it," Theo cut in, a smile appearing on his face as he stepped up and held his hand out for me to shake. "You're more than welcome to stay, and I'm Theo by the way."

"Dean," I greeted.

Katie turned to me, hope swirling in her eyes at the notion of me staying, and I knew, without a doubt, that I couldn't leave. Not now. Not after she'd been through so much. It'd be awkward, in my opinion, with her brother here, but if I could find a way to break the ice, maybe I wouldn't feel so out of place.

"So," I trailed, glancing back towards Theo, "What's it like living in London?"

It was later in the evening when the three of us sat in the living room, delving into the pizza that had been delivered just moments before. Katie and I were sat next together on the couch, close enough so that our arms were brushing every few seconds, and with Theo sitting in the chair adjacent, I wasn't about to pull her closer.

"So you've been driving his car?" Theo asked in astonishment.

Katie simply shrugged, swallowing the bite of pizza she'd just taken before replying. "I wanted to help, and it's not like he can drive with a cast." She directed a pointed look towards my injured leg. "Plus, he's got a pretty nice car."

Having already told him that I'd gotten injured in a car accident a few months ago, it wasn't surprising when curiosity flitted across his features. "My brother got it for me," I admitted sheepishly, answering his unasked question. I waited for the inevitable follow-up question about where my brother got the money, or if I'd grown up in a rich household, but it never came.

He moved on, asking Katie more about how her classes were going and how she was liking her job at the hospital –

all while I rested back against the couch cushions and faded into the background, letting the two of them catch up.

It was surprising however, when Katie pushed the conversation back towards me when she mentioned that I played basketball.

"So you're on the varsity team at Duke?" Theo asked, seemingly impressed.

I nodded. "Well I was. Right now I'm just trying to keep in shape so that I can get back on the court once I'm cleared to play."

"I tried to get Katie to play basketball a few times when we were younger," Theo said, reminiscing as he chuckled at a past memory. "She was absolutely horrible. No hand-eye coordination whatsoever."

A smirk pulled at my lips and I turned towards Katie. "Really?" I mused, "And how come you never mentioned this?"

I waited for her response – for her to blush or duck her head in embarrassment – but what I didn't expect was no reaction at all.

"Katie?"

When her eyes continued to stare straight ahead, a blank look glazing across them as she gazed right past her brother, an ounce of worry bubbled in my chest.

"Katie."

Theo's voice was louder and more pronounced, managing to shake Katie from the state she'd been in. Her skin paled and her breathing staggered for a moment, making my concern even more prominent.

"Sorry," she said quietly, looking ashamed, "What were you saying?"

Katie squirmed under scrutiny as neither of us replied, though Theo's eyes narrowed with suspicion, his gaze lingering daringly on his sister, making me wonder if I was missing something. He stood up, towering over the pair of us as anger overtook his features. "How have you really been these past few months?" Theo asked in a low voice.

Katie clenched her eyes shut. "Theo..."

He shook his head, disbelieving. "I can't believe you never mentioned it – to me, to mom, to anyone!"

"I'm fine," she ground out.

"You're not fine Katie." He raked his fingers through his already dishevelled hair. "You're zoning out and even though you're trying, those bags under your eyes aren't that easy to conceal. I was still around when you slipped the first time, and I can't just watch you spiral again."

My mind was spinning as I tried to figure out what Theo was talking about, but seeing an embarrassed flush colour Katie's skin, I knew this wasn't something I was supposed to be hearing.

"Just tell me one thing... when's the last time you've slept through the night?"

"Theo," she pleaded, tears springing to her eyes once again as she glanced my way quickly, "Please."

It wasn't immediate, Theo's reaction, but once his accusing eyes flitted away from his sister and towards me, they widened as understanding sunk in. "He doesn't...?" Theo trailed, and when Katie shook her head shamefully, he cast an apologetic glance in my direction. "Well then," he paused, clearing his throat awkwardly, "I think I'm just gonna go visit mom for a bit. Don't wait up."

As he spoke he slowly backed away, moving towards the entryway. The door slammed moments later, echoing throughout the entirety of the bottom floor of the apartment, the tenseness in the atmosphere filling the room with a deafening silence.

It wasn't surprising to me that Katie had turned her shoulder to me, her head hanging low in attempt to make herself seem small. "Katie," I paused, waiting until she met my gaze to continue, my eyes trailing over her features carefully with worry "What was he talking about?"

She looked up at me through hooded eyes, sighing as she began to fidget nervously. "I started having trouble sleeping when my mom first got sick a few years ago. I'd go from sleeping a few hours a night to not sleeping for days on end, and it really took a toll on me. I collapsed one day and was taken to the hospital, where they diagnosed me with insomnia, explaining that it'd been brought on by a combination of heavy stress, but also stemmed from a mild case of depression."

My eyes widened at that statement. Knowing that Katie – bright, beautiful, and full of life – had once been diagnosed with depression threw me for a loop, but it also proved to me that anyone could disguise the problems they were facing if they truly wanted to.

Pain wasn't only physical – it couldn't always be seen – and sometimes the people who hid their emotional and mental pain behind a masked exterior were the one who were hurting the most.

"I was on medication for about a year to help with my depression, but with time, both my depression and insomnia began to fade." She paused, contemplating her next words. "It wasn't until recently that I started having trouble sleeping again."

"How recently?"

She hung her head. "Beginning of term," she replied softly.

I hissed in through my teeth, realizing that, over the entirety of the time I'd known her, I'd been blind to the fact that she'd been suffering. "Why didn't you tell me?" I questioned, my voice thick with emotion.

"I didn't want you to worry," she said, her fingers fiddling with a stray string on the bottom of the oversized t-shirt she was wearing. "You'd just been in an accident and were starting to recover, and I didn't want you thinking that I was only helping you to ignore my own issues."

"I wouldn't have," I started, only to smile sheepishly as she shot me a look of disbelief. "Okay, maybe I would've, but you told me about your mom. You could've mentioned your insomnia then; I wouldn't have judged you."

"I know that now," she trailed off.

Inhaling deeply, I tried to wrap my head around it all – the depression, the insomnia, her family. I hadn't expected any of this when I'd met her that first night at the party, but now, sitting next to her after witnessing her breakdown and having her lay all her cards out on the table, I knew I couldn't imagine my life moving forward without her.

"So," I started a few minutes later, a lightness in my voice as I tried to rid the dreariness from the air, "That's how you get so much in a day?"

I'd meant it to be a joke, though the short bout of laughter that escaped her lips sounded dry and cynical. "It seems great doesn't it, having more hours in a day to get your life in order?" she asked, though she didn't wait for me to respond before continuing. "I thought so to, until the fatigue and drowsiness set in, and then even when I tried to sleep, I couldn't."

"Sorry," I stuttered, realizing my mistake, "I didn't mean to – "

"Don't worry about it," she sighed. "I didn't mean to go off like that. It's just frustrating, but I gave up trying to under-stand how my brain works a long time ago."

My next question stopped at the tip of my tongue as I held it back, worried about how it'd be received. I didn't do a good job at hiding my thoughts however, as Katie sent me a meaningful look, urging me to respond. "Would you be open to talking to the doctors you work with about this?" I asked carefully. "I don't know much about all of this, but if it helped to get you back on track last time, wouldn't it be worth a shot?"

I noticed her hands beginning to shake with anxiety as tears formed in the corner of her eyes, but she held them at bay as she said shakily, "I just don't want to disappoint my mom."

"You won't," I said adamantly. "Trust me, she'll be proud that you're working towards getting better."

A sad smile pulled at her lips, as though she didn't fully believe me, but for now, as I wrapped my arm around her shoulder and pulled her into my chest, it was enough.

Chapter 15

It was late in the evening when Dean went home. He was wary about leaving, especially after I'd opened up about my struggle with insomnia, but once Theo had returned, I'd reassured him that I'd be fine for the night. More so, I'd wanted to avoid the inevitable awkwardness that would transpire with Dean staying over while Theo was sleeping just down the hall.

Because while he had never been one to be overprotective, he was still my older brother.

I'd watched him go, waiting as the elevator doors had closed until I'd slipped back into the apartment, heading straight upstairs and to my room with hopes that, after an emotionally draining day, sleep would come easily. Though as I laid in bed, the time well past midnight, my mind was wide awake and my eyes had been drawn to the stars.

They were shining brightly – an endless possibility of wishes floating thousands of miles above.

Sighing as I rolled over, I knew that there was no chance of me falling asleep anytime soon. Weighing my options, I slid out from underneath the covers and tiptoed down the stairs to see the harsh glare of the television lighting up the living room. Theo sat on the couch, having yet to change out of the work clothes he'd arrived in, nursing a beer while his attention, though unfocused, was on the screen. A creaky step near the bottom of the staircase gave me away, and when his head turned towards me, he managed a small smile.

"Aren't you tired?" I asked, hugging my arms around my stomach consciously.

He shrugged indifferently. "Couldn't sleep," he said, though contradictory to his words, his voice was laced with exhaustion. A frown creased his forehead, his eyes surveying me for a quick moment before he tipped his beer towards me. "You want one?"

I surprised myself by nodding, stepping into the kitchen to realize that he'd not only bought a case of beer, but he'd also stocked the fridge with more food than the two of us would ever need. Grabbing two beers from the fridge, I headed back to Theo, dropping into the empty space beside him on the couch. He raised an eyebrow with concern at the beers, but when I sent him a pointed look, passing one off to him, he sighed, finishing off the one in his hand with one long gulp.

"Thanks," he muttered.

Twisting the cap off my own drink and taking a sip, I ignored the bitter taste, but couldn't ignore the obvious scrutiny Theo had me pegged beneath.

"What?" I asked, moments later, breaking the silence.

He took a swig from his beer. "Can you promise not to get mad if I ask you something?"

"Depends on what it is." Though I already knew, and as though it would protect me from his question, I pulled my knees up to my chest.

"I get why you don't want people to know much about your life. You don't want them getting too close to you, and even though Stella's still around, I left, and mom – " His voice shook slightly. " – Mom's not around." His words weren't so much an observation, but a fact. "But from just a few hours I could tell that you and Dean are close, so why not let him in?"

I dropped my gaze dejectedly as I took a deep breath. "I told him about mom a while ago," I said. "He had followed me to her room one day at the hospital and I couldn't hide it."

"Sounds like he was just trying to be there for you."

"That's the thing though; he wasn't. It was all one big mistake, and even though we'd been getting close, I hadn't even thought to tell him about mom until I had no choice."

"And even then, when you knew he was a good guy, why didn't you tell him about everything else?"

"I didn't want him to worry. He had his own pain to deal with; he didn't need my problems putting extra weight on his shoulders."

Locking eyes with him, I waited as he contemplated his next words. "You know, he said you guys were just friends when he answered the door," he said, "But I don't really believe that."

The vaguest hint of a laugh escaped my lips, shaking my head. "It's complicated."

He quirked an eyebrow. "I've got time."

Sighing, I went on to explain the things I'd skimmed over earlier that day. How we really met, the time Dean spent in the hospital, his struggles with his wheelchair and my determination to help, and then onto how close we'd gotten since. It didn't feel weird talking to Theo, in fact, I'd missed it, because while we'd been growing up, despite the age difference, we'd been close. I did find it amusing however, that when it was evident to Theo that I was falling for Dean, he resorted to swigging his beer as a way to deal with the developments.

When I'd finished, I sat there waiting, resting my empty bottle on the coffee table as he exhaled, finally looking as tired as I was sure he felt. "You weren't lying about it being complicated then."

"He's a great guy," I said softly, "And even though we both have our own problems to overcome, I don't think I can keep dealing with everything by myself."

He sighed. "I know how you feel," he trailed, but as I looked closer, I realized a familiar emotion was flashing across his features.

"Who is she?" I asked bravely, the longing in his eyes shifting quickly to surprise. My lips tilted upwards with slight amusement, having caught him off guard.

"A friend... a really good friend," he replied affectionately.

"I've heard that one before," I quipped.

He laughed. "I'm sure you have," he teased, though as he ran his hand through his dishevelled hair, causing it to appear wilder than it already had, he sighed. A solemn atmosphere descended on us once more, and this time, I couldn't hold back the fear brewing in my mind.

"We're going to be okay, right?" I asked, my voice just above a whisper.

Though there was pain in his eyes, he nodded, and needing the comfort, I cuddled up to his side. "We'll be okay kiddo," he replied, rubbing his hand along my arm, "Everything's going to be okay."

My eyes widened in shock when Stella arrived the next afternoon, a wide smile on her face as she dumped a bag full of junk food onto my bed.

"What's all this?"

After a restless night, I'd woken up far too early for my liking and had gone downstairs to eat breakfast with Theo, but after jumping in the shower, had decided to braid my damp hair into pigtails and slip back into the comfort of my pajamas.

"The essentials," she said happily, as though it was obvious. There were a handful of chocolate bars, two large bags of chips, and five different bags of candy – all accompanied by a large bottle of wine and two pints of chocolate chip ice cream. "I tried to grab everything you like."

"You didn't have to do all of this," I said softly, though I didn't object as I grabbed a bag of candy and sat back against my pillows.

It took a moment, but Stella's upbeat façade dropped when she sighed, taking the space next to me. "Yeah I did," she trailed, wringing her hands nervously as she met my gaze. "Friday was a mess. You looked so broken, and I immediately knew why, which just made the guilt that much more prominent as I watched Dean comfort you."

"You don't – "

"I realized after you left that you'd called me," she continued, not stopping as I tried to interject, "But since I was with Holden I didn't answer, and I don't even know if I could've done anything to help, but I would've been there for you."

When she paused for a moment, I took the opportunity to speak. "Really," I pressed, knocking my shoulder against hers, "It's okay."

She sighed. "You know it's not. I'm your best friend, I should've been there for you."

"Stella..."

"And I'm sorry I didn't tell you about Holden. I wanted to, I just didn't know what to say."

My lips edged upwards into a small smile. "You didn't have to tell me," I said, and as she opened her mouth to object, I shook my head. "I already knew."

Her eyes widened. "How?"

"I mean, it wasn't for sure," I shrugged, "But considering you were going on a lot of dates, and Holden always seemed to mention to Dean when he was busy, it didn't really take a genius to put two and two together."

"Then why did you look so shocked?" she asked, biting her lip nervously.

"If you didn't notice, I was kind of a wreck that night," I mused. "Plus, the fact that you were practically naked took me by a bit of a surprise."

A deep blush spread across her cheeks, causing me to laugh, though it died down as I saw the giddy smile pulling at my best friend's lips. "He's just a really good guy, and I'm not even sure if we're dating or if he's completely over his ex, but he makes me happy."

"Then that's all that matters right now," I said, smiling encouragingly.

Seemingly content, she studied me for a moment. "And what about you?" she asked, quirking an eyebrow, "Was Dean the support you needed on Friday?"

"Trust me," I said, my voice dropping lower as I shifted my gaze away, my cheeks tinging red as I did so, "He was enough."

And because I knew I wouldn't be able to keep it from her for long, I told her what had happened. How I'd kissed him, and how he'd kissed me back, and how I wished that everything would just go back to normal so I could be with him.

But sometimes, wishes took longer to come true for the ones that desired them the most.

When my tale of embarrassment had finished, and Stella had appropriately gasped and chuckled along, we decided it was time to make a dent in the junk food she'd brought. Bringing up two glasses for the wine and two spoons for the ice cream, we spent hours just relaxing – giggling about non-sense and reminiscing about the simpler times.

I managed to steer the conversation away from my mom for the most part, and after two incredibly painful days, I needed the lightheartedness Stella offered to get me back to feeling like myself.

With the bottle of wine long gone, and all of our sweet cravings satisfied, Stella and I were lying comfortably on my bed. We'd set my laptop up at the foot of the bed, an old romantic comedy that we'd both seen several times playing on the screen, and it was just getting to the good part when my bedroom door was pushed open, the knock following.

Theo, who had kept to himself for most of the day, presumably keeping busy while trying to fight off the jetlag, stepped into the room. He was dressed in an old college hoodie and a pair of black sweatpants, his hair sticking up in all directions, and it was a strange sort of comfort knowing this was the most casual I'd seen him in a long time. "You know you're popular today," he stated, propping the door open wider so that I could see the person standing behind him.

Dean.

With his hands in his pockets and his shoulders tensed slightly, a smile still graced his lips as his eyes landed on me.

"Hey," I said, propping myself up on my elbow as I sent him a questioning look, "What are you doing here?"

Theo slipped away quietly as Dean stepped forward. "I just wanted to check on you," he explained, two rose coloured spots of embarrassment filling his cheeks, "To make sure that you were doing okay."

"I'm all good," I said, more bashfully than I normally would have, and it may have had something to do with the wine I'd consumed over the past few hours.

"She's also a little bit tipsy," Stella pointed out, a smirk on her face as the two of us turned to face her. "And since you're here," she continued, directing her words towards Dean, "I guess it's time for me to head home."

"Don't you mean to mine to see Holden?" Dean mused, quirking an eyebrow.

Rolling her eyes but not denying it, I didn't give her a chance to inch any farther away as I grabbed her arm, stopping her. "You don't have to go," I said, and watching her gaze flicker between Dean and I, I moved closer to the middle of the bed. "There's room for both of you."

She didn't move and didn't speak as I bit my lip anxiously, though I could tell by the way that Stella and Dean were looking at each other, they were having some sort of silent conversation centered around me. When she sighed, I took that as a bad sign, but was quickly relieved when she moved to lay back down.

"Are you sure this is what you want?" Stella asked, sending me a knowing look, but I nodded.

I knew she was only trying to give Dean and I some time alone, but in that moment, as Dean took the empty spot on the opposite side of me, that wasn't what I wanted. "Right now," I started, my voice clear despite the shyness to it, "I need both of you here."

Cuddling closer to Dean as he pulled me to his side, I reached out and grabbed Stella's hand in comfort, knowing that while today was for regenerating, my problems and pain wouldn't simply fade away because I spent one afternoon with a smile on my face.

And as we turned our attention back to my laptop screen, a sinking feeling stewed in the pit of my stomach, telling me that I'd need both of them by my side for what was to come.

Monday was a mess.

The weekend had been a roller coaster – full of ups and downs – but once the ride came to a stop, I landed back on the ground, my steps wobbly as I tried to find a footing.

I'd tried to go about my usual routine, and for the most part, considering I'd gotten a surprising amount of rest the night before, it was fine. It was when I began to zone out in lectures however, that I realized I wasn't completely okay. My thoughts drifted frequently to how I'd be able to step foot in the hospital again, knowing that just floors above me, my mom might be taking her last breath.

But as I dropped Dean back at his apartment, knowing that I was scheduled for my next shift in less than an hour, I found it difficult to unclench my hands from the steering wheel.

"Hey," Dean had said gently, placing his hand on top of one of mine before squeezing it with encouragement. "You'll be okay. You're stronger than you think, and as soon as you're done with work you'll be able to see your mom."

With those words in mind, I'd hopped on the next bus with a better mindsight. That however, had been hard to maintain as I walked the hospital corridors. It was evident that, as soon as I passed through the main doors, word about my mother had spread. Many eyes glanced over me, some – belonging to my coworkers – lingering, while others moved on as though they saw nothing of importance.

I tried to keep my head held high, ignoring the looks of sympathy that were thrown my way, and while I was working, I pushed myself to focus solely on the patients I was helping. By the time I made my way up to my mother's room that night, there had been no update on her condition and her doctor had already gone home, but that didn't stop me from sitting there and talking to her, even though I knew there'd be no reply.

The days continued on, and while my mood slowly began to lift as the attention on me faded, it crumbled right back to the ground when my mom's doctor informed me that their attempts at curing her were in no way positive. The increase of medicine had done nothing for her body and the extensive chemo she'd been put through had done more harm than good; making her even frailer than she'd been before.

Her days were numbered, and that scared the hell out of me.

December also brought exams, which, while providing somewhat of a distraction from the horrors of my life, did little for my health. Trying to juggle studying and work should've been simple, but with my determination to spend as much time with my mom as possible; Theo and I spending hours in her hospital room at a time, my insomnia had worsened. It was getting to the point that, even though I didn't sleep, I didn't feel tired, and when I did manage to catch a few hours of shut eye, a bit of caffeine was enough to get me through the day.

It was unhealthy and wrong, and though everyone – Dean, Stella, and Theo – was encouraging me to talk to a doctor, I could never find the time or the strength.

As I walked out of my final exam of the term in the middle of December, I felt the relief of one weight lifting from my shoulders, but the heavier and more prominent one was still pushing me down. Unlike my classmates, I didn't have much time to celebrate as I headed towards the bus stop at the edge of campus, hopping on just before it pulled away and towards the hospital.

Because today, after nearly four months of healing, Dean was getting his cast taken off.

Finding a spare seat near the back of the bus, I spent the majority of the ride with my headphones in, my gaze locked to the view only partially visible through the frost covered windows. Just as the bus was pulling up to the hospital, the ringer on my phone came alive, and I looked down to see Dean's name flashing.

"Hey," I greeted as I stepped off the bus, seeing my breath cloud in front of me, "I just got here."

"And I went in early," he countered, sounding more chipper than usual.

"So you've already got it off then?" I asked, matching his blatant enthusiasm.

I could almost imagine him nodding, a smile on his face. "My leg is officially able to breathe again."

"That's great." Swiveling my head around the lower floor lobby, I tried and failed to spot him. "Where are you?"

"I'm in the waiting area on the third floor."

Moving towards the elevator, I stepped into the empty lift and pressed the button for the third floor. "I'll be there in a few seconds," I replied, ending the call and hitching my bag up further on my shoulder.

When the elevator doors opened again, I immediately spotted Dean. He was leant over the administration desk, handing back a stack of forms he'd presumably finished signing, and an easy smile rested on his lips. As he stepped away from the counter and his eyes landed on me, they flashed with a blend of intensity and excitement. With his newly acquired freedom, he moved quickly towards me, wrapping his arms around me tightly and spinning me around, causing a laugh to bubble from my lips.

"What was that for?" I asked as he finally set me down, though I couldn't seem to shake the grin that pulled at my lips.

"I thought it'd be fun," he shrugged, causing me to roll my eyes in amusement. "So," he started again, wiggling his eyebrows suggestively as he looked down at me, "Notice anything different about me?"

Playing along, I ran my eyes over him quickly, tapping my chin as though I was thinking. "I don't think so... wait," I clicked my fingers together. "You got a haircut, didn't you?"

"No," he said, chuckling at my response, "But I probably need one soon."

As he snaked his arms loosely around my waist, my act fell and I smiled up at him. "So what did the doctor say after you got your cast off?"

"He said I could start training again," Dean replied, the joy he felt laced around every word. "I'm still booked for three physiotherapy sessions a week for the next month, but after that they'll fully re-evaluate my injury and tell me if I'm ready to start playing again."

Lifting myself up onto my tiptoes, I placed a gentle kiss on his cheek, meeting his eyes as pulled back. "I'm happy for you."

Dropping his hands from my waist, one of them sought out my own, threading our fingers together as he squeezed my hand. "And I'm ready to celebrate," he chirped in response. "Anywhere particular you wanna go?"

The thought flew into my mind without warning, and while the rest of this day was meant to be about having fun, I knew I didn't have it in me to leave the hospital without seeing my mom.

"Not really," I replied, biting my lip guiltily as I lowered my gaze, "But do you think we can make a pit stop first?"

His features softened, not needing to ask anything further. "Of course."

Stepping back into the elevator with Dean by my side, I leaned on him for support, because lately, every visit with my mom caused a whirl of nerves to flow through my veins. This time however, it was different, because I was hoping that she'd be awake. I could count the number of visits since her health had nosedived that I'd seen her awake on one hand, and while I was happy that she'd been able to see Theo, I also wanted her to meet Dean again. This time, for real.

Leading him to the hospital room, my grip on his hand tightened, and when I pushed open the door, I was overcome with happiness and relief when I saw a nurse handing my mother – who was sat up and fully awake – a glass of water.

"Hey mom," I spoke shakily, feeling the tears well up in my eyes.

Waiting at the edge of the room as the nurse finished checking over my mom, it wasn't more than a few minutes later when she slipped into the corridor, giving us a moment of privacy. My eyes trailed over my mom as her lips, cracked and worn out, pulled upwards. Her skin had lost practically all of its colour, verging on a dullish grey, and even with an immense amount IVs attached to her arms, I noticed how hollow she looked, as though there was no more muscle separating her skin and bone.

"Hi sweetie," she replied, her words sounding strained and breathless. When she looked past me, her tired eyes settling on Dean, I felt him tense up beside me. "And it's Dean, right?"

I noticed him gulp as he nodded, clenching his free hand as he pushed it deep into his pocket. "Yeah, it's good to see you again."

"Likewise," she said, a soft tone to her otherwise croaky voice, "Though last time I do remember you weren't so up-right."

Chuckling lightly, Dean managed a smile. "I've got a whole group of people to thank for that," he said, flitting his gaze to me momentarily, "Including your daughter, who never gave up on me."

Flushing, a deep crimson colouring my cheeks, I was speechless.

"Well," my mom started, a spark in her eyes that just seemed to further my embarrassment, "I'm glad she has you around."

Wanting to steer the conversation away from mine and Dean's complicated and budding relationship, I pulled two chairs up next to my mom's bed and started rambling on about school coming to an end for the holidays. She no doubt could tell what I was doing, but went along with it, pulling Dean into the conversation as she asked him if he went to Duke and what he was studying.

Watching the two of them talk as though we weren't in a hospital room, and instead just sitting together in the comfort of our living room, was comforting. I wanted my mom to see that I wouldn't be completely on my own when she was gone – that I could still live a full life and be happy with the people I've grown the closest to.

And maybe, on some account, I wanted to prove that to myself as well.

When the nurse returned not long after and I saw my mom's eyelids drooping low, I knew today's visit was over. For the first time since we'd entered the room, I pulled my hand from Dean's and leant down to place a gentle kiss on my mom's forehead, she whispered, "He's a good one Katie."

Leaning back to see her lips tilting upwards, I choked back a sob, simply nodding in reply, because I knew that if I opened my mouth, a strangled cry would escape.

Stepping back to Dean's side, the act of holding hands was almost thoughtless, and as he raised his free hand in a wave, both of us were surprised when she spoke again.

"Dean... can I ask you something?" Her voice was wavering as I saw the signs of her nodding off, but Dean's eyes were full of curiosity, his forehead crinkled as he nodded. "When I can't... can you make sure that Katie always has something to smile about?"

Her words caused my throat to catch and the tears in my eyes to fall, knowing that what she was truly asking was for him to watch out for me when she was gone. I noticed the surprise on his face at her request, but as her eyes fluttered shut, he removed his hand from mine and wrapped his arm around my shoulder.

"I can do that," Dean replied, his voice raw with emotion as his gaze slowly moved from my mom to me, "I promise."

Chapter 16

Katie's mom passed away two days after Christmas.

I'd gotten the call while enjoying the holidays at my parent's house in California, and as soon as I'd pressed the phone up to my ear to hear Katie's sobs on the other end, my blood ran cold. Her voice was strangled and hard to understand, but the words 'she's gone' were difficult to ignore.

There was a moment where my mind blanked and I had no idea what to do, though with the looks of worry plastered across my family's faces, I shook myself out of it, suddenly knowing exactly what I had to do.

I had to go back to her; to be there for her.

Ryan was probably the most supportive of everyone, because while my parents understood why I needed to head back home, they didn't know how much I cared for Katie – how much my chest was aching knowing I was miles away when she needed me. With a few quick calls, my brother had arranged a private plane for me, and within hours of receiving the devastating news, I'd packed up my things and was

40,000 feet above the ground, counting down the minutes until I'd land in North Carolina.

It was past midnight when the cab I'd caught at the airport pulled up in front of Katie's apartment, though I didn't get out right away. Instead, I sat in the back seat, my lip pulled in between my teeth as conflicting thoughts ran through my mind.

Would she be asleep? Could I wait until morning? How was she dealing? Did her and her brother need time alone to process things before I stepped in?

Shaking myself out of my head as the driver looked at me with annoyance, wondering what was taking me so long, I sighed, handing him a twenty-dollar bill and grabbing my bag as I stepped out onto the sidewalk. Pulling my cell phone out of my pocket, I dialed Katie's number, holding my breath as it rang, but letting it out slowly as the call went to voicemail.

Deciding to try the buzzer, I stepped up to the door and hit the button next to Katie's apartment number, and just when I was about to turn around and head home, a tired and familiar voice came onto the intercom.

"Who's there?"

Theo sounded exhausted, and whether it was because I'd woken him up or due to an emotionally jarring day, my reply was shaky.

"It's Dean," I began, wanting to say more – to explain why I was here – but the door buzzed, allowing me in before I could continue.

Heading up to their apartment, I was jittery in the elevator, and when I knocked on their door quietly, watching as Theo opened it to reveal his disheveled appearance and tired features, I felt my stomach sink with doubt. I didn't know what to do in a situation like this – I'd never lost someone close to me – but in that moment, I knew it was too late to turn back.

"I know it's late," I started quietly, meeting Theo's red-rimmed eyes, "But I just wanted to make sure she was okay. And I'm sorry," I added, pausing as I clenched the strap of my bag harder, "About your mom."

"Thanks," he replied, his voice slightly hoarse, though the sadness that overtook him as a result was enough to make my throat lodge with despair. He stepped back, letting me in as he nodded vaguely to the staircase. "And she's upstairs. Hasn't left her room for most of the day."

Nodding almost robotically, I gulped, knowing he was watching me as I turned on my heel and headed up to see her.

By the time I reached her door I was shaking from nerves, wondering if this was the wrong move, but as I brought my hand up, my fingers digging tightly into my palm, I rapped lightly. Standing there anxiously, I knocked slightly louder when there was no response. "Katie..." I trailed, "It's Dean."

Filling with worry as another moment of silence passed, I was able to breathe easier as I heard shuffling on the other side of the door before it opened. Katie stood there, her hair pulled into a messy bun and an oversized hoodie draped over her body, which I realized, after a second glance, was one I'd lent her a few weeks back. Tears stained her face, her eyes and nose were swollen red, and pain was etched prominently into her features.

She looked broken, and dropping my bag to the ground, I stepped forward quickly, wrapping my arms around her as though it would put the pieces of her heart back together.

Collapsing against me almost instantly, I could feel Katie begin to shake as she cried, which only caused my hold on her to tighten as she slipped her own arms around my waist loosely. There wasn't much I could do in that moment but be there for her, and if there was a way I could curb her suffering, I would.

As she teetered off balance, I rearranged my hold on her, lifting her up so that one of my arms supported her legs and the other rested under her back as she pressed her face into my chest. Kicking the door close when I stepped into her room, I immediately noticed the tissues scattered across her bed, and with some careful maneuvering, I dropped Katie into the middle of the mattress, cleaning up the mess quickly before crawling into bed beside her.

"She's gone Dean," Katie sobbed, hiccupping between words as she clutched at my t-shirt. "She's really gone."

I knew my comfort wouldn't change the fact that she'd lost the one person she relied on the most in life, but not knowing what else I could do, I drew her closer to me, smoothing over her hair slowly. I wanted to say something that would make her feel better, or crack a smile at the least, but nothing came to mind. "Shh..." I trailed softly, any other words getting caught in my throat.

Resting my chin on top of her head, we laid there for hours, my arms a type of cocoon – shielding her from the cruel reality. When her shallow breathing evened out, I turned my face into the pillow, knowing that she couldn't hear or see me as the tears I'd been holding back finally fell. I cried for Katie, because I regretted not being by her side the moment she found out, and I cried for her mom, who would never get to see the strong woman that Katie would grow up to be.

But when morning came, my tears were dry and my resolve had built back up.

Through tired eyes, I noticed the effects that her mother's passing had already had on Katie – the sadness that had taken her over – creasing and blotching her skin. Doing my best not to wake her as I pressed my lips gently to her forehead, I remembered the promise I'd made to her mom. I couldn't see myself leaving Katie's side for the next couple of days, and I knew that if I stuck around through the worst of it, when the time came, I would be there to see her smile.

In the days that followed, I came to learn that when you lost someone, you didn't lose them all at once. Instead, it felt like standing in the wreckage of an earthquake – the aftershocks continuing to cause an impact well after the initial damage had been done.

Watching Theo make arrangements for the funeral, Katie helping out where she could, simply made everything that more real. As they made the necessary phone calls to their friends and family, their faces mirrored that of distress and pain, as though they'd been punched in the stomach every time someone answered the phone. Dealing with the visitors that dropped by however, seemed just as agonizing. With almost every guest came a new kind of freshly cooked food, and while it seemed like a kind gesture, I knew as the days wore on that it was becoming more of a hassle, having to face each new visitor with a fake smile as they accepted the condolences.

A majority of the time however, I spent consoling Katie. Whether it was holding her close as she cried on my shoulder, or getting her out of the apartment in an attempt to get her mind off of everything – I was there for her.

There were times, when the two of us were alone, where Katie tried to conceal the pain she felt, masking her features so that they appeared as a blank canvas. She'd steer clear of the subject of her mother, building up a wall to keep her emotions at bay, and these were the moments that were the most concerning.

After all, how did you help a person who didn't want to be helped?

But even through the frustration and the trying times, I stuck by her side, not caring to leave just because things became difficult.

And when I awoke on the 31st of December, my arms wrapped securely around Katie, I became hyper aware that she was shaking uncontrollably, and it wasn't because of the cold.

Today, Katie and Theo would be saying goodbye to their mom one final time.

Bringing my hand up to her face, I cupped her cheek as I wiped away the stream of tears. "Today's going to be hard,"

I said truthfully, continuing over her sniffling, "But you'll get through it."

"I don't know if I will," she replied in a wobbly voice.

Meeting her gaze, there was no disguising the thinly-veiled fear shining in her irises. It suddenly dawned on me that, in that moment, she was less concerned about saying goodbye, and incredibly worried about messing up her speech. "When you're up there today," I started gently, "Nobody is going to be judging you. That's your moment, and when you're speaking, the only person that should matter is your mom."

"But what if – "

"No what-ifs," I shook my head, giving her an encouraging smile. "You're stronger than you think you are, and if you're feeling skittish or worried, just look at me."

Her lips pull up hesitantly with gratitude, and while it wasn't quite a smile, I knew it was a step in the right direction.

Kissing her forehead, my lips lingered a moment too long before I pulled away, knowing that, for the first time since I'd landed back in North Carolina, I was leaving her side. Her and Theo had to be at the church early, a few last minute arrangements still needing to be made, and while I was comfortable in the loungewear I'd more or less been living in the past couple of days, I knew I needed to head home and change before the service.

As I got ready, my mind kept circling back to Katie – wondering what she was doing and how she was coping – only coming to a screeching halt when I stepped into the church to see her and Theo standing at the front.

There were already a lot of guests in their seats, and among them I caught eyes with Ryan, who had Zoe and Abbie seated next to him, as they'd made a detour on their way back to New York, wanting to be an extra source of support. I spoke with them for a few minutes, exchanging nothing more than meaningless small talk, but I couldn't help the fact that my focus was wavering, my gaze repeatedly flitting over to Katie.

Excusing myself when I got the chance, I headed slowly towards the front of the church, slipping through the group at the front and standing off to the side as not to interrupt. Seeing the fake smile that pulled at Katie's lips, a near exact copy of the one her brother wore as they greeted guests, made my gut twist painfully, knowing that she was putting on an act for these people. However, when her eyes found mine through the dwindling crowd, the veil that had been concealing her sadness dropped as I stepped closer.

"Hey."

"Hey."

Both of us stood there quietly, not knowing exactly what to do as the time drew closer to noon, though when I noticed her hands were shaking, I reached out and wound my fingers around hers. "Just remember, I'm here if you need me."

I received a small, inconspicuous nod in reply, her grip on my hand tightening as we took our seats and she leaned closer to me, almost like she thought I'd suddenly disappear.

But squeezing her hand in support, I silently affirmed I wasn't going anywhere.

As the priest began the service, speaking kindly of her mother and what it meant for her memory to live on through all of us, Katie stayed strong. Through the prayers, the hymns, and the short speeches made by several of those in attendance, she kept a tight hold on her emotions, but when it was Theo's turn to stand and pay his respects, her resolve began to crumble. Her nails dug deeper and deeper into my palm, and knowing she was up next, nervous goosebumps rose on her skin.

And when it was time, Theo gave her a hug as they both stood in front of the casket, and I watched, waiting as she took a deep breath.

"My mom's cancer was never her defining feature, as it was always overshadowed by the light in her eyes and the smile on her face. Maybe that was why I was optimistic about her recovery, why I thought her sickness was only a small battle she had to fight, but unfortunately, she couldn't continue fighting forever." She paused, biting her lip as her eyes flickered towards me. "Growing up without a father, my mom always made sure that Theo and I were showered with love. She'd make us pancakes on Saturday mornings, had taught both of us to ride our bikes without training wheels, and as we grew older, always encouraged us to follow our dreams."

"She was my best friend and my biggest supporter."

She exhaled a choked-up breath, holding back tears as her eyes moved over the crowd of people gathered in the church. It was then that I realized, that hearing Katie's speech, most of the guests, including myself, had been brought to tears.

Bringing my hand up to wipe the tears hastily away from my face, I watched as Katie stood bravely, glancing over her shoulder as she spoke to her mother's casket.

"It hurts me that you're gone. You won't be there to congratulate me when I graduate and you won't be there to see me marry the love of my life one day, but even though I can't see you, I know you're watching over me, huddled next to dad with a proud smile on your face. I'll never stop missing you mom, and you'll always be in my heart."

A silent hush fell over the church as Katie stepped down, kissing her hand before pressing it to the picture of her mom that was displayed, blown up big enough for everyone to see.

By the time she sat down next to me, the priest had taken the front again, and as everyone listened to him explain where the burial would be taking place, Katie pressed a tight fist to her lips as the tears she'd been holding in finally began to fall.

Despite the chilling winds that had descended on the cemetery, everyone huddled together on the snow covered grass, bowing their heads as flowers were placed atop the casket.

I, on the other hand, stood back from the crowd, my partially clenched fists pushed deep into my pockets as I watched Theo hug his sister close.

"Why are you all the way back here?"

I shrugged in response, glancing at Ryan as he stood next to me, as to not make a scene, with a quizzical look on his face. "She needs to be with her brother right now," I replied honestly, "And the rest of her family."

I'd ridden in the car over alongside Katie and her brother, but as they stepped out together, trying to appear brave as they squeezed each other's hands for support, I'd stayed back.

Casting my eyes over the frosted landscape, there were only a handful of familiar faces. I could see Holden standing next to Stella, not at all deterred by the rest of her family that had come out to show their support for their daughter's best friend, and Zoe was standing out by the gates, holding Abbie close and waiting for Ryan to join them.

"We're gonna head off," Ryan said, nodding off towards his fiancée, "But just remember, don't get down on yourself. Katie will slowly return to the girl you met a few months back, it'll just take some time."

My lips tugged upwards slightly. "I know," I sighed, running my fingers through my windswept hair, "It's just the waiting that's hard."

"But it'll be worth it in the end."

After saying goodbye, I waited until their car was nothing more than a blur in the distance before turning back to see the casket that held Katie's mother being lowered slowly into the ground.

When there was nothing more anyone could say, the sea of strangers began to make waves, spreading out and disappearing without a trace. Holden however, caught my eye as he left, giving me a nod of encouragement as he could tell that I was planning on braving the weather and sticking around.

It felt like I was intruding on a private moment, watching as Katie rested her head on her brother's shoulder and cried, but my feet didn't seem to want to move. Evidently the both of them were distraught, using today as closure as they came to the end of one chapter of their lives.

Sometime later, whether it was minutes or hours I didn't know, Theo was the first to pull away. Kissing Katie's temple, he left her to wrap her arms around her waist in support as he turned and headed towards the gates. Before he could disappear however, he noticed me standing there. With not even a flicker of surprise in his features, the look that glazed over his eyes was purely grateful, as though he was telling me to watch out for her; to make sure that she would be alright.

Not able to stand back any longer, I weaved my way through the narrow paths between headstones. The closer I came the louder Katie's sobs became, echoing through the wind and pulling at something within my chest. When I was no more than a few feet away, I noticed her shoulders tense as she no doubt heard the crunching of snow beneath my feet, but as she turned her head, her posture relaxed fractionally when she noticed it was only me.

In that moment it was the temperature that caused a chill, but the situation – standing beside an open grave – which numbed the both of us.

"Did you know that I haven't seen most of my extended family in years?" Katie asked, not directly facing me as she kept her gaze glued to the ground. "My aunts, cousins, and even grandparents," she listed, "None of them have called or visited since they learned that mom was sick. It's like they forgot she was suffering, and now, today, they all showed up as though they'd been supporting her every step of the way." I noticed a vein in her neck had begun to pulse with anger as I moved to stand beside her. "It took my mom dying for them to finally come around."

The sheer intensity of her words was overwhelming, and as the last word rolled off her tongue, a strangled sob passed through her lips, her hand rising to press hard against her mouth. I wanted to say something supportive, or anything at all that would help her feel better, but any intelligent response I had got stuck in my throat, "Sorry," being the only word I could mutter.

Katie sniffled, and though she wiped at her tears, it didn't do much to keep them from falling. "You have nothing to be sorry for," she said in a small voice, turning towards me as she spoke.

A sad smile pulled at my lips as I wrapped an arm around her shoulder, pulling her tightly against me. "Yes there is," I replied softly. "I'm sorry that you lost your mom, and I'm sorry she's not going to be able to see you thrive the rest of your life."

My words only seemed to cause her tears to fall faster, her hands gripping desperately at the fabric of my jacket. "It's not fair," she wailed, "It's just not fair."

"I know," I replied quietly, moving my hand in slow, comforting circles on the small of her back, "I know."

Chapter 17

Losing my mom had caused a gaping hole to open in my chest – one that couldn't be covered or ignored, no matter how hard I tried. It required stitches to carefully pull the jagged pieces back together, and dealing with the grief coursing through my veins would take time.

After all, when you lost someone close to you, moving on was an uphill battle that couldn't be fought in a day.

As the New Year broke, I found myself surrounded by constant support. The university was still in between terms, which meant that classes were on break, leaving Stella, Dean, and even Holden, spare time to stick by me and make sure that I didn't get tripped up by sorrow. My supervisor at the hospital was also incredibly understanding, giving me an extended amount of time off before I fully stepped back into my life again. This I was thankful for, as even the idea of stepping back into the place my mother had taken her last breath caused a panic to ignite in my chest, though I knew eventually I'd have to face the pain.

Every time I saw the family portraits scattered around the house, or noticed a forlorn look grace Theo's face, I was brought back to the memories I carried of my mom. The family dinners, our over-the-top birthdays, her celebrating with me when I'd gotten accepted to Duke, and the two of us watching Theo graduate university. And while it hurt to think of those times, it also helped me realize that, even though she wouldn't be around anymore, she would be forever ingrained in my mind.

I'd thought I was slowly healing, but when I woke up on the second Monday of January, knowing it was the day that I was meant to start my last term of university, I was unable to move from my bed.

Theo had left the night before on a red-eye flight back to London, and though I'd known he couldn't stay forever, his absence made me, once again, feel suffocated from the loneliness of the apartment.

The familiar aching spread quickly, feeling as though I'd been thrown off balance and pinned to the ground, and suddenly every thought of heading to campus was drowned out by pain.

After all, if I couldn't save the person closest to me, how would I be able to help others? What was the point of it all?

My mind was all-consuming. My surroundings faded away as the wrenching torment washed over me, overwhelming and dizzying as I felt my eyes slowly sliding shut. Dazed with fear, my sleep was plagued with flashes from my mother's hospital room and her funeral. With every new, depressing thought, all I wanted to do was wake up, but it seemed as though hours passed, my mind fighting against me each step of the way.

Finally, when a shaking sensation overtook my body, I was pulled from the nightmare inside my head. It wasn't until I opened my eyes however, my blurry vision taking a while to focus, that I realized my subconscious wasn't causing my sudden movements, but rather, someone attempting to rouse me from my sleep.

"Katie? Katie?"

Blinking incoherently, I recognized the increasing worry that came with each call of my name, only stopping when an indescribable groan passed through my lips. It was Dean, his eyes filled with concern as our gazes locked, slowly dimming as relief washed over him.

"What are you doing here?" I asked groggily, raising my head slightly. "What time is it?"

I noticed the corners of his lips tug upwards, though it was more of a grimace that graced his features. "It's half past eleven."

Dropping my head back down to my pillow, I brought my hand up, dragging it through my straggled hair. "Shit."

A short chuckle escaped his lips as he dropped his bag next to my bed, though as he took a seat on the edge of my mattress, a more serious expression was pointed towards me. "When you didn't show up this morning, I just jumped on the bus with Holden, figuring you'd just hitched a ride with Stella," he explained, his fingers mindlessly winding around my own. "But when my first class was over, Holden texted me to say that Stella hadn't heard from you this morning, so I knew something was wrong."

I sighed, rolling onto my side and meeting his eyes. "You didn't have to come and check in on me you know."

"Yes I did," he replied softly, "Because not too long ago, you did the exact same thing for me."

For a short moment, I didn't understand what he was talking about, but then my thoughts flashed back to September. Him – confined to a wheelchair, not wanting to move forward as he contemplated not returning to school, and me – giving him advice on how to get back onto his feet. It was the exact same situation now, except this time the roles were reversed and he was playing the part of knight in shining armour.

"If you hadn't come by that morning," Dean continued, "Even if it was just because Holden had called you, I don't think I would've left my room."

"And that's why you're here?" I raised an eyebrow. "To repay the favour?"

He shrugged, but the sincerity in his eyes shone bright. "Maybe, but only if you want to talk about the reason why you're still in bed."

"I wish I had a reason," I trailed, my voice just above a whisper. Squeezing my eyes shut for a minute, I tried to calm my heart beat, which was rapidly increasing, with slow, deep breaths. "It's just... I thought I was doing okay. I thought I was dealing with everything."

"You are," he insisted, "But just because you're picking yourself up, that doesn't mean you're not going to fall back down every now and again."

I smiled sadly, noticing an undecipherable light flicker in Dean's eyes as I did so. "Maybe it's the fact that Theo left last night; that once again, I'm on my own."

"You know that's not true."

"But it felt like it," I said adamantly, getting frustrated with myself for feeling this way. "This morning when I woke up, the thought of going to class, pretending that I could actually help people, made me sick to my stomach. I couldn't do anything to help my mom, so who's to say I can help anyone else?"

"Katie," he began gently, "You know there's nothing you could've done – "

"I know," I sighed, "It's just hard."

"And it'll be hard for a while," Dean said honestly, "But that doesn't mean that by becoming a nurse you won't be helping people. There'll always be people recovering from surgery or needing to keep up to date with their shots. Plus, when accidents happen and bones are broken, nurses are there to help get the damaged back up on their feet." I saw him nod down to his leg, which had healed immensely since his accident.

"But – "

He shook his head. "No buts." He paused, running his hand up the length of my arm until his fingers splayed wide on my neck. "You once told me that you wanted to help others," he said softly, "And if that's still what you want, you can't just give up because things are difficult right now. But if your heart isn't in it anymore, take some time and figure out something new. Your mom would be proud of you either way."

Tears had come and gone over the past couple of days, but now they were welling heavily in the corners of my eyes. "How do you know exactly what to say?"

"Dumb luck?" he offered, which caused a real smile to pull at my lips. He pulled me closer, kissing my forehead and lingering there as I let myself sink into his comforting embrace. "But really, that's just what I would've wanted to hear if I was in your position."

"And it helped," I mumbled under my breath, feeling significantly better, and more relaxed than I had hours before, "So thank you."

"You're welcome."

Realizing that, while he probably should've been heading back to campus, bringing me along with him, Dean wasn't letting go. And if he wasn't leaving, I was content on idling in his support a little while longer.

Tomorrow, I promised myself. I'd face the music tomorrow.

As January faded into February, bringing an increase of snow and a drop in temperatures, I felt as though I was slowly making progress; each day seemingly a little better than the last. My classes were hands-on and engaging, specializing our skills so that we'd know the ins-and-outs of working as a full-time nurse after graduation, and while the theory was heavy, I found myself enjoying it. I hadn't realized it before, but my degree, along with the hospital, would always be a connection I had to my mom. This also made it easier to jump back into work, Claudia easing me back into the fast-paced environment, and the generosity of the rest of my co-workers, offering their help whenever I needed it.

Something that I hadn't expected to do however, was talk to my supervisor about the troubles I'd been having with insomnia. He hadn't been surprised, given my drowsy and scatter-brained behaviour before my mom's passing, and had taken the information as a professional, recommending me to the hospital's sleep specialist, along with a therapist who I could talk to about the stress that was weighing me down. I was prescribed a small dosage sleeping pill, which helped to get my sleep patterns back in line without much of a side effect, and talking to someone who would in no way judge me had been a great help with healing,

The cracks in my heart were still there, and I knew they'd leave scars, but glue was currently holding me together, and without another hard blow to the chest, it was unlikely that I would crumble.

It was four weeks later however, as I sat alone in the campus library with my notes laid out in front of me, when Dean brought up an idea to help get my mind off of everything.

"Hey there pretty lady," he said teasingly, not at all lowering his voice as he appeared beside me, sliding into the open chair.

I rolled my eyes, though a smile graced my lips as my attention shifted from the page I'd been reading. "Hey, how was the gym?"

Once the term had started and Dean had gotten a feel for his classes, a lot of his spare time had been focused on getting back into the swing of basketball, working hard for what he wanted. He was still using the gym after the team practiced, though I was sure his coach had figured it out by now, and after he worked on getting his skills was up to par, he'd work-out using the machines on campus.

"Good," he nodded, pulling a water bottle out of his bag, his hair matted to his forehead with sweat as he chugged from it.

"So good you forgot to shower when you were done?" I mused.

He narrowed his eyes playfully. "You know I would hug you right now if I wasn't so nice," he said, causing me to laugh, forgetting for a moment where we were. People all around us were looking our way, annoyance and anger filling their gazes, and I ducked my head in embarrassment. Dean had also seemed to pick up on the attention we'd gained, lowering his voice as he continued, nodding to the work on the table. "So, what are you working on?"

"Nothing really." I shrugged, collecting the loose papers into a pile before sticking them underneath the front cover of my notebook. "I have a lab assessment tomorrow morning, so I was just looking over my notes and my review from last week."

He nodded in understanding, though the hint of confliction in his eyes made me wonder if he wanted to say something more. Before I could ask however, he spoke up.

"You're working tonight right?" he asked hesitantly, and I nodded in response. A bout of confusion filled my head though, knowing I'd already told him this. "And what about tomorrow?"

This time I shook my head. "I've got tomorrow and Saturday off, but I work a full shift Sunday, why?"

"Well," he started, pausing to collect his words, "The basketball team has a home game tomorrow night. I haven't
been to one all season, and I thought that, if I wanted to
talk to my coach soon about playing again, I should probably
go out and show my support." He spoke quietly, and not
just because we were currently in the middle of a library. It
seemed to me as though he was genuinely scared. "And I
was wondering – actually kind of hoping – that you'd want to
come."

My features softened, noticing how uncharacteristical-
ly nervous he was. "Of course," I replied, sending a
half-crooked smile his way, "But you do realize that I know
next to nothing about basketball, right?"

His eyes were bright at my response, thinly-veiled amusement swirling around in his irises. "Don't worry," he replied
happily, bumping his shoulder against mine, "I'll explain it to
you."

Waiting in my apartment the following night, I was dressed
casually – a pair of denim jeans, a loose white t-shirt, and a
thick grey cardigan covering my shoulders – picking at a stray
thread on my shirt as Dean buzzed up.

"I'll be right down."

Deciding to forgo a purse, I slipped my license and a twenty-dollar bill into the back of my phone case, and once I'd
locked the door behind me, pushed my keys into the front
pocket of my jeans as I waited for the elevator.

Stepping out onto the sidewalk, I pulled my cardigan tighter around me, suddenly regretting the decision not to bring a jacket as the chilly night air nipped right through my clothes. Dean was leaning against the driver's side of his car, having parked in an empty space across the road. He noticed me almost immediately, his smile brightening as he stood straighter. When I was sure it was safe to cross, I scurried quickly across the pavement, narrowly avoiding a small patch of ice that had formed right in the middle of the road.

"Hey," Dean greeted, pulling me into the warmth radiating from his body, "You ready for this?"

"You mean am I ready to spend the next couple of hours watching a bunch of guys dribble a ball and try to shoot it in a net?" I asked teasingly, gazing up at him with a twinkle in my eyes, having only remembered the main bits of the sport he'd explained to me.

He grinned. "Exactly."

I laughed as I pulled myself from his arms, quickly rounding the front of the car before sliding into the passenger's seat.

A few weeks back, once I'd started therapy and began sleeping through the night, Dean had brought up the possibility of him driving again. There had been a moment where I'd been stunned, having been so used to the way things had been going that climbing into the driver's seat felt like second nature, but as I handed him back the keys, I'd felt an immense amount of respect for him.

He wasn't sitting back and letting his fear conquer him – he was facing it head on.

He was shaky at first, but I was there to calm him down, turning down the volume of the radio so that he'd be able to completely focus on the road ahead of him. By the time that first week of driving had come to an end, he appeared to be relaxing. His shoulders weren't as tense, his gaze wasn't so jittery, and his grip on the steering wheel had loosened.

Now, as he pulled off of my street and towards the university, Dean was completely at ease. His seat was pushed far back, making room for his legs as he increased the pressure on the gas, and he drove with only one hand, the other resting comfortably against the glass of the window.

We reached the university in no time, and Dean turned on his signal light, heading towards the parking lot closest to the gymnasium. When he'd rolled to a stop in a spot next to an old, beat-up truck, he cut the engine, pulling the keys out as the two of us got out.

It turned out that a college basketball game actually pulled in quite the crowd, and a five-dollar admission was charged at the doors. When I'd gone to pull out my fare however, Dean had already handed the lady working the money to cover for the both of us, accepting two navy blue wristbands in return before handing one to me.

"Thanks," I muttered in acknowledgement, securing the band around my wrist as we stepped into the gym.

The only time I'd ever stepped foot into the building before that night had been to see Dean, when the whole gym had been empty except for the two of us. Tonight however, the noise was next to deafening. The stands were already half full, still a while to go before the game started, and while some people seemed to be talking loudly with their friends, others were watching and dancing in their seats as the cheerleaders pumped up the crowd. Faces were painted, handmade signs were being waved, and everyone appeared to be having fun.

"Do you mind sitting by our bench?" Dean asked, his words, a bit louder than usual, shaking me out of my thoughts. "I think I see a few free seats."

When I nodded in agreement, not really bothered with where we sat, Dean's hand reached for mine, leading me around the edge of the court and towards an empty spot on the bleachers big enough for the both of us. We squeezed our way through the crowd, stopping six rows up and taking a seat.

There wasn't much to do as we waited for the game to start, and disregarding the cheering coming from every direction, the two of us drew out the time just talking, only pulled into the spectacle the crowd was putting on when the lights dimmed slightly and both teams ran out onto the court.

Basketball, and sports in general, had never been something I'd been interested in, but being in the middle of such an energetic crowd, it was hard not to get swept into the excitement.

Being the home team, the Duke players were dressed in white jerseys with blue trimming, and when the first whistle went, the crowd quieted down a bit as the ball was thrown up, only to return immediately as we got a hold of the ball. The intensity began right away – jump shots landing effortlessly in the net, brutal fouls as players got tossed off their feet, and both teams running up their score.

I'd never expected to enjoy myself as much I was, and when I glanced next to me, seeing Dean just as into the game as the rest of the crowd when one of the players on our team got another basket, I was glad I'd agreed to come.

When the first quarter ended, the players barely had enough time to grab water from their bench and listen to their coach before they were thrown right back onto the court, but when half-time came, both teams retreated to the locker rooms, leaving the crowd to settle down a bit.

"You want to hear a funny story?"

I turned to look at Dean curiously, noticing that instead of watching the cheerleaders take the court, his eyes were trained on me. "Sure."

"Ryan and his fiancée, Zoe, got together at one of my high school basketball games," he said, amusement lacing his words as he recalled the memory. "During the half-time of our games, our school had used a kiss cam for entertainment, and when I got Zoe and her daughter to come with Ryan to the championship game my senior year, I organized for them to get put on the big screen."

"Really?" I asked, a light smile spreading across my lips. "So you're the one who got the two of them together?"

"Not really," he shrugged. "I kind of just gave my brother the push he needed to ask her out." Nodding in understanding, I hadn't even realized that my gaze had begun to wander, curiosity filling my eyes as they travelled across the crowd, until I heard Dean chuckle next to me. Turning towards him and quirking an eyebrow, I waited for him to say something. "There's no kiss cam here, you don't need to worry."

Despite the fact that I knew he was simply teasing, I couldn't help the blush that rose up my neck and coloured my cheeks. I excused myself quickly, suddenly needing the bathroom as I noticed the smirk playing on Dean's lips. When I returned, the teasing glint in his eyes had dimmed, and, noticing the cheerleaders heading back to the sidelines, I realized I'd made it back just in time.

Raising an eyebrow as I noticed a large bag of popcorn now in Dean's possession, he just smiled, offering some to me as both teams came back out.

The players huddled around the bench just a few feet in front of us, and while none of his former teammates noticed Dean in the crowd, his coach's eye flitted our way, causing Dean to tense up next to me. The coach's gaze didn't linger, but he nodded inconspicuously at Dean, acknowledging his support as he turned back to the players.

Dean's posture didn't relax as the game continued, and instead of applauding along when the Duke players began to run up the score and pull ahead, his hands were clenched tightly.

"You okay?" I asked worriedly, no longer concerned with the game.

Snapping out of his anger-filled head, he turned to look at me with a blank look in his eyes. "I'm fine," he said levelly, not fooling me one bit as he flashed me a fake smile.

"Umm, we can go if you want," I offered a few moments later, leaning closer as I lowered my voice.

It was as though his mood did a complete twist in the seconds that followed. His body relaxed, his eyes gleamed happily, and an unforced smile greeted me. "No it's okay," he shook his head, popping a handful of popcorn into his mouth. "Sorry, I just had something on my mind, but I'm good."

I let it drop as I nodded hesitantly, turning my attention back to the court.

Having once mastered the skills it took to tuck your pain away and mask it with happiness, it was easy for me to notice when others did the same. And as my gaze continuously found Dean's, I knew he that was what he was doing – I just couldn't understand why.

Chapter 18

We won.

I'd hoped that to be the outcome – to be able to leave the game with a smile on my face knowing that I watched my teammates play their hearts out, but what I felt as the crowd dispersed was the opposite of happiness. It may have been the reaction I fronted, but inside, there was anger and resentment tugging at my chest.

'They won,' I thought sardonically, 'And they did it without me.'

In the depths of my mind, I think I had subconsciously been hoping that without me the team would be struggling. That they'd be good enough to win, but nothing extraordinary. Now, seeing the crowd still buzzing, I realized that they were doing just fine without me. I was just another player; one who was completely average and easily replaceable.

Not wanting to get caught in the middle of the celebration, Katie and I stayed seated on the bleachers, though I noticed the way she was squirming uncomfortably. "Shouldn't we be going?" she asked hesitantly.

"Trust me, it's better to wait it out," I replied, shaking the near empty bag in my hands so that the popcorn kernels at the bottom jumbled around. "The traffic in the parking lot gets heavy quick, but by the time I would usually leave the locker rooms, most of it would be cleared."

A sense of understanding fell across her features. "Oh," she said nervously, "I didn't realize you wanted to stay and see your friends."

Hoping she didn't notice how my muscles tensed for a second, I realized that it had sounded like I was trying to stick around to see my teammates, which really wasn't something I was keen to do just yet.

I cleared my throat. "Actually – "

"Dean!"

Too late.

My chest tightened as I plastered on a smile, turning to see Dallas, Matt, and a few other guys coming from the locker room. I didn't know if Coach had mentioned that I'd been in the crowd, but as they moved towards Katie and I, it was evident that I couldn't run away. I wasn't a coward.

"Hey guys," I said, holding back the resentment as I stood up, Katie following me down to the court, "Good game."

"Thanks bro," Dallas said, stopping in front of me with a grin on his face. "We didn't expect to see you here tonight."

I shrugged. "Thought I'd show my support."

"And you're back on your feet," Matt chimed in. "Does that mean you're cleared to come back?"

Any conversations the rest of the guys had been having had come to an abrupt halt, all of them seemingly interested in my response. "Not yet," I said slowly, noticing disappointment flash across some faces, while others looked relieved, "But I've been training for a few months, so I should be back soon."

Truthfully, I had an appointment booked for the following week, and while I was sure I'd get the clearance to play, I didn't want to say that now and have to deal with the repercussions if it didn't happen.

"Hopefully you'll be back for playoffs then," Dallas said, sounding genuinely hyped, "That's when we're gonna need you."

"Dude," Matt cut in, "Why don't you come to the party tonight?"

All the guys, whether they were sincere or not, quickly shouted and hooted in agreement, leaving me momentarily stunned, not able to shake the discomfort that crept up on me. When I'd been injured, none of them had given me a second thought, not really bothering with helping me out or checking in on me, but now that I was back on two feet, they appeared eager to hang out again.

"What do you say?" Matt asked, noticing my hesitance as a smirk pulled at his lips, "If I remember correctly, you used to have quite a lot of fun at our parties." His eyes shifted towards Katie, who until now had gone seemingly unnoticed by the rest of the guys. "And of course, this little cutie is welcome to come too."

Ignoring how he was immediately clapped on the back by a few of his teammates, I turned towards Katie, leaning down slightly, my breath fanning the side of her face as I whispered, "We don't have to go if you don't want to."

Pulling back, awaiting her response, there was a small part of me that hoped she just wanted to go home and end the night here. Instead, a small smile tugged at her lips, a contradictory action to the blank look in her eyes as she shrugged. "I'm not gonna be the buzzkill here Dean," she replied. "If you want to go, we can."

I wanted to tell her that this wasn't what I really wanted. I wanted to get out of here and shut off the conflicting voices in my head, but at the same time, I also didn't want to look like the bad guy and reject the invitation.

Forcing back a sigh, I smiled. "Just tell me where it is and we'll be there."

Half an hour later we were parked a block away from Dallas's house. I'd taken the keys out of the ignition but hadn't moved to get out, clasping my hands tight around the steering wheel as I watched people I only vaguely remembered passing by in a hurry as they tried to escape the cold.

From what I remembered, Dallas's parents were workaholics, often leaving him alone for days at a time. They knew about the parties he threw, but as long as nothing of theirs was broken when they got back, they didn't really mind.

"You know, if we were going to be sitting in a car tonight, I might've thought about bringing a jacket," Katie mused, causing my attention to turn to her in surprise, not having realize how long we'd been sitting here.

"Sorry," I muttered, dragging a hand stressfully through my hair, "I guess we can go."

Reaching for my door handle, I was pulled back as Katie's hand wrapped around my arm. "Are you sure this is what you want to do tonight?" she asked, a blend of curiosity and skepticism glossing across her features. "Because if you'd rather just go see a movie or something, I'd be okay with that."

"This is what I'd do almost every weekend before my accident. It's what brought the team closer together, because we didn't just see each other at practice, we spent a lot of our free time together," I revealed. I left out the part that was eating away at me the most – that what I'd come to realize over the past couple of months was that the guys and I had partied together because we'd had nothing better to do. "So maybe, if I can get through tonight, it won't be as awkward as I think it'll be when I get back into the game."

This was something I believed to be untrue, because I knew that if I got clearance to play again, there was sure to be a shift in the dynamic that the team had built up over the course of the season.

"Okay then," Katie said softly, and because she recognized that I needed it, she squeezed my hand encouragingly, "Let's go."

The house was easy to spot, a mass of guests crowding the porch and doorway as the bass from the music reverberated all the way out to the street. It was surprising the neighbours weren't doing anything to shut the party down, but I guess having lived next to Dallas for a while, they'd grown to expect the antics.

Holding Katie's hand tightly in my own as we stepped into the house, I glanced around, failing to recognize anyone, but that didn't stop others from greeting me as we made our way towards the kitchen. There were less people there, and I was surprised as Katie was pulled into a conversation with someone she'd known from her program, introducing me quickly before they begun discussing the lab they'd completed earlier in the day.

I stood there awkwardly, not really having much to contribute to the conversation when a small commotion caught everyone's attention. Turning slightly, I saw three guys enter the kitchen, all at different stages of drunkenness, and Dallas, who happened to be the tallest and soberest, noticed me immediately.

"Adams," he grinned, making a beeline towards me before clapping me on the shoulder, "Glad you could make it." He nodded towards the fridge. "You want a beer?"

I was about to shake my head and tell him I was driving, but Katie nudged my hip before I could reply, causing me to look back to her with a crease between my eyebrows.

"If you want to drink, I don't mind driving back." I quirked an eyebrow and she rolled her eyes with a vague amusement. "Really. I was the one driving for the past four months. I think I can handle getting behind the wheel one more time."

"There," Dallas begun, a teasing undertone to his words, "Now you have no excuse to not let loose."

There was a beer in my hand no less than a minute later, and in attempt to calm the nerves of uncertainty I'd been experiencing, I chugged a good amount of it quickly. After thanking Dallas, he'd retreated back to the crowd in the living room while I, seeing a genuine smile on Katie's face, stepped closer to her to join in on the group's conversation.

An hour later, I was beginning to thaw out to the idea of being there. The alcohol was doing its job to calm my nerves, I'd joined in on a game of beer pong - partnering with Matt to completely annihilate a pair of rookies, and I found myself laughing as one guy, who'd clearly lost some sort of bet, stripped down to his boxers and took off running in the snow.

Grabbing another beer from the fridge as my other hand held Katie's, I enjoyed the buzz that I was beginning to feel as we headed towards the living room. It had become even more packed as the party gained momentum, but when I spotted my teammates, the two of us headed in that direction. These guys had been my 'normal' for years, more or less since I'd started at Duke, and even though I'd thought it'd be awkward integrating myself back into this scene, in that moment, it seemed effortless.

"I'm telling you," one of the guys slurred, having drank quite a lot so far as he threw his arm over the person next to him for support, "It was like she expected me to quit basketball when we started getting serious. The training schedule apparently interfered too much with the time I was 'supposed' to be spending with her."

His use of air quotes caused a few laughs, but Dallas was the one who replied, slapping him on the shoulder in support. "That sucks man," he trailed, "But if she didn't get it, then what more could you do?" There was a mutual hum of agreement that could barely be heard over the music. "What about you guys?" Dallas asked, turning towards me as I had my arm around Katie's shoulder, keeping her close. "How long have you guys been together?"

I could feel a hot flush spread down my neck and colour the tips of my ears, and out of my periphery I noticed that Katie's jaw had dropped in surprise. A bright red hue coloured her cheeks, and the both of us were struck speechless.

"Um..." I cleared my throat, dropping my arm from around her as I dug my hand deep into my pocket, "We aren't together."

Dallas quirked his eyebrow, his eyes flitting between us for a moment before his mouth ticked upwards in a smirk. "Sure," he drawled, clearly not believing me as he brought his red plastic cup up to his lips, "Whatever you say."

This simply caused me to stutter, clenching my beer a little tighter than necessary as I realized my inability to get my words out was only playing against me. Eyes were on Katie and I, most of them twinkling with amusement, and as I glanced at Katie to see her ducking her head and biting her lip anxiously, I grabbed her hand.

"We'll be right back," I muttered, not caring what it looked like as we moved further into the crowd. I heard a few teasing jabs meant for us, but I ignored them, only stopping when our bodies were safely hidden amidst a sea of people. "Sorry about them," I offered semi-awkwardly, leaning down so that she'd be able to hear me.

She seemed shy all of a sudden, her arms crossed protectively across her chest. "Don't worry about it," she replied, an attempted smile accompanying her words.

Before I could say anything more, a few people tried to squeeze by, pushing me towards Katie as we were jostled around. It was only when I steadied myself that I realized that my hands had landed clumsily on her waist, pulling us together so that our chests were touching, and her eyes were wide with surprise, but whether it was due to the trip up or our proximity, I didn't know.

The music suddenly sounded louder to me, enhancing all of my sense at once. It may have been the alcohol swirling around my brain, but as my hold on her loosened slightly, I raised an eyebrow and motioned to the people moving rhythmically around us. "You dance?"

She avoided my gaze for a moment, casting her eyes around the room. Everyone that surrounded us was either dancing or trying to move through the crowd to find their friends, and when she realized this, she looked up at me with apprehension crossing her features. "Not really."

When her head ducked shyly, nerves radiating off of her, I did the only think I could think of in that moment to loosen her up – I began to dance. I wasn't good by anyone's standards, and was sure I was making a bit of a fool of myself in the process, but as Katie's resolve slowly began to melt, I knew my efforts were paying off. Her eyes softened as I continued dancing even as the songs changed, and as the beat began to pick up once more, I saw her slowly begin to sway side to side.

"You know you can do better than that," I teased, causing a blush to colour her cheeks.

"I told you, I don't dance," she replied meekly.

A wicked grin spread across my lips as the alcohol flowing to the deepest corners of my mind faded any logical thinking I could possibly possess. "We'll see about that."

Without a second thought I was suddenly pulling her closer, letting my hands fall from her waist as I sought to intertwine our fingers together. She stumbled at first, eyes wide, but after she realized that nobody was paying a significant amount of attention to us, I saw her begin to let go, my grin widening as she did so.

The way we were dancing was in no way intimate – our arms in the air, flailing badly to the beat and taking up a little too much space. Others were surely taking notice of us as the kept at it, but in that moment, their opinions didn't matter. Holding Katie's hand high in the air, I watched her twirl goofily around in spot, a wide smile on her lips.

Dancing with her brought me a kind of joy that I'd long since forgotten about. I was letting down all my walls and doing the craziest things – including my own rendition of the chicken dance, which earned the fullest laugh from Katie and sounded like music to my ears.

We had nothing to worry about in that moment – our problems pushed to the back of our minds as we made the most of the night by having fun.

It felt like we were dancing for no time at all, but when both of our breaths began to come out in pants, we realized that we'd been at it for a while.

"That was fun," she said breathlessly, resting her hands on my chest as our movements stopped.

"Yeah," I smiled, "It was."

She nodded off towards the kitchen. "I'm gonna go grab some water," she said, trailing her fingers slowly away from my body as she moved, "I'll be right back."

My eyes followed her retreating figure as she squeezed her way past unfamiliar faces, and once she'd disappeared from my view, I found myself latching on to the spot I'd last saw her for the moments that followed.

It was only then that I realized how fast my heart was beating, and my chest felt like it'd been scorched by fire, the burn fading slowly and imprinting her touch onto my skin.

Though my brain was hazy, one clear thought formed. 'Shit was I in deep.'

As I stood in Dallas's kitchen, once again surrounded by my teammates, Katie wasn't by my side.

After our dance, she hadn't found her way back to me, and when I'd finally left the dance floor, deciding to try and look for her, I'd had no such luck before I was pulled into a conversation about how the basketball season was shaping up as it came to an end. I was only half paying attention to what they were saying, realizing that the clock in my peripheral read well past midnight.

Just as a gnawing begun in the pit of my stomach, thinking that she'd left without telling me, or had gotten into some kind of trouble, I saw her making her way towards me. I noticed that she'd let her hair down, allowing the blonde shield to cover half of her face.

"Hey," she said, her voice quiet.

Putting my half empty beer down on the counter, I lazily draped an arm around her shoulder, pulling her closer to me. "Where have you been?" I asked, a smile on my face and my eyes glittering with happiness now that she was here. "I've been missing you."

I hadn't noticed that the conversation had died down, the guys more interested in watching Katie and I with amusement clouding their eyes.

"I just stepped out to get some fresh air," she replied, her breath fanning the side of my cheek as she spoke.

Her eyes trailed over my face in a calculating manner when I didn't respond right away. She was close enough that if I moved forward just a few inches we'd be within kissing distance, and at that thought, my heart sped up into overdrive, knowing that was exactly what I wanted. As I made to move closer however, she stepped back.

"I was actually thinking about heading home soon," she said shyly, touching the hem of her shirt self-consciously, "But if you wanted to stay then – "

"No," I said, cutting her off abruptly, "We can go."

It was almost as if she was shocked that I'd agreed to leave, stopping short for a quick minute before she nodded. Grabbing her hand, I tossed a quick goodbye over my shoulder to the guys and let her lead me through the madness that the house had become.

When we reached the front door, stepping out into the chilly winter air, it actually felt refreshing as we headed for the sidewalk.

"I didn't do anything tonight that upset you, did I?" I asked worriedly, suddenly questioning myself as I realized she had yet to say anything as we neared the spot I'd parked the car. "Because I was trying to make this night fun. Was the dancing too much? Or – "

Katie was quick to set me straight as she shook her head venomously. "It wasn't you, don't worry," her voice soothing and soft in the night breeze, "I'm just not the party type of girl."

Needing more of a verification in my drunken state, I asked again for clarification, "And that's why you wanted to leave, right?"

She smiled, albeit a little sadly, and shrugged. "Yeah." Katie nodded. "I'm sorry if I'm ruining your night."

"You're not," I clarified as we reached the car, though I knew the slur in my words was starting to become noticeable in the absence of the loud music. "You're actually making it better."

The drive back to Katie's didn't feel as long as it should have. The conversation between us was sparse, but the silence wasn't uncomfortable. In fact, it was rather soothing, the radio playing lightly in the background as the headlights tore through the night and guided us home.

With Holden having casually mentioned to me earlier that he was having Stella over for the night, I knew he wouldn't have cared if I'd gone home, but I hadn't thought twice about asking Katie to crash at hers.

We'd fallen asleep next to one another a countless number of times, and while it shouldn't have been any different tonight, as we rode the elevator up to her apartment, it felt different. Neither one of us was hurting or in need of company tonight. Over the course of the past couple of months, we'd grown so close to each other that things like this just didn't seem out of the ordinary – they felt normal.

That very fact however, was what caused an unsettling feeling to grow in my stomach, accompanying the one already present due to the alcohol I'd consumed.

Sharing a bed was something that couples did, but Katie and I weren't in a relationship. We were there for each other, made each other laugh, and could always make the other smile when they were feeling down. I had told Katie back before her mom's death – the night she'd kissed me – that I wanted her, and that feeling hadn't gone away.

Yet something was missing; I didn't know if she felt the same way.

The guys tonight had even seen it, because the more I drank, the more my true feelings came to light. It was in the way we touched and interacted, the subtle gestures that told the story we were too afraid to tell on our own.

Resting my head against her pillow that night, my eyes trained on her as she moved around her bedroom getting ready for bed, I tried to think of ways to show her how I felt, though they all seemed too over-the-top, and not at all something that she would appreciate. When she slid in next to me however, leaving only a sliver of space between us, my mind had only one track.

I could feel myself slowly drifting as she said, "Goodnight."

And before I could fully process the ramifications of my actions, I leaned forward, my lips slowly capturing hers.

My eyes were closed, unable to see her reaction as I kissed her, though the stillness of her lips against mine gave me a clue as to how surprised she was. I brought my hand up slowly, cupping her cheek as the pad of my thumb rubbed softly against her skin, my lips still gentle yet demanding.

The kiss didn't last long – a few seconds at most, but it did its job in showing Katie that my feelings were there, and they were unlikely to fade anytime soon.

"Goodnight," I replied, my breath fanning her lips as I pulled back.

As my fingers dropped from her cheek, I cuddled further into the sheets, which were now warmer as a rush of heat ran through my blood. The surprise on Katie's face was evident; her cheeks flushed pink, her jaw gone slack, and her blue eyes wide. That image was the last thing I saw as my eyes fluttered shut, welcoming the sleep that washed over me with the hopes that my dreams would be haunted by the beauty that laid beside me.

Chapter 19

Dean had managed to steal my breath away and fall asleep all within the same minute, and as his breathing evened out, I was left wide awake.

My eyes were focused on the ceiling, the night air floating somberly around the room as I tried to process what had happened. The kiss wasn't what was bothering me, as it wasn't the first time it'd happened, but rather the fact that his actions had been completely effortless. I hadn't expected it and had frozen at his touch, but that hadn't stopped a shiver from running down my spine at the light friction he'd created. Even now, a dimmed tingling sensation lingered, and I found myself raising my hand to my mouth, running my fingers over the crevices of my lips that had captured a warmth that'd been missing before.

It was hard however, to decipher whether his intentions were true. Glancing over at the man beside me, he seemed peaceful in his state of rest, but that didn't stop a sinking feeling from settling over me. I wondered if he'd even meant to kiss me at all, or if it was just the result of him having a few too many drinks.

When I tried to close my eyes, it was as if time slowed down. The only thing I could see was a vivid replay of his lips on mine, and not just that night, but from months back, when I'd been vulnerable and had indulged in the bliss accompanied his kiss.

In the rush of it all, I'd forgotten to take my sleeping pill and had no clue as to when I'd finally been able to shut my brain off. The lack of sleep caught up with me the next morning however, as I was awoken by a shrill ringing just as the sun began to graze the horizon.

Lifting my head from my pillow, my vision still hazy, I tried quickly to locate the sound. It wasn't my alarm clock or my phone, but when I saw Dean's phone lighting up on my desk across the room, I rolled over to shoot him a look of annoyance. It faded quickly however, when I saw that he was sleeping right through the noise, a small smile on his lips as his chest rose and fell rhythmically.

Heaving a sigh, I inched out from underneath the covers, my bare feet cold against the floor as I made my way across the room. Just as I reached to shut the sound on his phone off, the ringing came to a halt, irking me slightly, but when it started up back up not even a minute later, I grabbed the phone quickly.

Zoe.

Biting my lip with indecision, I looked up to see that Dean was still very much asleep, and hoping that he didn't mind, I slipped out of the room, heading downstairs as I answered the call. Not able to get a word in before Zoe's voice flowed purposefully through the speaker, I heard her ask, "Has Ryan talked to you about renting your tux yet?"

Her words were rushed, "Sorry Zoe," I paused, "It's Katie." My voice was timid as I rounded the back of the couch, sitting down and tucking my legs beneath me. "Dean's actually sleeping."

I'd only met Zoe a few times, most of them during the stint Dean had had in the hospital after his accident but knowing she was engaged to his older brother made me feel somewhat at ease talking to her.

"Oh, sorry Katie," she replied, sounding a little surprised, though she masked it quickly. "I didn't mean to wake you up."

"It's okay," I trailed, picking at a loose thread on my pajamas, "Though I'm not so sure Dean would've answered your call if I hadn't."

She chuckled. "I'm guessing he's gonna be a little hungover then when he wakes up," she stated with amusement, "Because that's the only time I've ever seen him sleep through anything."

"Probably," I mused, glancing back towards the staircase as though he'd suddenly appear.

"Well good luck with that," she said. "I'm sorry for calling so early. Ryan had an overnight shoot, so when he got home an hour ago, he ended up waking me up. But since I've got you, would you mind asking Dean to talk to his brother about his tux rental for May? I don't want to be worrying about that closer to the wedding, and knowing both of them, they'll likely put it off until the last minute."

"Uh sure, no problem," I said, suddenly realizing that a small amount of nervousness had seeped into my words as a question circled the forefront of my mind.

The line was quiet for a moment, almost as if she was waiting for me to say something else, but I didn't. When it was evident that I wasn't going to be the one to talk next, she asked, "Everything alright Katie?"

"I, uh," I cleared my throat, biting my lip anxiously, "Can I ask you something?"

"Sure."

"You've known Dean a long time, right?"

A light laugh escaped her lips, resonating her amusement through the phone as she replied. "Ever since I started seeing Ryan four years ago, yes. Why?"

I sighed, dragging my fingers backwards through my hair. "I don't know, it's just, last night – "

"Uh oh," she said, cutting off my mix of words, "What did he do?"

"Nothing," I replied, shaking my head as though it'd help me get my thoughts straight. "I went with him to the basketball game yesterday, and even though it seemed like he didn't want to, we went to the after party with his teammates. The night picked up a bit and he appeared to be having fun, and when we got back to mine everything seemed normal. We'd slept in the same bed before so that wasn't awkward, but before he fell asleep he kissed me and I completely froze."

I stopped my rambling, chewing nervously on my lip as she was quiet for a moment, mulling over what she'd heard.

When I heard her release an airy breath, I certainly hadn't expected for her to say, "Finally!"

"Finally?" I repeated with confusion.

"Come on Katie," she mused, "You and I both know that the two of you have never been just friends." I opened my mouth to interject, but Zoe simply continued talking. "Dean's accident and your mom's passing made the both of you push your feelings aside and focus on what was important, but now that you're both moving on with your lives, or at least trying to, I think you're both inching towards the line that separates the two of you being just friends and something more."

I knew she was right, of course, but that didn't mean there wasn't a small pull in my chest at the possibility of coming clean with my feelings. "And what if it doesn't work out?" I asked, my voice quiet, feeling as though I'd shrunk to half my size.

Zoe was quiet for a moment. "You're scared," she stated bluntly, though there was compassion and understanding laced around her words.

"I'm terrified."

"Well don't be," she said, as though it was that simple to calm my racing heart whenever he was around. "From what I can tell he cares about you a lot, and all you have to do is be brave enough to start that conversation about being something more."

"So I won't be making a fool of myself?"

"No Katie," she said softly, "And, if you're anything like I was a few years back, you'll be a lot happier when you get everything off your chest."

"Thanks," I said, genuinely thankful for the advice.

"Anytime."

Hanging up the phone, I sat still for a few moments, relishing in the silence that blanketed the apartment as I breathed deeply. It didn't know how much time I had before Dean would wake up, but I knew I had to build up the confidence to talk to him before he did.

It just so happened that Dean didn't wake up until it approached mid-day. There were no floorboards creaking as I showered and got dressed, or any clues that he was here at all as I made myself breakfast, deciding to make the most of the quiet time.

When he finally came downstairs, the clock hanging on the wall showed it to be quarter past twelve. I was sitting on the couch, my back to him, with my notebook and a textbook laid out in front of me, and at the sound of his footsteps echoing heavily through the room, I turned my focus away from my assignment to see his dishevelled appearance.

"Well, it looks like Sleeping Beauty is finally awake," I teased, laughing a bit as he responded with an emphasized groan.

My eyes trailed over him, and while he was in the same clothes he'd changed into the previous night before falling asleep, they somehow looked much better in that moment. His t-shirt, while slightly wrinkled, was clinging to various parts of his chest, and his sweatpants hung dangerously low on his waist. I found myself flustered as I followed the defined lines of his hips as they disappeared below the soft fabric, though I came to my senses and flitted my gaze away before he realized what had caught my attention.

It was the kiss that suddenly had me noticing these things, because while I'd always found Dean to be good looking, this morning, every little thing about him seemed to be amplified.

Clearing my throat, I saw him yawn as he brought a hand up to rub the sleep from his eyes. "I took the pain relievers out of the bathroom and put them in the kitchen in case you needed them."

Despite the way his hair stuck up at odd angles, I still found the way he grinned in response undeniably attractive. "Thanks," he said, turning on his heel to head towards the kitchen.

As he left my sight, I brought my bottom lip between my teeth, contemplating my next move for a few seconds before slowly rising from the couch and following in his footsteps.

Entering the kitchen, I stopped, hovering in the doorway as I watched Dean swallow two pills and locate a glass for water. Brought back to the previous night, I'd remembered being wary about the party as soon as Matt had mentioned it. I wasn't that big on parties, especially the ones with packed houses, but I'd held back my emotions and gone with Dean.

That wasn't to say the evening hadn't been enjoyable. In fact, I'd found myself having fun. I'd felt comfortable enough to pick up a conversation with people I'd recognized from class, and while Dean's teammates found too much amusement in insisting that him and I were an item, the moment he'd pulled me away from them and started dancing, my spirits had lifted.

It was just at the end of the night, when I'd stepped outside to get some air, that I'd realized how much my life had changed over the course of a year. I'd gained someone who I could truly count on, started a job that would lead to a bright future, and had begun to spread my wings instead of keeping to myself. However, at the same time, I'd also lost the person who'd been closest to me. That realization had put a slight damper on my mood, and I knew as soon as I'd found Dean that he'd sensed as much, but there had also been a part of me that felt proud, knowing I was finally branching out.

" – long?"

Realizing I hadn't been listening and had zoned out, I shook myself out of my thoughts. "Sorry, what?"

Dean quirked an eyebrow in response, but nonetheless, repeated him. "I asked if you'd been up long?"

"Oh," I replied, leaning back against the wall adjacent to the entryway, "Yeah. Zoe called your cell early this morning, and since you didn't seem to want to wake up, I answered it and couldn't really fall back asleep after that. I hope you don't mind."

"Not at all." He shook his head, grimacing as soon as he did it. "What did she want?"

There was no waver to his voice or hint to his tone that suggested that the way he'd kissed me last night was anything more than a drunken moment. For all I knew, he didn't even remember it at all.

"She just wanted to remind you to call your brother and get your suit sorted out for the wedding."

"Okay," he nodded, not saying anything more.

When a lapse in conversation ensued, both of us unsure as to what to say, the awkwardness surrounding last night's turn of events finally began to build. Dean was fidgeting with his, now empty, glass, avoiding my gaze as I peered at him, trying to get a sense of what he was thinking. His features remained unreadable however, not giving away a clue as to what was going on inside his head.

"Look," Dean sighed, breaking the silence eventually as he dragged a hand through his hair, "About last night – "

"It's okay." I found the words tumbling out of my mouth before I could stop them, because while I couldn't be certain about what he would've said, judging by his tone, it didn't sound good. I saw the confusion flood his features as I pushed my feelings aside. "You don't have to say anything."

"But I do," he pushed, staying where he was as he threw an apologetic look my way. "I'm sorry that I dragged you along to the party last night. When Matt asked I felt pressured to say yes, and when you said you didn't mind, I didn't have it in me to say that I didn't actually want to go."

'That's what he wanted to say?' I thought. "You didn't?"

He dug his hands deep into the pockets of his sweatpants and shrugged. "Not really. I mean, before last night I hadn't talked to any of those guys in months, and if I hadn't of been drinking, I probably wouldn't have been all that fun to be around." His reply was honest, which I found endearing in the moment. "Plus, I think the best part of the night was dancing with you."

My lips twitched upwards, the memory vivid in my mind. "Ditto."

Once again however, I was brought back to the simple brush of our lips less than twelve hours previous, and I knew that while dancing was fun, it fell short of being the number one moment of the night.

"Actually," he started again, clearly nervous as he cleared his throat, "That's a lie." His words mirrored my thoughts, and suddenly I found my heart speeding up in anticipation, nerves coursing through me as I wondered what he'd say next. "The best part of the night, even though it was a little hazy, was falling asleep next to you and having the courage to kiss you goodnight."

It was exactly what I'd wanted to hear, but instead of a smile, a surprised look took over my face as I tried and failed to stop the blush that rose on my cheeks.

"Katie, I – " Dean paused mid-thought, his words appearing to fail him. "Last night wasn't a one-off," he said finally, sounding more determined as he met my gaze, "Or at least I don't want it to be.

"I don't either," I mumbled shyly, finding my voice.

My words seemed to boost his confidence as his lips twitched slightly, a glimmer of hope swirling in his eyes, though the expression on his face still stood quite serious. "I know I shouldn't have done it when I was drunk, but at least it's out there now," he said. "I told you once that I wanted you – that I wanted to be more than friends, and that hasn't changed. I just didn't want to push you when you weren't ready. After you lost your mom, I knew that I couldn't expect you to want a relationship because your heart was broken, so I was there for you, and if you still need more time, then I'm happy to wait on the sidelines."

The warmth in my chest expanded quickly, filling every bit of empty space as I realized just how much he wanted this. "I don't need more time," I said, just above a whisper, as though I thought speaking too loud would break us from the moment.

"You know what I'm asking, right?" he asked, as he moved closer slowly. "I want to take you out and not have to think about whether it's a date or not. I want it to be certain. I want to be able to call you whenever I need to just because I want to hear your voice, and fall asleep with you in my arms whenever I can. And I want to be able to kiss you – every time you smile and every time you take my breath away."

What scared me in that moment wasn't what he was saying, or how, as he stepped impossibly close, he looked at me through hooded eyes, waiting for a response. Instead, it was the way that, even though his proposition was forward, I found myself wanting the exact same things.

His eyes darkened as they dropped to my lips, and when I swept my tongue across them, they flitted back up to meet my own. "Katie," he trailed, his voice low and barely audible, his breath fanning my lips, "You're a whole new kind of tempting."

That was all it took for the switch to flip, my lips twitching upwards as a spark of confidence ignited. My hand crossed the invisible barrier between us and rested on the side of his waist. "Then what are you waiting for?"

For a moment I wondered if I had been too forward, as it wasn't normally my style, but when his hands rose to my cheeks and his lips grazed mine, my eyes fluttered shut and all of my worries were forgotten.

This was different from the times before; unrushed and all-consuming. The passion was overwhelming as our lips moved together with equal fervour, each of us giving just as much as we took. He would nip at my bottom lip and I would let my tongue explore his mouth for a moment. It was a dance of sorts, and one where both of us took the lead.

The back and forth went on for a while, and when I finally pulled back with a desperate need for air, I found that my hands had snaked their way underneath the fabric of his shirt.

"Where do you think you're going?" he asked softly, his eyes shining brightly with happiness as the pad of his thumb stroked the faded blush along my cheeks.

Before I could respond he was pulling me back to him, our lips meeting again with an intensity so strong, I didn't know how I could ever tire of it.

"So," he started, quite some time later as I rested my head against his shoulder, "How would you feel about a date?"

I shifted slightly, his hand slipping from the ends of my hair that he'd had between his fingers as my gaze met his. "Tonight?" I asked wondrously.

His eyes gleamed happily as his shoulders shrugged. "I don't see the point in waiting." He paused. "That is, if you're up for it?"

The edges of my lips pulled upwards and I leaned forward to press a kiss softly against his cheek. "That sounds perfect."

"Great," he chirped, a bit too happily, and I found myself giggling into his shoulder. "Do you have anything particular you want to do?"

I thought about it for a minute, scanning my memories of anywhere in the city that would make a good date. I tried remembering places that Stella had mentioned, restaurants I'd passed while on the bus, and even places I hadn't thought about in years, but nothing particularly special stood out to me. If I was being honest with myself, it didn't matter where we went or what we did, it was this right now – the closeness and intimacy, that made for a memorable time.

And with that thought I suddenly had the perfect idea, though I wasn't sure how Dean would feel about it.

I think he sensed that I was worried about something, as a sudden crease formed above his eyebrows. "Something wrong?"

I shook my head, my hand resting gently on his chest. "No, not at all," I said, speaking nervously as I continued. "I was just wondering how Chinese take-out sounded to you? And maybe a movie?"

Surprise flitted across his features momentarily, noting how simple my request was, but when a smile appeared on his lips and he pulled me in closer, I could feel my heart speed up ever so slightly.

"Sounds perfect to me."

Chapter 20

You're not working tonight, right?

Glancing up from my phone, I realized that the professor was still running over the same slide that she had been for the last ten minutes, and when my phone buzzed a few moments later with a reply, there was no guilt in my mind as I looked down at the screen.

No, why? Got something planned? x

The symbol for a kiss that appeared at the tail end of her message caused an immediate smile to appear on my lips. It'd been a few days since the moment at her house, where I'd taken the risk and laid my feelings out on the line, and I had yet to fall back down from the cloud I'd stumbled upon. Katie was great; thoughts of her running through my mind every moment of the day, and everything with her was effortless, which stemmed from the trust and relationship we'd built over the last couple of months.

It's a surprise. ;)

Though I was itching to tell her, I left the message at that, hitting the send button before tucking my phone back into my pocket.

The rest of the lecture seemed to breeze by, though when I tried to pay attention, my plans for that afternoon circled my mind. I knew it was unconventional, that was a given, and while it wasn't something I'd thought about before speaking with Stella earlier in the week, I'd figured it would be fun.

I was one of the first ones out the door when the lecture let out, eager to put my plan into motion. Stepping out into the quad, I was just one student within the crowd, but through the throng of people I easily spotted Katie waiting near the edge of the building, a grin blossoming on my face as I neared her.

"Hey," I greeted, leaning in close to plant a quick kiss on her lips.

She'd only spotted me at the last minute, her blonde hair obstructing her view as it blew wildly with the breeze. As I pulled away, her lips twitched upwards and she hitched her bag higher up on her shoulder. "Hey."

"How was your day?"

It seemed completely natural for me to lift my arm and toss it over her shoulder, pulling her closer to me as we headed for the parking lot.

"Good," she nodded. "I only really had my lab today, but I got a bit of studying done while I was waiting for you." Her gaze suddenly shifted upwards as she tilted her head back, excitement flashing across her features. "And I'm just a little curious to see what this surprise is you have planned."

A smirk pulled on my lips as I chuckled. "You'll just have to wait and see."

My amusement grew as we settled into the car and I pulled off of campus, watching the curiosity on Katie's face grow as I headed in the direction of our apartments. It was apparent that she was trying to figure out where we were going as her eyes repeatedly scanned our surroundings, but as I turned onto an unfamiliar street, a determined crease formed above her brows.

It wasn't long before I pulled into a parking lot across the street from a small plaza, deliberately backing into the spot so that our backs would be towards the building. Katie's hand was quick to reach for her seatbelt, but before she could climb out of the car and spoil the surprise, I grabbed her hand and held her back.

"Remember how I said this was a surprise?" I asked, a mischievous look flooding my features as she nodded slowly. "Well, you're going to have to close your eyes then."

Incredulity spread quickly across her face as her eyes widened marginally. "You're serious?"

"Mhm," I nodded. "If your eyes are open you might figure it out beforehand, so if you want to get out of this car any time soon – "

"Alright. Alright," she grumbled under her breath, though from the way the edges of her mouth were tilted upwards, I knew she wasn't all that bothered by the request.

Once her eyes were shut and I'd waved my hand in front of her face for good measure, I stepped out of the car, rounding the front before opening Katie's door and helping her out.

Our hands were intertwined as I led her towards the shop on the very left side of the plaza, a bell dinging overhead as we stepped inside, only to be hit with a sickly sweet smell.

"Where are we?" Katie asked, seemingly in awe even though her eyes were still closed.

Letting go of her hand, I took a step back and stood behind her. Both my arms weaved their way around her waist and my head rested on her shoulder as I whispered, "Open your eyes."

Katie's eyes fluttered open, widening as she took in her surroundings. The cake shop was fairly quiet at this point in the day, being well past the afternoon rush, with only a few customers filling up the booths situated next to the windows. The mixture of scents in the air was wafting towards us from the display cases to our left, full of small, delectable treats.

"How – " she began breathlessly, the rest of her words getting caught in her throat as she realized what was going on.

Despite the layers I had on, as my arms tightened around her, I could feel her body heat slowly seeping through to my skin. I kissed her cheek softly, a tiny smile playing on my lips. "Happy birthday."

Her expression filled with surprise. "I don't understand... I never told you – "

"When your birthday was?" I finished for her, lifting an eyebrow as I turned her around to face me. "Luckily, Stella happened to ask me what my plans were for today a few days ago, or else I wouldn't have known. Don't you think it would've looked bad if I hadn't done something for my girlfriend's birthday?"

A smile tugged at her lips at my use of the word. "Sorry," she sighed, bringing her hands up to rest on my chest, "I've just never really celebrated my birthday much the past few years."

"Which is why, this year, I thought we'd do something special."

The curiosity returned to Katie's features, clearly realizing that she was missing something to all of this – and she was. I'd gone one step above simply bringing her here to buy her a cake, but before I could reveal my plans, the doors to the back swung open. A petite woman emerged, her grey hair pulled back from her face and a flour covered apron hanging around her waist. She smiled as she noticed the two of us, looking pointedly at me as she spoke. "I'm guessing you're Dean?"

"That'd be me."

"Come on back then," she said cheerfully, motioning for us to follow her.

Intertwining my fingers through Katie's, I guided her towards her real surprise. As soon as she'd stepped through the door, the wariness in her gaze disappeared, being replaced quickly with disbelief and joy.

The three tables that were usually spread out had been pushed together, a white table cloth thrown over top, and a few of the chairs had pink and purple balloons tied to them. There were four place settings set up with all the tools we'd need for the afternoon, with the extra two being for Stella and Holden, who were standing on the other side of the room with smiles on their faces.

"Surprise!" the both of them greeted, causing Katie to laugh and shake her head in amusement as she turned to me.

"What is all of this?"

"This," I paused, motioning around the small room, "Is a cake decorating class."

"It was my idea," Stella popped in excitedly, causing me to roll my eyes as she threw a smirk in my direction. "I've brought my little cousins here a few times, but after talking to the owner," she continued, smiling at the lady beside us, "She let us rent out the room for the rest of the day and decorate a few cakes by ourselves."

"Just as long as you all remember to clean up after your-selves when you're done," the lady said in a kind voice. Ges-turing to the other door in the room – the one that led to the kitchen – she continued, "Now, what kind of cakes would you all like?"

After the four of us had given our orders, consisting of two chocolate cakes, one vanilla, and one red velvet, the lady headed to the back and left the four of us to get situated. There were bowls of icing scattered across the table, as well as knives, candles, piping bags, and other small utensils I had no idea how to use, though once each of us had a cake in front of us, we were given a quick crash course in decorating.

Even out the icing before layering it. Be creative with the sweets and designs. Make sure to twist the top of the piping bag closed.

The tips were helpful, but it didn't fix the fact that I didn't really have much talent when it came to art and being creative.

Half an hour later, all of our cakes were slowly beginning to come together. Holden and I were in the same boat, not really knowing what we were doing and coating out respective cakes with way too much icing and no real design.

The girls however, were concentrating hard and paying close attention to detail. From across the table I could see Stella piping a few roses on the top of her red velvet cake, which had already been iced with cream cheese frosting, and it looked like she was almost done. Katie, on the other hand, had gone the more spontaneous route and, after icing her chocolate cake with chocolate icing, she'd used a small piping bag to drizzle melted white chocolate on top. She was now using a metal scraper to smooth out the icing on the sides of her cake, and was eyeing the large M&Ms that sat in the middle of the table.

Music was playing from Stella's phone – a supposedly inspirational playlist she'd put on shuffle that was meant to get us into the decorating mood. I, however, knowing any further decoration would just make my cake worse, was content with sitting back in my chair and watching Katie. I don't think she even realized, but about ten minutes later, as she placed the last sweet atop her cake, she looked my way.

A faint blush spread across her cheeks as she realized my eyes were already on her. "What?" she asked timidly, swiping at her cheek as though she thought she'd gotten icing there.

"Nothing," I replied, a smile tugging at my lips. I reached across the table to grab a small plastic sign that read 'Happy Birthday', and careful not to ruin the design she'd created, I gently placed it onto the top of her cake.

There was a pause as her features softened, her hand reaching across the table for mine. Seconds later, with her fingers brushing mine, she leaned towards me, capturing my lips with hers. The kiss was soft and sweet, and when she pulled back, I caught the gleam of happiness in her eyes. "Thank you."

Leaning in again, I aimed my lips for her cheek. "Anything for you."

It was a picture perfect moment, that was, until I felt a small blob of icing hit the side of my face.

Narrowing my eyes as I turned to the couple across from us, I saw Stella covering her mouth with her hand as she attempted to hold in her laughter, though she gave me a hand as she pointed a finger in Holden's direction.

"What?" Holden asked, the smirk on his face giving him away. "I figured that if we already have to clean up, why not make a mess first?"

Raising an eyebrow at his logic, I didn't have a chance to reply before I felt more icing being wiped onto my face, this time, from the girl beside me.

Katie grinned as I turned to her, licking the rest of the icing off of her finger. "He's right," she grinned wickedly.

Shaking my head in amusement, I quickly reached out to grab a bowl of icing from the middle and dotted a bit on the tip of her nose. "You're on."

Katie's birthday ended up being an afternoon to remember – the four of us laughing through a messy food fight and somehow, finding a way to make the clean-up enjoyable as well.

It was fun and it was freeing, and while I didn't mean for it to be, it also served as a welcome distraction, because the next morning, instead of heading to campus, I found myself waiting anxiously in the waiting room of the hospital. Today was the day of my doctor's appointment, and if everything went according to plan, I'd get cleared to play again.

I didn't know how to feel, and as a result, all of my emotions swirled together in a large melting pot, causing an unsettling feeling to bubble in my stomach as the white double doors pushed open. An unfamiliar nurse in mint-green scrubs appeared, her unruly brown hair falling down past her shoulders as she glanced down at the clipboard she held.

"Dean Adams?"

Despite the fact that my legs felt like jelly, I stood up, following her back through the narrow hallways until she directed me into an empty room.

"Your doctor will be with you shortly," she said matter-of-factly as I took a seat on the thin, crinkly paper that covered the examination table. Pulling on a pair of clean gloves, she continued, "In the meantime, I'm just going to check your blood pressure, as well as a few sensitive points around your injury."

Nodding, I couldn't find the words to speak.

Sliding the pad that would read my blood pressure up my arm, the nurse secured it properly before pressing a few buttons on the machine. When the beeping began, she took a step back, taking a seat in front of me as she examined my knee. My breathing was controlled as I tried to stay calm, but as the pad tightened around my bicep, my leg began to bounce anxiously. This appeared to cause the nurse a great amount of annoyance as she tested the reflexes of my leg, having to tighten her grip on my skin to keep it still.

Once the pad around my arm deflated, I slid it off, handing it to the nurse. "So," she started, stepping across the room to grab her clipboard to document her notes, "There's nothing out of the ordinary with your vitals, and your injury site seems to be healed." She paused, clicking her pen closed as her gaze lifted back up to me. "Just sit tight. I still have to print out your physiotherapy record, and once I get that to Dr. Richards, he'll be in to see you."

"Thank you," I replied, my voice low and somewhat timid as I spoke out for the first time, receiving nothing more than a nod of acknowledgement in response before she left the room.

Left alone, I found my gaze wandering around the room. The walls were plain white, an abundance of small machines were scattered around the room, and a few printed out warning signs hung next to the desk that reminded all members of the staff to wash their hands on the regular and always dispose of contaminated products.

It wasn't much, and with nothing else to occupy my thoughts in that moment, my worries about how the conversation with my doctor would go began to eat away at my mind.

What if things didn't go my way? What if there was nothing more I could do? Would the game I loved slip through my fingers?

When the door creaked open minutes later, a glimpse of the doctor's white coat was the first thing I saw.

"Dean," he nodded in greeting as he stepped into the room, "How are you today?"

Although my mind was still whirling with possible scenarios of how this would go, I managed to swallow my worries and say, "As good as I can be."

A light chuckle escaped his lips at my obvious nerves. "Then I guess there's no point in prolonging what I have to say."

My palms started to sweat and the seconds ticked by agonizingly slowly as I waited silently for him to continue.

"According to the records your physiotherapist has submitted, you've been putting in an ample amount of effort in getting yourself back into shape. It says here that you've been working out all of your muscles regularly and accepting the tips he's given to rid any pain from your injury site. Is that correct?"

Nodding, I clasped my hands on my lap in front of me.

He took a moment to jot something down in his notes. "That's a great start, but just know that it's only going to get harder from here."

I blinked in confusion as he trailed off. "So that means...?" I trailed questioningly, not wanting to succumb to the sinking feeling in my stomach that was waiting to burst.

"I'm clearing you to play."

Those five words were all it took to lift a giant weight off my chest, all worries immediately fleeing from my mind. "Seriously?" I asked breathlessly, needing clarification that I hadn't imagined those words.

A small smile formed on his lips as he nodded. "Your injury has healed nicely over the past couple of months due to your determination to get to where you once were," he explained. "I can say with confidence that there's no chance of re-injury from working under an extended amount of stress and pressure. When you get back into the game however, you have to remember that you're not up to the caliber you once were. Maybe with time you will be, but as you readjust, there's a good chance that there'll be times when the muscles around your knee will cause you pain."

I'd thought about getting back onto the court for real since the moment I'd woken up in the hospital after my accident, and hearing his words in that moment was like music to my ears.

"I understand," I spoke lowly, my voice filled with disbelief and gratitude, "And thank you."

"I'm just doing my job."

Standing in front of my coach's door the following afternoon, I felt my heart beat racing into overdrive. Throughout all of my classes I'd barely paid attention, my thoughts frequently flitting back to the conversation I'd had with my doctor as he'd written me the clearance note I'd earned.

The same note that was now in my hand, being held onto tightly as I raised my hand to knock.

"Come in," I heard my coach's booming voice respond almost as soon as my skin had met the wood, and following his orders, I closed my eyes for a quick second and took a deep breath as I twisted the handle.

Stepping only partially into the room at first, I saw that he was sitting behind his desk, papers that held game plays and old scores scattered across it. His eyes widened marginally behind the spectacles he wore as he realized it was me there to see him, though his surprise was quickly masked as he waved me further into the room.

"Come have a seat."

Shutting the door behind me, it felt as though my steps were calculatingly slow as I made my way to the chair directly across from him. Dropping my bag to the floor and taking a seat, I managed to pull a nervous smile onto my lips. "Hey coach."

He nodded in acknowledgement. "It's good to see you Dean," he said kindly. "I noticed you were at the game on Friday."

"I was," I affirmed. "I thought it was about time I started to show my support for the team again, giving that my knee finally healed up."

It was a way to gauge his thoughts – bringing up my injury and the fact that it would no longer affect my ability to play, but when his expression remained neutral, I knew the conversation would be a lot more difficult than I'd first believed.

"I can see that," he said levelly, his gaze dropping to my leg momentarily.

When it was apparent that he wasn't going to continue, I cleared my throat and broke the silence. "That's actually why I came to talk to you," I said, my voice partially strained with fear. In that moment, my nervous brain couldn't predict which way this conversation would go, and while I hoped for a shot to prove myself, the note in my hand became heavier by the second. Lifting my hand and placing the piece of paper on his desk, I continued. "I've been in physiotherapy since my accident, trying to get my body back to the way it was, and just yesterday, my doctor cleared me to start playing again."

Flitting his eyes between me and his desk, he reached for the piece of paper. Slowly unfolding it, he took a moment to look it over, but as his lips drew together in a grim line, my hopes slowly started to diminish.

"Dean – "

Panicking, I cut him off. "Before you say anything," I said in a rush, "I want you to know that I've been working really hard. I'm just steps below the fitness regimen you had us following last season, and ever since I've gotten my cast off, I've been finding time to practice my skills in the auditorium."

"I'm not doubting what you're saying," he said, an author-itative tone to his voice that caused me to sink lower in my seat. "I don't always leave right after practices, and I've seen you in the gym on more than one occasion. You're just as good as you've always been, but that's not the problem." I sighed. "Every year, players graduate, get drafted or drop out, and I'm tasked with bringing together the guys that are left to make a team. It takes work, and now that we're nearing the end of the season, I don't know how you'll be able to transition back into the game."

Frustration and devastation fought to worm their way into my mind, but I pushed right back, not letting his words deter me. "You know me coach." My eyes flashed with determination as they met his steely. "I'm a hard worker. I put my all into this sport, and I earned my place on this team. I never wanted any of this, but the world threw me a curve ball and this is me fighting back." There was still apprehension clear in his features, and I only had one last plea in me. "Just give me a chance to show you that I can do this."

He was quiet as he eyed me carefully, clasping his hands together atop his desk. "I understand your situation, I do. Lots of players on my team have gotten injured over the years, but what I've learned is that it's what they do once they've recovered that shows the strength they truly have. The team has readjusted since losing you, and things are different now," he stated, and I could feel my heart sinking with every word, "But I'm not going to lie and say you haven't been missed."

My eyes widened in surprise. "Are you saying...?"

"If you really want this," he began, stressing his words, "Show up at practice tomorrow. If you can show me that you're capable enough, and can get back into the swing of how things work on my team, then I'll put you in the line-up for next Friday's game."

My lips curled upwards as I breathed a sigh of relief. "Thank you," I said, standing as I felt an immense amount of joy radiating off of me. "I won't let you down."

The vague outline of a smile appeared on his lips as he nodded. "Just don't make me regret it."

Chapter 21

Walking into the gym, the crowd was already beginning to hype themselves up. Just like the last game I'd attended, the cheerleaders were dancing to the upbeat music in the center of the court as the clock on the scoreboard counted down the minutes until the game would start.

This time however, instead of accompanying Dean to the game, I'd dragged Stella along.

"Do you see him?" she asked, tightening her grip on my wrist as she overexcitedly scanned over the handful of players stretching and warming up at either end of the gym.

I shook my head, only having to glance quickly at the Duke players to know that Dean wasn't out here. "He's probably in the locker room with the rest of his teammates," I replied, straining slightly as I raised my voice.

"Okay then," she sighed, though her excitement didn't fade much as her gaze shifted to the bleachers. We were hovering near the entrance of the gym with other people swerving around us, some occasionally bumping into us in a rush to find seats. "Oh," Stella chirped, grabbing my wrist as she pointed across the court, "I see Holden, come on."

Following her, I quickly spotted Holden as he stood up, waving to get our attention. As the two of us got closer, climbing the bleachers to where he sat, I noticed he'd saved enough room for the both of us.

"Hey," he greeted, kissing Stella quickly as she squeezed past him, taking a seat on his left as I sat to his right.

Taking a handful of the popcorn from the bag in his lap, Stella smiled at him and raised an eyebrow with curiosity. "How long have you been here?"

"I came with Dean."

"So you've been here a while then?" I asked with the tiniest amount of surprise laced around my words.

Holden nodded in response. "I went to find something to eat first, but yeah, I was here when everyone was still warming up."

"And Dean – "

"Was warming up with the rest of the team," he said, answering my unasked question with a smile of amusement.

My lips tugged upwards shyly, feeling slightly guilty that my worries were so transparent. Last week, when Dean had mentioned that he'd talked to his coach, I'd been nervous for him, but had masked it with congratulations. His determination was admirable, but thinking about it realistically, I didn't know how well Dean would fare joining the team again.

"He'll be fine," Holden continued reassuringly when I didn't relax. "I've been to too many of these games to say otherwise."

Although it was a good attempt, it didn't do much to calm the nerves that were slowly causing my hands to shake. However, when an outburst from a group of students behind me made me jump, their faces all painted as enthusiasm radiated off of them, I realized that I'd zoned out momentarily and that both teams were now emerging from the locker rooms.

Dressed in their white jerseys, my eyes bypassed each Duke player until they fell on Dean. Despite the fact that he was now without his glasses, as I'd gone with him earlier in the week to get contacts for the nights he'd be playing, I recognized him easily. Seemingly fitting right in with his teammates as they all circled around the coach, it reminded me of the first night we'd met.

He was purposeful, athletic, and confident.

Even though it didn't surprise me, it was slightly saddening to see Dean stick to the sidelines as the starting line-up took to the court. I watched as one of his teammates took the jump ball as the first whistle went and the game began. The crowd was into the game, and right from the beginning it was obvious that there was a rift between the teams. The game was intense and the score was close, and while I could've easily been swept into the excitement like the rest of the crowd, I found my eyes frequently flitting to Dean. His leg bounced up and down anxiously as he watched the game, and every time the opposing team scored his hands would clench by his sides.

My worries must've been clearly written on my face, because as Holden glanced in my direction, he spoke up. "He's just not used to starting on the bench," he pointed out, noticing where my focus laid. "He'll get his chance; the coach knows what he's doing."

I gave him a tentative smile, but before I could respond, both of our eyes were brought back to the court as a collective groan of protest erupted around us.

The referee had blown his whistle loudly, stopping the play as one of our players was down for the count. I recognized him from the party a few weeks back, and as he wrapped his hands around his ankle, I noticed a player from the opposing team standing only a few feet away from him, seemingly satisfied as a sly grin appeared on his face. Figuring he'd intended for him to get hurt, a crease formed between my brows as I, along with the rest of the crowd, watched the injured player limp off the court with the help of his teammates while our coach shook his head in frustration.

What sent a thrill through me however, was when he motioned for Dean to stand up, speaking to him quickly before clapping him on the shoulder and pushing him onto the court.

"See," Holden said, grinning and joining in on the applause as his best friend entered the game, "I told you."

When the whistle blew again seconds later, I was shaken out of my state of surprise and cheered along as we were given the ball to inbound.

All of the players had their game faces on, and unlike the first quarter of the game, I was pulled right into the action.

Routing for Duke, I cheered with every shot we made and held my tongue with every shot the opposing team sunk in response. Dean was playing his heart out, slipping easily back into the game that he loved as he dribbled past players and contributed to our team's rising score. Every time the ball was passed to him, I was forced to bite my lip and contain the proud bursts of energy that were coursing through my body. It seemed to me that he was an unstoppable force on the court, only taking quick breaks when he needed a refuelling, and that wasn't lost on the other team.

When the last quarter began, it seemed like their strategy was to double team Dean, no matter if he had the ball or not, in hopes that without him our offense would shut down.

It was easy to see that this frustrated Dean to no end as he tried his best to dribble and deke them out, but to no avail, he settled for being the one to draw the defense away from the play. Astonished at his selflessness, I watched as he let the rest of his teammates use the open space to draw up the score.

It took longer than it should've for the other team to pinpoint his strategy, and just before the clock hit zero, as Dean was left open a few steps outside the three-point line, the ball was thrown his way. He had only seconds to line up a shot, and aiming it the best he could, his feet left the ground as he used the extra momentum to propel the ball towards the basket. The ball was in the air as the final buzzer went, but when it swooshed through the net effortlessly, the crowd leapt to their feet in celebration.

"Way to go Dean!" I screamed with delight, clapping happily as I ignored the chuckles of amusement coming from Holden and Stella.

It was a loud crowd, full of screaming fans and supportive families, but even through it all, I saw Dean turn away from the celebration his teammates were having in the middle of the court and meet my gaze. My smile was wide and my cheering overdramatic, and as I saw him grin in return, I knew that everything he'd worked on over the past few months was worth it, even just for this infinitesimal moment of joy.

"There he is," Holden announced in an overly amused voice almost half an hour later when Dean emerged from the locker room, "The man of the night."

His teasing words reverberated off the gym walls, echoing across the room and gaining a few people's attention. Many of them turned away when they realized nothing of importance was happening, though I couldn't ignore the girls that were lingering in the gym, their gazes locked on Dean as they giggled and whispered amongst themselves.

I had no reason to be jealous however, because as Dean neared where the three of us sat on the bleachers, he rolled his eyes at Holden, and the moment he sat down next to me, his features softened.

"Hey," he said, the corners of his lips tilting upwards as he swiftly pulled me closer.

Freshly showered, his hair was damp and smelled of a citrus tree in the middle of a forest – a scent that suddenly appealed to me much more than it ever had before.

A smile matching his graced my lips, though before I could say anything, he leaned down to kiss me. Although a pleasant shiver trailed down my spine, I hadn't expected it, and raised one of my hands to his chest to push him back slightly. "People are watching."

"You care about that?" he asked, a slight teasing tone to his voice as he quirked an eyebrow.

I shrugged, a little self-conscious. "Not really, I just, I didn 't..."

Noticing that I was stumbling on my words, Dean simply chuckled, pulling me closer again as he pressed his lips against my temple. "If you don't like PDA, all you had to do was say something," he said quietly, his breath fanning the skin next to my ear.

A soft blush spread across my cheeks as I scooted along the bench, putting a sliver of space between us in an attempt to recover a fraction of the dignity I was losing.

"Well, I think Stella and I are gonna head out now," Holden started, turning the attention off of me as he grinned at his best friend. "Congratulations on the game, and hopefully you didn't fuck up too much that the coach will actually let you play again."

Dean guffawed. "Thanks for the support," he mused.

Holden chuckled in response while my forehead frowned with curiosity. "You guys are leaving?"

Stella shrugged. "Not everyone wants to spends their night surrounded by a stream of sweaty basketball players," she said jokingly, casting her eyes towards Dean as she said, "No offense."

"Non-taken."

"Besides," she continued, a smirk on her face as she weaved her hand through Holden's and led him down the stairs of the bleachers, "It seems like you two need some time alone."

My blush intensified as the pair quickly disappeared, leaving Dean and I to ourselves as the rest of the stragglers slowly began to vacate the gym.

I cleared my throat, tilting my head upwards to catch Dean's eyes and said, "So, what do you – "

"Adams," I heard one of his teammates, Dillon, shout from across the court, cutting me off as he looked between the two of us, "You coming?"

I assumed he was talking about the inevitable after party that was happening to celebrate their victory, which, if I was being honest, didn't appeal to me in the slightest in that moment. I kept my thoughts to myself however, not wanting to influence Dean's decision. If he wanted to celebrate tonight, he deserved to.

"Not tonight," Dean responded, his voice loud enough for them to hear. My eyes widened with surprise, not expecting it as I saw him shrug his shoulders in a not-really-feeling-it sort of way.

I was very much aware that the guys were still watching us, and an uneasiness settled into the pit of my stomach, thinking they'd blame me for his sudden disinterest in partying or send a teasing jab our way. The wave settled just as fast as it grew however, as the reply he got was much more understanding than expected.

"Okay man," Dillon said, nodding in acceptance, "See you at practice Sunday."

Waving back at him, Dean watched as they all left without him. "You didn't want to go?" I asked, confusion creasing my forehead.

His eyes were bright as he turned to face me. There were no tells in his features to hint at whether he was bothered or upset, instead appearing simply content with his decision. "Just not in the mood for a party tonight," he shrugged, directing a soft smile towards me, "And I had something a bit more relaxed in mind."

"And what would that be?" I asked slowly, quirking an eyebrow despite the fact that I knew I'd follow him wherever he wanted to go.

"Come on," he said, turning back to face me after he'd stood up, extending a hand towards me, "I'll show you."

I expected him to lead me towards the parking lot, after which we'd head home or stop off somewhere for some food.

What I didn't expect however, was to be wandering around the campus late at night.

Snow was falling lightly as we walked, and with no real route in mind, our footsteps carved a path in the snow while the chilling air nipped at the rosy skin of my cheeks. Shoulder to shoulder, our intertwined hands hung between us, and with the glare of the moon the only real light we had, the darkness consumed us.

"You played great tonight," I said, and while my words were quiet as they laced around the wind, there was an undeniable proudness to my tone.

"Thanks," he replied, though I noticed his smile didn't reach his eyes, which were once again hidden beneath the frames of his glasses.

Stopping mid-step, I turned towards him. "Was there some other reason you didn't want to go out tonight?" I asked hesitantly. "Did your coach not notice how well you were playing, or – "

"Katie," Dean cut me off, "nothing happened." He'd moved his hands to my shoulders during my short ramble, but as he took a step back, they retreated to his pockets. "Coach was actually impressed, and depending on how Scott's ankle looks, he said I might be starting next game."

"That's great."

Expecting a grin to appear, I was even more perplexed as the only movement on his lips was a slight twitch. "It is," he started, pausing for a moment, "But something just felt off."

My features drew together in confusion as I waited for him to continue.

He sighed, stepping further away from me as he sought out the old wooden bench that rested just a few feet behind us. Not caring about the thin layer of snow that covered it, I followed his movements, taking a set next to him. "I didn't tell my family that I'd been cleared to play," he admitted.

"Why not though?" I asked, resting my hand on top of his thigh. "They would've been excited to know how far you've come."

"I know that, and maybe, that's exactly why I didn't." He paused, his words settling into the silence that drew out between us. "Not so long ago, basketball was the only thing

I was focused on. It's why I came to Duke; because they'd offered me a full scholarship and it was my best chance at getting to play professionally. I never saw a future for myself that didn't include a large crowd, the game I love, and a group of teammates I could count on, which was why I couldn't let myself get distracted by getting into relationships or focusing too hard in classes."

"Last season I started to notice the scouts watching me, and when I didn't get drafted, I knew that this would be my year. I was ready – I didn't have anything tying me here, but then the accident changed everything." His fingers found mine again, his expression completely neutral as his gaze locked with mine. "What I first saw as a bad thing turned out to be a blessing in disguise. I got to see my life from a new perspective, and things like building solid relationships and learning to love the program I'm in came naturally once I'd realized what I'd been missing. Basketball was a part of my life for so long, and I'll always love it, but I'm not so sure about playing professionally anymore."

There was the smallest of smiles pulling at his lips once he finished unloading his thoughts, his mind no doubt lighter, not having to keep all of these doubts inside.

"Your parents will understand," I responded a few beats later. "They'll just want to see you happy, and I'm sure Ryan will be supportive."

"I know," he admitted, "I think I just wanted to figure out for myself what I wanted before bringing them into the mix."

"Then thank you for trusting me with this," I said softly, squeezing his hand. "And whether or not you play, it doesn't matter to me. I'll still be here to support you either way."

He leaned in close, now completely at ease as he pressed his lips against my forehead and I relaxed against him. "I never doubted otherwise."

Chapter 22

Stirring awake as the morning sunlight seeped into Katie's bedroom, I didn't have to open my eyes for a smile to form on my face – the memory of last night having invaded my dreams, and even now, still playing vividly in my mind.

After a particularly long Friday night shift, I'd been there to meet Katie as she stepped off the bus, walking back with her to her apartment as we'd planned to finally relax and unwind. With the end of term slowly creeping up on us, the both of us had been letting the stress of the situation get to us. There was only two weeks left of classes before exams started, and that left little time before things began to change and we were thrust into the real world.

The night had started as I'd expected, with a movie on the television and the two of us cuddled beneath a blanket on the couch. It had quickly taken a turn however, as one kiss turned into two and so on and so forth. We'd barely made it ten minutes into the movie before our hands were wandering and our mouths were moving feverishly against each other, at which time we'd vacated the couch in favour of the bedroom.

With our clothes shed, and our hearts beating wildly, our bodies were a tangle of limbs beneath the blankets, moving in sync as we created a rhythm all our own.

Now, as I rested peacefully beside her, my arm thrown over her bare waist with my fingers splayed out, I could feel her chest rising and falling at a steady pace, telling me that she was still very much asleep.

Undeterred and still unwilling to open my eyes, I inched closer to her. My knees pressed against the back of hers, the curve of her butt fit nicely against my hips, and I tilted my head so that it rested just above her shoulder. We fit together like a puzzle – one that I didn't want to take apart.

Settling back into the pillows, I allowed my breathing to slow down, eventually matching Katie's as I fell asleep once more. An hour later however, I stirred again. Blinking my eyes open to the rays of light streaming in through the window, my gaze immediately fell to Katie, who'd shifted in her sleep. She laid on her stomach now, her head tilted towards me, and it didn't take me long to notice that, as a result of her change in positions, the covers had slipped partially down both of our bodies. The blanket was bunched around her waist, exposing the milky skin of her bare back that seemed to enchant me. My fingers were drawn to her body immediately, tracing circles on her skin as I focused my attention to the bottom of her spine.

I moved forward, pressing my lips against the bare skin of her neck, and as I pulled back, I felt her slowly begin to squirm awake.

"Good morning," I muttered, my voice slightly scratchy and heavy with sleep. The pattern I was drawing had become more intricate, spreading every which way as the warmth of my fingertips met the chilled skin of her back.

She hummed in enjoyment, and as a low chuckle escaped my lips, her eyes fluttered open. "Good morning," she replied, smiling so wide it made her eyes gleam with happiness.

"You know I could get used to this."

"Yeah?" She quirked an eyebrow, turning onto her side, exposing herself as she rested her palm against my chest. "Which part?"

The look in her eyes told me she knew exactly what she was doing to me, and as enticing as she was, I didn't let my gaze drop from hers as I pulled her tight against me. "The part where I wake up to the most beautiful girl in the world."

Saying exactly the right thing had its benefits, and as Katie leaned in to kiss me, I happily obliged, letting her take the lead as her tongue slipped slyly between my lips. It was the perfect morning kiss, languid and effortless, her hands weaving up to pull gently at my hair.

It ended abruptly however, as I was forced to pull back when a yawn escaped me.

"Tired?" she mused.

"After last night?" I asked, a teasing smirk remaining on my lips as I yawned again. "I'd say I could use a few more hours in bed."

She giggled, catching the double meaning behind my words. With her head resting softly against the pillows, her gaze locked on mine as I propped myself up with my elbow. There was a pause before she spoke however, her features softening with gratitude, and an emotion that was beginning to resemble love. "Thank you," she said quietly, "For last night."

I had inkling as to what she was insinuating, but not completely sure, my brows drew together in confusion, pushing a stray lock of hair behind her ear as I waited for her to explain.

"You didn't expect everything all at once," she continued shyly, the apples of her cheeks colouring faintly with a blush, "You went slow, you took your time, and I don't know," she shrugged her shoulders with embarrassment, "It just meant a lot to me."

"You're the one who put your trust in me," I murmured, pressing my lips against her forehead, "And for that, I should be thanking you."

As she snuggled further into my hold, there was nothing else to be said as the two of us laid there basking in the silence. Sometimes it was just nice to enjoy the moment and cherish the little things. The way her hair smelled of freshly picked apples, how I could feel her heart beating steadily against my chest, and how, even during a stressful time, we could take the time to just breathe easy.

Just because we were finally peaceful however, that didn't mean that time suddenly stopped. In fact, if it was possible, it seemed to speed up.

"We should get up soon," Katie said after another twenty minutes had passed, though the words didn't hold much conviction as she stayed exactly where she was.

"But it's Saturday," I protested, tightening my grip on her waist. "We can lay here for as long as we want, and I'm more than okay with staying here a little while longer."

Rolling her eyes as she finally pulled back, she also reached out to grab the covers, pulling them up to cover her chest. "You know we can't," she sighed. "I have assignments to finish up and revision to do for all of my classes, and I know you have at least a few term papers that aren't close to being finished."

It was deflating to know that she was right, because with her shifts piling up over the next two weeks and my basket-ball practices becoming more frequent with playoffs in full swing, we needed to make use of the day.

"But can't that wait a few more minutes?" I asked softly, a slight begging tone to my voice as I planted a row of kisses across her face, ranging from the tip of her nose to the apples of her cheek.

A grin appeared on her lips as she laughed beneath me, and I knew my offer sounded just a bit appealing to her in that moment. "Five more minutes," she said, trying to be assertive but failing miserably, "And that's it."

"Five more minutes it is."

"Done," I announced, overdramatically clicking my mousepad as I saved the final draft of my paper.

Katie's eyes widened with surprise as she looked up from her notes, casting a dubious look my way. "Seriously?"

The five minutes had extended into an extra hour that morning, and by the time we'd finally rolled out of bed it was going on eleven. With a soft blush grazing her cheeks, Katie had pulled on a robe and headed down to whip up brunch while I hopped into the shower, permanent happiness etched into my features.

We'd gotten to work eventually though, not able to prolong it once the time edged closer and closer to noon.

Now, having been working on a term paper for my virology class for the last six hours straight, I felt a sense of accomplishment wash over me knowing it was finally complete.

"Yeah," I replied proudly, "Twenty-six pages strong."

She cracked a smile. "That's great."

I nodded, closing my laptop and pushing it to the side as I swung my feet over the edge of her bed. "And it also means I can finally have something to eat," I said, standing up and stretching my hands above my head. "Do you mind if I cook dinner?"

When she didn't reply immediately, I noticed her eyes were focused on the skin of my waist that was on display where my shirt had risen up. Clearing my throat with amusement, I watched as she blinked a few times, snapping herself out of the daze before sending a guilty smile my way.

"Are you sure? We can order something in if you want."

"I'll cook, it's not a big deal," I shrugged. "Plus, I really need a break after staring at a screen for hours."

Reaching into the large bag of chips next to her – which was the only real food we'd had since we'd migrated upstairs and started studying, she sent a small smile in my direction. "Okay."

Quirking an eyebrow as I hovered in the doorway of her room, I asked, "And it's okay if I use anything in the fridge?"

"Go crazy," she replied teasingly, holding my gaze for a moment as I chuckled before her attention turned back to the notes she was revising.

Walking into the kitchen, I had a vague idea of what I wanted to make. I'd seen a few chicken breasts in the fridge when I'd come down earlier to grab something to drink, and searching through the cupboards, I quickly found half a bag of pasta that was just waiting to be cooked. However, as I bustled around a bit, collecting various spices and ingredients, my plans slowly began to change. I'd spotted a few unused candles stored on one of the top shelves, as well as a bottle of white wine at the back of the fridge, and as a new idea started to formulate, my excitement for the night ahead grew.

Over the next half an hour my eyes flitted towards the stairs frequently, every sound making me worried, as I didn't want Katie to come down and ruin the surprise. When everything was ready however, I was able to relax, pleased with the setup as I took a step back and slowly headed back upstairs.

Katie's tongue was poking out the side of her mouth when I knocked on her bedroom door, breaking her concentration as her attention shifted towards me. My palms were beginning to sweat as I smiled at her, nodding back down the hallway as though nothing was out of the ordinary. "Dinner's ready."

"Great," she sighed happily, leaving her notes be as she moved towards me, standing on her tiptoes to kiss my cheek, "Because I'm starving."

Motioning for her to lead the way, I followed her down the stairs, hanging back as she reached the bottom and stopped in place.

I'd shut most of the lights off, successfully dimming the entirety of the downstairs after I'd scattered candles around the room. Their wicks were burning slowly, casting off a soft light and delicious scent, and as Katie's eyes took in the rest of the setup, her eyes widened with wonder. Having pushed the coffee table off to the side of the living room, I'd found a few large blankets in the storage closet and laid them out, resting the pillows from the couch on top. The food was set up next to the blankets, ranging from the chicken pasta I'd cooked to a small bowl of pretzels and a platter of fruit and veggies that'd been cut up. I'd also found two wine glasses and set them down on either side of the unopened bottle.

It took Katie several seconds before she turned to face me. "What is all of this?" she asked, her voice filled with awe. "I thought you were just cooking dinner."

"I did," I replied, stepping down the final few stairs so that I stood right in front of her. My hands trailed down her arms before my fingers weaved their way between hers. "I just added a few little extras."

The laugh that escaped her lips was light and full of happiness. "I can't believe you," she said, wrapping her arms around my waist tightly as her head tilted back to gaze up at me.

"There's only so much studying someone can do in a day – even you, so I thought we'd relax the rest of the night."

I had expected some sort of pushback, even if it ended up being a feeble attempt, but when she smiled and nodded in agreement, I was a bit surprised. "Sounds good to me."

The conversation was sparse as we ate, the both of us comfortable on the blankets and simply enjoying the time, but once we'd finished with the food, Katie fit herself snuggly against my side, her elbow locking with mine as the both of us sipped slowly at our wine.

"I didn't even know I still had these," she said quietly, and when I shifted my gaze to follow hers, I noticed how she ran her hand over the fabric of the blankets.

My eyebrows furred together. "What do you mean?"

"Theo and I used to build forts with these when we were younger," she reminisced, a far off look casting over her face. "Every weekend up until he started eighth grade, the two of us would pull together the dining chairs, throw these blankets over top, and then secure it all with a few heavier knick-knacks that mom had lying around and bungee hooks. We had this little portable DVD player that we'd watch movies with, and then we'd fall asleep in a pile of pillows." Her lips twitched, a conflicting mixture of happiness and sadness swirling in her eyes as she recalled the memory. "Both of us never let our mom help, but she'd always watch us struggle making it with a smile on her face."

I hugged her closer as her words ran out. "Sounds like fun," I said quietly, not really knowing how else to respond.

"It was."

Covering her hand with mine, I rubbed my thumb over the back of her palm. "You miss them?" I asked, though I already knew the answer.

Dropping her head down to rest on my shoulder, her eyes flitted up to meet mine as she gulped down her emotions. "Everyday."

"Thank god you guys called," I heard Stella announce with relief about an hour later, "I was just about getting ready to throw my notes at the wall."

"She's not lying," Holden pitched in, the both of them appearing in the living room seconds later, trailing behind Katie.

Once the mood had lightened between Katie and I, we'd repositioned the pillows and had laid down in each other's arms. Cuddling was the perfect way to fill time, but when our conversation started to drift off onto random roads, we'd thought inviting Stella and Holden for a movie night was a good idea.

We'd cleaned up the food but left the blankets how they were – the setup perfect for the four us to just sit back and unwind.

"I'm sure it wasn't that bad," I chuckled, watching as she rolled her eyes and slipped off her jacket.

Stella raised an eyebrow. "Have you ever tried condensing America's entire history on dealing with their surroundings countries onto just a few pages to study from?" she asked, receiving a simple shrug from me in return. "And that's only for one class!"

"Don't worry," Katie mused, "Nobody here will be quizzing you about anything history related tonight."

"And just think," I added, "In a few weeks, it'll all be over."

Sighing, she settled into the blankets, pulling a pillow onto her lap as she plucked at a loose thread. "That's not exactly reassuring." Sending a confused look in Holden's direction, he shook his head, silently letting me know not to push the topic as he dropped down next to Stella. "But tonight's not about that," she continued, her mood shifting almost instantaneously as a smile reappeared on her lips, "Tonight's about eating way too much popcorn and watching a few movies to get my mind off of everything."

My eyes met Katie's as she made her way towards the DVD collection, and though she bit her lip with worry, she shrugged, not knowing what was going on.

"So," Katie started, gesturing to the stack of movies, "What'll it be?"

Once we'd all agreed on a comedy, the movie trailers began playing as Katie went around the room and blew out most of the candles, leaving only a few lit so that we weren't surrounded by pure darkness.

When the beginning scenes of the movie started just a couple of minutes later, Katie having made herself comfortable next to me, I chuckled under my breath as I realized the situation resembled closely to the one of the night before.

"What?" Katie whispered, her breath warm against my neck.

A smirk formed on my lips as I turned towards her, my lips touching her temple as I replied, "Let's just try not to have a repeat of last night."

Leaning back slightly, I saw the tinge of red gloss her cheeks – the reaction I'd expected as she buried her face in the fabric of my shirt. Laughing lightly, I kissed the top of her head, rubbing my hand up and down the skin of her arm.

What I hadn't expected was for Stella to overhear my words, quickly turning towards the two of us with a curious look in her eyes. "And what exactly happened last night?" she asked, raising an eyebrow.

I could see the outline of a smirk appear on Holden's lips behind her, having quickly put two and two together, and though I was on the verge of giving a cryptic response, I was stopped when my phone buzzed in my pocket. Pulling it out to see my brother's name flash across the screen, I teased a smirk as my gaze flitted between the two girls. "I'm sure you can get Katie to tell you," I said, watching as my girlfriend's blush spread down her neck when I moved to stand up, "But I've got to take this."

Stella's eyes narrowed in suspicion, and though it was dark, when she noticed the colour of Katie's cheeks, and the way her gaze had dropped to her lap, her eyes widened in understanding.

"Oh my god! Katie!"

Laughing quietly as I made my way into the kitchen, my voice was full of amusement as I answered the phone. "Hey Ryan."

"You sound a bit too cheery for someone who's studying for their last set of exams," he pointed out quickly.

Leaning back against the counters, I lifted my free arm up to cross it against my chest. "Yeah well, I decided to take a break from all of that for the night."

"And I'm sure it's deserved," Ryan replied, though my smile slowly started to slip as he continued, "But if you're still serious about this job right after graduation, then you're gonna have to put a lot of work in on top of studying. I managed to talk to my friend and he – "

I couldn't listen to another word as I released a shaky breath and cut my brother off. "Ryan," I said, dropping my voice low, "This isn't really the best time for this conversation."

The guilt that I'd pushed down began to circle around my mind as my gaze lifted out to the living room. I could see Stella gushing and overwhelming Katie, but as her eyes met mine for a quick moment, there was a small smile on her face.

"You haven't told her." It wasn't a question, but a fact, and as I let my silence fill the line, it was all the reassurance Ryan needed to confirm his statement. "You have to talk to her Dean."

I brought my hand up and dragged it through my hair stressfully. "I know," I sighed, "But I can never find the right time."

"It'll never be the right time."

It was painful to think about doing, but as I closed my eyes, I resided, "I know."

In truth, I was withholding everything because I didn't want things to change, but I knew in my heart that it was inevitable – they would whether I was ready for it or not.

Chapter 23

The light spring breeze tousled my hair gently as I sat in the quad, my review notes in my lap as I waited for Dean's exam to finish. It was crazy how fast time had flown by, and now, as the end of a chapter neared, I found myself strangely okay with moving forward.

Maybe it was everything that had happened over the past year – it all piling up to make me a stronger person, but whatever the reason, with just one more exam to go in a few days' time, I was ready to step out into the world as a university graduate. I'd been offered a new position at the hospital, starting in just over a month, and I couldn't wait to see what else was in store for me.

When a mass of students began to pile out of the biology building across the lawn, I closed my notebook, tucking it into my backpack as my eyes scanned the crowd. Dean was one of the last ones out, his grip loose on the strap of his bag when, amidst the swarm of people, his eyes met mine and his lips turned up at the edges.

"Hey," I greeted him, my hand reaching for his as I leaned up to kiss his lips. "How was the exam?"

Dean shrugged as I pulled back. "It was alright I guess," he replied. "A lot of the content was crammed into the questions, but overall it wasn't that bad."

"That's good then," I said encouragingly, squeezing my fingers gently between his.

"Just one more to go," he sighed, pulling me closer as he pressed his lips against my forehead, "And then it's over."

There was a dreariness to his words that I could tell he'd tried to disguise. Over the past few weeks, whenever the topic of the future had come up, Dean had appeared to be happy, excited, and sometimes even a little nervous about what was in store. I'd slowly started to notice however, that while there was a smile on his face and a lightness to his words, the happiness never seemed to reach his eyes. He was putting up a front for one reason or another, and while I wanted to ask him about it, I also didn't want to push.

"Can you believe it?"

He shook his head as his eyes scanned the campus around us. "Sometimes I wish it would all just pause so that nothing would change." Dean's voice was quiet, his honest thoughts beginning to seep out into the open. "Or at least just slow down."

I didn't respond right away, searching the corners of my mind for words of encouragement, though nothing came. Instead, I raised my hand to his cheek, stroking the skin that grew a small layer of scruff. Our eyes met, and though I saw a hint of indecisiveness swirling in his irises, a glimmer of a smile appeared on my lips, causing his features to mirror my own.

"How about a coffee?" I asked softly, a hopeful and cheery tone to my voice. "My treat."

"That sounds great."

There were plenty of places to grab a cup of joe on campus, but figuring the best thing for Dean in that moment was to get off of campus, I suggested William's, the small diner just a few minutes away that Stella and I had frequently visited over the years. It was fairly busy for this time in the afternoon, though most of the customers appeared to be students, filling up the tables with identical piles of paper as they studied.

Dean and I found an open booth near the window, sitting down across from one another as a waitress came over to take our order. Not long after she turned away with fresh scribbles on her notepad, she reappeared with our coffees, as well as the chocolate chip muffin I'd ordered for the two of us to share.

The silence between us grew heavier as I sipped at my drink, not knowing what to say as I noticed the far off look in Dean's eyes. I wanted to enjoy this moment that we had free, but at the same time, I wanted to know what was bothering him so that I could help.

Biting my lip, I nudged the muffin, which had only a piece missing from the side, towards him. "Dean," I said, worry etched into my features, "Is there something bothering you?"

My question seemed to do enough to snap him from his daze as his brows furred together. "What do you mean?"

"I don't know," I replied, my gaze dropping to the table, "You've just seemed a bit off the past couple of days."

There was a short pause before he replied. "Just the possibilities I guess." As I lifted my head, Dean ducked his. He gripped his coffee cup tighter, fidgeting slightly in his seat. "With basketball really over, I think I'm just trying to understand what comes next." His voice quieted to a whisper. "And I'm scared."

I'd had an inkling that his recent mood had to do with the fact that basketball was now over for him. After his team had made the playoffs, they'd gotten through their games with ease, up until they'd reached the Elite Eight, where their team hadn't been strong enough to fight off Oregon to make it to the next round.

Scouts had taken interest in him, especially as his skills became more evident the more he played, but as far as I knew, he'd stuck with his gut and denied the offers he'd gotten.

Reaching across the table, I rested my hand on top of his. "You don't have to figure everything out right away."

Dean diverted his gaze away from me, unable to meet my eyes as he said, "I know."

It was clear to see, at least to me, that there was something I was missing – something I couldn't grasp at. I pulled my hand back, lifting my cup to my lips as I waited, a calculating look in my eye. I wanted him to trust me, to not feel afraid to share what he was feeling, or what was bothering him, but as the silence dragged on, my shoulders began to slump.

"New York," he blurted out, biting his lip after his nervous outburst as my eyes widened. "I mean," he cleared his throat, taking in a deep breath, "How do you feel about New York?"

Confusion fell over me as I tilted my head to the side, trying to understand where this was going. "Uh, I've never actually been there," I replied slowly, "So I don't know. Why?"

"Well, you know that Ryan lives there, right? With Zoe and her daughter?" I nodded, and as he began to spell it out, I started to understand. "Do you think, maybe, if you gave it some thought, you would want to – "

I cut off his stammering as a light bout of laughter escaped my lips. "Dean," I said, a giddy amusement to my tone, "Are you trying to ask me to your brother's wedding?"

Dean froze as the words left my mouth, his eyes growing wide. Suddenly, his expression made me believe that I'd overstepped and read the situation wrong.

Maybe that wasn't what he was going to say and I'd just made a fool of myself.

Just as I was about to backtrack, Dean's shoulders posture visibly relaxed, the vague outline of a smile twitching on his lips. "Maybe," he said shyly, an unreadable gleam appearing in his eyes.

I breathed a sigh of relief. "Of course I'll go with you," I said, the thought of exploring the city causing excitement to run through my veins. "I think it'll be cool to get to see a bit of New York, and I'm sure the wedding will be beautiful."

He took a bite of the muffin that had laid forgotten on the table, swallowing it before adding, "It's on the weekend of the 20th next month, just so you know."

I nodded, making a mental note to book that weekend off before a curiosity filled my mind. "Is that really why you've been skittish all week? Because you didn't think I'd want to go to a wedding with you?"

A flush overtook his cheeks, paired with a wobbly smile as he looked at me. "I didn't know if you'd want to," he replied, his words still shaky with outstanding nerves.

"Well then," I said, a genuine smile pulling at my lips, "Doesn't it feel better now that I've said yes."

"Yeah," he breathed out, "Sure does."

"Any chance you're up for taking a break?" Dean asked as we sat in his bedroom the following afternoon, his eyebrow quirked upwards as I lifted my gaze to meet his.

A smile pulled at my lips when I noticed his expression – a strange mixture of eagerness and exhaustion. His eyes were gleaming with hope and his hair was a mess, his fingers having worked their way through the strands numerous times over the past couple of hours. I had to admit, he looked cute, but I didn't let myself dwell on it much as I shook my head in reply.

"I really want to," I started, "But I also want to finish these next few chapters before I do."

Even though I was determined not to break my productivity, I could understand where his need for a break came from as I watched him sigh. I'd only arrived as the time struck close to twelve, and from the state of Dean's room – papers scattered across it as though a small tornado had wrecked through the space – he'd already been hard at work. Now it was nearing four 'o'clock, and besides the impromptu make-out session that'd taken place not long after I'd walked through the door, we'd been studying the entirety of the past couple of hours.

"Would you mind if I ran to the store on the corner to pick up some food?"

"Not at all," I shook my head, though I looked at him with doe-wide eyes and a sly smile as I continued, "And I wouldn't say no to a frozen pizza."

He chuckled as he moved towards his closet to grab a sweater. "I'll see what I can do," he replied, coming back over to me to plant a chaste kiss on my lips before heading out of the room.

The minutes that followed were quiet, allowing me to focus my concentration on my review notes, going over the important parts with a highlighter and starring the key words and phrases that I had to remember. By the time a familiar ring tone sounded, breaking me out of the zone I'd entered, I had almost completed a full chapter.

Glancing at the side table, I realized that Dean had left his phone. It rang three times before I leant over to peek at the screen, reading Zoe's name, and without hesitation, I reached to grab it.

"Hey Zoe," I said, leaning back against the pillows as I answered the call, "Dean's just gone to grab some food."

"Forgot his phone, did he?" she asked with a light laugh.

"Yeah, he did." I paused for a moment, picking up my pen to continue with my notes. "Anything particular you want me to pass along?"

"If you could, that'd be great." I nodded, waiting as I heard the vague sound of paper shuffling around. "Can you let him know that the moving truck will be at his apartment the day after you guys graduate. We'll be there of course, to see you both cross the stage, but I don't want him pushing his packing to the last minute when we'll only have about an hour to load up the truck before we have to leave to catch our flight."

When she first started talking, I thought there'd been a mistake – that Zoe had meant to call somebody else, but as she continued, each word hitting me harder than the last, I knew in my gut that this was no mistake.

Dean was moving out to New York, and he hadn't even bothered to tell me.

"Did you get that?" Zoe asked when I didn't say anything, snapping me out of my thoughts.

There were plenty of ways to respond – with denial or with anger, but as I breathed in deeply, I tried to keep my voice as level as possible as I bit down hard on my lips. "Yeah," I forced out, keeping my tears at bay, "I've got it."

She sighed in relief. "Thank god, and look, I'm really sorry Katie, but I'm gonna have to let you go. I have to get Abbie to her dance lesson."

"Don't worry about it," I replied, having to disguise the drop in my voice as a cough. I didn't blame her for this, as she more than likely assumed I'd already known, but that didn't help at lessening the pain I could feel growing in my chest. "Have a good night."

"You too."

The line disconnected moments later, the phone slipping through my fingers and landing on the bed with a dull thud.

My notes forgotten, I found my gaze to be unfocused as small puzzle pieces began to fit together in the chaos of my mind. How he'd leave the room when his brother called, the way he'd been acting the past couple of weeks, the nerves he'd had when bringing up New York – they all seemed insignificant on their own, but together they painted a heart-breaking picture.

Since I met Dean there'd never been an instance where he'd been the one to cause me pain – always the person that I'd relied on for support, whether it was simply to listen or as shoulder to cry on. This time however, he was the one with a grip on the hammer that had the strength to tear my heart to pieces.

As I sat alone, I could almost hear the cracks starting to form, slow and unexpected, but I knew it was only a matter of time before everything fell apart. After all, the calm before a storm only lasted for so long.

Minutes later, I couldn't count how many, I heard a key rattling, the sounds of footsteps and plastic bags following.

"You're in luck," Dean announced, his voice travelling down the hall as he moved around the main room of his apartment. "I managed to snag a frozen pizza and a few other things we can whip together to make a meal." When I didn't reply, my head still ducked, his footsteps grew louder until he stood in the entryway of his room. "What do you think? Have an early dinner, or wait it out a while longer?" My lack of movement and response finally registered with him, his forehead creasing with worry as he took a tentative step into the room. "Katie?"

"New York."

Two words that caused his muscles to tense up and his face to flush white as a ghost. His eyes flitted down to his phone, which still laid beside me, though he said nothing as his lips pulled into a straight line.

"Zoe called," I continued levelly, though the anger the seeped into my words was clear. "When were you going to tell me that you're moving to New York?"

Dean flinched backwards at the power behind my words, but when he didn't deny it, I felt the tears begin to line my eyes.

"I was, I – " He was stuttering, causing the pain in my chest to grow by the second. " – shit, just let me explain."

"Explain?" I repeated incredulously, my voice rising. "Deciding to move isn't something that happens in the blink of an eye. It requires a plan – some thought. So why should I expect you to tell the truth now, after you've been keeping it from me for who knows how long?"

"I didn't know how..."

"So you thought it'd be easier for me to hear it from someone else?" I asked, the first tear falling as I stood up, moving closer to him so that he couldn't divert his eyes elsewhere. "How did you think I felt, hearing Zoe talk about you having to pack up all of your things, and that your flight was the night after we graduate?"

"I'm sorry," he said, barely waiting a second after I'd stopped speaking. Dean lifted his hands to my shoulders, and though my tears continued to fall, I didn't push him away. "The day after I told you that I was thinking about leaving basketball behind, I had a long talk with my parents. They wanted the best for me and were really supportive, so when I told Ryan, he mentioned a friend of his in New York – one of Abbie's friend's parents who runs a research facility on the outskirts of the city. Ryan told me that he'd talk to him, and pass on my phone number."

"I didn't want to tell you and get my hopes up," he continued, a pleading look in his eyes, but there was also a detectable amount of happiness as he spoke, "But at the beginning of March he got in touch with me. He said that they had an entry level lab position available in their genetics center, and I interviewed over Skype the next afternoon. It all happened so fast, and by the end of that week he'd let me know that the job was mine as soon as I graduated." He sighed. "I never meant to keep it from you, but every time I thought about telling you, I thought about everything that you've already had to go through this year. I didn't want you to think that I was leaving you too."

There was a small part of me, behind the fragments of my heart that hung loosely together in my chest, that was happy for him. He'd found an opportunity and went with it, but that didn't change the fact that he'd kept it from me.

Stepping back from him, I choked out my next words. "But you are – you're leaving, and you didn't trust me enough to be supportive."

"No," Dean shook his head, reaching for me once again, "That's not it."

"It is," I said, avoiding him as I hurriedly threw all my things into my bag, throwing the strap over my shoulder, "And I can't be around someone who doesn't know how to be honest – with me or himself."

The distraught look on his face was almost enough for me to regret my words, but shaking my head and clenching my eyes to slow the stream of tears, I turned away from him and made my way quickly towards the front of the apartment.

"Katie – " he said, following me as I slid my feet quickly into my shoes and reached the front door, "Katie, wait!"

My vision was blurry as I looked back at him, twisting the doorknob and throwing open the door as I did so. His eyes were lined with tears as well, and the expression on his face appeared as though he couldn't quite believe what was happening.

Somehow, over the immense pressure on my shoulders, the lodge in the throat, and the pain in my chest, I managed one final word before I walked out of his apartment.

"Goodbye."

I looked a mess when I jumped on the bus, which was just pulling up at the stop as I passed by, though travelling away from my apartment was a much better option than heading home. I had no doubt in my mind that Dean would've come looking for me when the shock wore off, or called Stella with worry, but I didn't want to see anybody in that moment. I just wanted to be alone.

With my gaze on the window, watching as the spring rain splattered gently across the glass, I let my thoughts wander and the pain wash over me. It was all-consuming, and while

I tried to keep my tears to a minimum, the effort itself was too much.

It was only when I noticed where the bus was nearing, the roads hauntingly familiar after my mother's death, that I felt the need to pull myself together just a little bit. The view of the cemetery was distant, but nonetheless, I hit the button next to me. When the driver pulled to a stop a few moments later and I stepped off the bus, the weather didn't deter me as I headed towards the gate.

There weren't many others out, and the pair that I did see were huddled beneath a black umbrella as they bowed their heads in front of a lost loved one. My gaze didn't linger however, as I made my way towards the spot I'd never forget, not needing to count off the headstones I passed because my feet carried me there all on their own.

When I reached the spot, I cared not for the wet ground or the clothes I wore as I sank to my knees and allowed a fresh round of tears to fall. It'd been a few weeks since I'd visited, choosing to talk to her in my dreams instead of making myself susceptible to the pain of staring at her gravestone. Seeing the flowers that rested in front of it, seemingly fresh, reminded me that I wasn't the only one that missed her, and as my hand trailed across the cold granite, tracing the letter of her name carefully, I let all my restraints go.

"Mom..." I trailed, a strangled sob escaping my lips, "Why did you have to leave? I need you here."

Like always, the lack of response caused a deep and blazing sadness to fall over me, and mixing with the pain that already burned in my chest, my mind was whirling with a mess of emotions.

"He's leaving, and I don't know what to do." I shook my head, clenching my eyes shut as I hiccupped through the tears. "I'm going to be alone again, and I'm not ready for that."

Trying to even out my breathing proved difficult, though as I looked up to the sky, letting the raindrops fall against my skin, I asked, "Why does it have to hurt so much?"

It took a few moments, but as I blinked my eyes open, I realized that the sky was clearing up and the rain drops were lessening by the second.

I didn't believe in much, but I did believe that my mom had heard me. She was always next to me, and though she could no longer stand beside me, she'd be there to guide me along the bumpy road ahead.

It was uncharacteristic, especially since the ache of this afternoon was still fresh, but a ghost of a smile twitched on my lips as I dropped my gaze back to my mother's gravestone. "I miss you mom," I said, emotion clouding my words. "I miss you so much."

Chapter 24

I didn't know how I managed to get through my last exam with the memory of Katie walking out on me replaying constantly inside my mind. I was unfocused and torturing myself, though once I set my pen down and handed in my exam, I was able to breathe a small sigh of relief.

It wasn't long-lasting however, as the minute I stepped out of the building, the freedom of university propelling me forward, I was brought back to the reality that I had managed to make a mess of my future.

I had a family who supported me, graduation to look forward to, and a new job on the horizon, but I didn't have what I truly wanted, and that was Katie.

In the days that followed, I did all I could think of to reverse the damage I'd done, though having had the chance to get to know Katie, it wasn't unsurprising that my efforts went without reply. The calls went unanswered, the messages unread, and when I'd found her on campus studying with

Stella, the two had quickly packed up and left without much more than a second glance.

She was avoiding me, and what hurt the most was knowing that I'd given her a reason to.

"Katie," I started as soon as I heard the familiar message of her voicemail end, "I know you probably haven't listened to any of these, and I don't blame you. I should've bucked up the courage to just tell you that I was leaving, but I was scared of your reaction." A dry laugh escaped my lips. "Funny how things ended up like this anyways." I sighed. "But I am sorry – really, I am."

My words trailed off as I ended the call, though as I slumped back against the couch cushions, the front door was thrown open with a bang.

Stella stormed in not even a moment later while my eyes, which had widened in surprise, watched her movements, hoping that she wouldn't see me. It was no use however, because as frustration overtook her features, it quickly dissolved into anger when her steps halted and she turned to glance at me. Shaking her head, I could clearly hear her mutter the word 'asshole' under her breath before she continued further into the apartment, heading for Holden's bedroom as she slammed the door behind her.

Holden, who'd entered the apartment closely behind Stella, sighed, raking his fingers stressfully through his mop of hair as he turned to look at me, a pointed look in his eyes. "You fucked up man, big time."

My chin dropped to my chest as I sighed with regret. "I know," I replied sadly, tightening my grip on my cell phone as I tapped it nervously against my leg, "Trust me."

He didn't say anything else, simply giving me a nod in acknowledgement before heading towards his room.

It seemed that with each passing day, as my attempts at communication went unanswered, the hope in my chest began to crumble. Slowly my calls began to dwindle, and it wasn't long before I was forced to accept the truth. If Katie wanted to see me, she'd do so when she was ready.

That didn't stop me from moping as graduation loomed closer, and when the day finally came, I felt just a bit displaced. The pictures that I'd imagined having of the two of us together – those would no longer happen, but that didn't stop my mom from cooing over me in my apartment before the ceremony, a plethora of boxes surrounding us as she smiled proudly at me.

I adorned my cap and gown with the rest of the graduates that afternoon, crossing the stage with a sense of accomplishment as I was handed my diploma. I could hear my family cheering in the crowd, and as I let my gaze trail over the sea of students filling up the gymnasium, my eyes locked with Katie's, a rush of joy running through me as I saw her hands coming together in applause.

When the ceremony was finished, a mass of chaos ensued on the lawns outside. Everyone bustled to find their friends and family, and while I knew exactly where I was meant to meet my parents, my steps were slow as I hoped to catch a glimpse of Katie. It wasn't long before I spotted her, her blonde hair sweeping gently in the breeze and her gown un-zipped to reveal the dress she wore underneath. It surprised me however, to see her chatting happily to her brother.

As if she'd felt my eyes on her, she turned towards me a few moments later. There was apprehension in her features, and I could see the confliction swirling in her irises as Theo cast a confused, then protective glance my way. I kept my place, not deterred, and was glad that I did.

Moments later, I saw Katie's lips pull upwards hesitantly, offering me a smile as she mouthed 'congratulations'.

The will to walk over to her flooded my chest, though I fought hard against it and stayed where I was, a grateful and congratulatory smile gracing my lips as I returned her sentiment.

I was giving her space, no matter how much it crushed me inside.

A hand clasped down on my shoulder and our gaze was broken. "She'll come around," Ryan said slowly, "But you can't stop living while you wait."

I turned to him, the edges of my lips now straightened. "I know."

"Now come on," he nudged me, an uplifting tone to his voice, "I don't think mom wants to miss getting pictures of her university graduate."

Laughing along with him, I let myself be pulled away to join my family. Pictures were taken – Holden being pulled into a fair few of them, and when the crowd at the university began to disperse, I jumped in the car my parents had rented as we headed out for dinner.

It was a joyous night of memories, though when I awoke the next morning, it was overshadowed by the fact that boxes lined the edge of my room.

I was leaving, and only had a few hours left in the city I'd called home for the past four years.

My mind wandered as I packed up the remainder of my things, and with an uneasiness settling in my stomach, I knew I couldn't leave things like they were. I spotted one of my notebooks on the top of a pile that was yet to be packed away, and without thinking much about it, I grabbed a pen and began to write down everything that Katie needed to know – whether she wanted to or not.

Katie,

Thinking back to the night we first met, I still smile at how effortless it was to talk to you. You were everything I didn't need at the time – a beautiful distraction that would force me off the track from a professional basketball career. But, even though many could categorize the night of a life-threatening car crash as the worst of their life, I think of it as one of the best – because of you.

If I was given a chance to go back and rewrite the last year – to never get in a car crash, to go about the year the same as the last three – I wouldn't change a thing. Changing the terrible things would also mean changing the wonderful things. It would mean never getting to know you; never having the chance to fall in love with you.

You said that I wasn't being honest with myself, and to some length, you were right. I'm leaving, and there's nothing that can be done to change that because I'm excited to start off new. I want to experience living in the city, working in a field that I've always found interesting, and just enjoy the chances I'm given.

However, when I held back the truth from you, it wasn't because I didn't think you wouldn't have been supportive. In fact, I'm sure if I'd just sat you down and told you, you would've been happy for me. I held back because telling you I was moving to New York wasn't the only thing I wanted to say to you.

I wanted to ask you to come with me. To join me on a new adventure.

I knew you'd grown up here and that this was the city that held so many memories for you. This is the place where your best friend lives, where you have a stable career path ahead of you, and where your mom is buried. North Carolina is your home, and I was afraid that if I asked you to leave, you'd resent me for taking you away.

This sounds silly now, but it's the truth.

I love you Katie, and I only want the best for you. You have my number, and if you ever want to talk, I'll pick up in an instant.

I'm so incredibly sorry Katie.

Love, Dean.

The words came easy, and as I sat back to look at the page, I knew that everything was true.

"Dean?" Holden called as he pushed open my door, one hand plunging deep into his pocket as the other rested against the wood, "The moving truck just pulled up outside."

My eyes widened at his words, not having realized that the time had already flown by. My family were busy in the kitchen, labeling the finished boxes and making sure nothing was left behind, though they also believed me to be doing the same in my room. My flight was in just over four hours, and I didn't have much time left before we'd be heading to the airport.

He must've seen the slight panic in my features as I tore out the page from my notebook and folded it in three, taping it sealed before I scrawled Katie's name on the back. "What's wrong?"

"Nothing," I replied hurriedly, tossing the rest of my supplies into a spare box, "Just, um, would you be able to finish packing these? I have something I really need to do."

His eyes flickered down to the paper in my hand and a wave of realization washed over him. "Yeah, of course." There was an understanding smile pulling at his lips as he stepped further into the room. "You know I'm going to miss you, right?"

I grinned back at him. "You'll be living in Philadelphia – that's not so far away."

"It's still weird... to know that after three years in this apartment, it's just coming to an end."

"We knew it'd happen eventually," I shrugged, though I did feel a sharp sting of nostalgia as I thought about everything the two of us had been through since we'd met. The ups and downs were a part of the friendship we'd built, though now as he began packing up the last of my things, I knew I thought of him as more of a brother than anything else.

"Yeah," he sighed, though he turned to face me with a look of encouragement, "Now go. I'll cover for you."

I smiled gratefully. "Thank you."

Slipping past my family, I ignored their questions about where I was heading, breaking into a jog as soon as my feet hit the sidewalk. Katie's building wasn't far, and as it came into view, my steps slowed and my heart raced.

Nerves came alive in my mind, and as I slipped in the first door, I knew that there was no going further. Turning to the mailboxes that lined the wall, I thanked the heavens that they were a little old so that, as I pulled at the locked door for her apartment, the top cracked open just enough for me to quickly slide the letter inside.

A weight slipped off my shoulders as I walked slowly back to my apartment, knowing that I'd done all I could do to get Katie to see how sorry I truly was.

When the moving van was fully packed just over an hour later and I watched it take off down the road, there was nothing left to do. A wind picked up gently, running through the spaces between my fingers as I waved goodbye to Holden one last time, and it was as if the city itself was wishing me off.

And by the time the sunset dawned the horizon, I was strapped into my seat beside Abbie, waiting as the plane began to speed up down the runway. My gaze was glued to the window, watching everything grow smaller and smaller as I said my final goodbye to the city and the girl I'd fallen in love with.

"And this is where you'll be working."

From the conversations I'd had with my boss over the phone, and through the research I'd done online, I hadn't expected Millennium Science Laboratory to be as big as it was. Their offices filled the entirety of a three-floor building, and they had a warehouse extension on the ground floor that housed their state-of-the-art research labs.

It was slightly overwhelming, suddenly being thrust into an environment I'd only yet been exposed to on a classroom scale, but it also sent a thrill of excitement through my veins.

"Don't worry about too much right off the bat," my boss continued, motioning around the small office that now belonged to me. "You'll be in training for a few weeks – assisting with two of the major projects our genetics sector is working on. It'll take a while to get used to the procedures and methods we use, but when you've begun to fully grasp the ropes, we can sit down and talk about what you're interested in working on going forward."

I nodded, still a tad in awe of everything I'd seen so far this morning. "Sounds good to me."

"Oh," he continued, holding up his finger as it pointed towards the cupboard to my right, "And before I forget – you've been set up with basic safety equipment, though if you ever require anything extra, don't hesitate to ask."

Opening the latch on the cupboard door, I saw two pairs of goggles, a brand new lab coat, and a small basket full of ear plugs and latex gloves.

"You probably won't need much of it today or tomorrow, as you'll just be going through our training seminars online and getting your certifications in order." He chuckled as he nodded towards the computer set up on my desk. "Not the most exciting thing around here, but it's got to get done."

And so I watched as he showed me which files to read over and briefly explained the website that the training took place on, making sure to ask if I had any questions before he left me to myself.

He'd been right in saying that it wasn't the most thrilling start to my job, but I understood that it was necessary. I spent the majority of the day working through the different seminars, stopping only when I'd struck up a conversation with the man in the office next to mine, who offered me a bit of advice after having been working with the company for over five years, and to take a lunch break with a few of my colleagues when they'd asked me to join. When I saw the clock in the corner of my screen pass five however, I shut down my programs and said goodbye to the people I passed as I headed for the parking lot.

Ryan had driven my car from North Carolina to New York while I'd flown with Zoe and Abbie, and though it was nice not having to memorize the complexity of the public transit system, the silence that accompanied driving alone was just a bit lonely.

The streets were full, as expected, and it took more than half an hour before I pulled up to the gated community where Ryan lived, and where I was staying until I found an apartment. Scanning the entry card I'd been given, I eased through gates as they swung open and pulled into the third driveway on the right, noticing that the spot beside me was empty.

As soon as I stepped through the front door, Ryan's voice echoed loudly off the walls as he asked, "How was your first day of work?"

"It was good," I started, stepping into the living room only to halt as I noticed the expansive mess. My eyebrows rose in surprise. "What is all of this?"

"Wedding stuff," he replied, looking wide-eyed and stressed.

"And Zoe left you to do this yourself?"

Ryan sighed. "She went to go pick up Abbie from dance and told me to do what I can, and now I get why girls get so worked up over wedding planning – it's a lot of work."

I chuckled lightly, dropping down next to him on the couch. "Then I'm guessing you want help?"

He didn't miss a beat as he pushed a pile of unfolded name cards towards me. "Make sure all of these are spelt correctly with that list." His hand pointed vaguely in the direction of a slightly crumpled piece of paper. "If they've RSVP'd, fold them and set them aside."

Nodding in understanding, I couldn't help but throw a few jibes at him as I noticed a few of his high profile friends on the list of guests.

It was strange, seeing him as anything other than the dorky older brother I'd grown up with.

The two of us simply chatted as we worked, the time passing easily, though when I reached to grab one of the last name cards in the pile, my eyes glazed over the name and my movements froze. This caught Ryan's attention only a few moments later as he sent a confused look my way. When he glanced at the card in my hand however, his eyes widened slightly as he plucked it quickly from my grasp.

There was a moment of silence that passed between us as a spike of anger surged through me. "Why is Katie's name still on this list?" I asked, my teeth grinding. "Did Zoe want me to see this?"

"No," Ryan said softly, an apprehensive look in his eyes. "She just thought that maybe the two of you would make up over the next few weeks."

"Don't you get it? We aren't going to get back together." Which was what I'd resigned myself to understand as the days passed and I had yet to hear from her. To add to the madness circling the forefront of my mind, I could hear Zoe and Abbie as they bustled into the house. "I left and Katie won't talk to me," I continued, an unreasonable frustration in my voice as I turned to the entryway with a narrowed gaze in time to see Zoe turn the corner, "And it's all your fiancée's fault."

Her eyes widened guiltily, not knowing exactly what was going on, but it was apparent she had at least a vague idea.

"Hey," Ryan said, his voice defensive as I turned back towards him, "Don't try to pin this all on her. I told you to tell Katie as soon as you'd gotten the job, but you wouldn't. You told us you had, so Zoe had no reason to not bring it up when talking to Katie."

"If I would've known," Zoe continued nervously, "I never would've – "

I let out a groan of frustration as I dropped my head, my eyes resting against my palms as I grabbed at my hair. "I know... I know it's my fault." The looks of pity that came from both my brother and Zoe were ones I chose to ignore. "I just... I really want to hear her voice again – for her to say she wants to work this out, but I don't think it's going to happen."

It wasn't neither of them that replied, but instead Abbie, as she sat down beside me on the couch and hugged me from the side. "She will," she said supportively, "Because she'll want to see you happy."

The mind of an eight-year-old was an interesting one, and while I truly wanted to believe her words, the smile that I gave her in response didn't quite manage to reach my eyes. "We'll see."

Epilogue

Stella's eyes were wide as they skimmed over the letter Dean had left for me. She'd snatched it from my fingers with anger when she'd arrived, though it was slowly dissipating into an unexpected softness.

"Wow," she said once she'd finished reading, her gaze lifting to meet my nervous one as we sat on opposite sides of the couch, "That's – "

"I know," I sighed, conflicting thoughts running through my head.

Since I'd returned from work to see that letter waiting for me in my mailbox, I'd been apprehensive and nervous about opening it. I'd wanted, on some level, to keep the situation black and white, which was why I'd put so much effort into dodging Dean's attempts at talking everything through. I wanted to keep believing that he'd been wrong, but the longer time went on, the more I began to realize that my thoughts were blurring.

Dean surely had a reason for keeping his plans from me, though up until I'd opened his letter, I hadn't been able to pinpoint exactly what it was.

He had wanted me to go with him.

That realization had thrown everything in my head off balance. Over the past couple of days, I'd been slowly driving myself crazy thinking of how things might have happened differently if I hadn't been the one to answer his phone that afternoon. Would he have truly asked me to join him in New York, or would he have left me in the dark?

The questions were maddening when I didn't have the answers, and in desperate need of a second opinion, I'd called Stella and invited her over. I knew that I could count on her to help me sort out what was going on inside my head – she always had, or at the very least, just listen as I talked through everything.

"What are you going to do?"

I dropped my head, running a hand through my hair in frustration. "I don't know," I trailed, "I mean, he's already left. What can I do?"

"You can call him," she shrugged, her voice soft and some-what unsure.

I raised an eyebrow in surprise, not expecting her to have a complete change of heart so quickly. "And say what?" I asked. That was my main problem, as the thought of dialing his number and hearing his voice again had crossed my mind many times after reading his heartfelt words, though I'd always talk myself out of it, not knowing what to say.

"You don't have to say much," she replied. "Just listen to what he has to say."

"But what difference will it make? I'll still be here and he'll still be in New York... there's too much space separating us." It was only when I noticed a mask of sadness flit across Stella's features that I realized what I'd said and an apologetic look filled my gaze. "Sorry," I continued quietly, "I didn't mean – "

Her lips twisted upwards slightly, though the attempt at a smile was dull and sad. "It's okay, it was for the best."

Holden and her had decided to end their relationship amicably after realizing that she was staying in town while he was heading back to Philadelphia; his hometown where he'd managed to find a job. They'd parted as friends, no hard feelings on either side, but I could still see that Stella was hurting. Holden had been the first guy she'd been serious about, and it would take a while before she'd be completely over those feelings.

"Besides," Stella continued, her mood lifting as she spoke, "Just because long distance wasn't in the cards for me, that doesn't mean it wouldn't work for you and Dean."

Having never believed that long distance could work, especially when the relationship itself was still quite new, I said, "Stella, we're more than 400 miles apart."

She was quiet for a while, mulling over her next words before she met my eyes. "Then don't do long distance."

A crease of confusion graced my forehead. "So what?" I asked, not exactly sure what she was trying to say. "You're saying I should call him and listen to what he has to say, and then just tell him that it won't work out?"

She shook her head, an undecipherable emotion filling her gaze. "No," she said softly, "I think you should go to New York."

My eyes widened and my breath caught in my throat. The possibility had been in the back of my mind, but I'd kept it tucked away, not wanting to think about it when I'd lived in Durham my whole life. "B-but... I can't," I stuttered incoherently once I'd regained some semblance of thought.

"Why not?"

"I have my job, and you're here, and my mom..."

"Would want you to be happy," she finished for me. I opened my mouth to respond, though I couldn't think of any reason other than the pure craziness of the suggestion. "You're making excuses," Stella stated simply. "You can find a job as a nurse anywhere, and there's really nothing else holding you to this city."

"But – "

"Katie," she interrupted, not allowing me to make further excuses, "You love him, right?"

The question took me a back, because although Dean had written his feelings clearly in his letter, I hadn't yet expressed my emotions out loud. However, it wasn't a question as to whether I did or didn't love him, but rather a question as to when I'd taken the plunge, and looking back on it, I couldn't pinpoint the exact moment if I'd tried. It was all the little things; a mix of the support he'd given me over the past few months, urging me to take care of myself, and simply being there for me when I needed him.

I'd fallen in love with him – slowly, without even realizing it was happening.

"Yeah." I nodded my head slowly, pulling my lip between my teeth. "I do."

"Then go." She spoke as if the answer was simple, but maybe, on some account, it was. "I think you'll regret it if you don't."

A sad, yet grateful smile lifted the edges of my lips upwards, knowing in my heart that she was right. "I'll miss you."

"I'll be fine," she shrugged, a teasing grin appearing. "Besides, I've always wanted to be one of those girls who flies to New York in her spare time."

Laughing along with her, I leaned forward to wrap my arms around her shoulders, knowing that even though distance would soon separate us, this relationship was one I saw lasting for years to come.

Despite having already agreed to continuing on full-time with the hospital, my new job hadn't been set to start until the middle of May, which still left me time to change my mind.

It took me a few days to get my thoughts in order before I'd plucked up the courage to talk to my supervisor, telling him that I'd ultimately decided not to return for the position I'd been offered. Sitting in the chair across from him, I'd been fairly antsy, my nerves flying dangerously around the pit of my stomach, but in the end, it had gone a lot smoother than I'd expected.

After explaining the situation to him, he'd understood completely, surprising me when he offered to call in a few favours to his colleagues in New York to inquire about any available positions.

"You haven't had the easiest year," he'd explained, "But your will and drive to succeed never failed to win out over the challenges you've been faced with."

I'd felt as though a weight had been lifted from my shoulders when I'd left work that day, knowing that I was putting my plans in motion, and I had a supportive system behind me urging me on.

Suddenly, the number of days leading up to Ryan and Zoe's wedding began to grow smaller and smaller, and with it, the chaos in my mind slowly started to dissipate. Relocating on a whim wasn't the simplest of tasks by any means, but with each thing I crossed off my list, it became clear that this was the path I was meant to be on.

The only thing I was slightly concerned about was actually facing Dean, who I had yet to call, thinking it'd be better to simply show up at the wedding and let things run their course. I had been smart enough to call Zoe however, talking my plan through with her after I'd made sure I was still welcome on their special day.

And when the 20th of May arrived, I found myself waiting nervously outside the venue as the security on site checked me in, allowing me to pass through.

While it had been drizzling earlier that morning as I'd gotten ready in my hotel room, the sky had since cleared, a few white clouds filling the blue sky as the dew glistened on the grass, casting the perfect weather for a beautiful wedding.

Inside, the guests were all beginning to take their seats, as there wasn't much time left before the ceremony was set to begin. Sliding quickly into a row near to the back, I waited as the rest of the seats around me began to fill up, not wanting to be seen just yet.

It wasn't long before a gentle hush fell upon the gathered crowd and a pianist began to play, filling the room with soft, melodic music.

Glancing at the front as everyone stood, I saw Ryan, his features calm and collected as he watched the bridesmaids and groomsmen make their way down the aisle. It was clear, seeing the gleam in his eyes, that he was waiting patiently to see Zoe, and Dean stood right beside him, a proud smile on his face. He looked the same as when I'd last seen him, the only difference being that his hair was slightly longer now, and had been styled neatly for the occasion.

Not wanting to draw attention to myself, I let my gaze fall back to the aisle as a girl, who looked to be Zoe's maid of honour, began her slow trek up to the front of the room.

The music swiftly transitioned into a classic wedding march, and when Zoe finally came into sight, everyone was in awe. Her dress embodied bohemian style – a mix of lace and flowing material that had cut-off sleeves and a short train, and a delicately made flower crown was weaved into her up-do as she cascaded down the aisle.

While no-one accompanied her to give her away, her daughter walked in front of her, dropping flower petals with a wide grin on her face. What caused a smile to bloom on my lips however, was the fact that, despite the crowd of people watching, Zoe's gaze was locked firmly with Ryan's, and both of their faces shone with bliss and unprecedented love.

The ceremony was short, with personalized vows that brought tears to everyone's eyes, and a sweet kiss that sealed together a promise for their future.

As they made their way back down the aisle, Abbie in front of them while their hands were intertwined, I couldn't help but smile. The moment was broken for me however, when I noticed Dean and the maid-of-honour following closely behind them, letting my hair fall in front of my face as I faded into the crowd.

The celebration started quickly afterwards, and though I knew the odds of running into Dean were slim once he'd disappeared to help with the wedding photos, it didn't stop the nerves from bubbling up inside of me.

The reception area was set up beautifully with simplistic table layouts that matched the rustic floors and slightly dimmed lighting of the bohemian theme. There was music playing from the speakers next to the DJ booth, an open bar off to the side of the room, and as the seats began to fill up, the buffet table did as well.

I knew that any moment Dean and the rest of the wedding party would walk through the doors to join the festivities, which led me to lingering by the corner, hoping that, as I sipped at a glass of wine, I'd fall into the shadows. My mind began to wander as spikes of nerves and anxiety flooded my body, second guessing my idea of showing up here as my heart started to race.

"You know," an amused voice trailed, causing me to jump as I was knocked from my thoughts to see Zoe standing just a few feet away from me, "I was beginning to think you'd changed your mind about coming."

A blush just a few shades lighter than my dress coloured my cheeks as I shook my head. "I didn't."

She quirked an eyebrow. "Then why are you hiding?" she asked, her lips lifting upwards as she nodded to where Dean stood with Ryan and a few other people, having not noticed me yet. He was so close, yet still so far away. "He feels bad about how he left things with you," she continued genuinely, catching my attention once more, "But I think he just wanted to give you time and space."

I stumbled to come up with a reply as a small wave of guilt washed over me, but I didn't get farther than a word or two before Zoe started to speak again.

"Don't worry, you don't need to explain yourself," she mused, and my shoulders relaxed with relief. Her gaze flitted back to where Ryan and Dean stood, though this time, having felt his wife's eyes on him, it wasn't long before Ryan turned towards us, Dean eventually doing the same. "Trust me," Zoe continued, sincerity lacing her words, "Relationships aren't easy, but if you're willing to put in the work, then you know you have something special."

I couldn't find the strength to respond, too enraptured as I watched Dean's movements freeze once he'd noticed me. His eyes blinked several times before they widened, almost like he needed to make sure that I wasn't just a figment of his imagination. Our gazes were locked, and while the evident surprise settled into his features, I held my breath, waiting for him to make the next move.

I barely even registered Zoe slipping the nearly empty wine glass from my hand and wishing me luck as she headed over to be with her husband, only noticing how jittery I'd become as Dean slowly began to walk over to me.

The expression on his face was entirely unguarded, every emotion visible to me as his steps halted directly in front of me. There was silence between us for a moment, the pair of us completely zoning out the rest of the party as we immersed ourselves in our own little bubble. "You're here," he breathed out, his eyes gleaming with a sense of disbelief as they took me in.

A faint smile glossed my lips as my eyes skimmed quickly over the suit he wore, not at all oblivious to how breathtakingly handsome he was. "I am."

"Did Ryan or Zoe call you?" Dean asked, his brow furring, "Because I didn't tell them to, or – "

"No actually," I started shyly, cutting off his tangent as I played nervously with the hem of my dress, "I called them."

"You did?"

I nodded. "I wanted to know if I was still allowed to come today."

His hands moved into the pockets of his dress pants as he let his shoulders fall with a sadness that washed over his entire body. "You could've called me."

I bit my lip and shook my head. "No, I couldn't have. I didn't want to settle things over the phone, especially when I couldn't figure out what to say."

There was a short pause before he spoke again, the sadness in his features being overshadowed with hope. "And now?" he asked, "Have you figured it out?"

"I have, but it's only one question..." I trailed.

"Anything."

I took in a deep breath. "Did you mean what you wrote?" I asked, my voice soft as I desperately tried to ignore the way my heart hammered inside my chest. "In the letter?"

He stuttered for a moment, clearly not expecting me to be blunt right off the bat, but it didn't take him long to gain control over his emotions, a measure of apology filling his irises. There was no denying the confidence and sincerity in his voice as his replied, "Every word."

And that was all I needed.

Happiness soared through me as I took a step closer to Dean, the ends of my shoes touching his as I brought my hand up to cup his cheek and leaned upwards, pulling his lips down to meet mine. The kiss was light at first, but when Dean's arms moved around my waist to pull me closer, responding with a delicious rhythm that made my toes curl, the kiss intensified.

I could feel him smile against my lips, causing a wondrous chill to travel down the length of my spine and I sank into the familiarity of his embrace. The kiss spoke volumes as our lips continued to find their way back to one another – conveying just how much we'd missed each other, and that although we'd spent time apart, our feelings hadn't faded. As I pulled back however, finally allowing myself to catch my breath, I knew there was something I still needed to say.

"I love you too."

His eyes widened in disbelief and a wide grin split his lips as he gazed down out me. "Really?"

My smile matched his as I rested my hands on his chest and nodded. "I think I have for a while," I admitted, "I just needed a bit of a push to realize it."

I felt his grip tighten on my hips, as though he was afraid that I'd take back my words if he let me go. "I need you to know that I really am sorry," he said, releasing a shuddering breath that hit the side of my face and caused my skin to tingle. "I never wanted to hurt you, but I thought that if I told you everything that was going on inside my head, you'd feel overwhelmed and think I was crazy for falling for you so quickly."

"It's okay," I replied with understanding, "I get why you were scared. When I first read your letter, it was all a bit much. I was second guessing everything, but it didn't take me long to realize that those kinds of words couldn't have been made up."

"They weren't," he pressed. "Like I said, I meant every word."

I lifted one of my hands so that my fingers slid across his cheeks. "I know," I said softly, "And if I'm being honest, before all of this, I'd never once thought about leaving North Carolina. It's where I grew up and where my home was, but with your letter constantly on my mind, I began to realize something. A home isn't necessarily where someone falls asleep at night, but rather where they can truly be themselves without having to put up a front, and I feel most at home when I'm with you."

I still had one hand resting on his chest and could feel the erratic beating of his heart as his eyes gleamed with astonishment. "But what about Stella?" he asked carefully, as though he needed full reassurance before his excitement could prevail, "And your job at the hospital?"

"Well, Stella's actually the one who pushed me to come here."

Dean pressed his lips briefly across my forehead. "Remind me to call her and thank her a thousand times over."

"Sure," I laughed as he pulled back. "And as for my job, I told my supervisor I wasn't going to take the position."

"You did?"

I nodded, my lips twisting upwards as he looked at me like I had lost my mind. "He was understanding, and didn't think twice about calling a few places around the area to see if they had any available positions for me." I could finally see the joy and excitement fill Dean's gaze as he came to a conclusion all on his own, just waiting for me to say it out loud for confirmation. "In fact, I've got a few interviews over the next couple of weeks in the city, and I was wondering, if you're still looking around for an apartment, maybe I could help you when I'm in town."

A string of kisses was how Dean chose to respond, pecking my lips repeatedly as he said, "You. Are. Amazing." The kiss that punctuated the last word was more solidifying, with him caressing my lips until the both of us were breathless.

"So is that a yes then?" I asked, pulling back slightly with a grin on my face, "To seeing what the future has to offer?"

"Hmm... I don't know. I'll have to think about it," he said, though it was evident by his teasing tone and the happiness that settled into his features that he'd already made up his mind. "But in the meantime, how would you feel about dancing?"

It was the first time since I'd locked eyes with Dean that I let my gaze scan over the room. The reception was in full swing – plates full of food, the bride and groom making their way around to greet everyone, and a few people daring enough had already made themselves comfortable on the dance floor. The night was just beginning, and already, everyone seemed to be enjoying themselves.

Turning back to Dean, I let my hand fall to intertwine with his and smiled. "I thought you'd never ask."